A chill raced over her. The air around them screamed in alarm.

Yoshi grinned, slick and crooked. "And I'll take you, too, Gwen."

The goon behind him whipped out a gun—metal flashing like fire, barrel aimed straight at her. *Think, Gwen. Think. How can you turn this asshole's hubris to our benefit?*

She took too long. Griffin burst like a kraken from Vaillancourt Fountain.

Water gushed upward from the low pool, assuming the strong, lean shape of Griffin's human body. Translucent waves flowed over the valleys of his stomach muscles. White froth cascaded over his square jaw and the hard cut of his arms. His torso darkened, solidified. Water droplets skittered across his skin, soaking in. From the waist down he remained a brilliant, shimmering waterfall balancing on the fountain's bubbling surface. Frighteningly beautiful, unmovable as rock.

One of Griffin's arms went liquid and shot out, fast as a bullet, to wrap around the stunned bodyguard and yank him forward into the fountain. Griffin's watery legs flowed over the Japanese goon, holding him under the surface. His chest and shoulders heaved with channeled fury.

Gwen transformed her own arm into a liquid whip and snapped it at the *Mendacia* box sagging in Yoshi's fingers. Reversing the suction, she peeled it from his grasp and flung it back into her own hands. As her arm returned to solid, she felt the familiar, cool tingle of ebbing waters.

LIQUID LIES

HANNA MARTINE

BERKLEY SENSATION, NEW YORK

THE BERKLEY PUBLISHING GROUP
Published by the Penguin Group
Penguin Group (USA) Inc.
375 Hudson Street, New York, New York 10014, USA
Penguin Group (Canada), 90 Eglinton Avenue East, Suite 700, Toronto, Ontario M4P 2Y3, Canada
(a division of Pearson Penguin Canada Inc.) • Penguin Books Ltd., 80 Strand, London WC2R 0RL,
England • Penguin Group Ireland, 25 St. Stephen's Green, Dublin 2, Ireland (a division of Penguin
Books Ltd.) • Penguin Group (Australia), 250 Camberwell Road, Camberwell, Victoria 3124, Australia
(a division of Pearson Australia Group Pty. Ltd.) • Penguin Books India Pvt. Ltd., 11 Community
Centre, Panchsheel Park, New Delhi—110 017, India • Penguin Group (NZ), 67 Apollo Drive,
Rosedale, Auckland 0632, New Zealand (a division of Pearson New Zealand Ltd.) • Penguin Books
(South Africa) (Pty.) Ltd., 24 Sturdee Avenue, Rosebank, Johannesburg 2196, South Africa

Penguin Books Ltd., Registered Offices: 80 Strand, London WC2R 0RL, England

This is a work of fiction. Names, characters, places, and incidents either are the product of the author's
imagination or are used fictitiously, and any resemblance to actual persons, living or dead, business
establishments, events, or locales is entirely coincidental. The publisher does not have any control over
and does not assume any responsibility for author or third-party websites or their content.

LIQUID LIES

A Berkley Sensation Book / published by arrangement with the author

PUBLISHING HISTORY
Berkley Sensation mass-market edition / July 2012
Copyright © 2012 by Hanna Martine.
Excerpt from *A Taste of Ice* by Hanna Martine copyright © 2013 by Hanna Martine.
Cover photo by Claudio Marinesco.
Cover design by Rita Frangie.
Interior text design by Tiffany Estreicher.

ALWAYS LEARNING   PEARSON

For Mom, who would have been so proud.

ACKNOWLEDGMENTS

I would like to thank the wonderful people who helped make the dream of my debut novel become a reality.

Early on, the Online Writing Workshop for Science Fiction, Fantasy and Horror was instrumental in teaching me how to give and receive critiques. Among those who read the earliest first chapters—and whose comments would eventually steer the book in the direction it needed to go—were Rae Carson, Aaron Brown, and Joanne Anderton.

Jodi Meadows, Rhea Ference, and PJ Thompson read my first complete draft and provided valuable comments about editing and pacing that I still carry with me today.

Jill Myles also helped with my early drafts, and her support over the years has humbled me. Perhaps even more importantly, she was the one who pointed me in the direction of the Romance Writers of America (RWA) and said, "I think this might be good for you."

Without a doubt, the publication of this book never would have happened without the encouragement and wisdom of the Chicago-North chapter of RWA. My deepest gratitude to you all. To my Aphrodite Writers, whom I also met through RWA, your passion and advocacy is inspiring.

Katie Junttila, one of my oldest and dearest friends, critiqued the manuscript from a reader's (not a writer's) perspective, and opened my eyes to so much.

Clara Kensie astounded me with her acute observations. This book is better because of her.

Erica O'Rourke and Eliza Evans are two of the smartest women I've ever met and I trust their opinions regarding craft, the industry, and social media implicitly. I'm privileged to call them critique partners, but even more blessed to call them friends.

Holly McDowell's honesty and spirit have pulled me over many humps, and she has been my unfailing champion when I needed it the most.

Without Ellen Wehle, this book, and my writing in general, wouldn't be a quarter as good. And that's not an exaggeration.

In 2000, I told my husband I wanted to fulfill my life's dream and become a writer. He's always supported me—even when I turned down fun things to sit in front of my computer— and I love him for it.

And finally, to my agent Roberta Brown, whose unparalleled enthusiasm, initiative, and drive made this all happen; and to my editor, Cindy Hwang, for believing in unusual stories, the power of voice, and for saying *yes*.

Thank you, thank you, thank you.

ONE

Deals always went down near water.

At 3 a.m. Gwen Carroway and the Chairman of the Company waited in an idling limo on the Embarcadero. To the left, the bay curled around a sparkling San Francisco. To the right, water poured incessantly from Vaillancourt Fountain's hulking mess of squared concrete tubes. Water everywhere—soothing her, whispering to her, offering her protection.

She peered through the tinted windows. On the opposite side of the fountain, two male figures in dark suits appeared between a line of palm trees. Their steps slowed as they started across the angular half-moon of the plaza.

"They're here."

Her father, Chairman Ian Carroway, stopped poking at his phone and set it on the seat next to his thigh. "You sound a little nervous. Are you?"

She sucked in air through her teeth. "Maybe a little. New client jitters, I guess. It'll pass."

His sharp, brown eyes warmed as he patted her knee. "You've done this a dozen times. The Company trusts you. *I* trust you."

She blew out a breath and tilted her face to the jagged line of city buildings cutting into the night sky. "I know, I know. I just wish it wasn't so out in the open."

The phone buzzed and her father reached for it again, thumbs dancing across its face, as he typed one thing and said another. "The location is for their comfort, not ours. You'll be fine, kiddo."

Still "kiddo" to him, and she was closing in on thirty.

When he finished typing, he didn't put the phone down, just held it loosely in one palm. Did he sleep with that thing?

"Are you sure you don't want me to come with you?"

She waved him off. "Yes. I want to do this myself. But thanks."

Maybe if the Board saw how ambitious she was—how devoted and beneficial to the Company—they would vote her into their ranks before her next birthday. And wouldn't that be an accomplishment? Wouldn't that prove to her people that she'd do anything for them, including committing her life to better theirs?

Because of her gift, she was the only person in the Company capable of making international deals, but she wanted to be so much more. She wanted to lead. She wanted to take what her father had grown and make it even stronger.

Gwen patted the bulge in the pocket of her black blazer and opened the limo door. The dome light illuminated her father, who nodded confidently and shooed her off with a grin. His belief in her gave her strength. She would not let him down. She would not let her people down.

A beige Subaru slowed behind the limo, honked, then swerved around. Gwen hopped onto the curb, suddenly and frighteningly conscious of the way the limo's interior light cast a spotlight on the important man inside. Secrecy was paramount. She slammed the door, extinguishing the light, and the limo pulled away on silent wheels, leaving her alone in the plaza.

She closed her eyes and breathed, absorbing the combined sounds of the bay's lapping waves and the roar of the fountain. Opening her eyes, she channeled her father's panache and squared her shoulders. She walked steadily around the fountain, resisting the urge to tug at the yellow strands of her hair that swirled in the unpredictable breeze.

The new client was Japanese, the Company's first from that country. The actual buyer was too important to retrieve the product himself, rich enough to send others to do his business, and obsessed with anonymity. Just like everyone else willing to pay the Company's high price of vanity.

The lead Japanese man approached Gwen with shallow steps. A lock of inky black hair bounced across his forehead, and he used a palm to slick it back. Per the Company's instructions, he clutched a cheap, nondescript briefcase. His companion, striding with purpose at his heels, stood a full head taller and weighed double.

She walked among Primaries every day. She lived in their city without self-consciousness or worry that they could differentiate her from anyone else on the street. But when deals went down and the Company cracked open the door to their private little world, it was impossible for her not to feel vulnerable. Like she was opening the drawbridge and inviting the enemy inside the castle.

That was the source of her nerves, she realized. She didn't fear for her own safety or that she couldn't close the sale. Despite monstrous confidentiality agreements, every deal the Company made threatened to reveal more of themselves to the Primaries, and that scared her more than anything.

There were reasons humans were called Primaries: they were here first and there were far, far more of them.

Even though the wealthiest of the Primaries craved what her people had to offer, they regarded the Company with caution and a measure of disdain. After all, Gwen's people, the Ofarians, were special. No matter how much money the Primaries threw at the Company, they could never physically possess Ofarian magic.

But the Company could sell it to them in a bottle.

Gwen stopped near the lip of the fountain, where the tangle of concrete and rushing water guarded her from the intermittent headlights on the Embarcadero. She let the clients come to her. The smaller Japanese man walked determinedly, with a laser-like focus. His bodyguard made sweeping assessments of the surroundings with his eyes.

Go ahead, she thought. *You won't find anyone but me.*

The men pulled up a few feet away. The shorter man passed the briefcase to his bodyguard and retrieved a business card from his pocket. Presenting it with both hands, he bowed and spoke in quick Japanese. "I am Yoshi. Mikatani regrets being unable to come personally."

"Yoshi." She handed him her own card in the same way and bowed deeper. Japanese spilled off her tongue, coming as easily as her native language. "We spoke on the phone."

As Yoshi straightened, he looked pointedly over her shoulder. "Your chairman could not make it?"

She dipped her head. "It seems both our employers are busy. I assure you your business is safe with me."

"Gwen Carroway. Vice President, International Relations." He smiled as he read her card aloud, though the smile was oily and unforthcoming. She didn't like him at all. When he looked up, the gush of the fountain reflected in his night dark eyes. "Your Japanese is excellent."

"So is my Greek. And twenty-two other languages."

Another smile, this one wider and slimier. His teeth looked like they'd been knocked out and shoved back in by a third grader. She understood very well that she was in the business of lies, but she was supposed to sell them, not buy them. She desperately wanted out from under his stare; she wanted this deal done.

"Do you have the remainder of the payment?"

Yoshi gestured to the briefcase. "Do you have the product?"

"Of course." The subtle lift of her shoulders, the overly casual demeanor—she'd stolen them both directly from her father.

Reaching into her pocket, she withdrew a shiny, graphite-colored box the size of a cigarette pack tied with a red silk bow. The name *Mendacia* wrapped around the package in silvery embossed script.

Yoshi's eyes clamped on to it. He licked his lips. "Does it really work?"

They'd been out in the open for a while now and the covetousness in his expression set her on edge. Her knees locked and she prayed he wouldn't notice her legs shaking. Maybe she should just walk away from the deal . . . except that the Ofarians depended on her and her sales, not only for the money *Mendacia* brought in, but also for the jobs and security it provided.

"After Mikatani-san's foot is amputated, use this potion as directed and no one will be able to tell. His body will seem whole. To anyone watching, he will walk without a limp." She tilted her head, another *trust me* gesture borrowed from Dad, the king of sales, the master of persuasion. She couldn't resist needling Yoshi; he rubbed her wrong in so many ways. "But I have already convinced Mikatani. I don't need to sell it to you."

Another swipe of Yoshi's palm across his forehead. At last he ripped his gaze from the box. "No, of course not. I just find it hard to believe. A potion to cure what the most advanced diabetes doctors cannot?"

She jiggled the box, the bow flopping from side to side. "Not cure. *Appear* to cure. To hide."

She anticipated his reaction. Expected to see disbelief cloud his expression. That usually happened with first-time clients. Only Yoshi didn't indulge. His black eyes narrowed in a way that suggested pleasure, not doubt. "Is that all it can do? Make ailing octogenarians save face in front of their investors?"

Mendacia was far more than that. It was the Ofarians' honor. Only the most gifted of her people were selected to learn the craft, and it was the hard work of those chosen ones who essentially supported the entire race.

The Primaries would never know that. They'd get what they paid for. Nothing more.

"It's glamour," she said, taking care not to look away from Yoshi's eyes. "It can do almost anything." Related to the user's personal appearance, that is.

She raised the box and made an obvious glance at the briefcase. "The instructions to activate the spell are inside the box. I personally translated them and wrote out the words phonetically using Japanese pronunciation. If Mikatani-san has any questions or concerns, please call me directly."

The errant lock of hair fell over Yoshi's forehead again. This time he didn't shove it away. "That's exactly what I wanted to hear. I'll take the *Mendacia* now."

She extended the box, the red bow a splash of color in the dimly lit, deserted plaza. Yoshi hurried forward and snatched it a little too greedily. Sweat beaded on his skin underneath the flap of hair.

A chill raced over her. The air around them screamed in alarm.

Yoshi grinned, slick and crooked. "And I'll take you, too, Gwen."

The goon behind him whipped out a gun—metal flashing like fire, barrel aimed straight at her. *Think, Gwen. Think. How can you turn this asshole's hubris to our benefit?*

She took too long. Griffin burst like a kraken from Vaillancourt Fountain.

Water gushed upward from the low pool, assuming the

strong, lean shape of Griffin's human body. Translucent waves flowed over the valleys of his stomach muscles. White froth cascaded over his square jaw and the hard cut of his arms. His torso darkened, solidified. Water droplets skittered across his skin, soaking in. From the waist down he remained a brilliant, shimmering waterfall balancing on the fountain's bubbling surface. Frighteningly beautiful, unmovable as rock.

Time slowed as Griffin's furious dark eyes met Gwen's. They spoke paragraphs in that moment. She had no time to be pissed off he'd interfered before she'd called for backup. Together they silently assessed the danger. Made plans. Then time caught up, resumed normal speed.

One of Griffin's arms went liquid and shot out, fast as a bullet, to wrap around the stunned bodyguard and yank him forward into the fountain. Griffin's watery legs flowed over the Japanese goon, holding him under the surface. His chest and shoulders heaved with channeled fury.

Griffin, Gwen's personal protector. Griffin, the man the Board wanted her to marry.

The bodyguard thrashed facedown in the shallow pool. Griffin allowed him to break the surface and breathe. Just long enough for him to plead for his life in Japanese. Gwen didn't translate.

She transformed her own arm into a liquid whip and snapped it at the *Mendacia* box sagging in Yoshi's fingers. Reversing the suction, she peeled it from his grasp and flung it back into her own hands. As her arm returned to solid, she felt the familiar, cool tingle of ebbing waters.

Yoshi made a strangled, squeaking, unmanly sound in the back of this throat. His empty hands shook.

She walked to the edge of the fountain, where the briefcase of money floated. Under Yoshi's bug-eyed stare, she plucked it from the water and spoke the Ofarian words to dissolve every molecule of water from its surface and the stacks of money inside.

"Something tells me," she swiveled back to Yoshi, "that Mikatani isn't aware of your actions tonight." No response. "Let me guess. You had a better offer? Thought to take me along with the *Mendacia*? Force me to change the command words to make it do whatever your new clients wanted?" Yoshi gulped, defeated. "You do realize that by violating our contract you've just single-handedly forfeited fifty-one percent of Mikatani's holdings to the Company?"

Yoshi sagged as though his own body were made of water. "Please. I beg you. He'll kill me . . ."

She set the briefcase on the fountain's lip and ran her fingers along its edges. A great surge of anger and confidence bubbled inside her. She wondered if that was what drove her father and the rest of the Board day in and day out. That feeling of secret superiority and advantage. How dare a Primary think he could pull one over on the Company?

She knew what she had to do.

She looked to Griffin, whose eyes were almost as tortured as their captives'. A muscle in his jaw twitched. "Gwen," he said through clenched teeth. "Just give the order."

Usually the Board collectively passed down the sentence. She'd been in the boardroom in the past, when they'd decided a Primary should die for knowing too much, but she'd never been the one to slam the gavel.

It was Ofarian law and it was necessary, but that didn't mean she had to enjoy it.

Plus, there were two offenders. Griffin couldn't handle both of them at the same time and she . . . well, maybe here was where her cowardice finally showed its ugly face.

She faced Yoshi. "I'm sure the death Mikatani will give you will include pain. Humiliation. I understand saving face is very important to your people. It's why you're here in the first place, isn't it?"

"Please . . ." Yoshi begged.

"I'm willing to give you a choice, Yoshi. I can let you go and you can try to run from your boss—which I'm sure will be impossible—or you can die right here." She glanced at the bodyguard still gasping in the water. "If you go now, your man dies. I'll trade your life for his. Who's it going to be?"

Yoshi, made all the more tiny by his round-shouldered fear, pointed one shaking finger at the goon gurgling beneath Griffin's liquid legs. "Him." Then he turned and ran.

TWO

Yoshi sprinted across the plaza and disappeared into the city, his black hair and suit blending in with the shadows. The sharp beat of his loafers on pavement faded to nothing. Gwen fumbled for the signal switch clipped inside her lapel that would call the limo back.

"Gwen." Leashed panic lifted Griffin's voice over the rushing water. "What the hell are you doing? You let him *go*?"

She had, hadn't she.

She stuffed the *Mendacia* box back in her pocket and scooped up the briefcase. "You can't take care of them both at the same time, Griffin."

"Don't tell me what I am and am not capable of."

She glared in the direction where Yoshi had run. "I could say the same thing to you." His nostrils flared. "I can't take a life. I'm not trained, physically or emotionally." No, she was corporate, through and through.

"He'll talk."

"Dad will call Mikatani the second the limo comes. Yoshi's as good as dead."

Griffin was still half water, towering above her. "I hope you know what you're doing."

She did, too. Leaders had to own their decisions and she'd stand by hers.

The limo screeched around the bend and braked where it had dropped her off earlier.

"Get in the car." Trouble darkened Griffin's eyes, and the slant of his mouth turned grim.

She understood. He didn't want her around when he drowned Yoshi's henchman.

The past fifteen minutes settled like ice in her bones, and she stumbled to the limo without remembering the walk. She fell into the seat, unclipped the signal switch, and tossed it in the corner.

"Kiddo? Gwennie?" Her father scooted closer. "You're shaking. What happened?"

When she removed the *Mendacia* box from her pocket and couldn't read the name for the quivering of her hand, she knew it to be true. His hand squeezed her shoulder, forcing her to look at him.

She swallowed hard. "Call Mikatani. Tell him to come pick up his trash."

"What do you—"

The door flew open and in tumbled a naked Griffin. "Go," he yelled at the driver, then turned to scan the windows for witnesses. The limo lurched away from the curb and sailed down the Embarcadero.

Her father shifted seats so Griffin could sidle next to Gwen. She fought the urge to scramble away.

She'd seen Griffin naked once or twice before, but only during transformation. Ofarians didn't need to be naked to change, but it took extra effort to maintain outside objects as liquid, and he'd been waiting in that fountain for a good thirty minutes before Yoshi showed up.

Though she averted her gaze, she was still acutely aware of Griffin tugging the black pants of his security uniform up his bare legs. He'd stashed his clothes next to the whiskey carafe, and when he stretched forward for his black shirt, the lean, strong muscles in his shoulders and back bunched.

Any woman in the world would pant at the sight of him. Any woman except Gwen.

She turned to her dad. "Go on. Call Mikatani. Let his people deal with the translation on their end. I'll talk if I have to, just can't promise what I'll say. I think you'll be better with diplomatic relations right about now."

"What happened?"

She told him, Griffin silent beside her. Before she was even finished, her father had gone fire red in the face.

"Forget Mikatani," the Chairman blurted. "We're hunting that son of a bitch right now. Griffin, get on it."

Griffin opened his phone and mumbled orders to his security team. In minutes, tens of plainclothes Ofarian soldiers would be scouring the city for Yoshi. Come sunrise, SFPD would be saddled with not one, but two mysterious deaths of Japanese nationals.

"And you," her father said, "you shouldn't have let him go."

One awful lesson learned. The Board position slipped out of her immediate reach. She'd have to make up for that.

Adrenaline seeped from her body in stuttering waves, and she sank deeper into the seat. From underneath it all floated the *tap tap tap* of her father's fingers, back on his phone again.

She let the rock and jerk of the limo carry her farther and farther away from what had just happened. How could she remedy this? How could she save face in front of the Board?

"Sir, if I may," came Griffin's quiet interjection. The Chairman nodded for him to continue, but he was looking out the window, his expression clouded.

"The international deals," Griffin said, "they're getting riskier."

Gwen sat up straighter, not liking at all where this conversation was about to go.

The Chairman pinched his lips between his fingers and sighed. "You're right. They are. Because foreigners aren't scared of us yet. The Americans are because we've been doing business with them for almost a century. Our existence is protected here. Fear breeds secrecy."

Griffin nodded vehemently. "And is this a new threat? Assholes like Yoshi wanting to grab Gwen? Get her to reconfigure the potion? I don't like it. Not at all."

"Gwen," her father said, "is your safety really worth this?"

He turned sad eyes to her, and the emotion behind them struck a deep, bitter chord.

Ofarians weren't immune to vanity. Though her father was closing in on sixty years old, tonight he looked barely forty. She didn't like facing him when he did *Mendacia* and the glamour made him look like the photo above his mantel in which she was a little girl on his knee. Seeing him young was like looking into the past, and she wanted more important things—things other than his wrinkles and softening gut—to change instead.

She wanted her mom back. She wanted her sister to have been smarter, more loyal.

"Whoa, whoa, whoa." She spread her arms between the two men. "Going global was my idea. Think about everything my division has done for Ofarians in the past seven years. Because of me, we've tripled *Mendacia* production and our earnings. We have everything we could possibly need. More, even. Our people are the happiest they've ever been."

"Right," the Chairman said, clamping a loving hand on her knee. "So maybe we should scale back. Be more selective in our international clientele. Try instead to expand our American base."

"I have Griffin," she argued. "It's his job to keep me safe. The whole race trusts him. His security team is impenetrable."

She risked a look at her protector, but he was staring at his lap, his mouth a straight, white line. He hadn't had much say in his role when the Board handed it to him when he was sixteen. He didn't have much say about it now.

She couldn't help wondering if part of the reason he was so amenable to a marriage with her was to improve his station in their society.

"Please." She held her father's hands now. Though they looked smooth, they felt dry and wrinkled. "This is what I have. What I was born to do. I'll do what I can to keep *Mendacia* viable overseas, then campaign to be admitted to the Board. I have so many ideas, Dad . . ."

He tugged his hand out. "You understand why I worry, don't you?"

"Of course I do."

"We're on the same side, Gwennie. We both want what's best for our people."

"And I can do things for them that no one else can. I'm the first Translator born since we came here. Don't shut me down."

She'd been hearing she was special since she hit puberty and accidentally learned Spanish over chicken flautas and virgin strawberry margaritas in a Mexican restaurant. The Board had gone into a tizzy and the very next day she'd been assigned a protector, the same man who would eventually hand-pick and train Griffin before retiring.

"*Mendacia* is a gift to our race," she went on, and her father nodded with pride. "It's let us figure out how to live as Secondaries in a Primary world. Besides"—she sat back with a grin—"you know I'm dying to know how it's made."

The Chairman wagged a playful finger. "When the Board votes you in, my dear. Not a moment sooner."

She couldn't wait.

"So I can scout the job in Moscow next week?"

She'd already booked her and Griffin's flight, giving herself five days to learn the language and study the culture and potential client. This time it was an heir possibly linked to crooked money.

"I want extra guys," Griffin said, and her father acquiesced.

As they pulled up in front of her apartment building, the limo slanted at a steep San Francisco angle, a text came through Griffin's phone.

"Got 'im," he said. *Wow, that was fast.* "They'll detain him at a neutral location until I get there. If you don't mind, sir, I'd like to wait until after we've met with the Board."

Gwen threw a look of relief at her dad, who was watching Griffin like a proud father-in-law to be. She lunged for the door, eager to get away. "Good night. Or good morning, rather."

She stumbled out to the sidewalk, her vision a little blurry, her legs a little shaky from the adrenaline crash.

"Gwen. Wait." Griffin climbed out after her. He leaned back inside to apologize to the Chairman, who was already back tapping at his phone.

Griffin jogged the few steps to her, then stood with his legs planted wide, arms crossed over his chest, like he was trying to root himself to the spot. Or keep himself from touching her.

"You got a gun pulled on you tonight." His expression was as dark as his hair and clothing. "You can try to act tough, but I really need to know if you're all right."

She blinked up at him, so ready to say, *Yeah, of course! Fabulous!* "I will be," she replied, because this was Griffin and not a Board member. With him, she didn't have to pretend.

His brow creased and his eyes dipped to the sidewalk. There

was more. He wasn't moving from that spot until he'd said it, so she stayed put.

"What the hell were you thinking, not calling for me? I heard everything that was happening with Yoshi. I heard how shit was going south fast. Why didn't you?"

"Because I thought I could handle it."

"Gwen . . ."

"All right. Because I knew you had my back and I was trying to figure out what he wanted and what more he knew. If this was a bigger threat than it seemed."

She bit the inside of her cheek. There were too many emotions on Griffin's face—none of them bending in her favor.

"Don't do that again," he said.

"How about, don't make a move unless I say?" Big, awkward moment. She'd never pulled rank like that before and it made his jaw clench, though he didn't respond. At considerable length she asked, "Are *you* okay? With what I had you do?"

"Yeah. Fine." It was the most she'd ever get out of him on the subject of acting executioner.

His arms dropped to his sides. He wasn't much taller than her when she wore heels, and his every movement had a careful grace, as though he'd planned it moments ahead of time.

"Want me to walk you up?" A casual question, but his eyes begged: *Please, please can I walk you up?*

She looked away. "It's late. Or early, however you want to look at it."

He cupped his jaw in the crook of his hand between thumb and forefinger and gazed down the street. They'd known each other so long that she recognized the sign of his barely controlled frustration. He said, "We haven't hung out at your place in a long time."

Not since she'd first heard the rumblings from the Board about their impending marriage match.

She shrugged. "Still looks the same."

"That's not the point and you know it. We haven't stopped being friends, have we?"

Her head dropped back on her neck, heavy as a sack of flour. "Of course not."

It had taken a while to get to this place, to friendship. All through junior high, Griffin had picked on her so much she'd

spent a lunch or two crying in a bathroom stall. He hadn't cared
that she was a Translator or a Board member's daughter. Then
her assigned protector wanted to retire when Gwen finished
high school; he tested every boy her age and guess who came
out on top?

She and Griffin had resented the new relationship, but duty
to the Ofarians rose above all. By the time they graduated high
school, they fell into friendship. The best kind.

Until the Board shook up eleven years of closeness by wanting the only known Translator and the man sworn to protect
her to procreate. They'd never say as much, but they were hoping she'd birth a child with her gift. The official engagement
announcement hadn't come yet, but it would.

And then they'd be married. Sleeping together.

Griffin rolled his eyes, reading her panic. "I'm not talking
about sex, Gwen. I'm talking about *talking*."

He made perfect sense. She couldn't throw away their relationship over a bit of discomfort. It was how the Ofarian marriage system worked. *Every* man and woman suffered initial
panic. In this regard, she wasn't remotely special.

And this was Griffin. Brave, beautiful Griffin who'd always
be there for her. She opened her arms.

He swept across the sidewalk as silkily as if he were still in
water form. They embraced hard. She couldn't deny it; he felt
like home. The cologne he'd worn forever, the lean, athletic build
of his body, the caring circle of his arms. That moment reminded
her of the first time they'd hugged when she was seventeen.
When the Ofarian doctors had told her family their race wasn't
immune to cancer and that her mom didn't have long to live.

"Gwen." He drew a deep breath and blew it out, warm, into
her hair. "The way I feel about you has . . . changed in the past
few weeks. It may have even changed before that."

She fell perfectly still. "I have no idea what to say to that."

"You don't love me. I know."

She stepped back, trying not to make it seem like she was
pushing him away. "Of course I love you."

The wry grin he gave her restored some of their long-
standing camaraderie. "But not in that way."

Primary and Secondary women lusted after this man. She'd
seen it happen plenty of times. She shouldn't have him. He

deserved a woman who looked at him with heat that rivaled a summer afternoon.

She picked her next words carefully. "It'll change for me. I have no doubt in my mind. Look at all the great Ofarian marriages. Look at all the terrific kids and families. And look how our work is setting up such incredible futures for all of them. We'll get there. I know it."

Maybe if she kept repeating that, she'd believe it.

He raised his thick black eyebrows and took her face in his hands. For a second she thought he'd kiss her, and she tensed. But he didn't.

"We will," he said, and backed toward the limo. "Call you later?"

"Absolutely."

The limo pulled away, heading for the Chairman's manor in Pacific Heights. She turned for her door . . . and realized she'd left her purse, with her cell phone and apartment keys, back at the office. She reached for the signal switch to call back the limo, but she'd pulled it off on the Embarcadero. In the chilly predawn it was way too early to knock on her neighbor Martha's first-floor window and ask for her spare. The idea was to avoid attention and suspicion.

Company HQ was only three blocks up and two blocks over, uphill. Even though Yoshi was in custody, Griffin and Dad and probably the whole Board would likely have a heart attack if they knew she was out on the streets alone. She weighed her options. Sit out in the open on the front steps for another few hours, or be at HQ in ten minutes.

Settled. She'd call Griffin from her office.

So she walked, high heels gouging into her feet and the suit she'd been wearing for going on twenty-four hours feeling itchy and dirty.

Later, after grabbing said purse from her bottom desk drawer, she called Griffin, who apparently had fallen asleep just inside his apartment door.

"Be there in ten," he slurred, sparing her a lecture.

"Mind if I go around the corner to grab a coffee? Don't think I'll be sleeping now anyway."

A big pause. "Okay. But stay in the restaurant until I get there."

HQ was in the middle of the block, the all-night diner just south around the corner. She started for the restaurant, mouth stretched wide in a yawn and the sky beginning to pale low over the Berkeley hills.

Then she wasn't on the sidewalk anymore.

Hands ripped her off her path and threw her against a wall. Her skull rattled. Her vision winked out. A great blossom of pain exploded on her crown and tore its way down her spine, detonating a bomb of fear.

When she came to, Yoshi's bared and crooked teeth filled her terrified sight. He held her immobile, forearm like iron across her chest.

THREE

Who the hell had Griffin's forces nabbed? Some poor, unsus-
pecting Japanese man on a sunrise walk?

"If you touch your magic"—flecks of Yoshi's spittle splashed
her cheek—"the whole world will know what I know."

Of all the threats he could throw at her, it was the only one
that could make her listen.

He shoved a cell phone in her face, the screen reading the
name of a recognizable Japanese news service. "I have other
contacts. CNN. Our government. Yours. I recorded what you
did. What *he* did."

No. *No.* The Ofarians themselves didn't even have recorded
evidence of their powers. It was the most important Ofarian rule,
the one drilled into children's heads the moment they understood
speech. *Leave no shadow.* In situations like at Vaillancourt Fountain, Ofarian moles working inside the authorities and in Primary
security firms would have already erased any camera footage
that proved Ofarians were ever within fifty yards of that place.

The Company's client contract and confidentiality agreement was so huge it could prop open the door to a safe. But
since Yoshi's attempted theft had already forfeited the majority
of Mikatani's empire, he was a walking dead man. He had
nothing to lose, and it showed.

"What do you want?" She clawed for every last bit of strength.
Any weakness on her part would only make Yoshi stronger.

"I want in." His Japanese slurred with desperation. "You'll
hide me from Mikatani and give me half of the assets you take
from him." He jiggled the phone. "And I'll keep the secret of
your little magic shop."

The second most important rule in the Ofarian world? No Primaries allowed inside. *Ever.*

It was violation of that rule that gave Griffin such a haunted look sometimes.

"No way," she ground out.

Yoshi bounced her head against the wall. Stars pecked at her peripheral vision. Breath struggled inside her crushed chest.

Not fifteen feet away, the hulking shape of a drunk man shuffled by on the sidewalk. Chin tucked to chest, he ambled with stuttered steps. Of course, when Griffin was not by her side and she could not touch water, the world would send her a huge guy lost in an alcoholic haze. Still, he was her only hope. She opened her mouth.

"You cry out," Yoshi snapped, "and I press *send*."

His thumb twitched over the green button. The screen showed a tiny movie icon labeled "fountain."

The only defense she had left was to stall. When Griffin didn't find her at the diner, he'd go looking. The sun would touch the city soon, its rays slicing through the shadows night left behind. People would begin filling the streets. Yoshi wouldn't be able to hide them then. All she had to do was buy some time.

"You don't realize what you're asking," she whispered. "You don't know what you're messing with."

He laughed. That forced laughter of crazy people. "I know exactly what I'm . . ."

Someone grabbed Yoshi's shoulders from behind and threw him to the side. *Threw* him. But he still had a decent hold on Gwen and she flew off balance, too. She struck the ground hard, elbow smarting.

Parting the messy curtain of her hair, she peered up to see a giant of a man holding Yoshi in a death grip. The stranger's back was to her, but she recognized its shape—the wide shoulders, thick arms, and muscular legs—as the "drunk" who'd stumbled by moments earlier.

She sent out virtual feelers, testing the stranger's signature, looking for magic. Wondering if he was one of Griffin's. Nothing. This man was a Primary.

He was a tornado wrapped in human skin and he shook Yoshi hard enough she felt it in her own teeth.

"I don't know what the fuck you guys were saying"—no

trace of alcohol in his deep voice, just thunder rolling over gravel—"but I know when a woman's being threatened."

She didn't translate, but then, she didn't have to. Yoshi, flailing uselessly, eyes wide, clearly got the message.

The stranger glanced over his shoulder at her, still sprawled on the ground. "You okay?" When she didn't answer right away—could only stare at his hard profile and ponder how she was supposed to get out of this cleanly—he barked, "You speak English?"

She rubbed her throat where Yoshi's arm had tried to carve a trench, and hobbled to her feet. "Yes. I do."

The stranger wrangled Yoshi around, and now she and the big man looked directly at each other. "You okay, then?"

He was something to look at. The muscles in his arms bunched tight beneath his gray T-shirt. His head was shaved and round, and veins protruded from his thick neck. He wore faded jeans with frayed hems and scuffed workman's boots, and he held Yoshi between his powerful, widespread legs so that Yoshi's loafers barely grazed the asphalt.

The way the stranger stared at her, hard and unflinching, made her fear she'd been thrown from one threat into the arms of another.

"I guess," she said.

Yoshi started babbling in Japanese. "Just let me go. Give me the chance you gave me before. I'll leave. You'll never see me, never hear from me again." Yet his eyes drifted tellingly to his cell phone, lying half-hidden under a cardboard box.

"Sorry, Yoshi. That was a one-time offer."

Protocol dictated he should die. Right then and there. But she had no Griffin and she had no weapon. Even if she had one, she couldn't outright kill someone in front of a Primary. She didn't think she could kill anyone, period. If she called in the security team, how would it look to the stranger when a van full of black-clad soldiers pulled up and stole Yoshi away? Would they take the stranger, too, even though he knew nothing?

Damn Primary. Saving her and screwing everything else up.

She snatched up the phone, turned it on, and dialed. It rang only once, then voicemail picked up. She used her most formal Japanese. "Mikatani. Yoshi's been very, very bad. You'll find that over half your assets are now in the hands of the Company, per our contract. And there will be no *Mendacia* coming your way. Yoshi thought someone else deserved it more than you. His body is in San Francisco. Come get it."

Popping out his phone's memory card, she dropped it on the ground, stabbed it three times with her stiletto heel, then slid the shards into her purse. When she looked up, the stranger cocked an eyebrow at her.

Yoshi squirmed, unintelligible Japanese streaming from his lips. The stranger held him seemingly without any effort. When he removed one hand, a moment of panic stabbed into her. Was he going for his phone?

She thrust out her hands. "Don't call the cops!"

He froze, just his eyes flicking up to hers. His were blue, blue like ocean water, and they widened with speculation and . . . was that amusement?

"Don't worry," he said. "Wasn't planning on it."

He flexed the fingers of his free hand, cracking them, then resumed his grip on Yoshi. Sunlight struck the tops of the two-story buildings rising on either side. He looked up into the brightening light and then out at the street. His feet shifted, the only sign of anxiousness she'd witnessed in him thus far.

But he didn't ask what this was all about. It didn't even look like he cared.

Neither one of them wanted the cops involved. She didn't care about his reasons, only that they were on the same page. They watched each other. Assessing. She fought the urge to defend herself, to tell him that she was normally perfectly capable of holding her own.

"So what now?" he asked.

Griffin had acted when she hadn't wanted him to, but this man waited for her to call the shots.

When she didn't answer, the stranger added, "If I let him go, will he follow you?"

"Don't let him go. And yes. He probably will."

Deep creases dug into his forehead. "So . . . leg or arm?"

Said so matter-of-factly. Like he did this every day. She shivered.

She paused, but couldn't really understand why. She'd already ordered Griffin to kill Yoshi's bodyguard. But that had been Griffin and it had been Company business. This man was a Primary, and he'd been nudged into the Ofarian world.

She walked around Yoshi so she could meet his wild, pleading eyes. "Leg," she said in Japanese.

Yoshi thrashed like his henchman had in the fountain. She turned to the stranger. This close to him, she could sense the tension in his body, see up close the way his muscles moved beneath his skin. It was like standing next to a campfire. Inviting and intoxicating at first, but ultimately dangerous if you stood too close for too long. She stepped back.

"Leg," she told him in English.

The stranger bent low to Yoshi and growled, "You talk and I'll find you."

That she did translate.

He lifted an arm and drove his elbow down into Yoshi's cheek. Yoshi collapsed to his knees, the caps making a horrible, hollow sound on the pavement. He screamed, high and vibrating, and it echoed out on the street.

They wouldn't be alone much longer.

The stranger's head snapped up. He met Gwen's eyes and gripped Yoshi's ankle. He didn't ask her to leave, as Griffin had. This time, she would own her decision and watch it being carried out. The big workman's boot came down hard. There was a sickening crunch and another scream.

She started to breathe heavier and her palms hurt where they tightly clasped her purse strap.

Heavy footsteps came at her. A large hand grabbed her elbow and pulled her out onto the sidewalk. The stranger steered her downhill and she didn't look back. Yoshi's groans faded but didn't disappear.

All around them the city was awakening. Over it all drifted the wail of a police siren, coming closer. If Griffin was anywhere near the diner by now, he would hear that, maybe even come running, but she had no way to contact him while the stranger guided her away.

She wanted to run, and the big man must have sensed it because his clamp on her arm tightened. He held her back, kept her in check, wordlessly slowed her pace. He was right, of course. Running would only draw attention.

He ducked into an alcove behind a corner convenience store

already inhabited by trash cans and a hissing orange cat. He pulled her next to him, flattening her against the wall, one giant arm across the front of her shoulders. Her heart pounded so loudly she didn't hear the screech of new sirens until the flashing lights sped past, heading uphill.

With a foreign sense of helplessness, she realized she was more than a little out of her element. If she were alone or with other Ofarians—as she usually was—she'd be an innocuous puddle by now. And yet . . . this guy seemed to know what he was doing in evading the cops.

When she chanced a look up at his face, he was already watching her. He raised a deliberate eyebrow then returned his focus back to the sidewalk. How long did they wait there? One minute? One hour? At last he tugged her back out onto the sidewalk and they continued walking downhill, but at a much slower pace.

They stopped outside her apartment building.

The whole time she thought she'd been following him, when really it was the other way around. Wasn't that the classic mark of a con man, to let the victim think they were the one in control? This guy was a master. But a master at what?

Three blocks away, the squawk of an ambulance answered the blurt of a police car siren. Gwen desperately needed to call Griffin and tell him she was okay and that Yoshi had been picked up by Primary medical. Or maybe he was already on scene, pretending to be a bystander, and noticing that she wasn't there.

The street she lived on had four lanes, and now that the sun had fully risen, a smattering of people moved along the sidewalks. Cars pulled out of parking spaces and drove off. A line of vehicles began to form at the streetlight at the bottom of the hill, another line of customers in the Starbucks at the opposite corner.

"Just relax." The stranger's voice was still incredibly deep, but the grit and tumble of the aggressive storm had passed. "People notice panic. Breathe deep, in and out now."

He turned her to face him. The sound of his voice, pouring over her like honey, drew her eyes to his face. He leaned closer. "Come on now," he coaxed through a whisper. "Deep breath."

She started to comply, then . . . "Cop."

The white car stopped at the bottom of the block, idling at the corner. The policeman inside swung his head in their direction. Gwen flinched but her companion was faster. He reached out and pulled her body into his. She stiffened, resisted.

"If you dive for the door," he said near her ear, "they'll notice. Put your arms around me. I'm just a guy walking a girl home after a date that lasted all night. Nothing strange about that."

Except everything. Nothing about the last five hours had been remotely ordinary.

How did he do it? How did he put such force and focus into his words yet make his body act so natural?

His command pulled a string somewhere inside her. She slid her arms around his waist, finding him warm and taut through his T-shirt. Her ear pressed against his hard chest, and when he asked, "What will your neighbors think if they see you out here with me?" the soothing rumble of his voice made her sigh. She caught it too late.

"Nothing." She barely knew any of them except Martha, and even she was still just a casual acquaintance.

Not too long ago Griffin had embraced her in this very spot. And here she was again, in the arms of a complete stranger—a *Primary*.

Why wasn't this more awkward than it should be?

"What about the guy?" His voice swam around her, inside her. He was everywhere.

"The guy?"

"With the broken leg. Will he talk? Should I worry about you?"

"Me? What about you? You're the one who broke his leg."

Was that a chuckle? Gwen couldn't tell; he masked it by shifting, drawing her closer. "I can take care of myself." Then: "The cruiser's moving."

She couldn't see over the not-quite-a-stranger-anymore's wide shoulder, but she heard the whir of the cruiser's engine, the slow friction of its wheels on the asphalt.

He expelled a hard breath. "It's gone." He didn't release her. And she didn't push away. Somewhere inside those tense few seconds their embrace transitioned from alibi to personal. No space existed between their bodies. Their chests and hips and knees pressed together like two people who actually knew each other. He was firm and enveloping and smelled like delicious danger.

"I need to go." She didn't move.

"Tell me." His head dipped lower. "Is it too early in the relationship for you to ask me up for coffee?"

She shoved against him, nearly jumping away. Safely outside of his aura, she looked him up and down. The tension his body had owned in the alley had dissipated. He now stood relaxed, sitting slightly into one hip, big arms dangling easily at his sides. But it was his eyes, those sea-depth eyes, that spoke of his attraction. Or did it merely reflect hers?

She wasn't shocked that he'd asked, but because, for a split second, she actually considered it. Instantly, horrifically, she understood what had just clobbered her over the head: the Allure.

The Allure: the desire for what you could never have. The longing for the other side. The intense attraction to a Primary, not because you wanted to spend the rest of your life with him or her, but because they were *different* and you wanted them *right now*.

They actually taught it in Ofarian sex ed. Ofarian parents had to talk about it with their blushing prepubescent kids. Gwen remembered those talks vividly, remembered thinking to herself: *Why would I ever want to be with anyone who's not like me?*

And she hadn't. Until today.

He smiled and it transformed him. Holy stars in hell. A single dimple slashed deep into one cheek. Early sunlight caught the crystalline blue of his eyes. Easy crinkles radiated out from their corners.

She drew in a lungful of air then let it out slowly. If he thought himself forward or strange for asking to come up to her place, he didn't apologize. He didn't say anything.

Looking into his eyes felt too intimate, so she dropped her gaze. Though his head was shaved clean, the stubble on his cheeks and chin burned silver and gold. The tilt of his head was infinitesimal. A smudge of dark below his ear caught her eye. The black line of a tattoo peeked out from the neckline of his T-shirt. It snaked around his neck and stretched for his ear. He swallowed and the tattoo danced. As he crossed his arms over his chest, his sleeves rode up, uncovering a tease of similar lines on his hard left biceps.

She fought an overwhelming desire to tug up the T-shirt

and discover just how much of him it covered. Ofarians didn't get tattoos.

"Do you feel safe here?" he asked, nodding at her building.

He didn't ask about Yoshi, why he'd grabbed her, and she realized this guy never would. The reasons behind her predicament didn't matter, only that she was safe now. To him, it was just another day. That frightened her . . . and gave her a weird sense of security.

"I do," she replied, and meant it. Because the second she got inside, she would dial Griffin and let him know she'd made it home.

"Good." Another small smile touched his lips. "So . . . you want me to walk you up?"

Griffin's exact words. Spoken from the exact spot Griffin had stood not so long ago, and where they'd talked about their impending engagement. And here she was, actually playing with the thought of giving in to the Allure.

It hurtled her back to reality.

Why was she still standing there? How had she let herself be corralled by a pair of strong arms and crinkly eyes and a voice that promised things she hadn't even let herself fantasize about? She didn't like how she'd allowed this strange man a too-long look into the window of her life. She didn't like her response to him. Not because he wasn't worthy, but because he wasn't Ofarian.

She backed toward the door. "No, I don't."

He raised his hands and lowered his chin. "Sorry. Understandable. Forget I asked. I'm no danger to you."

And that *was* the danger, wasn't it?

"I'm . . . I have to go." She whirled away from him. Her hand shook as she dug out her building key and jiggled it in the lock. It took two tries. All the while she felt his eyes on her back . . . and other places on her body that made her frantic to get away before the sensations turned her back around.

As she bounded up the stairs, every step washed cooler air over her. It squelched the heat of his chest against her cheek and erased the imprint of his arms around her back. She had no business remembering either.

FOUR

Reed Scott clanked his coffee cup on the tiled countertop.
Nine-thirty a.m. He'd been at the counter of the family-style
brunch place since seven, injecting himself with caffeine and
eating for two. His gut didn't feel right, and he couldn't tell if
it was the sick worry and excited anticipation that always came
before a new job . . . or her.

He clutched a folded newspaper in one hand, but the words
were in Chinese for all he knew. Every story, no matter how
sappy or morbid or anger-inducing, sent his mind circling back
to the events of that dawn. A blurry black-and-white photo of
a protest in France had somehow morphed into a vivid, color
image of the blonde. How screwed up was that? Her makeup
had been a little smudged and her hair had been tangled in the
back where that asshole had ground her skull into the building,
but still she'd radiated strength. Fortitude. Intelligent reason
and courage. And she'd been bothered by the fact that Reed
had helped her.

There was a whole hell of a lot of mystery there. When it
came to women, secrets didn't do much for him. He had his
own to deal with, thanks.

But he hadn't imagined it, had he? That spark of connection
between them? That lust? The entire situation was crazy, so
maybe it was all in his head. So why hadn't she pulled out of
his arms when it was safe? Why had he seen those brown-
bottle-colored eyes melt for him, just for a second, before she
turned and ran inside?

The phone in his jeans pocket buzzed and he jumped, rat-
tling the coffee cup on the counter. The waitress, an attractive

forty-something pinning order tickets to the cook's overhead clip, glanced his way again. She'd been making eyes at him all morning, and had even slipped him a free apple turnover.

He took out the new, disposable phone purchased at an all-night convenience store and flipped it open. The moment he'd bought it, he'd texted the number to the one person who needed to have it. "Yeah."

"Is this . . . the Retriever?" The female caller was trying to hide her snicker but the smile in her voice came through loud and clear.

A stupid code name, but he hadn't given it to himself. A long-ago client had called him that, and it had spread like wildfire. In this line of work, word of mouth meant everything.

Call the Retriever. He'll get you who you want. For a price.

Now more than ever he wore the anonymity like shield and sword. With Tracker gunning for him, he needed all the protection he could get. Of course, it would have been smart to lie low and not take on any new jobs after bailing on Tracker's contract, but Reed wasn't wired that way.

Phone in hand, potential client on the line, an invisible wall rose up inside him, dividing Reed Scott, the man, from the mercenary who collected the Retriever's substantial paychecks.

Slam. Lock.

It was the only way he could survive, keeping the two separate. The only way he could live with himself sometimes.

"Yeah, that's me," Reed said. "You must be Nora."

"Yes. It's good to finally speak to you myself. I do hate electronic communication." Her soft, wisp-thin voice was not at all what he'd expected.

"Tonight," she said, jumping right in, which he always appreciated, "you'll meet with my two colleagues, Xavier and Adine." She told him where to go and at what time, and he committed the info quickly to memory. Never rely on print or pixels, if you could help it.

He frowned into the phone. "Not you personally?"

Dealing with henchmen was never on the top of his list, but he'd take a chance on it this time based on where he'd discovered her money was coming from and what he heard in her voice.

"No, no," she chuckled. "I'm too old to travel that far."

Everything she said—even things she didn't—added small clues to his arsenal of puzzle pieces. Before he'd meet with her two people, he'd do more homework. If it came down to playing dirty, he'd need his own bargaining chip.

"They'll give you information on the target," she said.

Chin to chest, he kept his voice low. "Delivery point? Timeline?"

"That, too. Everything you'll need. Upon your acceptance of the job, I'll forward the second twenty-five percent of your payment."

The first twenty-five had already made a comfortable home in his off-shore account. Potential clients needed that much just to open the lines of communication with him. Nonrefundable. It secured secrecy and gave him clues about those who were paying him. His connections were very good at unraveling the most complicated of knots. When he wanted, he could track clients hiding behind multiple networks of bank security.

For instance, he already knew where Nora's money came from. Or from whom, rather. And it was a very, very good piece of information.

"Fine," he told her.

"I hope you can help us." She hung up.

His mind buzzed, setting off a dazzling chain reaction throughout his whole body. This old woman had thrust the starting gun into the air and pulled the trigger. The challenge of a new job sent him exploding from the starting blocks. The Retriever lived for this rush. Sometimes it was a short sprint to the finish line, to target delivery. Sometimes it was a long slog. Didn't matter. Jobs gave him what he craved: that intense concentration, the severe separation from everyday life, the high that could last for days or weeks.

Only after did the guilt set in.

Only after would he dream of another life. The life he might have had, had he once possessed any kind of foresight or courage or goals.

"You finally done?"

The waitress splayed her arms on the counter in front of him. Her lipstick had worn away everywhere but a faint line around her lips. The only reason he noticed was because of the way she was smiling at him.

Unlock. The wall between the Retriever and himself fell.

Reed looked down at his two desiccated plates of pancakes and corned beef hash, and saw how his fist had tightly crumpled the *Chronicle*. "Think so." He unfurled his fingers to spare the newspaper a sweaty death.

"Nothing else?" She leaned slightly forward, her eyes drifting to the bit of tattoo just below his ear. "My number, maybe?"

The blonde's eyes had found the tattoo, too, but he'd enjoyed her curious gaze. He'd even turned his head so she could see more.

He recognized the look on the waitress's face, that desperate need to escape your skin, if only for a little while. They both wanted out. They both wanted another chance, a rewind. Maybe she'd fallen on hard luck early on. Maybe she'd busted her ass right out of high school to support a family. Maybe she'd just got trapped in a bad life track, and no matter how hard she tried, she couldn't wrench the wheels out of the rut.

But Reed was not the key to the doors of her past or future, and she was not his. Not even for the little time she was clearly offering.

He gave her a small, sympathetic smile. "Thanks, but I have to say no."

She nodded without anger or judgment, and glanced at his bare left hand. "Taken?"

He laughed shortly. "No." At least, not in the way she was talking about. He was taken, but the chains that held him were made of adrenaline and money and lack of other options.

The only long-term relationship he'd ever had—and even that label could be debated—hadn't done what it was supposed to. He'd failed at it because he'd been selfish enough to want it to be something other than a relationship. He'd wanted a cure, a way out. A good enough excuse to leave his business. She'd wanted *him*, though, and the job refused to give him up.

Reed slipped a fifty under the check, tapping it twice. "Take care," he told the waitress, and ducked out into the sunshine.

He'd never been to San Francisco. Countless things to do and only one that truly interested him. He could try to convince himself he wanted to see the blonde again because of the awesome way she'd stomped on her attacker's cell phone and hissed foreign threats in his face, but the truth was, he worried about her a little bit. And he liked the way she'd felt in his arms.

Toeing a bit of crumbling sidewalk, he gazed around at the concrete waves of the city streets, rolling in all directions. She had made it pretty clear that her secrets were her own. Who was he kidding?

The blonde's apartment was six blocks north. He headed south.

FIVE

"Tell me, Gwen. Before we go in there. Please."

Griffin's hand slammed shut the glass front door of Company HQ before Gwen could open it, forcing her to look at him.

"I don't want to have to say the whole thing twice," she replied evenly.

He licked his lips. "It's going to look bad for me when you tell the Board I wasn't at your side. That I left without making sure you were safe inside your place."

She'd thought the same thing, only there was another angle to consider. "Maybe. But you wouldn't have caught the real Yoshi otherwise. You followed the ambulance to the hospital and took care of him there, right?"

His nostrils flared and he did that chin rub again. He'd had to kill two Primaries in less than twelve hours.

"Besides," she added, "Dad was with you when you took off. If they hold you accountable, they have to point the finger at him, too. And we both know that's not going to happen."

That seemed to let him breathe easier.

"Walking to HQ alone was a stupid, stupid idea that I'm embarrassed to say I ever had, and I'm sorry."

He reached out, hesitated for a moment, then dragged a soft hand around her skull and down the back of her clean hair, the action tender but not uncomfortable.

After stumbling into her place at daybreak, she'd finally gotten ahold of Griffin on his cell phone, and told him the ambulance he'd likely just seen near the diner held the real Yoshi. She'd assured him she was safe at home, and he'd raced to the hospital. Then she'd taken a shower, spending a long time under the hot spray scrubbing off Yoshi's attack . . . and trying to rid herself of the Allure. She'd had more success with the former than the latter.

"Thank you for saying that," Griffin said. "Look, I know you want me to apologize for acting without orders back at Vaillancourt Fountain, but you'd be dead or taken if I hadn't have done something."

She opened her mouth to refute that, but realized it was pointless. They were both wrong. They were both right. They could run in verbal circles all day. But the Board was waiting for her report.

"Can we go in now?" she asked.

Wordless, he released his hold on the door. He tagged so closely behind he practically clipped the four-inch heels of her knee-high boots. She supposed she'd have to get used to it; the Board wouldn't let her sneeze without Griffin handing her a tissue from now on.

One security guard nodded at Griffin, their boss, as she and Griffin skirted around the semicircular front desk. The other guard squinted at a bank of monitors. Both wore heavy cloaks of *Mendacia*, disguising them as portly and inattentive when in reality they were two of Griffin's best. Threats were more likely to be careless if they thought security was lax.

Gwen walked quickly past the rows of false elevator fronts and went right for the fountain against the back wall. Twelve feet high, water gushed from the ceiling and burbled over a mass of smooth, giant, and artfully stacked rocks. She placed her palm against a cool, round stone at shoulder height. The water came alive at her touch, sliding over her hand to cover her wrist, glove-like. She called to it in silent Ofarian, and it answered, testing her identity.

"How'd you break Yoshi's leg? Water's not that strong," Griffin asked behind her.

For a moment she lost her concentration, then she regained it.

The wall behind the fountain shivered and melted, its two halves drawing apart in a liquid curtain that dissolved to mist. A mixture of *Mendacia* and water magic, and the ultimate barrier between Primaries and Secondaries.

Gwen pulled her hand from the stone, spoke the Ofarian

words to absorb the water from her wrist and hand, and turned to face Griffin.

His face was impassive. "I'm not going to like it, am I?"

"Probably not," she acknowledged, and turned to enter the main floor of Company operations.

Around a hundred Ofarians worked here at HQ, but that wasn't indicative of all who were involved in *Mendacia* or with the Company in a peripheral manner. Almost two thousand Ofarians in existence and each and every one had something to do with the product, whether it was related to business or security or even washing the floors at night. Like the Primary world, their jobs depended on their level of education, their drive, and their connections.

If you worked at HQ, you were part of the ruling class. If you worked in the Primary world—whether in technology or government or law enforcement, with the purpose of identifying then hiding any leaks of Ofarian movement—you were considered cunning and extremely intelligent. If you worked at the Plant, well, you were considered very special.

Gwen and Griffin wove through the maze of sky blue cubicles, buried in the dense murmur of office activity and the gentle susurrus of the waterglass windows. The boardroom was at the far end of HQ. She prayed she wasn't late.

"The Chairman?" he asked.

"Hey, Casey," Gwen called to her dad's secretary, who waved back, her shoulder holding a phone in place at her ear. "No," she said to Griffin, flicking a warning glance in his direction. "He won't like it either. None of them will."

She was glad she couldn't see his reaction.

The Board was all assembled. Their hazy shapes appeared through the waterglass walls dividing the boardroom from the general Company employees. A thin veneer of enchanted water streamed slowly from floor to ceiling, enclosed between two layers of glass, and it completely shut out the voices inside. Gwen should know; she'd spent many hours trying to eavesdrop—trying to rechannel the magic to allow her to hear—during her internship years. She'd been known to attempt it again as a vice president.

The waterglass in the building's main windows looked like

gold-tinted, reflective glass from the outside, but it prevented any Primaries from seeing in. It canceled out heat-seeking devices. It stopped projectiles. It made them anonymous. Safe.

If the entire Board was already gathered, she didn't want to keep them waiting. She knocked twice and let herself in, Griffin trailing.

She walked into chaos.

An argument raged across the table. The Board had divided itself along its usual lines: five members siding with Dad, four with Jonah Yarbrough, the Vice Chairman and Director of Production. The two men had never gotten along personally and clashed repeatedly when it came to Ofarian matters, but that was one of the reasons they'd been chosen to lead together. Checks and balances. It wasn't perfect, but it also meant the leadership wasn't a monarchy. Dad was the face, the spiritual and cultural leader. Jonah ran everything else.

Gwen caught only tidbits of the loud disagreement.

". . . responsibility as leaders . . ."

". . . have to stay out of there . . ."

". . . if we won't, someone else will . . ."

In the middle of the screaming, Jonah, standing at one end of the long steel and glass table, saw her and turned. Beneath his carefully moussed hair, his calculating eyes met hers and narrowed. He pressed a button on his laptop. The image projected onto the large wall screen vanished.

But not before she saw it.

A map of the world. Brightly colored dots speckled every continent. Places in which she'd already opened business, like Abu Dhabi and Shanghai. Places she'd targeted next, like Saint Petersburg and Montreal. And places she hadn't tapped yet as possible markets, like Santiago and Copenhagen. Even in her brief glance of the map, she could discern no rhyme or reason to the colors over certain areas. They didn't match her research.

"Gwen." Her father came around the table. The Board fell suddenly and eerily silent. Ian Carroway was still dressed in *Mendacia*, and she wondered if it was left over from last night or if he'd done another hit this morning before coming to the office.

The hug he gave her was both tight and terse, meant to tell her that as her father he was glad she was okay, but as her Chairman, he had many, many questions.

Quickly she laced her fingers into the flat prayer position simulating water and spoke the traditional Ofarian-language greeting of elders. Beside her, Griffin did the same.

Straightening, she nudged her chin toward the now-blank screen. "Were those my territories?"

Several Board members exchanged inscrutable looks. Jonah's face was equally devoid of clues.

"Ah, no." Dad waved a hand and gave her a warm smile. "You'll be briefed on all that later."

That was most likely true, but it would be the watered-down version. The one with only a few more details than Casey the secretary would get. If they would just let her pull up a chair here on a permanent basis, she was confident her fresh voice would help calm the argumentative waters, so to speak. These men and women were like lifer Congressmen, set in their ways and deaf to new ideas.

Jonah wouldn't look at her. He shut his computer and shuffled papers, then sat and crossed one leg over the opposite knee. She battled with Jonah almost as much as her father, but Jonah had been the very first Board member to back her proposition of expanding internationally. Jonah was her boss and he'd taught her a lot, even if they weren't each other's favorite person. Was he going behind her back now?

"Sir?" Griffin asked the Chairman. "Do you need me to stay?"

Dad frowned. "Absolutely. We need your side, too." He sat, rolled his chair back under the table, and folded his hands on the top. "Now what exactly happened?"

She and Griffin related their versions of the Vaillancourt Fountain disaster. Gwen then recounted every moment since the limo drove away—including the Primary. She told them every detail except that the Primary had seen her safely home. That their pretend hug had gone on longer than it should have. That he had kindled the Allure.

Beside her, Griffin stood as still as the rock fountain by the elevators. If he suspected anything, his posture gave no hint.

Through it all, she could feel Jonah's sharp gaze raking her with scrutiny.

When she was done, the boardroom erupted again, divided along predictable lines. As expected, the concern came down to Griffin's ability to protect Gwen. Never mind that her father had also been in the limo that had driven away. Never mind that her stupidity had led to Yoshi's attack.

Someone even mentioned dissolving their match and aligning her in marriage to someone better suited to watching over the Company's most valuable asset.

She reached out and took Griffin's hand, squeezing his fingers. To defend him would save his ass, but it would also endorse their betrothal. A decade of friendship won out. Even though the arranged marriage made her stomach sour, she certainly didn't want to be paired with someone she didn't know and might never respect the way she did Griffin.

She lifted her voice above everyone else's. "My protector did all he could." Her father raised a hand and the Board hushed. "Do not blame him for everything. He's not a scapegoat."

Griffin squeezed back. She slipped her hand out of his grip.

"I agree," said her father. "Griffin will remain in service to Gwen and us. The betrothal will go on as expected. Formal matching ceremony in two weeks. Elaine?" He raised an eyebrow at the Director of Travel and Client Events. "Your department will plan."

Elaine Montag tittered as she scribbled something on a pad. The hefty older woman was a shark in a grandmother suit. She put on incredible events created to woo the world's elite into signing gargantuan confidentiality agreements just for the privilege of talking to the Chairman about *Mendacia*. Gwen could only imagine what she'd put together for the betrothal announcement of the Chairman's daughter and the only known Translator. The thought made her weak-kneed, but not with happiness.

"Yoshi's memory card," her father prompted. "Do you still have it?"

"Yes." She dug the shards from the bowels of her purse. The Board breathed a collective sigh of relief.

As she dumped the little chunks onto the conference table, she stole a glance over Elaine's large, soft shoulder. A neatly typed agenda sat in front of her. "Others" was the first item. She and Griffin second.

Others. Other what? Ofarians? Impossible. They were

concentrated in California. A few more scattered here and there to cover Company long-distance issues, but outside that, the Company kept tight tabs on its people. Even those it exiled.

"Break for fifteen," Dad announced, and the Board milled around. He came over and clapped Griffin on the shoulder. "Take Gwennie home. Let her rest."

"No." She shook her head sharply. "I'm going to head up to my office. I have a lot of work to do."

Griffin gaped at her like she'd announced she wanted to evaporate the oceans. "Are you kidding? After last night? After this morning?"

"*Especially* after last night and this morning," she replied. And her father gave her such a grin of pride that she couldn't help feeling exhilarated.

"Fine then," Dad said. To Griffin, "If she's staying, come see me in my office. I need you to do something for me tonight." To her, "*Don't* leave here without a member of his security team."

She agreed, of course.

Though she was bone tired, hiding in her apartment and playing weak wouldn't get her on the Board any faster. It wouldn't improve the Company or bolster the quality of the lives of her people. She was Ofarian and born into ruling lines. She'd serve the Company in any way they wanted, then she'd lead it into the greatest age her people had seen since their arrival.

Everything depended on the health and success of *Mendacia*, and she'd do her damnedest to lift it to the top.

SIX

Gwen had been sitting alone in Manny's Pub so long her second Stoli on the rocks had turned to water with a splash of vodka. This place was a hole in the wall, a narrow bar sandwiched between a shoe repair and a wig shop. It hadn't been updated in at least twenty years, or cleaned in two. She liked it because it was unpretentious and far enough away from Company HQ that her people never came here. Perfect for when she needed to destress anonymously.

After seven the downtown worker crowd cleared out and you could hear a pin drop out on the street. It was nearing ten.

She wasn't truly alone. David, the third in her and Griffin's triangle of dear friends and part of her own private security team, watched Manny's from the burrito joint across the way. Far enough away so she didn't feel baby-sat, but close enough to keep her safe. She couldn't tell him what had gone on in the boardroom that morning. Anything that took place behind waterglass was confidential. That was Griffin's job as his boss, and she had no idea how David had been briefed.

Griffin had been sent away on Dad's errand, whatever it was. Knowing Griffin's skill set, she could only imagine.

She played with the lime in her drink, watching it swirl around the clear liquid. If she wanted to, she could separate the water from the vodka. Make it jump out of the glass and do a little jig on the bar. Just that tiny bit of melted ice called her, begged her to touch it. If she were alone at her house, she might do just that—stick her finger into the chill and connect with what made her unique.

Remind herself of who and what she served.

"Guinness," rumbled a deep voice at her right shoulder.

A half second later, she recognized it.

He pulled out the chair next to hers, wood scraping over tile. She turned slowly in her seat, allowing herself a full-on, toe-to-temple gape. *Him.*

She glanced at the door, waiting for David to burst in. Then she realized she'd never given Griffin or the Board a physical description of the Primary who had broken Yoshi's leg. She hadn't really needed to—he hadn't witnessed anything to compromise Ofarian safety, and she'd spoken Japanese to Yoshi. And then the stranger had disappeared.

Only to reappear now.

He'd thrown a black, half-zip sweater over the gray T-shirt, but he still wore those faded jeans and scuffed boots. The sweater made a valiant attempt to soften his appearance, but in the end served only to add to his hard bulk while intensifying his eyes, currently the color of ocean shallows. Above the sweater's neckline, the tease of tattoo curled just below his ear.

He threw her a small, unsure smile and gestured questioningly to the chair.

She should tell him to leave. He hadn't been in danger before, but if David walked in here and questioned who he was, could she lie? *Would* she lie? How could she ever explain seeing the Primary again who'd saved her ass?

The Board would see through any story. At best, they'd recognize the Allure. At worst, they'd think he knew about the Ofarians, and then he'd be hunted.

Even with those possibilities hanging over her head, even with the way his presence practically consumed the bar, and even though she noticed several patrons toss him nervous glances and make mental notes to avoid him . . . he brought her an undeniable sense of calm. It was like the moment on the street when he'd pulled her against him. She'd been tense and jittery all day, and at last she finally exhaled.

"Sure. Yeah. Okay."

Another glance at the door. No David.

The stranger settled on the edge of the chair and leaned his forearms on the bar.

Her heartbeat kicked up a few notches. "Did you follow me? Because I come here all the time and I've never seen you."

He pursed his lips. "Maybe you just never noticed."

"No. I'd remember *you*."

He seemed pleased at that, inhaling long and slow through his nose, his mouth curved in a hint of a smile. "Coincidence is a funny, funny thing, isn't it? I'm actually supposed to meet some people here in a bit."

She laughed. "Yeah, right. People who live around the corner don't even know about this place."

He held up his hands. They were big. Devoid of rings, wedding or otherwise. "I swear. They told me to come here. Stick around if you want me to prove it to you."

What kind of crazy was she to want to do just that?

Manny, the bartender and owner, came over and placed a pint of Guinness in front of the guy. Manny was short and lean, and even though he didn't employ a bouncer, Gwen had seen him kick out an unruly customer or two. Before he wandered off to the end of the bar, he eyed the newcomer suspiciously.

Gwen turned to her companion, who was watching his pint settle in slow, smooth, black-and-cream waves. It made her think of the ocean creeping up on sand.

They looked up at the same time. Their eyes met. He cleared his throat and stretched out a thick arm to tug up his sleeve and glance at his watch. A Cartier Chronograph, a real beauty. A real expensive beauty. She blinked at the piece, thinking it might be a fake given the wear on his boots and the apparel she would have considered ordinary. Then there were the facts that he'd been wandering the San Francisco streets before daybreak, broke a guy's leg without so much as a blink, and then eluded the cops with eerily good skill.

Yeah, the watch intrigued her, but it was safe to say it wasn't the only thing. The Allure made no judgments, only identified targets.

He opened his wallet to pay for his beer and she noticed the state of Washington stamped on his license. "Just visiting, I see."

Brow furrowed, he snapped the wallet shut. As sharp and fast as a clap, the dark look of the bruiser she'd met in the alley returned. Then, just as quickly, it disappeared.

"In town on business." He shrugged and shifted his gaze to

the yellowed painting hanging above the saw-toothed lines of the liquor bottles. One of the paintings had tilted to reveal the darker wall behind it.

He skimmed the scene in the bar at a measured pace, taking in the five other customers scattered toward the front, near the single window. It was too methodical to be leisurely—she'd seen Griffin and the others on his team do the same—though this guy put on a good act.

"Been thinking about you today." His eyes meandered back to her. "How are you doing?"

Thinking about her? What did that mean? And what could she say? She couldn't tell him about Yoshi's death, or that the Board was continually shutting her out of decisions she was desperate to be involved in.

"Better," she said. "Things are . . . better."

"Better, huh?" His eyebrows were sandy brown, giving her a clue as to what his hair might look like, if he had any. Would it be curly? Thin?

"Thank you for helping me. Before. I don't think I said that."

He shrugged like she'd thanked him for passing the nuts. He leaned an elbow on the bar, his torso twisting toward her. "You speak Japanese." It wasn't a question.

"Yeah." She shifted on her seat, resisting the urge to dive directly into her drink and mix with the vodka. "It's for my job."

"What do you do?"

"Sales." Her standard line to Primaries.

"Sell a lot in Japan, I guess." His pale eyes glinted.

She recognized a challenge when she saw it. What surprised her was that she was willing to meet it. "Sometimes."

"Must be interesting work, doing business in alleys before sunrise. Looked like a decent presentation to me. Hope you get the sale."

So this was how it was going to go down between them. Secrets hovered in the air, creating a twisted game. *Who will crack first and ask what the other was doing in the alley at sunrise? Who has more to hide and does the better job of covering it? How little can we actually say about ourselves and still talk?*

Gwen liked games.

"So what brings you to town? Surely it's not to play Superman to ladies in distress." She heard the smile in her voice before she felt it on her face. Was this flirting?

His eyes narrowed slightly, but he seemed eager to take the bait. "Work."

"And what do you do?"

Mr. Tattoo smiled so widely she thought the dimple might open a hole in his cheek. "I'm a freelancer."

"Freelancing what?"

"Hey, you're in 'sales.' I'm in freelance."

She saluted him with her diluted drink. Point for him. "Fair enough."

The mysterious freelancer lifted his pint glass to his lips, but watched her out of the corner of his eye.

"I don't know how I feel about you being here right now." She spoke the truth.

"Yes, you do." He smiled into his beer, carefully, skillfully, keeping his eyes off her. "You could've left when I sat down. You still could."

Yes, she could have. And should have. They both knew that.

The Allure opened its jaws and devoured her whole.

Manny ambled over and pointed to her glass. "Want another?" Code for: *You okay with this guy?*

She pushed her water-vodka away. "What he's having."

Manny shuffled off to pull another pint, and she tilted her head to take in the man who didn't quite feel like a stranger anymore. She wouldn't call him beautiful, not pretty like a celebrity. He was a *man*, gritty and real. He was a Primary, the thing her mom and dad had warned her about. He was the cookie jar on top of the fridge, and she was an immature child, waiting for her people to turn their backs so she could make a grab for it.

Mr. Tattoo turned slightly toward her. She loved the little rolls of skin where his neck met his scalp when he tipped back the glass to sip. It was a private spot that wouldn't have been visible if he hadn't shaved his head. She pretended he'd done it just for her.

Her phone, sitting idly by her elbow, jumped to life with a buzz and flash of light, blasting the wallpaper image of a painting by her favorite artist. Her first, panicked thought was that it would be David, questioning her status, wanting to know if she was ready to go.

A text message popped up: *So sorry about today. Home now. David says you're good. Come to my place?* Griffin.

"Let me guess," Mr. Tattoo said. "You have to go."

She slid a sideways glance at him, and he was obviously trying not to look at her phone. Now was the time to exit. The perfect opportunity.

The thing was, she wanted to talk to her curious freelancer—and wasn't that telling, that she was already thinking of him as hers?

She wanted to know, if only for an hour or so, that there was life outside the Ofarian world. She may love her people and its culture more than anything, but it was so very insular. All Ofarians knew it; it was why they were warned about the Allure and then turned a blind eye when one of their own tasted what they could not have. As long as it was not permanent. As long as the Primaries never, ever caught a glimpse of the man behind the curtain.

It might be shameful, but Gwen also wanted to know she was desirable to someone other than the man—no matter how wonderful he might be—the Board chose for her. Maybe a little flirtation in the Primary world might spark something in the Secondary. Maybe it might make her long for the same attention from Griffin.

But the truth was—as her eyes drifted over Mr. Tattoo's strong hands and thick arms, and she recalled with a shiver how they'd felt around her—Griffin was far, far from her thoughts.

I'm sorry too, she texted Griffin back. Then added: *Thanks, but no. Raincheck?*

As she clicked off the phone and tossed it into her purse, her hands shook.

"No," she told Mr. Tattoo. "I'm staying."

SEVEN

The confirmation threw wide open some sort of invisible door.
He set his empty glass on the bar with a bang and swiveled on
his chair to face her. He bounced a finger at her purse. "That
painting on your phone screen. It's Ed Ruscha, right?"

She blinked. Blinked again. He'd mispronounced the artist's name, but she didn't care. "You've heard of Ruscha?"

"Is that how you say it? I've only seen it in print."

"But you know his work?"

"Shocking, huh? I think that painting's in the Whitney, in
New York."

She tried very hard not to gape but didn't succeed. When
she could finally speak, her voice came out all breathy. "I didn't
know that. I've never been there." The strangeness of that
didn't escape her; she'd been to some of the most far-flung
cities in the world—Cairo and Helsinki and Seoul—but not
New York City, practically in her own backyard.

"So you've been there? Seen it?"

"Yeah." When he rubbed a finger across his stubbly chin,
the scratching sound drew her in. It drowned out the low hum
of the other patrons and the tinny music piped in from an
unseen radio. "I remember it because it's so strange. Odd but
great, you know? The big words, the colors. One of those pieces
that really strikes you, but you can't quite figure out why—"

"Exactly."

"Then I read about all the weird materials he uses as paint
and I just stood there and stared, trying to see them." He sat
back. "Actually took away some of the magic for me."

Her mouth went completely dry. She tried not to bounce on

her seat. No one she knew loved art as much as she did. Hell, she couldn't name a single Ofarian who knew a single *thing* about art. She didn't care if Mr. Tattoo didn't enjoy Ruscha as much as her. Talking about art was nearly an orgasmic experience.

"Really? But there's so much to be said in his work, especially through his materials. It's so simple, but he *makes* it more complicated."

He considered that, frowning, round head bobbing from side to side. "Maybe. But if you're talking late-twentieth-century artists, I think I like Cy Twombly better."

An image suddenly came to her, of what might have happened earlier that morning if she'd actually invited Mr. Tattoo up to her place for coffee. He would've ambled around her apartment, mug in one hand, thick fingers of the other trailing over the spines of her bookshelves perfectly lined with art books. Griffin thought the books were a waste of entertainment center space, but Mr. Tattoo's powerful torso would've tilted sideways to read each title. She loved that visual.

"I . . . I can't believe you brought up Twombly." Oh, God, she was stuttering.

"Why? Because I know him or like him?"

Somewhere in the midst of the conversation his hand had crept toward hers. Palm on the wood, he faced her, fully engaged. Something akin to wonder glistened in his eyes.

"Both." Her voice turned thin as paper. "I think he's brilliant. Something about the size of his canvases."

He grinned wickedly. "You like 'em big?"

"Yeah. I guess I do." Heat started in her chest and spread to her neck. "Where did you see Twombly's stuff?"

He pursed his lips, thinking. "An exhibition at the Art Institute in Chicago."

"Did you study art in college?" Maybe he was involved in the art world, and that's what had brought him here.

There was the briefest of pauses before he said, "No. No college." Then he ran a hand over his smooth head and mumbled, "Barely any high school."

Time to share something that made her a little sheepish, too. "I love art. Might be my most favorite thing in the world. But I never get to go to art museums. Too busy when I travel. I buy books instead. I have close to two hundred."

She knew she wasn't imagining the warmth in his blue eyes. "It's not the same," he said. "In person you can follow the brushstrokes, see the globs of paint. For some reason, I like seeing the signatures in the corners."

Damn, there went a sigh.

"Embarrassing confession time," he said, settling deeper into his chair. "I like to learn. When I'm in a museum, I even walk around with the headphones."

She laughed. "I would, too!"

"Don't get me wrong. I like the NFL, too. And barbecues. And I've been known to buy a swimsuit calendar and a sports car."

"Scared I'll question your masculinity?"

"Nah. I don't even necessarily *like* most of the art I've seen." His hand crept closer on the bar. All she could see was his face, could even pick out a tiny scar under his eye. "But I know what I like when I see it."

Even though they'd embraced on the street, the space between them in the bar was tighter, more pressurized. Without preamble, he draped his arm around the back of her chair and rotated it toward him. His long legs surrounded her knees. With one arm on her chair back and the other on the bar, he trapped her in the cage of his attention.

She sensed his unmistakable hunger. For *her*.

After all these years, she finally understood what had happened to Delia, her sister. It must have started something like this. A chance meeting with a Primary man. A smile that made her shiver. An engrossing, surprising conversation.

Six years ago Gwen had sided with the Board, even though it had almost killed her. She had thought Delia weak for choosing the Primary guy over her own people. Delia had paid for it with exile. And with her water magic.

The Allure was intoxicating. A tempting, evil drug that could snare you permanently if you weren't careful. At this point, surrounded by Mr. Tattoo's sizzling heat, trying it once and then going cold turkey seemed virtually impossible.

Disobedience had never felt so seductive.

"I like the way that skirt looks on you," he said, staring at her mouth. His tone changed. His words changed. They felt like a caress. "And those boots."

She took the compliment the way she knew how, by deflection. "Came straight from work. One of those days."

That tease of a smile again. "Yeah. It sure was."

When the denim of his jeans brushed against the small bare patch of skin between her knee-high boot and skirt hem, she gasped.

He leaned in, so close his breath ruffled the hair next to her ear. "What's your name?"

The rest of the bar dropped away like a trapdoor.

She turned her head just enough to make out the details of his tattoo. Leaf- and thorn-covered vines twisted around his neck, the tip of the last leaf resting just below his earlobe. She clenched her fingers, resisting the urge to touch it. To touch him.

Her voice came out in shaky threads. "Gwen."

She *felt* him smile. "Gwen. I'm Reed."

Reed nudged her hair with his nose, inhaling. "Tell me more about this Ed Ruscha guy."

She chuckled low. "Are you serious? Now?"

The hand on the back of her chair dropped to her knee. Palm covering the top of her boot. Thumb on her thigh. Fingertips dancing like snowflakes at the edge of her skirt hem. She stopped breathing.

"Actually, no." Chin stubble scraped just below her ear.

She forced herself to inhale. "Good. Because I can't think."

Reed pulled back enough for her to see his face again. "I really did think about you today. I wondered if what I'd felt this morning was wrong. Misplaced."

"I thought about you, too." For different reasons, but those didn't seem to matter anymore.

"Good. I'm glad to hear that."

"Where are you staying?" It slipped out before she could stop it. She couldn't take it back, and she realized she didn't want to.

His expression turned heated. "The Four Seasons. Just for tonight."

"I hear that's nice." And expensive. And a quick cab ride away.

"It is." He licked his lips. "Would you like to see it?"

His voice thrummed deep bass chords in her ears, sending quivers straight to her legs. He tightened his grip on her thigh, and she watched him react to her reaction.

She'd never wanted to be naked more in her entire life.

This was it. The one pass granted to her by the Allure. Forgiven only if it was temporary. She knew for a fact that Griffin had slept with a Primary a few months ago, before they'd heard the rumblings in the Board about their match. He didn't know she knew and there was no reason to confront him about it. Had it been just sex to Griffin? Or had he connected with that woman in the way Gwen connected with Reed?

No, she would *not* go there. It would only be sex for her, too. And by the firm, gentle way Reed touched her now, she knew it would be good sex.

"Yes," she whispered. "I'd like to see your room."

The smile he gave her was positively feral.

Vaguely, she heard the door to the bar opening, followed by the tickle of cool air on her back. Reed's gaze flicked over her shoulder. The lust in his eyes and the promise in the curve of his mouth vanished. Whatever he saw pulled down a cold, hard wall between them.

The speed with which he went from seductive to nonchalant made her gasp. When he removed his hand from her thigh, it was like taking away a blanket in the dead of winter.

"The people I'm supposed to meet are here. Won't take a minute. Will you wait for me?"

She nodded numbly.

He stood. "Told you I wasn't lying."

As she listened to Reed's footsteps walk away, she considered that maybe this interruption was a blessing in disguise. Maybe her ancestors were telling her that giving in to the Allure was a huge mistake.

Something started to poke at her subconscious. Something . . . *else*. Something other than dirty fantasies and race-driven guilt trips. She couldn't pin it down. It was a buzzing fly she couldn't swat. No matter how hard she tried, she couldn't concentrate on anything except the phantom feel of Reed's hands.

And then she couldn't hear or feel anything for the great *whoosh* in her head.

A new language swirled into her ears and drove itself into her brain. It had to work extra hard; her mind had melted into hormone-engorged mush.

If she were a Primary, the sound of a foreign tongue would

be nothing but background noise, but since she was a Translator, the new sounds solidified into mental building blocks. They stacked themselves. Slid next to and behind one another, formulating correct sequences. New words and cadences and grammar rules formatted in her mouth and in her mind.

Two people spoke this new language simultaneously, which always made her head ache and her body woozy at first. She gripped the edge of the bar to steady herself as foreign speech hammered its way into her subconscious. Manny came over, concerned, but she waved him away.

Once the initial shock of the Translation wore off and she released her death grip on the wood, a new set of alarm bells almost threw her off her chair.

Three things about this Translation were seriously off.

First, she already knew a few of the words because they were part of the ancient codes used to manipulate *Mendacia*.

Second, some deep, dark part of her recognized the sounds. Like she'd spoken them ages ago but had since lost them, and now she was pulling the language out from behind the thickest partitions of her mind.

Third, this language did not originate here on Earth, and neither did its speakers.

She jumped off her chair and whirled toward the newcomers. A man and woman. That persistent, buzzing feeling she hadn't been able to decipher not moments ago? She recognized it now.

Ofarians knew their own kind blindfolded. Their bodily signatures emanated something that existed above and beyond humanity. It wasn't a smell or sound; it was a *sense*. It's what made them Secondary.

These two were also Secondary, but they were not Ofarian. How was that possible? No other Secondaries lived on Earth.

Had David seen them? From across the street he would be too far away to sense their signatures, but had he at least noticed them? Maybe he'd be suspicious and jog over to Manny's to check it out.

But then, these two didn't stand out nearly as much as Reed, and David hadn't appeared when Reed had walked in. Gwen was on her own.

The fair-skinned man was taller and thinner than Reed. If

it weren't for his dour expression, the steely, unwelcome look in his eye, and the knotted blond hair dusting his shoulders, he might have been handsome. The woman was tiny, her posture betraying her timidity. She stood with her hands in her pockets, and stray brown hairs dangled out of her ponytail as if she'd slept on it then bolted out the door. It must have started to rain because their shoulders were darkened with water droplets.

Everything about them told Gwen to flee, to get away as fast as possible. Yet curiosity and fear rooted her to the spot. She had to know who they were, why they were here.

Why Reed headed straight for them.

"Is that him?" the woman asked in her language, pointing to Reed.

"It's got to be," muttered the blond man. As Reed reached them, the blond switched to English. "I'm sorry. We were looking for the Mexican restaurant."

"It closed five months ago," said the new kid in town.

The blond man nodded. "Retriever?"

Reed's smooth head nodded firmly. The taller man pulled a small, white envelope from inside his distressed leather jacket and handed it to Reed.

Gwen realized who they were. And she couldn't get past them to escape out the front door.

She wheeled on Manny. "Please tell me you have a back exit."

He twisted a bar towel. "You okay?"

"I'm fine. You don't need to worry. Just the exit."

He pointed. "Back of the storeroom. Opposite the john."

She walked fast toward the back, feet smarting in the high-heeled boots and trying not to draw attention by moving too fast. Shoving open the storeroom door, she saw the exit, partially covered by paper towel packages. As she threw the first one to the floor, she heard Reed ask Manny, "Gwen. You seen her?"

He sounded so calm and focused. Like he had in the alley before busting Yoshi's leg.

Manny, bless him, replied, "Hey, man. She left. Leave her alone."

Gwen tossed another package and found the doorknob, yanking it with all her strength. She burst out into the alley, fat raindrops smacking her in the face. Behind her, Reed barreled through the mess she'd made in the storeroom. She couldn't make it around the corner to David in time, and she couldn't sprint to the street and hail a cab before Reed caught up to her.

There was only one thing to do.

Cars sped by the mouth of the alley. A few people hurried past, hands over their heads to ward off the unusual late-September rain, but otherwise it was dark and she was in a dingy alcove.

She whispered Ofarian words. Her body shimmered, liquifying, and collapsed in on itself. It took extra effort and deep concentration to transform her clothes and belongings, too, but she did it. As a puddle, she pooled around the stumpy legs of a Dumpster. Raindrops splashed into her but did not mix.

The puddle served as one great big limpid eye, and from it she watched Reed charge into the alley. Head whipping around, he called her name. By the determined way he took off toward the street, she knew he wasn't just disappointed to discover his potential one-night stand had bolted. His desperation stemmed from his conversation with the other Secondaries, and the envelope they'd given him.

She'd been a fucking idiot.

She moved the puddle over the disgusting ground, oil slicks and hamburger wrappers and used chewing gum sliding underneath her. At the alley entrance she extended a trickle out onto the sidewalk and saw Reed run heavy-footed down the street. A taxi rolled down the opposite lane.

Ducking back into the shadows, she let go of her liquid form. She was a great beanstalk extending to the sky, the world returning to normal size as her body and clothing solidified. She felt heavy and clunky with retransformation, but there was no time to wallow in it.

Jogging across the street, she flagged down the approaching cab. "Swing around the corner," she told the driver before her ass hit the seat. "Stop for a sec in front of the burrito joint."

As he hit the meter and did just that, she flipped open her phone and dialed.

Griffin answered. "Hey, you. You coming over after all?"

"No. Meet me at my dad's. Fifteen minutes. Tedrans are in San Francisco."

EIGHT

Griffin clutched the keys to Gwen's apartment and put a finger
to his lips. You couldn't have paid her to talk at that point. He
inspected the door lock and knob, then ran his hands over the
jamb. With a frown of concentration, he slid the key into place
and pushed the door open. He thrust out a hand behind him,
silently telling her to stay in the hall. Obediently, she plastered
herself to the opposite wall. The pinch of her feet in her boots
felt way better than the flock of butterflies swarming in her
stomach.

Griffin moved through the entranceway and into the main
living space, switching on lamps as he went. Her place was
minimalist, mostly white. Very few areas in which to hide.
When he disappeared down the hall toward the bedrooms and
out of her sight, she started to bounce on the balls of her feet,
anxious. After reappearing and flashing her the "okay" sign,
he headed for the kitchen. Gwen rushed inside, shut the door,
and bolted it. All energy left her in a single breath, and she
sagged against the door.

Two nights in a row up well past midnight. Two nights in a
row of occurrences that threatened her life and challenged the
security of her people. *Exhausted* didn't even begin to describe
her state of mind.

They'd just come from the Chairman's manor in tony Pacific
Heights, where she'd spent almost three hours being grilled by
the Board. They'd been called out of their beds to hear her tell
them about Reed and the Tedrans.

All the Board members were now under careful watch of

Griffin's security team. In the wee hours, Ofarian soldiers were scanning the Board members' homes, setting guards. Some families chose to leave San Francisco, heading for vacation homes or any other destination a last-minute, red-eye flight would take them.

"Griffin. I'm scared."

He emerged quickly from the kitchen but stopped in the hall, one hand curled around the edge of a steel and glass armoire she'd splurged on at a designer's auction. He tried to smile reassuringly, but even he was greatly disturbed by what she'd seen tonight, and the smile turned out to be nothing more than an odd twist of his mouth.

"Then you can be scared for the both of us. I'm the one who's supposed to act all brave, right?"

She buried her face in her hands. They smelled like the bar at Manny's—of alcohol-stained wood and dusting spray—and of Reed. Even though she hadn't even touched him. Her whole body shuddered. "How the *hell* did they find us?"

"And what are they planning?"

When she removed her hands, Griffin was moving from window to window, checking the locks and the folds of the stiff, white drapes.

"Isn't the fact that they're here enough?" She finally got her feet to move, and shuffled farther inside, every sound of her narrow heels on the parquet floor a scream.

He swept an arm around her place. "Everything look okay? Like it was how you left it this morning?"

Had it only been this morning? It felt like she'd been away for weeks. A quick glance told her the place was immaculate, as always. She despised clutter; there wasn't much to disturb in the first place.

"Yeah." She threaded a hand through her heavy hair and kneaded her neck. "Looks fine." Griffin nodded and continued to circle around the living room, eyeing the molding between wall and ceiling.

"We should run," she blurted out. "Leave San Francisco."

"We ran once, a hundred and fifty years ago. Didn't do much good." He threw her a hard look. A soldier's look. He'd never flee. He'd stay and fight.

"The world is so much different now," she murmured, running a hand over the back of her white sofa. "We can't afford a war. We can't risk the exposure."

Strange, but the Tedran man and woman she'd seen didn't look like fighters. In fact, they looked just the opposite.

"I want to know *why* they're here." Griffin's voice punched through the heavy silence. "How they got here without the Primaries noticing. Don't you?"

Of course she did. But what she really wanted was to forget she'd almost slept with a man collaborating with the Ofarians' oldest and most formidable enemy. She scraped her fingernails over the upholstery, digging them in hard. Sick to her stomach and sick with herself.

Griffin moved to the powder room and flipped on the light. Her whole apartment was now ablaze. She started following Griffin around, turning off the lamps and lights when he was done searching, until only a standing lamp glowed softly between the two sofas and the dim glow of her bedroom stretched down the hallway. She felt better now. Hidden.

"If they know about the Company," he said, "they might know about *Mendacia*. There's no reason for them to target San Francisco unless they came for that."

The Board had said as much, too, hence the extensive protection measures.

She started to straighten a few books on her shelves, realized they were of Magritte and Mapplethorpe and Goldsworthy, and then stepped back as though they burned. Reminders of Reed everywhere. She'd have to get rid of all the pages she loved so much so she wouldn't constantly be reminded of her awful choice to try to indulge when she should have run.

She had to think of something else. Focus her brain on the problem.

"Do you think our ancestors could have learned the art of glamour from the Tedrans?"

He fingered a gray-striped pillow on the sofa and frowned. "What do you mean?"

"Well, the words to manipulate *Mendacia* aren't ancient Ofarian. We always thought it was a lost language, which is why we had so few words to work the spells around. But in reality the commands are Tedran. Maybe our ancestors learned glamour from Tedrans—maybe even secretly—and when we escaped slavery, we brought it with us. But since we knew so little of their language, we only had so much to work with. I'm just thinking out loud here."

"Anything's possible, isn't it?" Griffin scrubbed his face with his hands. He looked incredibly tired, his eyes beer-and-Jack-Daniel-shots red. He wore impeccably tailored charcoal gray pants and a baby blue, custom-made shirt, dressed like he was heading to the Velvet Club. Despite the three-o'clock-in-the-morning shadow, he still looked hot. The thought made her glance away.

"I'll take the couch." A hint of hope crept into his softened voice. Hope that she'd invite him to share her bed.

"You can use the second bedroom, you know."

He shoved his hands into his pants pockets. "Out here I can hear better. Keep an eye on the door."

They looked at each other for longer seconds than she wanted to count, until he broke it by going to the TV cabinet and removing the cable-knit throw she always used when curling up for a movie. She nodded at his back and turned down the hallway toward her bedroom.

She desperately wanted out of her work clothes, out of the pencil skirt and high boots Reed had complimented. Everything was tainted now. They were her favorites, and she didn't think she could ever wear them again.

"What else can you tell me about the Primary?"

Halfway down the hall, across from the bathroom, she froze midstep. "The Primary?"

When she turned fully back around, he was looking at her as though she were stupid. And she was, wasn't she?

"I told you and the Board everything." Everything except that she'd wanted Reed. Damn it, she could still feel his hands on her leg, the fluttering of his breath at her ear.

Griffin ran a hand through his short, dark hair. Somehow it still managed to look artfully mussed. He prowled around the coffee table, coming closer. "Tonight you told them what he looked like, that his name was Reed. You said he was kind of casual and reserved until the Tedrans walked in. Then he switched to all business."

The butterflies in her stomach whipped into a frenzy.

He reached the edge of the sofa but advanced no farther. "The Board didn't notice, but I did. You were talking to him."

His tone wasn't accusatory, which made her feel even more like shit. It was clear to both of them where this conversation was headed, and any attempt to veer it someplace else would sound lame and immature. She was a grown-up; she should answer for her decisions. And she respected Griffin too much to lie to him.

Slowly she moved back down the hall and leaned against the corner that opened up into the living room. But even after her I'm-an-adult pep talk, she had difficulty looking at him. "Yes. I was talking to him."

"About what?"

"Griffin, let's not do this now. It's three o'clock in the morning."

"Do what? I'm just asking a question. You actually talked to the guy who was clearly hired by our enemies to do something."

She exhaled long and lifted her eyes to meet his. "What do you think we were talking about?"

Griffin shifted on his feet and wiped his mouth as if he'd just eaten something bad. "He hit on you." She said nothing. "Did you let him?"

"I didn't stop him."

"Even though you'd met him twice in the same day under highly suspicious circumstances?"

She refused to wince at his rising tone. "I thought about it a lot, okay? I weighed *everything* in my mind. But we got to talking and . . ."

"What'd he say? Anything about us? The Tedrans?"

She rolled her eyes. "No. I would've mentioned that to the Board. To you. It was just conversation." Nice conversation. And flirting. And touching. Griffin just stared. "Look, I don't see the point in getting into everything we've ever done with other people. You already know all the guys I've slept with anyway."

"Jesus, Gwen. You mean you—"

"No! No, we didn't. But I thought about it." Reed's dimple popped into memory, and she blinked hard to erase it, but it refused to budge. "I wanted to. It was the Allure, straight up."

She'd never seen Griffin look so disgusted. "You wanted to. With the guy who just happened to save you from Yoshi. Who just happened to find you in a dive bar later that night." He was yelling now, and she was disappointed to find her own voice rising to match his.

"It was talking. Like two people who are attracted to one another talk. The second I figured out his contacts were Tedrans, I ran. You think I don't feel like a complete ass right now?"

His emotions shifted; she watched them play across his face. The red in his neck paled. His stance softened, his shoulders dropping. His eyes turned sad, even regretful. "Have we ever fought before? After I became your protector, I mean."

She thought about it and couldn't remember a time. This whole marriage thing had screwed with their relationship in more ways than one. "I don't think so."

With a heavy sigh, he sank to the couch and fixated on his hands, clasped tightly between his knees. They stayed that way for a while, physically whipped and emotionally fried. But there were other things that needed to be said, and she knew that neither of them would sleep until that happened.

"You know," he finally said, "I get the Allure now. I really do."

She crossed her legs at the ankle and pressed her head to the corner. Funny, they hadn't ever mentioned that word until tonight. And now was as good a time as any.

"With all the speeches we got growing up," he went on, "warning us about the Allure, about wanting something we can't have, it's easy to make vows when you're fourteen or fifteen and don't know what's out there. 'I won't ever do that,' you tell yourself. 'I'll be true to my people.' But it's so different when you're older. When you're faced with forever with someone you didn't choose yourself."

"I know about the woman. The Primary a few months back."

His thick, dark eyebrows lifted, then he gave a small, humorless laugh. "Of course you do. But I bet you don't know about the others."

Wow, okay. Strangely, it didn't bother her. "I'm not judging you, Griffin. Not one bit. I bet the vast majority of us gave in to the Allure more than once. Everyone except me, that is. But we know it's just temporary. It's not permanent. We understand where our true loyalties have to lie."

He raised his eyes to hers. "Except for Delia."

"Yeah. Well. She's an exception." Gwen couldn't think of anything more to say that wouldn't bring out long-dormant tears. She pushed away from the corner and started for the kitchen. "Want some chamomile tea?"

She could change while it steeped, and then she'd lie in bed and let the hot brew calm her nerves until she passed out and didn't wake until after the engagement was announced.

He brightened, and his tiny smile indicated a truce. "Sounds nice."

She knocked around in the kitchen until she found the tea-kettle and filled it with water, the normalcy of the action already calming her. As she set it to boil on the stove, she heard Griffin rise and start to pace the living room.

"How many times have I told you to take down this picture?"

She smiled. The framed photo sat among her collection of Art Deco architecture books. It was of her, Griffin, and David in high school. She'd dyed her hair a hideous platinum blond and had a love of shiny shirts. Griffin was doing his best Marky Mark impression, and a bespectacled, scrawny David hadn't yet learned how to lift weights. She thought it was hilarious; both the men had aged so well.

"Wow." His voice softened as his feet shuffled down the length of the bookcase, to a new photo. "That's a great one of you and me."

She paused in removing two mugs from the cabinet. Taken years ago, long before marriage had ever entered their consciousness, it was her favorite picture of just the two of them. They were more carefree then, less serious. She'd been working for the Company, of course, but she had yet to approach the Board about opening an international division. And he'd been her protector, but hadn't yet risen to head of security. In the picture, they had their arms around each other, cheeks pressed together, the effects of a few glasses of wine glinting in their eyes.

"Hey, Mr. Bodyguard," she called to him. "You forgot to check the balcony."

She was half kidding, but he swore, muttering something about being distracted. His quick footsteps crossed the floor. As she plopped tea bags into the mugs, she heard the click of the French doors and the hard heels of his shoes out on the balcony. Then a thump. Then nothing.

"Griffin?"

Ducking her head out of the kitchen, she saw the balcony doors hanging wide open, the curtains flapping. Griffin's body lay half inside the apartment, half on the balcony. She couldn't tell if he breathed.

Fear snatched her in its terrible jaws. "Oh, sh—"

She lunged for the front door, thinking *escape get the hell out of there RIGHT NOW run run run.*

Someone grabbed her from behind. He was huge and silent as wind. She kicked out. She squirmed violently, the terror taking hold and thrashing her body like a puppet. But the attacker held her fast with one massive arm.

She opened her mouth to scream but his other hand whipped around and clamped a damp swatch of fabric over her mouth and nose. She panicked, gasping for air. There was none. Some chemical sawed and hacked at her throat. It clawed its way into her head, making her dizzy and buzzy. Her vision doubled, then blurred. The room dove and twisted, and she lost all control of her muscles. The only thing left in her head was fear.

All sound swirled into a vacuum, fading softer and softer. The last thing she heard was a man's voice.

"Sorry, Gwen. I had no idea it would be you."

NINE

The angry buzz of a thousand bees roared through Gwen's head. The vibrations stretched to the tips of her limbs and beyond; no amount of concentration could control the shaking of her arms and legs. Her teeth felt like they'd been jammed backward into her gums and her mouth tasted gritty, like she'd been chewing on hair. She tried opening her eyes, but invisible concrete weighed down the lids.

Awareness came agonizingly slowly. After hours or days or years, the hum started to dissipate. Gradually, gradually it decreased to the perimeter of her consciousness. The shaking stopped, but her limbs now moved on a delay. When she got them to budge, it was never more than an inch, and even that left her panting with effort.

The fear still beat at her with a sharp club. Palpable, unrelenting, vicious.

Finally she managed to pry open her eyes. Though it was only a crack, she nearly cried, feeling victorious. Tiny red lights glowed around her. The world smelled of rubber and plastic carpet, the kind her grandma had lining the breezeway in her house in Pleasanton.

She recognized a few sounds. Pavement whirring beneath tires. The *whoosh* of cars intermittently passing in the opposite lane. She lay in the back of a windowless van, rocking as it barreled down a highway.

With a groan, she tried to roll over. The buzz wasn't the only thing inhibiting her movement. Rope bound her wrists and ankles, and she ended up gracelessly on her belly, chin gouging into the prickly fake rug.

At first she didn't remember what had happened, how she'd got here . . . then she remembered everything.

Griffin's body on the floor of her apartment. The intruder. She'd been kidnapped.

"Take it easy," said a smooth, deep voice. "It'll take a bit to come around."

That voice.

A small flashlight clicked on, illuminating a frighteningly familiar man. The black half-zip, the shaved head, and that maddeningly innocent-looking vine tattoo climbing up his neck.

"You!"

Fishlike, she flopped onto her back and tried to scramble away, but the sudden movement tossed her stomach and sent her head spinning. Acid leaked into her mouth and she dry heaved.

Reed started to reach for her, then changed course and instead banged on the wall dividing the back from the cab.

"I said to take it easy." Whatever soothing she thought she'd imagined coming from him before was gone now. "You'll probably throw up. I told them to expect this. We're stopping."

He stretched for her ankles but she snatched them away. "Don't touch me!"

Her stomach contracted. He was right; she was going to lose it.

The van slowed. They turned off the paved road onto one full of potholes and rocks. As the vehicle pitched side to side, her stomach echoed the movement. Reed shined the flashlight on her green face, blinding her, and swore under his breath.

He clamped the flashlight between his teeth and moved to her feet. She could either kick him off or concentrate on holding in the contents of her stomach. She chose the stomach.

He jerked the ankle ropes until they loosened, then he snapped them free and tossed them against the metal van wall with a clang.

At last the van stopped, brakes squealing. The passenger-side door opened and footsteps headed toward the back. The doors opened, and it wasn't too much lighter outside than it was in. She couldn't see who was responsible, but she had a really good idea.

Reed jumped out first then pulled her out by her ankles, her stomach protesting violently. The moment he set her on her feet, she stumbled away from the van on wobbly legs and vomited into a small bush.

Thick fingers brushed her neck. She flinched. Reed was holding back her hair. No one had held her hair while she puked since her college days at Cal. It wasn't any less humiliating now.

There was no end to the pain, to the grossness her body expelled. All she could think about was how horrified she was with herself. How she'd actually considered sleeping with this man. This kidnapper.

But that had been his plan all along, hadn't it? Pretend to hit on her in Manny's so she'd leave with him and save him the effort of breaking into her place later on. Only she'd foiled him by running out of the bar.

So where the hell did the scene in the alley fit in?

She wanted to throw up on Reed instead of the bush, but she was dry. She settled for spitting on his boots. Straightening, she yanked her hair out of his grasp and ignored the sharp pain at the roots. He held up his hands but didn't step back.

"You killed Griffin." The sound of his name made her nose tingle and her lip quiver, and she tried desperately to ignore and cover both. Stupid, silly woman. This man wouldn't cave to weakness. Only strength would earn his respect, and his ear.

Reed's face was a stone mask—a carbon copy of the guy who'd thrown Yoshi halfway across the alley—ghostly and expressionless in the moonlight. "No," he said, then glanced surreptitiously at the van. "He's not dead. I just knocked him out."

"She talking?"

The new voice was sharp with anger. The male Tedran she'd seen in Manny's leaned against the van hood, long, defiant arms crossed over his chest. He was leaner than Reed but no less intimidating. Reed used his sheer size; the Tedran wielded a mighty glare. He pushed away from the vehicle and stalked toward her, his tangled blond hair flapping about his shoulders.

Reed backed away like an obedient employee and went to stand in the glow of dull red created by the brake lights, not sparing her another glance.

The Tedran male bent over her, his face so twisted with hatred she stumbled backward under its force. For this man, the war between their two races had never ended. History was not history; it lived in the present. He still detested her people, and even though she was only one Ofarian, she wore a million faces.

And she was alone.

Desperate, she searched for an escape. The night hugged its pitch-black cape tight around its cold body. The lights of San Francisco—or any hint of civilization—were nowhere in sight. Her only company was the scant, scrub-like vegetation, the distant wink of headlights on the highway, and Reed, picking at his fingernails as though he waited for a bus.

The highway was too far away to run for. Not with the slug drug still lingering in her veins. Not with her hands tied. Not with Reed or the lanky Tedran on her tail.

Gwen looked for the other Tedran, the small woman who'd also been in Manny's, and found her behind the wheel of the van. She bent far forward, her neck craned to see what was going on outside. When Gwen met her eyes, she looked down.

"So you're her," the male Tedran said in Tedranish. "You understand what I'm saying?"

He *knew*. He knew what she was.

Hesitant, she nodded.

"Then we'll speak my language so that Muscle over there doesn't know what we're saying. You have as much to lose as we do if we're found out."

She stole a glance at Reed, who'd stopped picking his nails and now seemed fascinated with his boots.

The Tedran grabbed her chin and forced her to look at him. "That Primary is under orders to never leave your side. Don't even think of transforming to water in front of him. You don't want him to find out what you are any more than I do."

No, but if she touched water and got away, she'd send Griffin after Reed. He'd be more than happy to dispatch the guy who'd attacked him and taken his betrothed.

The Tedran's fingers tightened on her face. "I don't have a gun, Gwen. But I do have this." He reached for his back pocket and pulled out a syringe. Yellow, iridescent liquid sloshed inside the cylinder. *"Nelicoda."*

She stared, dumbstruck. *Nelicoda* neutralized Ofarian water powers. The Board kept some under lock and key at HQ. When Gwen's sister chose to love a Primary over her people, the Board had voted to issue her a massive dose, annihilating her power.

Gwen couldn't even begin to guess how the Tedran had gotten his hands on some.

All the rationalization *not* to run flew out the door. She whirled, started to sprint, and tripped. The Tedran snatched her bound hands before she fell and yanked her back. With a snap of the wrist, he flung her around and pulled her tight against his body. Legs braced wide, one of his arms clamped her shoulders to his chest. He was much stronger than he looked.

As he raised the syringe, she tried to kick out, but the angle was bad. She snapped her teeth at his chest, getting a mouthful of leather. Out of the corner of her eye she could still make out Reed leaning against the van bumper, perfectly rigid. Perfectly passive.

When the Tedran's body started to quiver all around her, something in his signature shifted. Not what made him Secondary, but what made him a man. A whole new level of fear kicked into her system.

With a growl, he stabbed the syringe into her neck. She cried out—at the pain of the needle, at the disgusting feel of the icy, slimy liquid sliding into her bloodstream. It worked fast, snaking its way into her brain and the tiniest corners of her body. The water power, her last line of defense, slipped away like the ebbing tide, leaving her empty. Naked. Helpless.

She was as worthless as any Primary.

Against the van, Reed bowed his head.

The Tedran shoved her away. She hadn't been wrong about what she'd sensed in him. Lascivious eyes raked up and down her body. But his mouth twisted into a snarl and he'd gone red in the face. He was disgusted by her, enraged by whatever perverted desires had skated through his system. She didn't know if she should be relieved or even more frightened. She went with the latter.

The Tedran flipped back his hair and jabbed a finger at her.

"I'd be lying if I said I'm not enjoying your fear. How does it feel to be the one not in control?"

The needle prick burned but she couldn't rub it. She wouldn't cry. "Who are you? What do you want with me?"

He considered her, his eyes turning distant for a quick moment. "I'm Xavier," he grunted.

"What are you doing here? How did you find us?"

His laugh stung like poison. A fist tightened at his side, but she refused to flinch. If he was going to hit her, let him. She wouldn't back down.

A hundred and fifty years of freedom wouldn't end here.

"My people will look for me," she said. "I saw you and that Tedran woman in the bar, when you met him." She jutted her chin at Reed. "I warned our leaders. They know you're here, and when they see I'm gone, they'll know it was you. They'll come for you."

"They will, will they?"

"I don't know who you thought we'd be, but we're not your meek little slaves anymore. We've built something here, something powerful." The strength of Griffin's conviction, spoken in her own apartment not hours ago, came back to her. "You want another war? Bring it. I guarantee you this time we won't run. And you won't win."

He smiled without teeth. She hated that smile. His gray eyes glittered like sharpened knives. He stepped closer then stopped abruptly, as if recalling his body's previous reaction to her. "No one is coming for you."

"That's only one of many times you're wrong."

"Oh, really?" He bent forward at the waist. Hands behind his back, he mimicked her position. "They think you're dead."

TEN

It had to have been her. Millions of people in the San Francisco area, and Reed had been paid to extract Gwen Carroway.

Fighting tears, she kept her chin lifted. Her vicious stare never left Reed's client. Even when Xavier had grabbed her and stabbed that awful-looking needle in her neck, she resisted.

Yeah, Reed saw all that, even though he leaned against the van and pretended to look away, bored. After fifteen years in this business, his peripheral vision was almost as good as his direct.

He'd also noticed the way Xavier had reacted to Gwen's nearness. You'd have to be a man of iron not to be affected by the way she looked and felt, only Xavier's reaction set off about a thousand alarm bells. Hatred ran deep in that guy.

Reed's worry for her tested the strength of the wall keeping the Retriever on the front lines. He couldn't let that wall down. Not now. The job was on.

Reed had no idea what Gwen and Xavier were saying to each other, but he knew the gist of the argument. It was always the same. Every job.

Why did you take me? What do you want? Please let me go, I'll do anything.

Except Gwen's defiant stance and spitting tone veered markedly off script.

Suddenly Xavier turned and stalked back to the van. "Get her," he snapped. "Let's go."

Reed pushed to his feet. At last he looked directly at Gwen. Whatever Xavier had just said slapped some of that defiance off her face. The square set of her shoulders fell, and her lips parted on words unsaid.

An odd discomfort burrowed under Reed's skin.

She didn't try to run. As he took her elbow, she felt like dough, pliable and shapeless. As he guided her toward the back of the van, he was glad she didn't say anything, because he had no idea how he could respond.

"Xavier," he called out.

The blond man's hand slid from the passenger side's door handle. "What."

"She's gonna puke again if we don't get something in her stomach. I don't want to be rolling around in vomit the rest of the ride."

Xavier rolled his eyes before hauling open the cab door. From inside he took out plastic-wrapped sandwiches and two bottles of water. He stomped over and shook them in front of Gwen's face. She just glared.

Even if her hands weren't tied behind her back, Reed knew she'd never accept anything from Xavier. Reed held out his hand. "Give 'em here."

Xavier slapped the sandwiches and water into his palm, and then climbed into the cab.

Reed opened the van's back door with a creak and tossed the food inside. He nodded at the dark interior. "Get in." When her eyes met his, the transferred weight of all the hatred she'd focused on Xavier almost made his knees buckle.

"Get in," he repeated. "Or I'll put you in."

She gave him that little chin lift, then stood on tiptoe to seat her ass on the bumper. She held his gaze as she leaned into one elbow and used it to haul herself in. Awkwardly, determinedly, she shimmied all the way in like a worm.

The van bounced under his added weight. Gwen looked supremely uncomfortable and he reached for her.

"Don't you dare come near me." Her voice twisted into a nightmare of hopelessness, fear, and determination.

He exhaled audibly through his nose and sat back, hands raised. "Was just going to try to help you sit up."

She blew errant strands of hair from her face. "I can do it myself." And she did, struggling and flopping until she'd propped herself against the van wall, legs curled to one side. She refused to look at him.

He flicked on the small flashlight again and pulled shut the van doors. After a pound on the cab wall, the van lurched into motion.

He settled opposite Gwen and set the flashlight at his feet so it speared the dark between them.

"If you want," he said, his voice barely audible over the engine, "I can take the ropes off your wrists. At least until we get there."

Her eyes flipped up to his, and if they'd have been guns, he'd be dead. "Trying to tell me you're not afraid of me?"

"It hurts to have your arms tied for so long. I thought I'd give you a rest."

"How thoughtful of you. I want to go home. Can you do that for me instead?"

"No, Gwen."

The sound of her name made his tongue feel full and his cheeks weird, as though someone else had been moving his mouth. Then he knew. It was Reed again, knocking on the interior wall, reminding the Retriever of what he'd done. Who this woman was to him.

The drone of the highway passing underneath filled the space between them for a long while, until she asked, her voice hollow, "Do you know where they're taking me?"

"No. Not my business to know. It's my job to see you get there in one piece, without any hitches."

"I'm a job," she whispered.

A few hours ago you might have been more than that, Reed thought.

But now that's gone, the Retriever countered.

"Were you paid to hurt me?"

"No. I'm not a killer. Retrieve and deliver. Then I'm out."

She rolled her eyes. "That's not what I meant. I'm talking about before. In the bar."

Oh. So this thing between them hadn't been just physical for her, too. She thought they'd paid him to mess with her emotions as well. Why did that sting more than it should?

She restored the challenge to her voice. "So you 'deliver' me. Then what? You're not supposed to kill me, but what if they do it anyway?"

"They won't. It's in the contract."

She laughed. Actually laughed. "But will you wonder what's

become of me after you fly back to Washington, or wherever the hell it is you come from? Will you feel sorry for what you've done?"

Usually he gagged his targets. It helped keep the wall strong and erect. He had a clean handkerchief in his back pocket, but couldn't bring himself to reach for it.

"I'm not your first, am I?" She stared at him down her nose, and he got the feeling she was used to going toe to toe with people who were technically more powerful than she was. He admired her for that.

"No," he replied, but that wasn't necessarily true. She was the first in one big way.

She smiled but there was zero joy behind it. "You're good."

"Why do you say that?"

"Because you got around Griffin."

The guy in her apartment, the one she thought he'd killed. The one grinning and holding her in that photo on her bookcase.

God, her bookcases. Stacked with giant tomes of art, just like she'd told him about in Manny's, in perfectly aligned configurations. The sight had definitely chipped at his wall. He'd almost walked out right then and there.

Change the subject. "He your boyfriend?"

"Something like that." Her face paled and she looked away. She wasn't very good at lying.

He couldn't resist. "If you have a boyfriend, why were you going to sleep with me?"

"You know, at this point, I can't really recall." But when her eyes trailed back to him, they rested for a moment on his mouth. Then they skittered away again.

He stretched out one leg and propped an elbow up on the opposite knee. "They don't know about us. I mean, about what almost happened. They don't know about the alley and they don't even know you and I were talking in the bar before they got there."

"Why on earth would that matter to them?"

He didn't know. But it mattered to him. Maybe, after she thought about it, it would matter to her, too.

The sandwiches sat at his hip. He unwrapped one—peanut butter—and offered it to her. She narrowed her eyes at him and he thought she'd continue to be stubborn—it wouldn't be the first hunger strike he'd faced—but then her lips parted and she nodded. He scooted forward, one leg arching over her baby-soft leather boots, and placed the sandwich at her lips. Her first bite was tentative; the subsequent ones were those of a ravenous beast.

"You'll take food from me but not Xavier?" he asked. "You trust me over him?"

She paused mid-chew. "You aren't . . . one of them. And I never said I trusted you."

When she was done, he cracked open a water bottle and held it as she drank until she turned her face away.

A smudge of peanut butter sat on her cheek. "You have some . . . right there," he said. Her tongue poked out, swiping around her mouth. "No. Wait. Let me."

As he lifted a hand, she darted away, her head snapping back so fast she smacked it against the van wall.

"You okay?" he asked. When she just stared, he reached out and ran a thumb over the peanut butter smudge. Her eyes dropped to his mouth again as he put his thumb between his lips and sucked the peanut butter off.

She stopped breathing altogether.

He sighed, lowering his hand to the outside of her thigh, and leaned in close. Fuck it. There wasn't anything to lose at this point. She wouldn't believe him, but at least he could say he tried.

"I didn't know it was you they wanted me to take."

Her chest sputtered into breathing again. "Bullshit," she snarled.

They were so close he could smell the sandwich on her breath. It mingled with the scent of her hair, which he'd practically inhaled back at Manny's. Nothing about that encounter had been false. "It's the truth."

"You were scouting me when you found me in that alley. You saved me so you could kidnap me later, make sure you got your paycheck."

He slowly shook his head. "Nope."

She kept going. "And then you followed me to the bar. You expect me to believe that was all coincidence? That you just happened to meet me in the alley and then in the bar? The very same bar the . . . Xavier walked into?"

"My flight in landed long before dawn, but I was too wired so I wandered the streets. Never been to San Francisco and wanted to see the sunrise over the city. Instead I found a woman being attacked by a crazy Japanese guy with an agenda I still don't understand. I did what I thought was right."

"You're a goddamn kidnapper."

He didn't refute that. "Then I got a good look at you. I had this asshole in my hands and I could barely take my eyes off you. Couldn't stop thinking about you the whole day, wondered who you were, if you were okay. That night I went to the bar where my clients told me to meet them and, bam, there you were. I don't believe in fate, but I thought you'd be a nice . . . distraction until I had to do my job." He licked his dry lips. "I just didn't know you *were* the job."

She took two deep breaths before biting out, "You're such a liar."

"I know how it looks, so I don't expect you to believe me. But I'm asking you to."

She raised her face to the dark roof, exposing her neck. "Why do you even care at this point?"

She didn't wear a necklace or earrings, so this long column of golden skin captured his attention. "Because I really was interested in you, Gwen."

When her head tilted back down, he found he'd moved in even closer, enough that his knee brushed hers. "I liked our connection. I liked our conversation," he murmured. "I wanted you. And I'm pretty sure you wanted me, too."

"Stop confusing me. I hate you."

What the fuck was he saying? The wall had caved in without him knowing. That had never, ever happened before. With terrific force, he evicted Reed from his mind. *Slam. Lock.* Up went the wall.

He pushed himself away and resumed his seat on the opposite side of the van. It was colder over there, but his head was clearer.

Suddenly Adine, the driver, let up on the gas. The van slowed then swerved gently to the right, onto the highway shoulder. He'd told Gwen the truth; he had no idea where they were taking her. But he doubted pulling over on the side of the road was part of it, considering he hadn't given another warning knock. The van stopped, the engine idling. No one got out.

Red and blue flashing lights leaked through the cracks outlining the back doors.

Oh shit.

When he turned to Gwen, she was already watching him. Man, her eyes were wide. Life boiled inside her, fueled by adrenaline and determination. He recognized it; he'd seen it in the alley. She was no weak-willed onlooker and she was dying to challenge him. She'd move, and when she did, it would be fast.

Slow footsteps came around the roadside edge of the van.

The moment Reed edged toward her, aiming to subdue, she went for it. She threw herself on the nasty carpet and drummed those sky-high heels on the metal van wall behind her. Thrashing like a fish, she screamed at the top of her lungs.

In his head it went on for minutes. In reality, it was more like a second or two.

She didn't know how to fight, but she knew how to kick. He fell on top of her, slamming her against the van wall. He clamped a hand around her mouth, the heel of his palm under her chin to keep her from opening up and going for the bite. The other hand slid around her waist, keeping her pinned between himself and metal. He threw one leg over both of hers and locked his ankles together.

The hard, sharp breaths through her nose heated his fingers. Though her muscles slackened, there was no resignation in those huge, dark eyes. She stopped fighting because she knew she'd won.

Fuck fuck fuck. Reed couldn't get control of his pulse. Fifteen years and he'd never come up against anything like this. Fifteen years and he'd never once been busted. For *anything*.

The cop's muffled voice filtered into the back. He seemed calm, casual. Reed heard Xavier's voice, too, but mostly Adine did the talking. He couldn't make out any words.

Any second now. Any second, those doors will open and I'm a dead man.

The cop patted the van's driver's side door. The footsteps retreated. Toward the back.

Beneath him, Gwen's body shook and the dim flashlight beam caught the mirth in her eyes. She was laughing at him. At his demise.

But didn't he deserve it? After all this time, all this tempting of fate and giving in to his vice, this was what it would come down to. He'd known it for years and thought himself untouchable. Smart enough to be above it.

No longer.

In his panic, Reed lost track of the footsteps. Was the cop standing just outside? Was he calling in the vehicle?

Gwen's head, with that mass of thick, gold hair, lolled against his forearm, her face turned up to his. Never, not once, did he consider releasing her.

The van doors never opened. The footsteps walked away. The police car's door slammed shut, and the cruiser pulled back out onto the highway, taking the slow circle of the flashing lights with it.

The van jerked as Adine threw it back into drive. Slowly— clearly waiting for the cruiser to get a good head start—they rolled back onto the road.

Reed's face dropped into the warm slope of Gwen's neck. "Holy shit. Oh, my God. They must've paid the cop off." He sagged into her, every contracted muscle losing its tension at once.

She bit his loosened hand. It didn't have the effect she wanted. He growled and tightened his hold around her body.

Her eyes were wild—beyond tears, beyond sorrow, beyond hopelessness. "Get. Off. Me."

"No." He changed the position of his ankles, dragging her even closer. "Didn't work out quite the way you expected it to, did it?"

For once, she was silent, and it disturbed him more than he wanted to admit.

"Look," he went on. "My job is to deliver you to them safely. They've paid me some serious cash and they've promised not to harm you. I'm going to make sure they uphold their end of the bargain. But *that*"—he released his viselike hold on her and pushed back, coming to his knees over her body—"*that* little stunt won't happen again."

He expected a fight, a smart remark. In a way, it was what he wanted.

What he got were her first tears.

ELEVEN

Daylight outlined the van's double doors. Gwen had fallen asleep; her body rocked with the swerving van. Reed wouldn't shut his eyes until the job was done.

After the cop incident, they'd climbed steadily up a mountainside and now they were descending, the vehicle making wide, gentle curves. It stopped every now and again—streetlights and stop signs. Could be anywhere in California.

The van made a sudden sharp turn and plunged down a steep incline, so steep Reed thrust out a boot heel to keep himself steady. Gwen's body slid toward the doors, but he grabbed her shoulders before she could hit the metal. The jolt woke her up. She looked blearily up at him as the van flattened out and came to a complete stop. Adine cut the engine.

Reed took his hands off Gwen and popped into a crouch. Showtime.

"Where are we?" Red streaked across her eyes. Makeup smeared all over her face.

The Retriever shrugged. "Not my business to know."

"Retrieve and deliver, right?" she snapped. "And then you're out? Must be payday."

Not meaning to, he frowned.

"Having second thoughts?"

There she went again, her presence a mighty hammer, banging away at his wall. This time it held steady. "No," he shot back.

The doors flew open and blinding sunlight streamed inside. Xavier braced long arms against each door and glared at Gwen. Then he snatched her ankle and pulled her out.

Reed was supposed to step back now. Got it.

The ground was loose gravel, and Gwen's heeled boots had trouble finding purchase. Xavier gave her a shove but her tight skirt restricted her and she tripped. Fell. The tiny pebbles drew blood from her knees. She didn't make a sound.

Xavier threw Reed a confused look. Reed blinked. Looked down. He was reaching for Gwen and hadn't even realized it. Disconcerted, he let Xavier lug Gwen to her feet, then drew back to survey the area.

Three stories of cream-stuccoed mansion angled around a garden yellowing in late season. A four-car garage stood off to the right. The gravel drive circled in front of it then retreated back up a steep hill into a tangled mess of evergreens and other trees halfway into autumn. The drive was the only exit, as far as Reed could tell from this vantage point. A small hut sat just inside the trees, an armed guard leaning out the window, watching. The dense foliage made for a wickedly secluded location. A tall fence surrounded the premises. Cameras dangled from the house's eaves, which meant somewhere there was a security control center. He'd seen plenty of compounds like this in his line of work.

Xavier barked something to Gwen in that weird language. All Reed caught was a name: Nora.

Adine, the small, quiet woman who'd driven the van, shot past Reed, her sneakers crunching on the gravel. Head down, brown hair blanketing her face, she pulled aside a vine to the left of the heavy oak front door to access a small metal box. Reed shifted positions to see if he could get a better look. ADT had nothing on an Adine Jones creation. He'd learned all about her and her inventions after he'd traced the source of Nora's down payment.

One side of the double front door opened with a click and Adine ducked inside as though the sky threw down metal-spiked basketballs.

As Xavier pulled Gwen inside, he threw over his shoulder to Reed, "She wants to see you, too."

And Reed wanted to see Nora to hammer home the "no kill" clause in their contract.

He stepped from the bright, crisp, early autumn day into the pages of an upscale home decor magazine. The marble foyer dropped into a sunken living room. Wide, white-carpeted stairs extended up to his right, an archway into the immense kitchen on his left. The entire back wall of the house was made of glass, twenty feet high, and it framed a view of a cobalt blue lake, expansive and glittering in the early sunlight. A few boats drew foamy lines across the water. On the opposite shore rose white-capped mountains.

A stone terrace wrapped around the back of the house, a cold, oval fire pit in its center. On that terrace stood a tiny, white-haired woman. Had to be Nora. Her appearance matched the voice. Nora turned from her place at the terrace wall and shuffled inside. In silent but obvious fear, Gwen watched Nora approach. Xavier gazed upon Nora with a perplexing sort of reverence.

Nora came up the few steps from the living room, her knees shaking. She wore a billowy tunic and wide-legged pants over a bony and frail body. Her white hair was cropped close to her head, flattened on a severe side part. Wrinkles made deep crevices in her face, and loose skin hung below her chin. She stared at Gwen with eyes as hard as black diamonds.

Xavier shoved Gwen yet again and said something else in that language.

Nora raised a terse hand to stop him mid-sentence. "Gwen Carroway," she began in the raspy voice Reed recognized. Nora talked more in the foreign tongue, her light tone filling the quiet in the cavernous room.

Gwen exploded. Streams of ugly, rage-filled, indecipherable words spewed from her lips. Nora took the attack unperturbed.

Reed realized, with a great deal of shock, that Gwen had no idea who her captors were or why she'd been taken. There were too many questions in her eyes, too much panic. And when Nora had first entered, Gwen had looked upon her in utter bewilderment. Again, the script didn't match the action. Almost everyone he'd been paid to retrieve was fully aware of the reasons behind his or her extraction. They'd feared it, expected it even. But Gwen . . . she was completely lost.

He didn't like that. Not at all.

Nora turned to Reed. "You." She waved a finger at Gwen. "Remove the ropes."

He moved behind Gwen, who stiffened. He picked

methodically at the knots, knowing exactly which loop to loosen to make the whole thing fall apart.

As the ropes fell away, she let out a small cry of relief. She winced as she brought her arms to her front and rubbed at her elbows. Reed backed away until his heels hit a wall.

Nora barked something else to Xavier. Xavier grabbed Gwen again and tried to steer her toward the stairs, but with her arms free now, she fought him. She lashed out in English, "I don't want to take a fucking shower. I want to know what you want with me."

Nora's eyes narrowed, no longer diamonds, but icicles sharpened to deadly tips.

Another wave of her skeletal hand and Xavier clamped his arms around Gwen from behind and dragged her up the stairs.

Reed really, *really* didn't like that.

Any other job he'd turn his head and go back to his employer, hand outstretched for the cash. This time, he watched the whole scene—Xavier hauling a wriggling, shouting Gwen out of sight—with bile in his throat and a clamp fastened around his heart. Xavier hated her. Men who hated women gave them the worst punishments.

What the hell sort of kidnapping was this? Ransom most likely. Gwen clearly either came from money or had made a ton on her own. If she was upper-level corporate and made international sales, maybe her company had a hefty insurance policy on her.

It was the only explanation Reed could come up with, but it didn't make much sense given what he'd dug up about Adine. He hadn't been able to find anything about Nora or Xavier. It was like they didn't exist. And he excelled in finding people who supposedly didn't exist.

"So," Nora turned to him, "I finally meet the mysterious Retriever." She smiled, but it was calculating, not remotely warm. "Or should I call you Reed. Reed Scott."

With that revelation, Nora snatched the playing board and tossed all the pieces in the air. He had no idea what game they were playing now, and he'd dragged Gwen into the mayhem.

"Come." Nora beckoned to the terrace. "We have a lot to discuss."

* * *

"You want to know what this is all about, don't you?"

Nora stood next to the raised fire pit, spotted hands laced at her waist. Her body was still as an iron rod, her mouth quirked knowingly.

"Nah." Reed leaned a knee into the stone and pretended to gaze out at the lake. "Not my business to know."

"Mm-hmm." She barely came up to his chest, but man, did she carry her weight. "What's going on here is highly guarded information."

"Told you. Don't care. I just want my money."

She picked at a loose piece of rock on the pit wall. "The Retriever," she said absently. "The dog."

Maybe clients had thought that before, but no one had actually ever said it to his face. Even if it were true.

"Do you want to know how I found out your real name?"

Couldn't lie about that. "Yes."

"You made a mistake." She lifted her black diamond eyes to him. "While you were running from Tracker."

Jesus, she knew about Tracker? *Don't react. Don't tense a muscle. Don't look away from her for a millisecond.*

"He wants you. Or more accurately, he wants the million you took from him. And then he wants your skin on his wall. But I told him he can't have you until you're done here."

How in the world could Nora and Tracker know each other? Was there some sort of twisted Yahoo Group?

Come to think of it, this job stank of the same strangeness the Tracker job had. The same uncomfortable mystery that had made him bail with Tracker's deposit now shrouded Nora's job. Only he couldn't bail. They had Gwen.

The muscles in his jaw began to ache, and he realized he was clenching his teeth. When he unlocked them, all that came out was, "Tracker."

"I didn't tell him the whole truth," she added.

"Oh?"

"I'm not an evil person, Reed. What Tracker wanted with that boy was . . . disgusting. I don't blame you for taking his money and skipping out. But the thing is, I can't have you running loose. You've seen us."

"I've seen a lot of people. I don't talk. Ever. Since you found me through previous clients, you know that."

She pursed her lips and tilted her head. "I'm willing to believe you, given your record, but I need assurance. Keep quiet and loyal to us, and Tracker won't ever know your real name."

Sounded so easy. But not quite. "I need assurance, too," he said with a nod toward the house, "that the target won't be hurt."

She thought him a fool; he saw it in the condescending flash in her eye. Let her think he was stupid hired muscle, that he didn't know what he was doing or talking about.

She pressed a hand to her chest. "We have a contract. That was one of your stipulations. I promise Ms. Carroway will get through this alive. She's no use to us dead."

He hid a smile. Nora had no clue he knew about Adine, the weight and value of the information he held over their little group. If anything happened to Gwen, he'd have Nora by the balls, so to speak.

"Good. So with that in mind," he added, because he wasn't about to let her have the last say, "I have a proposition."

TWELVE

Xavier released Gwen at the end of the long second-floor corridor. A small set of winding stairs led up to the third floor. The Tedran blocked the way back downstairs; the only way to go was up.

On the third level, two doors stood on the same side of a narrow hallway. It'd probably been an attic at one point, because the slanted walls cramped in tightly. Tiny metal boxes served as the door handles and Xavier moved to the first one. Instead of using a key, he slid his watch into a square slot on top of the box and a light on the side clicked green. Before Gwen could get a better look at the watch, he tugged down his sleeve.

"In," he ordered with a terse nod.

She just stood there, gazing into the plain room beyond. The steep slope of the roof made it feel smaller than it was. The floors were wood and covered with colorful, mismatched throw rugs. A double bed was shoved against the far wall, just under a triangular window that looked out over the glittering lake. Bleach-white linens, white iron bed, white dresser, white walls and trim . . . the decor gave her cell this false sense of little-girl innocence that made her want to vomit all over again.

It smelled of new paint. So they'd prepared this place just for her. How hideous. She reached up and ran a hand down the steep slant of the ceiling.

Xavier hovered in the doorway. Not even his big toe crossed the threshold. "Clothes are in the armoire. Shower's through there. Knock when you're done."

Though it was warm in that uppermost floor, Gwen wrapped

her arms around herself and shivered. Her voice sounded as ragged as she felt. "How'd you get the cop to leave us alone?"

She suspected the answer, and it terrified her.

Xavier glared. "My room is next door, through the bathroom. I'm the only one with access to these rooms."

The thought of Xavier sleeping not twenty feet away, and having to share a bathroom with him, creeped Gwen out.

He started to pull shut the door, then stopped. "And Gwen, I want to make one thing clear. You're here because Nora wants it. If it were up to me, I'd tie a weight around your ankles and throw you into the lake, along with every other Ofarian."

His silver-steel eyes held hers until the moment the door slammed closed. No door handle on her side. Not even one of those metal boxes.

The white armoire tucked diagonally in the corner matched the dresser but not the bed. Both pieces of furniture looked worn, their corners chipped. The armoire door squealed as she opened it. She fingered the stiff, new jeans shoved inside. Piles of T-shirts and zippered sweaters in a menagerie of colors lay in the drawers, the price tags all from a big box store. A pair of hiking boots sat on the bottom. All her size but nothing her style. But then, she'd never heard of an inmate who got to choose her wardrobe.

She snatched a random sweater and a pair of jeans, and stomped into the bathroom. Every fixture was white and plain and available at any chain home repair warehouse. Anonymous. Utilitarian. Not fixed up for anyone who'd be staying here for any length of time.

The box next to the door leading into Xavier's room blinked red. She slapped on the nozzle in the walk-in shower, turning it up to full blast and steaming hot.

The last twenty-four hours slammed into her with the force of a meteor hitting Earth.

She sank to the bathroom floor amid her new, crappy clothes. Great, wracking sobs tore through her body. Steam swirled around, thickening by the moment. She wanted to get lost in it. She wanted it to erase her surroundings.

Wishing had never been her thing. The only success she'd ever achieved had been through planning and hard work. Both seemed unreachable now.

When the tears eased up, she summoned the strength to stand and undress. The tall boots and pencil skirt lay crumpled in a heap. Reed's compliments about them rang in her ears, taunting her, and she cringed at her foolishness.

Using a towel, she swiped at the mirror, clearing a small hole. She barely recognized the woman looking back at her. Yesterday's makeup poured down her cheeks and made black trails toward her ears and mouth. The layers of her hair tangled together. The heavy slope of her shoulders and the curve of her spine displayed her defeat. She turned away in disgust.

In the shower she scrubbed her hair three times, her face twice. She lathered up and shaved. If she could peel off her entire top layer of skin, contaminated by Reed and Xavier and Nora's odious stare, she would.

She longed to transform into droplets, swirl down the drain, and flow far, far away. Bracing her hands on the white plastic shower stall, she just stood there under the pounding water. Concentrating. Reaching. Calling out.

The water didn't answer.

The *nelicoda* shoved her power into a cage and threw away the key, but she refused to give up. Focusing all her energy, she probed every millimeter of that cage. Eventually she found some hairline cracks in the chemically created bars, but they were only that—too thin to completely bust through in her weakened state.

How long would the dosage last? Would it fade out? Or would its effects just end? She vowed to keep testing it. If she could just widen one hairline crack, stretch through to the other side, even a sliver of her power would allow her to touch water . . .

The effort exhausted her and she was forced to abandon it. A weak and pitiful showing that left her breathless and hugging the wall.

"Who is Nora?" Gwen asked Xavier as they wove around the living room furniture toward the door in the glass wall. The tiny old woman stood on the terrace, looking out at the lake. "I mean, who is she to you?"

"Your people have Chairman Ian Carroway," he grunted. "We have Nora."

As Gwen stepped out onto the terrace, a fierce blast of

sweet-smelling freedom smacked her in the face. The cool air made her still-damp scalp tingle. The wind picked up, tearing turned leaves from the trees and tossing them about the stone. She dragged her stiff new boots through the crunch and wondered how far she'd get if she ran.

Not very far, by the looks of the fence encircling the property. Down the hill, a private dock stretched out into the water. An armed guard sat in a small hut on the rocky shore, his rifle trained on her.

Gwen went right for Nora, Xavier having to pick up his feet to keep pace with her.

"Where the hell am I?" she demanded.

Nora turned from the wall. Slowly, casually. "Do you feel better?"

"Skip the pleasantries."

Xavier finally caught up and grabbed her arm before she could reach Nora, the pinch of his fingers birthing bruises. "Sorry," he muttered to Nora.

Gwen squirmed out of Xavier's hold. "Where am I? If you didn't want me to know, you would've kept me locked up in the dark."

Nora raised her silver eyebrows and looked vaguely amused. "You don't recognize it? You've never been here before?"

"Where exactly is *here*?"

Nora laced her fingers before her. "Lake Tahoe."

Less than four hours' drive from San Francisco. Gwen held back a gasp of hope.

"Why?" Gwen demanded. "Why me? Why here?"

The small Tedran woman gazed back at her with an expression made of granite. Then she turned to Xavier. "You can go."

"But . . ." he stammered.

"We'll be fine. There's been a change of plans. Go back inside and you'll find out more."

Xavier scowled at Gwen, then turned on his heel and stalked back through the door, leaving her with Nora on the wide-open terrace. Alone.

With a sharp pang, she realized Reed was the only person outside this house who knew she was still alive. And he'd grabbed his gigantic paycheck and was probably already halfway back to Washington, or wherever the hell he was from.

She should be glad to be rid of him, to not be continually reminded of his duplicity and her stupidity. So why wasn't she?

Nora went to a wrought-iron table and pulled out a heavy chair with a screech of metal over stone. "Sit," she ordered, as if Gwen had a choice. Gwen settled on the very edge of the hard chair. She'd never be comfortable. She just wanted to be ready.

Nora tilted her head and regarded Gwen with an inscrutable expression.

"What?" Gwen snapped.

Without words, Nora reached into the billowy folds of the cape she'd draped over her shoulders and produced a small vial of silvery, viscous liquid. As she set it in the middle of the black table, the sun struck the vial in an explosion of rainbows.

A strangled sound erupted from Gwen's throat. She snatched the vial off the table and cradled it in her lap, shielding it from unseen eyes. She could barely breathe. "Where did you get this? *How* did you get this?"

Nora eased back in her chair, looking disgustingly satisfied at Gwen's fear and bewilderment. "It's not that hard. For us."

So Gwen's intuition about the van had been right, and Reed's assumption had been wrong. When the policeman had walked up, she'd felt the subtle shift in atmosphere, the familiar tingle. She'd been around it since she was old enough to understand the nature of her family's business. It had its own signature, one she could recognize as strong as any Secondary's.

She didn't want to believe it then, and she sure as hell didn't want to acknowledge it now. Looked like she had no other choice.

Xavier hadn't paid off those cops. He'd used *Mendacia* to disguise the van.

It's not that hard. For us.

Gwen put two and two together. If the language used to control *Mendacia* was Tedran, they could likely shape it into any illusion they wanted, not just physical glamour. They would know far more command words than the Ofarians. The Tedrans must have used it to fake her death. But how? Would her dad be able to see through it? Would any other Ofarian?

She fingered the bottle under the table, following its hexagonal shape by memory. It didn't have a label. Strange.

"*Mendacia* is extremely rare and extremely valuable. We know where every bottle is and how it's being used. How did you get this one?"

"Yes, I heard that's what you call it. *Mendacia*." Nora breathed stiffly through her nose. For a moment her icy veneer cracked and Gwen glimpsed a heavy sadness underneath. Then the chill swept back over. "It means 'lies' in Latin. Did you know that? You're selling liquid lies. And there's more than one lie in that bottle, other than how it's made."

Gwen was so enraged, and so utterly confused, that she couldn't dig her voice out of the hole it had fallen into.

"Tell me"—Nora's fingers drummed on the table top—"what do Ofarians teach their children about the war on Tedra?"

"Excuse me?"

"What do you believe happened on Tedra, all those generations ago?" She enunciated each word like Gwen was a slow first-grader, making Gwen want to lunge across the table. "What story is passed from Ofarian mother to child about your ancestors?"

What sort of trap was she trying to set? "You should know the story as well as I do."

Her dark eyes flashed with a hatred that mirrored Gwen's. "You know *a* story. You don't know *the* story. Tell me what you know."

"Why?"

As she spread her arms, the cape fell to her elbows, exposing her translucent skin, peppered with age spots and striped with blue veins. "Because you, my dear, are the one sitting in that chair, with *nelicoda* numbing your magic and with your own personal guard watching from behind that glass wall, making sure you'll do exactly as I say. *Now tell me what you know.*"

A shiver crawled through Gwen that had nothing to do with the autumn wind.

She couldn't look at Nora, so she stared at the vial of *Mendacia*, since it seemed to be creating the shadow falling over her predicament. There, on the sun-drenched terrace of her kidnapper's home, the smoky tones of her mom's voice came back to Gwen so strongly she might have sworn her mom was sitting right next to her. Nora was right; Gwen's mom had told her the story many times. But she wasn't going to just hand it to Nora. The snide Tedran would have to work for it by asking Gwen for specifics.

"Why did your people leave Ofaria?" Nora prompted in the silence.

Gwen fidgeted, delaying her response as long as possible. "Ofaria's atmosphere had turned poisonous, the ground no longer supported life. The survivors fled."

"And behold! They found Tedra," Nora added, with the sarcastic, exaggerated flare of a nasty children's storyteller, "a world of mostly water. A world practically made for a race connected to that element."

"But you didn't want to share your world, even with ailing refugees. Whatever Ofarians you didn't kill outright, you took as slaves. You separated families, destroyed the settlements. You stole our freedom."

Nora's nostrils flared and her fingertips twitched, but otherwise she sat maddeningly still. At least she'd gone quiet. Gwen barreled on.

"You created *nelicoda,* pumped us with it, and forced us to serve you."

Nora only stared back. "Go on."

Gwen was on a roll now. She liked throwing the past in Nora's face. "We revolted even though we were outnumbered and knew we would lose. A few Ofarians stole a ship and fled to find a new home. A hundred and fifty years ago they found Earth. We've been hiding ever since." Gwen slapped the table, making it jump. "*That's* the story I know."

She wanted to punch Nora's awful little smile.

"Now," said the old Tedran, "tell me about *Mendacia.*"

"No." Gwen leaned forward. "Tell me how you found us. How you got here without the Primaries noticing."

Secrets and bitterness tugged at Nora's lips. She steepled her fingers. "I will. But I want to hear what you know first. How do you think it's made?"

By the smug look on Nora's face, she thought she knew more than Gwen, and Gwen hated that.

"If you're looking for insider information, you're barking up the wrong tree. I don't know much." Nora waved an impatient hand and Gwen bit the inside of her cheek. "Very few

Ofarians are chosen to learn how to make it. Those who are picked leave everything behind and devote their lives to creating it in secrecy. Its rarity explains the price. That's all I know. If you want more, you've got the wrong woman."

Somewhere in the distance a leaf-blower revved up. She was jailed in the middle of suburbia.

"Is that what you wanted to hear?" Gwen demanded.

"No." For the first time, Nora looked at her lap. "No, I didn't *want* to hear that. But I knew I had to."

Nora stood abruptly and started to walk away.

Gwen jumped into her path. "Where are you going?"

Nora snapped her fingers at the glass wall and the door to the terrace opened and shut behind Gwen. Gwen assumed she knew who Nora had summoned, but when she glanced over her shoulder and saw who actually approached, her mouth dropped open.

Nora snatched the *Mendacia* from Gwen's grasp and stuffed it back into a hidden pocket. "Everything you just told me," she whispered, "is a lie."

THIRTEEN

Nora snapped for him, so, like a dog, Reed heeled, even though it made him cringe.

He felt better that it was he going to Gwen and not Xavier. Better, but still not good.

He fingered the strange device Adine had fit onto his wrist. It sported a tiny screen and a camera, and closed-loop, two-way communication with Nora. Futuristic and sleek. It was his key, so to speak, to his new job of protecting Gwen.

Let Nora think he just wanted the fatter paycheck. Let her think he was a panting, desperate dog. Hell, let Gwen think that. All Reed knew was that he didn't trust Nora or Xavier, or even Adine. Contract or no, Retriever or Reed Scott, he'd make sure Gwen got out of this alive.

As he moved to stand next to Nora, Gwen gaped at him in disgust. He gave her his coolest disregard.

"Reed is your shadow now," Nora told Gwen. "He'll make sure you go where I say, do what I ask."

There. He saw it in Gwen's eyes. It was gone now, but it had peeked its head out and shown its face, however briefly: relief. He didn't scare her half as much as Nora, which bothered him all the more.

She looked different now, scrubbed of all that makeup and out of those fancy clothes. Some might say she looked like any other suburban woman, but to Reed she looked like no one else. She never would.

He felt the sweep of her gaze as she took him in. Showered, shaved, changed—everything to indicate he was staying. Then her eyes fell on the odd watch and narrowed, plotting. The watch only made her situation worse. The GPS inside always told Nora where Reed and Gwen would be, and he was required to provide photographic proof of Gwen's location at specific intervals.

"You know what to do," Nora said to him. He nodded and Nora doddered toward the door.

"Wait." Gwen lunged for Nora, but the old woman didn't turn around.

Reed took Gwen's arm and pulled her back.

"Hey!"

"Stay right here," he growled.

Gwen shouted around his body, "We're not finished, Nora!"

He stepped into her line of sight. "She's done with you."

Pure hatred darkened Gwen's face and she tried to skirt around him. He danced to one side, then the other, blocking her way.

"She owes me answers."

"You're not getting around me."

They stood there, several feet apart, the space between them filling with silent challenge. "You are soulless," she said.

Good thing she turned away because he didn't know if he succeeded in disguising his hurt. Targets had called him many things before, but never that.

She went to the terrace wall, arms spread out wide on its top. He granted her a moment then approached, giving her generous space.

"I suppose you know everything I don't," she snapped.

"Not true." He shrugged. "I'm paid to know nothing."

"Oh, that's right. I hope I'm worth every penny."

He bent to rest on his elbows. "I couldn't tell you anything, even if I did know."

Couldn't? Or wouldn't? Even he didn't know.

"When I find out," she said, staring out at the lake, "I won't tell you. Even if you beg."

"I won't beg. It's not my business to know."

"What if they plan to kill me?"

He ran a hand over his newly shaven head. "I already told you. They won't."

"If you don't even know why I'm here, how could you possibly say that?"

"Jesus, how many times do I have to say it? I don't do murders, Gwen. Retrieve and deliver, that's it."

"How can you be sure? Once you're done and gone, they can do whatever they want with me."

That's why I'm staying this time.

He glanced back at the house, discreetly enough that their cameras wouldn't be able to tell. "I make it a point to know a bit or two about my clients. Bits they don't want out in the open. Let's just say I usually don't deal with the straightest of arrows. If they renege on the no-killing part of our contract, I expose their dirty little secrets."

He expected some relief, or maybe even a little bit of gratitude on her part. Instead her face paled. Her voice dipped low. "What do you know about Nora?"

Not Nora. Adine. He shook his head. "Can't say. We've already crossed a line."

She snorted. "And whose line is that?"

His head dropped between his arms. "Mine." He breathed deeply, looked at her sideways. "This is different from what I normally do."

"Not your typical kidnapping?" The bitterness in her tone tore at him.

"No. It's not. I've already broken my first rule."

"And what's that?"

"Get in. Get out." He couldn't help it; his gaze settled on her mouth.

The wall dividing Reed from the Retriever didn't just crumble. It combusted into tiny little pebbles. Reed stared at her and struggled to rebuild it. No use. He was flailing like a puppy thrown into a lake for the first time.

She drew a sharp breath. Held it. "Clearly it's about money."

"Not this time. It's not about the money."

"Oh really? So you're not getting more for staying on?"

Scrubbing a hand over his head again, he knew how the situation looked, but he couldn't refute it.

She shook her head. Her hair was wonderfully golden. "That's what I thought."

"Look." He straightened. He had to get a hold on the Retriever and heave him back in somehow. "I've seen enough rage in my life to know that Xavier would hurt you if he got the chance." By the shadow crossing her face, he could tell Xavier had already made the threat. "I convinced Nora to move him out of that room next to yours and put me into it. I hate watching how he treats you. He's a bomb, waiting for the match."

"Then maybe," she said softly, "you shouldn't have taken me in the first place."

He blew out a breath. "You think I haven't doubted myself? The wheels were in motion, the money had changed hands, and all I could do was try to steer the runaway train."

She sneered. "Does it always come down to money for you?"

He ground his teeth together hard enough to hurt. "Not always."

"But sometimes. Most of the time."

And she was right. God, he made himself sick.

"I've never lied to you, Gwen. Ever."

She faced him now, hip pressing into the wall, arms crossed over her chest. "If that's so, tell me straight up, to my face. Why are you still here? For the money? Or for me?"

He looked down his shoulder at her, and was surprised at how easily the answer came out.

"You."

Then with a *slam* and a *lock*, he raised the wall and vowed never to let it drop again.

The next morning Gwen stood at the triangular window of her bedroom cell, fingering the cheap, gauzy curtains and watching the lake absorb the sunrise.

She'd been locked in the room since yesterday afternoon, after her infuriating "discussion" with Nora. After Reed had told her he'd stayed on for her.

Last night he'd brought her a dinner tray, which she barely touched. They hadn't spoken.

Behind her the bathroom door cracked open. She could sense Reed's eyes on her back as strongly as she'd once felt his hands.

"Are you just going to stand there?" she asked, eyes still on the lake.

The door creaked. When she turned, Reed stood in the threshold, hands in his jeans pockets. If he was waiting for an invitation inside, he wouldn't get one.

His eyes flickered to the bed she'd made up nice and neat out of habit, and he frowned. She wondered what his bedroom looked like. If it was just as plain as hers. If he was obsessive-compulsive like her about squared corners and perfectly fluffed pillows. If his huge body even fit on the mattress.

Stop it. Her mind definitely shouldn't head in that direction.

They stared at each other, silent, the bed between them. Such a small distance, such a telling barrier. She could only imagine what she looked like: crazy tangled bed hair, black rings under her eyes, confusion and fear drawing lines across her forehead and between her eyebrows. But Reed . . . he looked incredible. Rested and strong and confident, like he'd done this a zillion times. Because he had.

He strode into the room and crossed directly to her, every step efficient and powerful. The ridge of his thigh muscles pushed against his jeans. He pulled up two feet away. The tense control over his expression and the rigidity of his posture melted—just a smidge, but enough for her to notice the switch. When his eyes dropped to her mouth, his lips parted.

Doubt and desire claimed the darkness behind his eyes. He drew in a breath, bent a tad closer.

Sweet Jesus, he was going to kiss her. Here and now. Conflicting responses opened fire on her brain. Though her back pressed hard into the wall, away from him, she tilted her face up to him and licked her lips.

"Reed. What you said yesterday . . ."

At the sound of her voice, he shook his head as if clearing himself from a trance. His stern demeanor slammed back into place. He shoved his fist between them, shattering the moment. His fingers opened to reveal a small, yellow *nelicoda* pill.

"Take this."

Wow, was she dumb. Letting herself get reeled in by that body and their early encounters and the way he looked at her as though he were caught in his own Allure trap. She recoiled.

He thrust the pill closer. "Nora said it wouldn't hurt you."

Hurt, no. Disable, yes. "What if I told you it did?"

"I wouldn't believe you. I'm sure you didn't know this, but you're a terrible liar. Everything you're thinking flashes across your face in neon lights."

She gulped. "Everything?"

He leaned in and she counted five age lines radiating out from each blue eye. The bright sun streamed into the window, shrinking his pupils to pinpricks. "Everything," he murmured, and she knew he wasn't just talking about the pill.

She crossed her arms like a child. "I won't take it."

A muscle in his jaw flexed. From his other pocket he whipped out a syringe swirling with glowing yellow liquid. With his thumb, he flicked off the protective cap. "Then it's this."

Something about the set of his mouth told her he didn't want to give her a shot any more than she wanted to receive it. He'd also said that he didn't like the way Xavier treated her—manhandling her and stabbing her with needles. She saw an opening and plowed through it.

"Neither." Not giving herself time for second guesses, she slid a hand around the back of his neck. The skin there was much softer than she'd expected, contrasting with the faint scratch of the places where he'd run the razor. She refused to be distracted by the feel of him. This had a purpose, and it wasn't pleasure. Rising on her toes, she went in for a kiss.

For a split second she thought she was home free. She'd give him the kiss of a lifetime; he'd walk away in a daze and forget about the *nelicoda*. Later on she'd ask to shower and then simply slip into the pipes and be gone.

He was quicker than Xavier. Stronger. He flicked the pill to the bed and grabbed her arm like a vise. Spinning her around, he clamped her back to his chest.

"God, you're the worst actress," he said in her ear. "You forget that I know what you *really* look like when you want me, that I know what your breath sounds like when you're turned on."

His words enraged and terrified her. She scrabbled for a response, but found none. *Nelicoda* stole the parts that made her Ofarian, but it had no effect on what made her human. Reed's nearness, the solidity of him, the generic soap scent mixed with what made him *him* . . . it all scrambled her brain.

His cheek pressed into hers. "I may want you, too, but it doesn't make me stupid. I still have a job to do."

When he pulled his head back, she winced, waiting for the

needle to bite her in the neck. Instead, he jabbed it into her upper arm.

Though the deed was done, he continued to hold her. Far gentler than Xavier, almost delicately. And she didn't pull away.

The *nelicoda* drifted icily through her bloodstream. Her head lolled on her neck, her hair rubbing against his chest. He inhaled sharply then went perfectly still. She shifted on her feet, her ass unintentionally brushing against the bulge in his jeans.

He flung her away as though she were poisonous. Perhaps they were, to each other. His face was frustratingly blank.

"You're going out with Xavier and Nora today," he said.

"Where?"

"Not my business to know."

Fear sent shudders down her spine. "I thought you were taking Xavier's place."

He stared at her for a moment, then pocketed the empty syringe and snatched the yellow pill from the bed. "Not today. There's nothing I can do about it."

FOURTEEN

The same white, windowless van that had stolen Gwen from San Francisco now idled in the circular driveway. Little Nora sat behind the wheel, Xavier in the passenger seat.

Reed pulled Gwen across the gravel. One hand gripped her arm while the other threw open the van's back doors. She stared into the black space inside and didn't want to admit that the ride would be much worse without him. Reed, the buffer between her and the Tedrans, her only lifeline to the outside world, had been severed from her as quickly as he'd been attached.

"You'll be okay," he said, quiet enough for her ears only.

"Don't say that." She refused to look at him. "You're in no position to make promises."

As she tucked her body into the cold, uncomfortable corner, Reed slammed shut the doors. Darkness and panic enveloped her. The van lurched into motion, climbing away from the house prison cloaked in normality, and into an ignorant world. Her whole body clenched up. Her lungs constricted, her breath coming in short, shallow bursts. She could barely see her fingers when she waved them in front of her face, so she squeezed her eyes shut and concentrated only on what she could feel. The cold shell of the van at her back. The scratchiness of the plastic rug. The new, cheap clothing that didn't fit right. Her body, still alive.

How long did they drive? One hour? Two? The road curved a lot, throwing her from side to side. They drove over mountainous terrain for a long while, then, when the ground flattened out, even longer.

Finally the van stopped, but neither Nora nor Xavier got out. A familiar hum poked at the back of Gwen's brain. Through the van walls came the dull tones of Nora's voice, speaking Tedran.

Nora was using *Mendacia* on the van. Despite her fear, Gwen was curious. How exactly were they using *Mendacia* on an object that couldn't swallow it?

The vehicle rolled forward again, drove a few minutes more, then stopped. The engine cut. Xavier's hard footsteps stomped toward the back. The doors flew open. Gwen blinked hard against the sunshine.

"Come here," he snapped. Then, when she didn't move. "Come *here*." They should have named *her* the Retriever.

Either she could do as he said or make him pull her out. She didn't relish the idea of his hands on her again, so she scooted to the bumper. Xavier snatched her wrists, whipped out a set of thin, white metal handcuffs, and snapped them on her. A white metal chain hung between her bound wrists, and Xavier used it to yank her toward him. He attached the loose end of the chain to the strange watch that Reed also now sported.

She sneered. "A fucking leash?"

Xavier ignored her and shut the van doors, his gaze sliding over her shoulder. "You were right," he mumbled to Nora. "Double the guards. What time is it?"

"Almost noon." Though she replied to Xavier, she watched Gwen.

Xavier had not just gone completely still, he'd turned a shade of white reserved for people who survived winters in the deepest parts of Alaska. His eyes glazed over. Gwen turned around to see what had made Xavier look like he stared into the face of his own death.

They stood at the far end of a parking lot plunked down in the middle of nowhere. The slab of black asphalt was surrounded by endless layers of treeless hills, worn down by time. Sparse vegetation sprinkled itself over the cracked land. The wind here raced icy and fierce.

A giant, gray box of a building rose from the edge of the parking lot. With no windows, it looked like a distribution center without truck bays or loading doors, or an abandoned bulk discount store plucked out of a dying suburbia. No billboard sat on its roof; no neon decorated its walls. In fact, there was no signage anywhere, not even an EMPLOYEE PARKING ONLY placard.

But there were employees, because two of them, dressed in deep blue uniforms, stood outside the lone gray door, chatting and smoking. Guns sat strapped to their hips.

Between Gwen and that door stretched rows of cars. All shiny. All high-priced. Most with Nevada plates.

"Xavier," Nora warned. "We're losing time."

At the sound of Nora's voice, Xavier snapped out of his disturbing reverie. He turned to Gwen with such disdain she thought he might strike her, so when he snagged the chain connecting them and pulled her closer, she flinched. Xavier was tall, probably six-foot-five. He loomed over her, his quick-pumping chest pushing out breath from his nostrils.

"Don't go wandering off," he said. "If you get too far away from me, I won't be able to hold the illusion. If you just appear out of thin air, they'll shoot before they realize who you are."

Tedranish burbled out of his mouth so fast and soft that Gwen couldn't make out the words. But she felt the wave of enchantment wash over them. Only after Xavier started across the parking lot, pulling her behind him, did she realize he'd never actually drunk any *Mendacia*.

"How . . ." she started, then stopped as another surge of magic careened into her.

They cleared the last row of vehicles in the lot and headed straight for the door. The two guards watching over it were Secondaries. She could sense their signatures as clearly as she felt the wind through the loose knit of her sweater.

Secondaries and . . . Ofarians.

Gwen dug in her heels and pulled back on Xavier's damned leash. *Hard.* "Help!" she screamed in Ofarian. "Over here! It's me, Gwen Carroway! Hey!"

One of the guards raised the last of his smoke to his lips and looked right through her.

Xavier circled around them, chain in hand, and pulled her tightly to his side. "They can't hear you. They can't see you. Now shut up and come with me." He stalked wide around the guards, tugging on the chain.

Would they really fire if she somehow disabled Xavier's

illusion? She had one of the most well-known faces in the Ofarian world, practically a Secondary celebrity, for chrissakes.
Surely their reactions wouldn't be that quick.

Sliding up against the wall next to the exterior building
door, Xavier checked his watch. When it hit noon, the door
swung inward.

Two new guards exited. Xavier bolted for the opening, dragging her with him. She stumbled, the cuffs gouging into her
wrists. The door was closing. Xavier ducked inside. Gwen had
no choice but to follow. As she slipped into the dim interior,
the door caught on her heel, stuttering in its otherwise slow
sweep, and drawing the attention of the guards.

Just inside, Xavier shoved her against the far wall. The two
guards who'd been outside now stepped in, one of them running his hand along the door and its hinges. He turned his head
and mumbled into a shoulder radio that someone needed to
check the main entrance door.

The whole thing took less than five seconds.

As the guards strode down the long, shadowed corridor and
disappeared around a corner, she rounded on Xavier. "What
the hell is going on? What is this place?"

"You don't know?" So much in his voice: rage, sorrow, hurt.

"No. I don't."

Xavier lifted his eyes above her head. Gwen turned . . . and
gasped so loudly she was sure Xavier's illusion couldn't have
kept it masked.

The square sign hung above the door. A stylized *M*, backlit
in eerie blue. The symbol Gwen had recognized before Big
Bird. The logo she'd been trained to think of as her future, her
life, and the wellspring of her people.

She was standing in the ultrasecret *Mendacia* manufactur-
ing facility, known as the Plant.

In the name of all the stars in the sky, how had the Tedrans
found it?

There's more than one lie in that bottle, Nora had said yesterday, *other than how it's made*.

"Come on," Xavier murmured into the darkness. "You have
an hour to learn the truth."

He didn't have to drag her this time. Morbid curiosity and
a profound sense of dread propelled her forward.

The initial corridor branched off into a maze of gray-painted, faintly lit hallways. Like the building's exterior, there were no signs inside. No YOU ARE HERE maps, no arrowed plaques directing them through the facility. Yet Xavier knew exactly where he was going.

He pulled up in a short, wide hall lined with doors spaced evenly apart. Each door had a small, rectangular window. The silence squeezed her in a giant fist. Everything smelled of disinfectant. A chill raked over her, and she hugged her arms to her chest, but not even a parka and electric blanket would do the job.

"In there." Xavier pointed to the middle door on the left side. He was so pale now he almost glowed. "Look."

She didn't want to. She was dying to.

She crept forward until the chain between them pulled taut, then she rose on tiptoes to peer into the wire-crossed window.

Inside, a row of cherry-sized lights traced where the gunmetal gray walls met the ceiling. An Ofarian man stood inside with his back to the door, the silver *Mendacia* logo stitched just below the curve of his collar. When he shifted to one side, she saw that he was not alone.

A woman with long, stringy, white-streaked hair sat bound to an awful contraption. A metal semicircle wrapped around her waist, clamping her lower body against the far wall. Unyielding chains attached her ankles to the floor. More chains around her wrists pulled her torso forward over a metal table, immobilizing her chin on a padded rest.

Above the table, right in front of the woman's face, hung a glass sphere the size of a basketball. Inside the sphere, spindly arms supported a tiny blue bowl.

The Ofarian said something to the bound woman and emphasized it with a sharp gesture.

The woman stared right into the sphere, the glass fogging with the bursts of her breath. Sweat started to stream down her temples and drip onto the table. In the chains, her hands curled into fists. Her face red and shaking, the woman started to cry. Gwen could not hear her, but she sensed it was the sound of indescribable pain and severe loss.

The air inside the sphere began to condense, transforming into a pale silver mist. It swirled, slowly at first, then faster and faster, churning into a tiny tornado directly above the blue bowl. Then it collapsed, compacting, its particles slamming together.

A single drop of luminescent silver liquid formed in midair, then dropped into the bowl.

The woman went boneless in her restraints. Her eyes rolled back in her head and her fists uncurled as unconsciousness claimed her.

All that for one drop. One drop that cost a fortune.

The Ofarian guard unstrapped her and roughly lifted her away from the contraption. Like a doll, he dropped her into a wheelchair.

As the guard finagled the wheelchair out into the hall, the poor, spent woman's chin dropped to her chest. Gwen wanted to go to her, grab her arms, and shake her and ask why, *why* would any Ofarian agree to do this to themselves once they knew the price.

Then, as the wheelchair rolled by and she caught the distinct Secondary signature, it hit her.

That woman wasn't Ofarian. She was Tedran.

FIFTEEN

Xavier hadn't been inside the Plant in a year and a half.

The monotonous, ashy walls stretched for him, tried to steal his energy, but they wouldn't win. Not this time.

As the wheelchair carrying 075B squeaked past, Gwen's shackled hands flew to her mouth. A long, low moan leaked from her throat. So she'd figured it out. She wasn't as stupid or arrogant as Xavier had thought.

Two years ago Nora had appeared out of a cloud of glamour in his cell. She'd told him she'd been observing him, that he was the strongest Tedran she'd seen. That she'd chosen him for a hero's task. It took her two months to convince him she was real, another month to prove a whole world existed outside the gray Plant walls, and three more months to coordinate his escape.

She needed an inside man, one who could help her free their people. One who wanted to make his captors suffer. Now here he was, in the moment he hadn't known he'd been living for: showing Miss Ofarian Princess what her people were really capable of.

Gwen's whole body heaved. The guard with the wheelchair spun to turn a corner. Another guard appeared wheeling 003AC toward the draining room. The last time Xavier had seen 003AC, the younger man had just barely gotten hair on his face. Now he looked good and used. The man in the chair might be only eighteen Earth years old, but his skin sagged off his face. Black half-moons pulled down the lower lids of his dull, life-less eyes. His thin, frail shoulders curved with severe defeat and resignation.

Xavier used to look exactly like that.

The two Ofarians paused to briefly exchange idle talk. Just a normal day to them, punch in, punch out. The 49ers, the traffic on Highway 50 . . . Once those things had been foreign words to Xavier. Still were, to an extent. He remembered lolling in those chairs, listening to the drone of the guards' voices. Not caring about anything, not even living.

Gwen spun back to him, her gold hair as wild as the look in her glassy eyes. Xavier drew himself up to his full height. Challenged her.

003AC's wheelchair headed for the room 075B had just left.

Though Xavier didn't watch, he listened to the clank of the restraints as the guard looped them around the young man's extremities. Xavier heard his faint protestations, then the whimpers, then nothing. Yes, the room was soundproof, but the sounds rang as loud as sirens in his memory.

"Enough," Gwen said. "I understand."

From just this little room? Xavier almost laughed. "Oh, no." He backed away from her heat and scent. She disgusted and frightened him, but he'd show her everything Nora wanted him to, even if it destroyed him.

"No. You don't know the half of it." He thrust an arm over her head, pointing in the direction 075B had gone. "Walk."

But when they reached a T intersection, he was the one who came to a halt. 075B had disappeared somewhere into the maze of corridors. Here the Plant branched off into various levels of hell. He'd learned all about hell after he'd gotten out. He'd learned an awful lot about an endless number of awful things. This place still topped the list.

Even though he resisted going forward, he looked into Gwen's pale face and knew he had to. Not for her. Fuck no, not for her. *Because* of her. She would be the one to make all this go away, to erase hell and turn it into some version of heaven.

The corridor to the right loomed dark, save for the intermittent circles of white light falling from the wall sconces onto the floor. Yellow-and-black tape striped across the double door at the far end. Wall spray paint declared it: CELL BLOCK I.

A jagged rock lodged in his throat. "Through there."

She watched him too intently, too many questions hiding behind her lips. His skin itched under her scrutiny. The wonder and horror in her eyes pissed him off. And he hated Nora a little bit for making him come here again.

They stopped in front of the closed doors.

"What now?" she whispered.

He turned to wait for 003AC to come back from the draining room. After a few minutes, the wheelchair swerved around the corner. As the guard pushed 003AC through the security doors, Xavier followed, forcing Gwen with him.

Inside the cell block, the dim green lights overhead made his stomach churn and his head swim with their insistent buzz. Even Gwen looked horrible in that light.

The long rows of iron bars stretched seemingly into infinity. When he was younger, the end of the block had seemed a world away. Now he could run it in a few seconds. And a year and a half ago, he had.

Though he hated to touch her, he reached back and pulled Gwen to his side against the bars to 003AC's cell. Gwen inched back. He shoved her nose into the iron, and she watched like she was supposed to. It was almost like when Adine had first shown him a horror movie and he'd covered his eyes and she'd laughed at him. That awful humiliation, knowing he'd been scared by something so fake.

This wasn't fake. Not remotely. And Gwen had to see it without childish hands over her eyes.

Inside the cell, the guard tilted the wheelchair and 003AC slid from the cushioned seat. He collapsed in a shapeless pile of skin and bone on a mattress shoved in the corner. The guard kicked the chair around and left, yawning. The cell lock clicked behind him.

Gwen didn't follow her kinsman. She remained locked on 003AC. The boy's eyes opened a bit, showing nothing but white. His body flattened on the mattress and his back expanded and contracted with deep, even breaths.

"Will . . ." She cleared her throat. "Will he live?"

"If you call this living."

Someone rustled, unseen, in a cell down toward the end. For a second he hoped he'd been heard, that his people knew he was coming for them. But that was impossible. Neither he nor Nora had made first contact yet; they'd been waiting to snag Gwen. Besides, Nora had apparently been sneaking into the

Plant for decades—observing, planning, waiting—and never once in his life had he sensed a thing.

Gwen's voice tightened. Snapped. "Will he be all right?"

"Eventually." He swallowed, and it hurt. "In twelve hours or so, when he finally comes around, they'll feed him. When his strength returns in a day or two, they'll send him back to that room. And so it goes. On and on. Until it kills him." When he turned to her, she was doing this thing with her throat—holding it tightly within her hands, as though choking herself.

"There's more."

She sucked in a breath. "How many of them are kept here?"

"Three hundred. Maybe more. That's not what I meant, though."

He tried to lead her to the end of the cell block, desperately needing to get out of there, but she paused before each cell. Most caged Tedrans had collapsed like 003AC. One, awake now, sat with his hands tucked into the hollow behind his knees. He stared at nothing, awaiting the appearance of a uniformed Ofarian.

Gwen's hands had moved from her throat to the long zipper of her sweater, where she clutched it with white knuckles. "Why can't they use their glamour to get out, the way you got us in?"

He pointed to the boxes strung up on the ceiling that filled the cell block with pulsing green light. "Inhibitors. They neutralize glamour before we can touch it."

"Like *nelicoda*."

"Yes, but if you take *nelicoda* while working with water, it'll kill the magic right away. The Tedran neutralizers only keep you from starting glamour. I started my illusion outside. Those things have no effect on us right now."

"That's why there were no green lights back there, in the . . ." She couldn't even say it.

A new Ofarian guard veered around the corner, stalking into the cell block.

"Oh, God," Gwen breathed, her fingers touching her lips. "I recognize her."

"A friend?" he asked bitterly.

"No. I don't know her personally. She applied for Plant duty a few years ago. I was there when the Board approved her appointment."

Xavier had hoped for that, that she'd know someone here. "So how does she like her job?"

Gwen's head whipped around. Ah, there it was, back again: the corporate slut programmed to defend her people. "The Plant is its own entity. Once people are accepted, they give up their former lives . . ." Her voice petered out.

He tugged her past Cell Blocks 2 through 5. The concrete floor gave way to wiry, industrial carpet. A few more Ofarians moved about the open spaces, some in doctor's scrubs, most in uniforms. They tapped at tablet computers and pointed into cells, mumbling to one another.

Xavier gestured to the row of barred cells lining one side of the wide, quiet corridor.

Her hands rose again, this time to her face. She advanced slowly to the bars, her mouth falling open. He joined her, hands in his pockets.

This cell, three times as large as the others, contained four young women.

111J was pregnant again. In Earth years she might be in her early twenties, not too much younger than Xavier. This would be her third or fourth child, he guessed. She lay on her side on a yellow couch, her head covered in thick, black hair resting on her outstretched arm. Her face was perfectly blank, her Tedran gray eyes dead.

The others were barely out of girlhood, their swollen bellies a contrast to their thin arms and legs. They sat in a circle, playing some sort of hand-slapping game and singing in Tedranish. On the outside, girls their age were just starting to learn to drive. Or getting their first after-school jobs. Or learning how to kiss.

These girls had never even heard of those things.

Only when Xavier had gotten out did he come to know why the Ofarians allowed the slaves to continue to speak their own language. Tedran words were needed to power the glamour. When a bottle of *Mendacia* went out, one of the slaves was forced to provide the client's specific glamour needs in Tedranish.

A glowing screen on the wall next to the cell listed each woman's classification code paired with a man's code.

Gwen's eyes swept over the soft rugs, the plush beds and

cushioned chairs, the shelves stacked with games and cards, and food and drink. The cinder block walls here were painted pleasant colors, and decorated with framed prints of mountains and flowers. Things the women would never actually see.

"There's incentive to get pregnant," Xavier said. "At least, the Ofarians think it's incentive. They impregnate the young girls before they know better, lure them with better rooms and food. And pregnancy puts glamour into dormancy, so they don't have to go to the draining rooms." He waved a hand at the ceiling, free of neutralizers. "That woman you saw when we first came in, she's probably sterile. Her only use is draining. She doesn't have much longer to live."

"Why not?"

"Glamour isn't meant to be squeezed out day after day, forcing it out of your body like a poison. The men"—he shook his head, feeling the bits of his own life stolen from him, the holes left behind—"we never live long."

He coughed, looked away. "Soon enough the women'll realize what it is they're continuing. They want to live more comfortably but they don't want to keep having kids, knowing what the little ones will have to go through."

Gwen's mouth twisted like she was about to spit out rotten meat. "Do they have a choice whether or not to get pregnant?"

Xavier looked back toward 111J. "What do you think?"

Gwen shrank away, mumbling, "I don't want to know anymore. I don't . . . we can go now. Get me out of here."

"Tough shit." One of the choicest phrases he'd learned on the outside.

On cue, from down a softly lit hall, drifted the sounds of children's giggles and the shrieks of new babies. There were pieces of him in there. For a moment he thought Gwen might dash for the nursery, and he was grateful when Gwen pinched her eyes shut and turned her head away from the kids' noises. If she'd gone down there, he didn't think he'd be able to stop himself from scooping up what he guessed was his and try to make a run for it.

If he did that, everything would end. All of Nora's work. The Tedrans' only chance at freedom. Revenge on the Ofarians. *Everything.*

There was one place left for Gwen to see.

Though it killed him, he dragged his heavy legs to the left. The new corridor curved sharply around, and the sight of it almost brought him to his knees. Damn Nora for making him come back. Damn Gwen.

He sagged against the wall, feeling the glamour flicker around them. He snatched it back under his control before it slipped away. The wall supported him. Breath labored in his chest.

"Xavier?" Gwen stood way too close, considering where they were about to head.

"Get away from me." He shoved away from the wall and marched around her. Into the Circle. She thought she'd seen the worst of this place? She thought she understood what Tedran lives had been reduced to?

She had to jog to keep up with his long strides. He didn't slow down.

The cells in the Circle were like pieces of a pie. The first time Adine had made him a real pie, it had been apple, and when she'd cut into it, making triangular shapes, he'd instantly flashed back to this place. With a growl and a sweep of his arm, he'd sent the whole pie against the wall. He still had yet to eat a bite of one.

The main corridor swept around the cells at ceiling height, looking down into the triangular-shaped rooms. Carpet here, too, but no shelves of food or games. Just a single mattress lying beneath bright, glaring lights and the pallor of green neutralizers.

The first occupied cell held a naked Tedran man and woman. They lay on the bed, curled into one another. The sight of skin on skin burned a bullet through his chest.

Gwen's voice went completely flat. "What is this."

Xavier looked at the floor. Safer that way. But the buzz in his brain and body and blood had already begun.

"No baby yet." He fixated on the tight nap of the beige carpet. "Poor couple combination. Bad timing. Fertility issues. Who knows? They haven't figured it out yet. But they will. They'll test each of them. Over and over and over. When they find a good stud, they'll just keep bringing the women."

"Oh, my God. Oh, my God. I thought . . ."

He wanted to bite something. Rip something apart. Stomp something into pebbles. "Just say it."

"I thought they'd do it scientifically. With needles. And petri dishes."

"Is that how *you'd* do it?"

"No!"

"The Ofarians think it's some kind of reward." He slashed at the air with a hand. "Like an orgasm will take all this away."

He'd never known the word *orgasm* either, only that they demanded he have one inside a woman.

She staggered to the next cell in the Circle. A naked Tedran man sat on the edge of the mattress, heels tapping incessantly, fingers rubbing together. Xavier didn't have to see proof. The Tedran man was hard. Hopped up. Waiting.

A door opened at the wide end of the pie piece, just below Gwen and Xavier's feet. The waiting man's prize entered: a naked Tedran woman. Head down, she shuffled forward. The man rose, visibly trying to calm himself, and slowly approached her. He took her hand. There was a gentleness to his touch, but it didn't soften what he was about to do.

The mattress creaked as the Tedran man climbed upon it. The woman reclined back and opened her thighs.

Don't look. Don't look. But not only did Xavier look, he stared. He felt. He wanted.

Gwen's chin touched her chest and she shuddered.

"Don't," he snapped. "Don't you dare look away. *They* don't." He jabbed a finger toward the narrowed tip of the cell where floor-to-ceiling windows revealed the central observation room. An Ofarian man and woman stood on the other side of the glass, watching as the Tedran man started to thrust into the prone Tedran woman.

The Tedran woman's arms draped out to the sides, not reaching for her partner. They rarely did. Her head lolled and her expressionless eyes drifted up to the walkway. She couldn't see Xavier, but it felt like she did.

The man pounded harder into her, the thin muscles on his arms straining as he held himself above her. The only way Xavier knew the man came was from the stiffening of his body, the silent grimace on his face.

Xavier remembered this part. It felt good for about half a second. Then the guilt and horror rushed in.

On the mattress the man did what Xavier always had: he touched the woman's face, brought her eyes to his, and said in Tedranish, "I'm sorry. Are you all right?"

Xavier swiveled away, angry, pounding blood gathering in his penis. *Fuck fuck fuck. Not here. Not now.* He punched his fists against his thighs and squeezed his eyes shut so tightly he saw stars.

"Xavier." Gwen came up behind him. "You were in here. Weren't you."

He shook his head, but not in denial. 267X. That was him.

"Xavier, look at me."

If he turned around, she'd see. *Fuck it.* There was no hiding it. One foot first, then the other, he slowly pivoted until he faced Gwen. She stared into his eyes, got the confirmation she wanted, then her eyes flickered down to his shame.

The erection pressed against his jeans' zipper. Aching. Immediate. A trained tool. "Don't worry. It's not for you. I'm a goddamn Pavlov's dog."

If it mollified her, he couldn't tell. She stood completely rigid except for the deep rise and fall of her chest.

"They lost me," he said. She'd seen his humiliation so the best he could do was use it to make her hear everything now. Maybe then he wouldn't feel it. "They lost me and they hate it. I was their prize, Gwen. I could get any woman pregnant they brought me, even the ones who'd had problems. Do you know how many kids I have? Because I don't. Wouldn't know them if they came up and shook my hand. My first time was at fourteen. *Fourteen.*"

She was crying now. Full-on crying. She clutched her arms at her waist and bent over, the sobs jerking her whole body. But he wasn't about to let her off now.

"All of a sudden it got worse about six, seven years ago. It was constant. *All the fucking time.* They had to build more nursery space. The women were constantly pregnant. The men were dying faster. Your people did this to me. To us."

"No," she wailed, her head shaking at the ground. "Not all of us. We didn't know."

Every word of hers repulsed him.

He pinched his own arm. Hard. Pain might take away the urge to breed. Pain and getting the hell out of there.

He glanced at his watch. "The guards will change again in five minutes. My glamour is starting to slip. Let's go."

He jerked the chain. She'd called it a leash, and at the time he hadn't appreciated her anger. Now he enjoyed it, controlling her.

He pulled her back out of the breeding Circle and almost ran right into a small group of four Ofarians huddled in the dimmer spot between wall sconces. He veered on one foot, stumbled, and took Gwen down to the ground with him. She fell right on top of him and he kneed her off as though she were a rabid animal. He jumped back to his feet.

Gwen remained sprawled on the floor, frozen and staring up at the Ofarians. Two Ofarians were dressed in Plant blue. A woman whom Xavier recognized as head of breeding wore medical scrubs. A fourth Ofarian wore a sleek black business suit, his silvery hair polished, his face authoritative and stern.

"Gwen," Xavier warned, jerking on the chain. "We need to go *now*. If we miss our window, the guards won't change for another hour. Nora can't hold the van illusion that long and I can't hold the two of us much longer."

"Wait." She dug in her heels. A new brand of terror washed over her face. "That's Jonah Yarbrough. The Company's Vice Chairman."

"We weren't expecting you," the woman in scrubs said to Yarbrough. "I apologize for the mess in the—"

"I didn't expect to come," Yarbrough interrupted. "There's been a security breach. I need to move the Plant again."

SIXTEEN

.

Only an hour earlier, Gwen would have done anything to get the Ofarians to know she was alive and inside the Plant. Now she sprinted across the parking lot as though she were being chased. Every pounding footstep stabbed a new shard of terror into her heart.

"Hurry," Xavier called over his shoulder. "It's getting harder to hold. If I'm straining, so is Nora."

They reached the van, its back doors open and waiting. Gwen threw herself inside without being told. Xavier snapped off the chain and slammed the doors shut. Seconds later, Nora pulled the van out of the parking lot in a tight curve.

Gwen felt like she'd polished off an entire bottle of *nelicoda* and had been pushed into the Arctic Ocean. Frigid numbness surrounded her body. The world moved like water just about to freeze. She could see it, sense it moving slowly around her, but she could not touch it or taste it or smell it.

Only one thought ran on a loop through her mind. *I am not a monster. I am not a monster. I am not a monster.*

When the van stopped, she wondered if she'd fallen asleep, because they hadn't been traveling long and they'd yet to climb up and over the mountains that surrounded Lake Tahoe. Nora opened the doors. A highway roared behind her. A sign on its shoulder proclaimed: CARSON CITY 34 MILES.

Xavier loomed behind Nora. "If he takes the cuffs off," she said, "will you behave?"

Gwen met Xavier's eyes. Now she understood all the anguish and embarrassment and wrath in that familiar hard look. It had taken more courage than she knew how to define for him to step foot in the Plant again. Every time she blinked, she saw the way he'd reacted in the breeding block. Hating his body's reaction. Hating her people. Hating her.

She held out her arms. "I'm not going anywhere."

Hesitantly he came forward, slid his watch through the handcuff lock, and stepped back as the metal fell away. She slid out of the van and took in her surroundings.

They'd brought her to a roadside rest stop, a dilapidated, sixties-era rectangle plopped into the dreary Nevada landscape. Nora led them past cobwebbed restrooms and a vending machine blinking an outdated Pepsi logo, to the picnic table farthest from the lot. The Tedrans took the bench facing the cars. Gwen sat on her hands to keep them from shaking, and her fingers gripped decades of travelers' carvings in the wood.

"I had no idea." Better to speak first, to take control of the situation. One of the first things she'd learned from watching her dad. "You have to believe me."

Nora gazed back at her, composed and chilly. "That can't be true."

"It is."

"The Ofarians who work in the Plant know. Your *leaders* know."

"No! Oh, my God, no. There's no way my father would agree to this. Not knowingly. Not willingly."

Impossible. Her father couldn't know the intricate, disgusting details of *Mendacia*'s production and still sleep at night. This was the man who'd withdrawn from the Company and from life for months after his wife had died. This was the man who'd cried when he gave the order to have his own daughter stripped of her powers and exiled.

He'd spent his entire adulthood guiding Ofarians in their problems, helping them find futures within the Company. He led their culture's rituals with solemnity and openness. He *loved* serving others, and Gwen had fashioned her goals after his example.

Was slavery the action of a man who valued life?

"My dear," Nora said, "he didn't have to agree to anything. The Plant's been running for generations. He didn't start it; he inherited it. And believe me, he didn't accept his chairmanship without knowing full well what atrocities he was endorsing. *Everyone* on the Board knows."

Gwen's head swam. How did Nora know so much about the Company's inner workings? It was a security threat a thousand times greater than Yoshi's little cell phone stunt.

"Look." She stabbed her fingers into her hair. "My father depends on Jonah Yarbrough to run the Plant as he sees fit. The Chairman delegates, the same as for all corporations. It's Jonah who's responsible. *Jonah*. I even saw him in there. Ask Xavier."

Nora's hard glare was shatterproof. She leaned forward ever so slightly. "Every one of you is guilty. Every. Single. One."

"You can't place the blame on Ofarians who have no idea what's going on. The janitors in our building? The secretaries? Me?"

Xavier bristled and looked away.

"But you're part of them, no? You sell the magic they're forced to make. You profit from their despair, their lives. Ignorance doesn't make you less guilty."

It was the first time Nora had raised her voice, and it made Gwen sit up.

She looked directly into those dark, hard eyes. All the eyes of the Tedrans in the Plant had been silver—*Mendacia* silver—but Nora and Adine's were nearly black as coal. "I had no idea how *Mendacia* was truly made. I swear."

Gwen saw her mistake the moment she'd made it. Nora wanted such strong emotion from her. It was her winning card.

"So fix it," Nora said, like she was telling Gwen to tighten the screw on a wobbly chair.

How? Gwen wanted to scream at the sky. Instead she chewed on the inside of her lip. "Obviously you have a plan."

"Obviously," Nora said with a dry grin.

"And it started with kidnapping me. Bringing me here."

"No, it started before that." Nora turned her head slightly. "Xavier?"

He'd inched to the very edge of the picnic table bench, as far away from Gwen as possible. He nodded. "It worked. They're moving the Plant again. Heard it with my own ears. Gwen did, too."

A few stray pieces of the puzzle clicked into place. "The

bar," Gwen said to Xavier. "You wanted me to see you and warn the Board."

"This whole thing didn't just happen overnight," he said. "We'd been following you from a distance for a long while. We knew you liked that bar, that you never went in there with any of your . . . people."

"It was the first step in a long plan," Nora added, drawing Gwen's attention back.

"How'd you know they'd move the Plant?"

"Because of Xavier. A year and a half ago, after I broke him out, they panicked and moved the whole operation to remote Nevada from the Central Valley."

A year and a half. Gwen's mind circled back. She recalled a period of a few days when the Board had sequestered themselves behind waterglass. When they'd emerged, they'd tried their best to hide the spooked looks on their faces, but she wasn't stupid. Her father had been in Palm Beach at the time, schmoozing a media heiress, and when she'd asked him about it, he'd told her vaguely that Jonah had it all under control.

Within days, everything seemed to go back to normal and she'd filed the scenario under "Things to Find Out Once I'm a Member of the Board."

Now she understood. One of their slaves had gone missing.

She eyed Xavier. "How'd you know how to get around this Plant then?"

He sneered. "The basics are the same. Same structure, same organization of cell blocks and death rooms. They could have lifted the Breeding Circle from the old Plant and dropped it into this one."

And they'd done it in a matter of days. *Great stars above.*

"Your chairman is clever. Swift," Nora said. "But now he's scared."

"I told you"—Gwen stabbed a finger into the table—"my father doesn't know."

Behind her, car doors slammed. She turned to watch a family pour out of a green minivan. Three children squealed excitedly at the sight of the sorry vending machine. Their parents called for them to walk, not run.

Xavier half rose, ready to tackle her if she attempted to run toward the Primaries or call out. No glamour shielded them and she knew the two Tedrans were drained from their earlier efforts; if Gwen wanted, she could end this all right here. Or start something else entirely. But exposure wasn't in either of their best interests.

She turned back around and laced her fingers on the table-top. "What do you want from me?"

Nora was so still Gwen thought she might have died sitting up. Then she took a deep breath and replied, "Return us back to the stars. Get us back to Tedra."

Gwen shook her head, sure she hadn't heard right. Neither Tedran's expression faltered. "That's impossible."

Nora's lips puckered around an invisible lemon. "Is it?"

"We have no connections in NASA or any other country's space program. We deliberately avoid anyone or anything involved in government."

"We don't need NASA." She mimicked Gwen's hand clasp. "We already have a ship."

If she hadn't just witnessed the destruction of an entire race at the hands of her own people, Gwen would have easily dis-counted the Tedrans as insane. "Explain."

"The ship that brought the Ofarians and Tedrans to Earth a century and a half ago is still here. Hidden and trapped. We need to know how to get it out, how to fly it again."

She almost fell off the bench. *"What?"*

"You heard me."

"So where is this supposed ship?"

The Tedrans shared a look. Nora answered, "At the bottom of the lake."

"Which lake?"

"Tahoe."

She laughed. She couldn't help it. "I'm sorry. You have me confused with someone else. I have no idea how to bring up a spaceship that's been lying at the bottom of Lake Tahoe since the mid-eighteen hundreds. And I can assure you that I wouldn't know how to fly it."

"But we know someone who does, and we want you to speak with him."

Gwen opened her mouth. No sound came out. Were those tears in Nora's eyes? No, couldn't be. But when Nora spoke next, her voice was reedy.

"I've been waiting so, so long for a Translator to be born. And here you are." She cleared her throat. "You will speak with Genesai, learn his language. He knows how to retrieve the ship. He knows how to fly it."

"So this Genesai is not Tedran?"

"No. He's . . . something else. Something else from the stars." Nora's eyes swung skyward.

"Does he look like us? Is he human?"

"Now he is. Well, humanoid, like all Secondaries." Nora narrowed her eyes. "When the Ofarians arrived here, they forced him into a human body. The new form didn't agree with his mind and fought with his spirituality. He is, for lack of a better term, insane."

Fascinating. "After all this time, he doesn't speak any English?"

Nora shook her head. "He doesn't speak any of Earth's languages, doesn't understand a word anyone says. He just babbles in his own tongue. We've never been able to decipher it. But a Translator can. *You* can."

Gwen pressed fingers to her aching temples. Something—a lot of things, actually—wasn't adding up. "How can you possibly know all this? How did you know about Genesai and the ship? And if all Tedrans are . . . slaves . . . how come you aren't?"

Xavier was gazing at Nora again with that strange look hovering between wonder and admiration. The old woman traced a graffiti heart with a gnarled finger. "Because I survived the crash into Lake Tahoe."

"Wait. *You* were in the crash?"

Nora evenly met Gwen's gape. "Tedrans live much longer than Ofarians."

"How old are you?"

Nora shrugged. "I can only start counting in Earth years. Time is . . . different up there. And I've had very little reason to use my glamour since I came here. I don't age as fast."

The quick peek at Xavier was not meant to be seen, but Gwen noticed. She remembered what he'd said in the Plant, about the draining of glamour aging and slowly killing the Tedrans. How old was he, if that was true? And how much time did he have left if they stole bits of him day after day?

Gwen shuddered. "They" were Ofarians. Her people. She'd take care not to forget it so easily next time.

She stared at the table for a long time, letting its splintered vandalism blur into her thoughts. Wind raced down the highway corridor, mingling with the constant whir of the passing vehicles. It was the only sound for quite some time.

When Gwen finally raised her head, Nora patiently regarded her.

"Tell me." Gwen's fists clenched. "You're dying to spill. All that talk yesterday about everything I knew about Ofarian history being a lie. If it's all a lie, tell me the damn truth."

Nora began to slowly roll up her sleeves. "Ofarians went to Tedra looking for a new home, that much is true, but they didn't settle peacefully. They weren't humble and grateful for the space we generously gave them. They thought the native Tedrans were simple and inferior. They thought us undeserving of our planet. So they tried to take it from us."

"But—"

"I was *there*, Gwen. I saw. I remember."

The animosity in Nora's tone and composure rivaled that of Xavier's. But whereas Xavier wore his hatred on his sleeve, Nora's boiled just under her skin and came out in her tightly controlled words. Gwen didn't know which she feared most.

"How did you get off planet?" she managed to ask.

"There was an uprising. It turned into an all-out war. The Ofarians thought us simple, but it was our planet and we knew it better than they did. Even though they were more advanced technologically, we outnumbered them, and we destroyed their crafts. We weren't going to let them get off our world and go destroy another. We wanted to kill them all."

Gwen sucked in a breath. How was that any better?

"I don't know how they found Genesai," Nora continued, "or where. All I know is that I was taken hostage, along with twenty or so other Tedrans. The Ofarians forced Genesai off Tedra and ordered him to find a new, habitable world. He crashed here."

"A crash. What happened?"

Nora's concentration drifted far away. "There were casualties on both sides, Tedran and Ofarian. So much death, so much confusion. What few made it to land overtook a small settlement

of Primaries. That's when they destroyed the Genesai I knew
and kept the handful of living Tedrans enslaved. Within days
I saw an opportunity to escape. It was run then, or never live
free again. So I took Genesai, cloaked us both in glamour, and
fled. We watched his ship sink." She gazed to the west. "I've
been protecting him ever since. Waiting. Wanting to return
home."

"Why didn't you leave before?"

"Besides the fact that it was 1852 and there was no way to
get down to the bottom of the lake?"

Gwen resisted the urge to roll her eyes.

"By the time the technology came around, the Ofarians had
already melded into Primary society and had established their
Mendacia empire. The twelve surviving Tedrans had been bred
into ten times that number. The early machinery they used to
extract the magic makes today's draining rooms look like play-
grounds. As the last Tedran who'd known freedom, it was my
responsibility to get them out. Can you at least understand
that?"

It was too fantastic to believe. Even for Gwen, who was
Secondary and, by nature, fantastical herself. No Ofarian
would ever believe that story. Gwen wasn't even sure if she did.
She'd been taught about her ancestors' suffering, and her
mother had been taught before her. And her mother before that.

He said, she said. It made her brain burn.

Except that mere miles from here, she'd witnessed the
enslavement with her own eyes.

She rubbed her arms. "Okay, so assuming I can learn to
communicate with Genesai, and assuming the ship can still fly
after all this time, how the hell do you expect to get the Tedrans
out of the Plant?"

This time Xavier answered. "Don't worry about that. Just
concentrate on Genesai."

Another assumption: that she'd help them at all.

She couldn't say what made her think of Reed at that
moment. Maybe it was the sound of the family piling back into
their minivan, then the buzz of the engine as it accelerated back
to the highway. So ordinary. So everyday. The Primary world
came and went all around, never knowing that Secondaries
existed among them. Or that some of them wanted to leave.

Reed kept saying that it wasn't his business to know why he'd been hired to "extract" her. Yet he'd stayed. For her. He claimed not to care about the reasons for her kidnapping. He claimed only to want to keep her alive. She wondered, if after witnessing an alien spaceship rise out of the murky waters of Lake Tahoe and zoom back into the sky, he would continue not to care.

Holy fuck.

She rounded on Nora. "You'll reveal us."

Nora's watery eyes widened and her narrow-lipped mouth curved into an evil smile. "My dear?"

"There's no way your plan could work without revealing us to the rest of the world. The Primaries'll know they're no longer the only ones on Earth—or in the universe. You'll leave us behind, knowing there'll be a massive hunt."

"Hunt?" Xavier smiled, and it wasn't pretty. "We'll tell them exactly where to find you."

He reached into his jacket pocket and threw a stack of photos on the table. They fanned out, displaying disgusting images. Tedran slaves being drained. Rows of babies without parents. Ofarian doctors standing over blank-faced women as Tedran men tried to get them pregnant.

"Keep them, they're yours. Enjoy."

Keep them? She could barely look at them.

"I have more"—Xavier leaned over—"documenting the Ofarians' wonderful little connection to water. Primaries love that stuff. As we're flying home, the U.S. government will know exactly where the aliens live."

The word *aliens* slithered out between his teeth.

She saw the scenario he envisioned, the one she'd been taught to fear all her life. Government pursuit. Mass captures. Lockups and tests. International panic.

Ofarians behind bars, just like the Tedrans in the Plant.

The air around the table stifled, turned noxious. *Think, damn it, think.* She swung her legs over the bench and jumped up. Xavier scrambled to his feet and started for her. She threw out an arm.

"I'm not going anywhere!"

She backed up a few steps to the edge of the rest area, where the dull earth sloped down into a barren ravine. On the other side, the land rose up like a giant wave, aggressive and dangerous and ready to crash over her. An arctic wind gusted under her sweater. Footsteps crunched behind her.

"I said I'm not going anywhere, Xavier."

But it was Nora. Five feet never looked so intimidating. "There's another way."

Gwen wanted to scream. "Another way to what?"

"Help us. Do what's right."

She crossed her arms. "How can you possibly talk about doing what's right when you want to inflict the same pain the Tedrans have faced on innocent Ofarians?"

Nora's lip curled. "Let's agree to disagree on the definition of *innocent*."

"There are *two thousand* Ofarians who have no idea what's happening. Why do they deserve punishment?"

"Do you want to save them? Do you want to keep them out of the public eye?"

"Yes!"

The wind whipped Nora's clothing about her perfectly rigid figure and ruffled her short hair. "Then destroy the Board."

"What?"

She shrugged. "And the Plant workers. Everyone who knows about the Plant and is instrumental in its function must die. Then stop *Mendacia* production, free my people, and let us live our own lives here on Earth."

Gwen's voice floated somewhere far away. She had to reach for it and drag it back. "Kill them?"

"Yes. Everyone. You don't want to believe who's really involved, but deep down you know. You know."

She was talking about her father. *No.* Gwen wouldn't believe that. And she wouldn't destroy her own father just to prove a point to Nora. Death plus death just equaled more death. There were no answers in that.

"After all the Tedran lives they've taken, cut short, abused. You don't think they deserve to die? It's the only way to be sure it'll never continue."

That didn't make any sense. There had to be another way.

Nora's sick words hammered into Gwen's head. "You know where the Board lives, where they work. Set up a bomb at

Company headquarters. Hire Reed to take out the Plant workers, for all I care. He looks capable."

Gwen threw a hand in Nora's face. "No. I refuse. I reject everything you've said to me and I refuse to do what you want. I'll cover my ears so I can't Translate Genesai. And I sure as hell am not going to murder my own father."

Nora looked simultaneously sad and pleased. She'd been waiting for Gwen to say that. Goddamn her. One hundred and fifty years to prepare and she'd thought of everything.

"Then we're ready to send information about *Mendacia* and evidence of the Ofarians' existence to the government anyway. If we're still going to lose, then we're taking you down with us. It's your choice, Gwen. You have to help us. It's just a matter of how you do it."

SEVENTEEN

Reed should have been thinking about how to elude Tracker.
He should have been researching where he'd gone wrong bad
enough to draw Nora's attention. He should have left Lake
Tahoe yesterday.

All he could think about, however, was Gwen.

He circled the house several times, inside and out, taking
inventory of the surveillance equipment. Ninety percent of it
was well hidden. The other ten percent was meant to be found,
to let him and Gwen know they were being watched. One tiny
camera spied on the narrow hall outside their attic rooms, but
as far as he could tell, their bedrooms were untouched. At least
they weren't perverted clients. Adine's futuristic watch dictated
where he could and could not go. It opened some doors, but
not all. A few perimeter gates but not the garage door to get
the cars out. No phones anywhere, and he'd had to give his up
as part of the contract.

The hired guards in the huts by the driveway and down by
the water were soft ex-cons. They eyed him curiously. Let them
wonder if he was like them. Let them wonder what he'd done
time for, even though he hadn't. He could take them if he
needed to, but he hoped it wouldn't come to that.

Nora was paying Reed to keep Gwen captive, even as he
was trying to keep her out of danger.

So fucked up.

This morning . . . he could still feel her hand on the back
of his neck, at the scratchy place where his skull shave was
starting to come in. She'd run her finger over it; he didn't think
she was aware she'd done it. But she sure as hell thought she

could pull one over on him. Pressing into him, going in for a kiss. Did she think she was the first woman target to try seducing him out of responsibility? He'd never been fooled by it.

Except this time, he almost was. Because it was Gwen, with the sexy, vicious, high-heel stabbing of Japanese men's phones. Gwen, with the easy banter and wit. Gwen, with that hair and those legs. Gwen, who never looked away from the faces of her challengers.

He took a seat at the breakfast bar in the immaculately clean kitchen. Gwen's place in the city had been this spotless—every inch of counter streak-free, every length of grout scrubbed and even-toned.

He hated that she was out there with them. Without him. He was wrong; he had lied to her. He didn't believe for a second she'd be all right alone with them.

The front door opened. Though his head snapped up at the sound, he casually leaned back to see if it was Gwen.

Nope. Adine.

The small, brown-haired woman clutched a large box in one hand and struggled to shut the door with the other. Could've been any frazzled person returning from any old errand. Except that Adine wasn't any ordinary person. From what intel Reed had gathered, that mind of hers was extraordinary. So extraordinary that the last Silicon Valley company she'd been contracted for couldn't keep its mouth shut. When word leaked out about some sort of strange composite she'd used in one of her doohickeys, more than just the CEO came calling. The government started to sniff around and she took off, taking her technology with her.

Now more than corporate America wanted to know her whereabouts. If anything happened to Gwen, Reed knew exactly where to point them.

Adine hurried across the foyer to the basement door, and grappled with trying to balance the box on one hip while freeing her wrist to access the lock with her watch.

He slid off the stool. "Need help?"

Adine jumped high enough the box top popped open and a bundle of wires peeked out. He pretended not to see them as she stuffed them back inside.

"No."

He kept walking forward. "You make these?" He raised his wrist. It was good to perpetuate the idea he was dumb as rock.

"Maybe." Shifty eyes.

"It work for the basement?"

One of her dark eyes—as dark as Nora's—sat slightly closer to her nose than the other, and she narrowed both at him. "Not yours, no."

He shrugged and started back for the kitchen. "Just curious." *About what the hell you're doing down there and what it is the government's so interested in.*

The basement door clicked shut behind her. Adine's muffled footsteps faded out.

He frowned into the sunset, the orange and pink light bouncing off the lake and striking the glass wall of the house, bothered by the fact that he *was* curious. Curious about Adine and her inventions. About Nora's connection to Tracker. About why they wanted Gwen.

Damn her. That woman had taken a giant spoon to his brain. Scrambled it all up. He couldn't afford that.

The front door opened again. He turned. His reason for staying entered.

Gwen looked two inches shorter and two days short of sleep. She looked like she'd hacked her way through a battlefield and just barely escaped with her life. Stomach tight, he scanned her body, looking for a limp or a grimace—anything to indicate physical pain. Nothing. Whatever torture they'd inflicted, they'd done to her mind.

She lifted her head—slowly, heavily, like someone being held underwater—and found him watching. Ghosts lingered in her eyes, specters of rage that had floated away to be replaced by helplessness and defeat.

This was not the Gwen he knew.

Her blank gaze traveled past him, to a point beyond the glass wall.

Something twisted hard in his chest. To prevent himself from clutching it, he threw on his most impassive mask and sauntered to Nora.

"Orders?"

The little woman patted at her silver hair, the gesture of a woman just returning from the salon. "Done for the day. Lock her upstairs."

Gwen was already climbing the staircase by the time he got to her, her cinder block feet thudding on each step. In the attic hallway she stood facing her locked door. He sidled around her, slid his watch into the lock mechanism, and held the door open. She moved hypnotically inside and sank onto the edge of the bed.

He'd done that to Gwen. She'd called him soulless, but she was the one without the soul. It had been ripped from her, and he'd handed the tools to Nora to do it.

He pulled shut Gwen's door and went down the hall to his room, mindful of the cameras. Inside, he checked twice to make sure his door had locked securely, then crossed through the bathroom.

She hadn't moved a millimeter from her perch on the bed. Head hanging, legs splayed out to either side, her arms dangled uselessly between her knees.

God, he was such a shit. He'd often imagined this devastation on the faces of his targets after he turned his back on them, but he'd never actually witnessed it. It sucked.

The solution, in his head, was remarkably easy. Throw Gwen over his shoulder and storm out of the lake house like a fucking action hero. The gates would open for him; the guards would fall with a good kick and punch.

That solution, in reality, could send him on the run and put a bullet in the back of her head when Nora found her. Of that, he had no doubt.

He was the only person on Gwen's side. He'd stick it out, do whatever Nora wanted him to do, and keep a protective arm around Gwen—if only to see the courage on her face, or the bright, daring spark in her eye again.

"Hey." He lowered himself to a wooden bench just opposite her. "How do you feel?"

When she raised her head, she didn't look at him, but out the small window at the lake. "Like I'm in quicksand," she murmured.

The sun had dipped below the far mountains, and the whole room was dusted in filtered shadows.

She swiveled her head and pinned him with a deeply tormented stare. "Do you know where they took me today?"

He opened his hands in a helpless gesture. "I told you. I know nothing. I'm paid to know nothing."

She considered him for a long while, then nodded sadly. "Okay. Yes. That would make sense. There's no way you could know."

Her despair was starting to scare him.

"You know." She straightened her spine and he heard a few faint cracks. "It's really easy to blame you for all this."

He wouldn't react. *Would not.* "If I hadn't done the extraction, they just would've hired someone else. I took the job for that very reason. I stayed because I didn't want anyone else with you. Be glad it was me, Gwen." Let her make of that what she wanted. He pushed up the sleeves of his shirt and balanced his forearms on his knees.

The expression on her face was completely undecipherable. Her dark eyes danced all over his face. When they returned to his, they stayed . . . and he saw in them what he'd seen at that sunrise on the San Francisco street. Like she wanted him, and hated herself because of it. He didn't blame her; he was more than mixed up about it himself.

"It's also easy to hate you," she said. "Except that I don't." From the wide plea in her eyes to the seductive fall of her lower lip, she screamed of raw desperation. "And I am glad you're here."

Neither of them breathed. God, she was so fucking beautiful, and how warped was he to think about that when her life had been ripped out from underneath her? He made himself look away. Her head fell into her hands. The sound that came from her throat was an amalgam of a groan and a sob, a frustrated laugh and an enraged shout.

"Hey," he said again, because he was stupid and didn't know what else to say. He fisted his hands so tightly the knuckle of a forefinger popped. He had to, otherwise he'd reach for her.

Her hands covered her face. She shook her head slowly, a few long, blond strands of hair getting snagged in the zipper of her sweatshirt. "There's a tornado in my brain," he thought he heard her say.

He couldn't tell her it was going to be okay, because he didn't believe that anymore. "Look at me." Too late he realized his hand had sprouted a mind of its own. He touched her knee and didn't take it away.

Slowly uncovering her face, Gwen looked at him in dazed wonder.

She wove a little on her seat. Her eyes traveled over him, inch by arduous inch. Had this been how she'd felt in Manny's, when he'd let himself touch her, smell her, discover her with his blatant stare?

He straightened, wondering what the hell he was supposed to do. What he *wanted* to do.

"I should go . . ." he began.

She launched herself at him.

They came together with a force that made him grunt. He caught her, one arm snaking around her narrow rib cage, the other hand hooking behind her knee. He pulled her legs around his hips, fitting her to him. Crushing her to him.

Their breath mingled in space a half-second before she devoured his mouth. The world went dizzy at her taste. Sweet from the silk of her lips and tongue, salt from the tears she'd shed before she stepped back into the house.

Fire licked through his body—fire that had been contained behind iron doors since the moment he'd tugged her against him outside her apartment. It raged free now, and he groaned into her mouth. Her answering whimper was tender and hot and . . . desperate.

Oh. What the fuck was happening?

Her mind wasn't in the right place. And he had to keep a clear head to get them both out of this alive.

He gripped her waist and pried her off him. "Wait." But she'd taken his breath and held it hostage, and his voice came out in a thin shred of a whisper. She dove for his mouth again, but he forced himself to duck away. "Stop. What are you doing?"

"Please." Those gorgeous eyes brimmed with tears. "Make me forget. Make me forget where I am and why I'm here."

He swallowed hard. Her heated gaze skipped to the tattoo where it escaped his collar and curled under his ear. She let out that incredible whimper again and bent to kiss the black lines on his skin. Right there, where the sensation of her moist lips shot straight to his dick. His chest vibrated with a moan.

"Gwen. Wait. I don't . . ."

Her hands slid down his chest, grabbed fistfuls of his T-shirt, and pulled it out of his jeans.

"Ah, Jesus. Gwen, I don't do this with clients."

She dropped her hips, the hot place between her legs grinding against his erection. She tightened her knees and growled into his ear. "I'm not your fucking client."

Holy . . . His body went completely rigid for one second. Two.

He paged through a million possibilities, but they all ended with him inside her.

Snatching both her wrists, he lifted them above her head. Noses inches apart, eyes meeting in furious lust, they breathed like they'd just staggered across a marathon finish line.

Peeling her off him like a wet shirt, he tossed her backward on the bed. She sprawled easily. No resistance, her head falling back, her spine arching. Goddamn, she was desire, all wrapped up in a tight little package that wanted him, of all people. She licked her lips and he wanted to tell her exactly what else she could do with them.

A new rush of blood raced for his crotch and he fell on top of her. The hard mattress didn't give her up. He felt all of her beneath him, every curve, every bone, every movement. She met his mouth halfway, their mouths grinding together like teenagers making out in the backseat of a car minutes before curfew.

He'd been ready for this in Manny's, when she'd teased him about the museums and he'd actually been truthful with her. When she'd smiled at him and laughed. When she'd told him to break a guy's leg and then stood there to watch it done.

This woman . . . yeah, she was more than a body. She was the one with the hammer who'd shattered his wall and destroyed the Retriever, the sorry-ass dog.

Her fingers tickled his waist as she fumbled at his shirt. "Take this off."

Gladly. He pushed off her and whipped off the T-shirt, tossing it somewhere far away. Gasping, she came up on her elbows and gaped at his chest. "Wow," she breathed.

He knew what she saw. The vine tattoo originated on his left shoulder. The mass of leaves and twirling stalks tangled down one arm, across most of his chest, and trailed down his ribs. She liked it; he could tell by the glint in her eyes and the not-so-subtle clue of her fingers snapping open her jeans.

He watched her, breath snagged somewhere halfway up his throat, as she slid the jeans from under her fine ass. She was taking too long. He reached over and yanked them off her long legs. The palest light coming through the window made her skin gleam. Her underwear was bright white and sat low on her golden hips. The flat place between her hipbones begged for his mouth.

She sat up and reached for his zipper, but he was a step ahead of her. He toed off his boots, ripped open the fly of his pants, and pushed them down and off. The hunger he saw on her face couldn't possibly match what he felt. No way.

Sliding a knee between her smooth thighs, he came back over her. Elbows outside her shoulders, he allowed himself a gentle touch and smoothed her hairline with his thumbs. The gesture seemed to startle her, and she jumped. For a moment, he could have sworn he saw a new sheen of tears draw across her dark eyes, but then it was gone and he was kissing her again.

His hands drifted to her ears, then her neck, then her chest. Something crinkled in her bra. Something sort of papery. Didn't matter. All he cared about was that she still wore too many clothes.

He flicked the zipper on her sweatshirt, started to draw it down. She swatted his hand away. "No. Just fuck me."

A melting glacier slid down his back. His lust snapped in half and crumbled to the floor. He shoved away from her and staggered back.

It didn't matter to her who he was. It could have been Xavier groping her, his cock halfway home, and she would have taken it. Anything to get her to forget, right?

Wow, did he feel like a fool. He deserved it, though. He deserved that sick feeling of wanting everything from someone and in return only being wanted in part.

Gwen blinked up at him, confused. Then she sat up in horror. "Reed. No. I meant . . ."

He plucked his jeans and boots from the rug and straightened, throwing a hand between them. "I know what you meant. What you wanted."

"I want *you*." The words seemed to shock her. She even touched her swollen lips.

He paused, his body straining to get back to her, his mind

dragging him in the opposite direction. "Think about what you just said. Then look at where we are. And ask yourself what you would believe if you were me."

Though it took every ounce of power he had, he gave her his back and retreated to his bedroom.

EIGHTEEN

The hard knock on the other side of the bathroom door jolted Gwen from sleep.

"You up?" Reed sounded gruffer than usual.

Maybe if she buried herself deeper under the blanket and pillows, he'd think she was invisible. Forget about her. Yeah right.

He pounded again. "Gwen, get up."

She didn't want to see him, didn't want to be here. Didn't . . .

"I'm coming in."

The door flew open. From inside her bed cocoon, she lifted a corner of the blanket and watched him stride across the floor. He stood at the edge of the mattress, a steel mask for a face.

"Up."

She was the worst kind of fool: the kind of person who knew she was doing something idiotic and did it anyway. Reed wasn't the same guy she'd wanted to sleep with back in Manny's. He never would be. What the hell had she been thinking last night? That she could erase the pain of thousands of Tedrans and Ofarians by fucking the guy who'd kidnapped her?

They needed *her*, not her orgasms. She was immature for thinking sex could be any sort of cure, however temporary, and beyond embarrassed that she'd attacked Reed and demanded what she had.

She pulled the covers down to her shoulders. "I'm sorry."

The headboard seemed to fascinate him. "Forget it."

Forget what exactly? That he'd grabbed her as eagerly as she'd jumped him? How his stubble had rubbed her skin wonderfully raw? The tattoo that spread organically across his skin and the fact that he was beautiful in the most dangerous sense of the word?

Stop it. She tried to hate him again, to get back the emotion she'd thrown away last night. He'd done the right thing by refusing her. Nothing good could come of them being together like that. The memory of his mouth and hands on her narrowed the focus of her senses to only him, and she couldn't afford that.

She sat up, holding the blanket high on her body. "It started off as one thing and turned into another."

He cut her off with a slice of the hand. "I'm taking you somewhere today."

"Where?" Only one place was possible: Genesai.

Now the lamp in the corner had his attention. He shrugged. "Not my business to know."

Of course. Twenty-four hours ago she would have spit those words back at him. Tried to make him feel guilty for how he'd ruined her life. Only now she knew the truth. Now she was grateful for his ignorance.

Or was she? Because now she couldn't hide behind loathing him. His presence in a house full of Secondaries compromised any chance she might have of escape. She couldn't risk exposing herself to him. Maybe he really had volunteered to stay to make sure she was safe, but what good would that do now? Gwen was as good as dead no matter if he stayed or not. And because he was more deeply involved, he'd never be free either. He'd be a perfect witness for the Primaries when the Ofarians were discovered. He could go on TV shows, write a tell-all about his intimate encounters with the aliens. Make millions. Maybe he'd love that.

What an ugly, ugly mess.

"You have five minutes."

"Are you going to tell Nora? About last night."

His shoulders rolled back, down. "No. I won't say anything. That wouldn't be good for either of us."

She sighed in relief and the blankets fell to her lap. He was in the middle of turning around, but he froze. A dark, scary look cloaked his face.

"What are you wearing?"

She looked down and pointlessly tried to cover her chest with her arms. All that did was push her boobs tighter against the gray T-shirt. Reed's T-shirt. The one he'd been wearing when they met.

After he'd left last night, she'd thrown off her clothes in disgust, as though they were the things that had twisted her focus. His discarded shirt had lain crumpled by the lamp, still warm from his body and holding his distinct scent.

Now he stared down at her, looking like he wanted to rip it from her body, and not just because she'd taken it without asking. His lazy gaze traveled from her shoulders down to the T-shirt hem stretching across her bare thighs.

His long legs brought him to her in three steps. He loomed above her, much like he had last night in all his fearsome beauty. A shudder skittered through his breath.

Touch me again. Push up this shirt. Slide inside me and take what you wanted to last night.

When he went to one knee before her, her fingernails dug unconsciously into her ankle. Her lungs refused to work. Only his eyes moved. They dropped to her mouth, and it watered in response.

He thought he was so good at hiding his desire, but she recognized the tight coil of his arm muscles and the little clench in his jaw. She'd seen them last night, moments before she took his mouth and gave him hers.

She recalled the disconcerting moment when, in the midst of their wild, hungry, half-naked clawing, he'd draped himself over her and cradled her head. Dragged featherlight fingers over her hair and face. Kissed her with an aching tenderness that switched the area of highest intensity from between her legs to her chest.

There was none of that in him now. Only hardness. Only duty.

He leaned in, an animalistic twist to his mouth. She gasped, wondering—and perhaps fearing—if he intended to give her what she'd wanted last night: sex that was hard and fast and devoid of any emotion except anguish. She no longer enjoyed the prospect.

He edged even closer. Her mind swam dizzying laps in a turgid pool.

Then his hand opened, and in his palm lay the syringe and the *nelicoda* pill. "Pick one."

Her arm still burned from where the needle had punctured yesterday. Keeping her eyes on his, she snatched the pill and popped it in her mouth. She moved to get up, maybe torture Reed a little by walking to the closet in only his T-shirt, but his fingers clamped on to her arm.

"Swallow it."

The rolling thunder voice made her shiver. Made her imagine another situation in which he might say that.

She looked past him, out the triangle window to the glittering lake surrounded by frosted mountains and trees painted in orange and gold. Using her tongue, she pried the pill out from where she'd stashed it next to her gums and gulped it back dry. The pill lodged in her throat then finally slipped down. She opened her empty mouth and circled her tongue.

Reed's hand slid from her arm and he rose gracefully.

"Five minutes?" she choked out as he walked away.

"You used up time with your little show-and-tell." His back was still to her. "Now you have two."

A silver Range Rover waited in the drive. No white van, no blindfolds, no funky handcuffs with leashes. Apparently, Reed didn't think he needed those. Cocky jerk.

And Nora wasn't exactly the trusting type, especially of Primaries. So why the freedom? What made her believe that Reed wouldn't double-cross her?

"Where's everyone else?" Gwen asked.

"Ran out of here like bats out of hell this morning. Nora was supposed to come with us but I guess she got called away."

She hadn't expected him to answer. That was a lot of information she wasn't sure she should have. Gwen looked to the east. Something was wrong in the Plant. Not much could rip Nora away from her chance to sit in on Gwen meeting Genesai, but her people could. Was it a problem with the Tedrans? Or the Ofarians?

"You're mine today," Reed said. "Don't think because she's not here that it'll be easier going. I have orders."

She thought he'd say something like that, but it barely registered. Her mind was on the Plant.

Reed pressed her into the Range Rover's passenger seat. She settled on the black leather, the interior warm from the sun, and debated all the options that had been thrown at her yesterday at the rest stop.

Translating Genesai's speech would align her with Nora. Ignoring him would send the government dogs on a Secondary fox hunt. Either way, innocent Ofarians would know a fear they'd only imagined. Secondaries would die. Everything came down to today. Everything depended on her.

She bent forward and buried her face in her arms. Reed slid behind the wheel and pressed buttons on the dashboard. A British woman's voice began a navigation sequence.

"Sit up," he said, toneless. "Put your belt on."

How nice of him to consider road safety. She straightened and pulled the seat belt across her body, clicking it down by her hip. Her eyes refused to face forward, however, and drew a long, slow line over Reed's body.

Those thick thighs spread over his seat. He wore new jeans, like her, but he still wore those beat-up, ankle-high workman's boots she'd noticed in the alley a few centuries ago. The black fleece coat stretched across his chest and arms, one of which draped over the top of the steering wheel, the other throwing around the stick shift.

She'd seriously screwed up.

BLN—Before Last Night—she could easily chalk up her desire to the Allure. Now she knew what he tasted like, how his hard muscles felt beneath his skin. What that tease of a tattoo had turned into.

What had he said to her before? That he knew what her breath sounded like when she was turned on? Well, now she knew that about him, and every time he exhaled, she found herself focusing on his mouth, wanting to hear it again.

Appalling, that thought, that she still wanted the guy who had stolen her then claimed to want to keep her safe. The guy who'd shoved her away and treated her like chattel. If she could slap herself, she would.

Now, though, his mouth was set in a tight line and he looked so determinedly forward she imagined him in a neck brace. He gunned the engine, his legs working the clutch and the gas to start the steep climb up the drive and out onto the road.

A heavyset man with a mangled ear and two missing fingers exited the driveway guard hut and circled around to Reed. As he checked out the display on Reed's watch, Gwen watched Reed assess the guy. She could tell without any verbal interaction: the guard, too, was a Primary.

Nora was a fool, to trust that money could buy loyalty. Her army consisted of Xavier and Adine. Xavier was damaged and volatile, and Adine was . . . hmmm, Gwen didn't really know what Adine was. Smart, definitely. Observant and careful. Shy, even. Odd traits for a kidnapper. Gwen had sensed a Secondary signature when Adine came around, but it was strangely weaker, as though masked or incomplete.

So Nora had been forced to hire Primaries to help. Where was all this money coming from? This sort of thing was Reed's job. Gwen had noted his Cartier Chronograph watch. Clearly the guy wasn't charging his clients minimum wage. And by the way he'd appraised the mean-looking guard, she guessed the fingerless guy with the gun operated on the same side of the law as Reed. Those types would need a pretty penny to stay reliable.

Nora was walking a fine line. Gwen filed it all away and kept her mouth shut.

For the next hour and a half, the British woman in the navigation system did the talking.

The Primary world lined the four-lane road snaking around the lake. Gwen watched it go by with a hand on the window. At a stop sign she tried the door handle. Locked, of course. No amount of pressing the lock mechanism worked either. Beside her Reed made a little sound like he was insulted she'd even try.

He veered off the main avenue and onto a two-lane road that stretched up into the mountains. Pretty soon the markings on the pavement disappeared. The tree growth turned denser, and the road made severe turns and sharp dips. She clutched her stomach to keep down the car sickness and tried to focus on a distant point to stave off the dizziness, but even the far points shifted too fast. The houses thinned out. Their sizes and general upkeep declined. She saw more pickups than BMWs.

The British woman told Reed to turn in twenty meters. He slowed, but Gwen saw no road or driveway. Then, as they got closer, two faint tire ruts swerved off the road and disappeared into a canopy of evergreens so thick the automatic headlights flicked on. The Range Rover came out the other side and face to face with another little green hut almost identical to those sitting around the lake house.

This time a woman exited and strode to the car. Though both her ears were still intact, she shared the same skeptical grimace as the driveway guard. Reed rolled down his window and held out his watch again. What was on that thing? The female guard looked across Reed at Gwen, and her frown deepened. Then she disappeared into the hut and came out with a bulging envelope. She passed it to Reed and waved him onward.

The bushes in front of the Range Rover parted. The SUV slowly drove through and into the opening of a tall, formidable gate extending through the trees. The tire ruts swooped into the forest and the gate clanged shut behind them. The land sloped steadily downward. Ahead rose a ten-foot-tall iron latticed wall. The tire ruts ended in front of it.

Reed threw the SUV in park and killed the engine. The lock on Gwen's door released. The sudden freedom was anticlimactic because they literally stood at the edge of the world. As she stepped out of the car, pine needles crunched under her boot, releasing their sweet scent. The forest clutched her so tightly she could barely breathe. There was nothing up here except icy gusts that liked to torment her skin, and the roar of the wind throwing about the tree branches.

"There." Reed stood to one side of the iron lattice, pointing downward. She went to his side, keeping a careful distance between them.

The iron wall had prevented the car from rolling down a steep decline. A path switchbacked down to a tiny shack. Its minuscule front porch rested on the ground, but the back half of the cabin balanced on stilts, hanging over a cliff that dropped into a hazy, quiet valley. The windows were dark, as if blacked out by paint or heavy drapes.

"I'm supposed to stay up here. Orders." He waved about the watch, but as she tried to steal a glance at it, its screen was disappointingly blank.

"Here." He slapped the envelope at her chest.

She took it, blinking in confusion. He just shrugged, as if to say, yet again, "Not my business to know."

So this was it. She was on her own. Nora trusted Reed would make her go inside that cabin at any cost, and Gwen believed he would, too. All that posturing about how he was here for her now had vanished. Maybe she could have used that before. Maybe, if she'd been smart and had actually thought through her actions before she'd tried to jump him, she could have manipulated his obvious desire to get him onto her side. But that was gone now. His position was all too clear.

He worked for Nora.

Reed leaned against the Range Rover's bumper, the car sagging a bit under his weight, and stared, absolutely expressionless.

Gwen turned away to face Genesai's shack.

Nora claimed to have told her the truth about the Ofarians and Tedrans, but really, wasn't her opinion as skewed as Gwen's own? Maybe Genesai knew something else entirely. Maybe he was the one who knew The Truth.

And maybe, just maybe, she could use it.

She marched down the mountainside, trying to ignore the nerves twanging all over her body. Nora had called Genesai insane. What did that mean exactly? Was he dangerous?

As she stepped onto the porch, the weathered floorboards were spaced so that she could see the pitch of the cliff under her feet. She gulped and tried to focus. The creak of the shack on its stilts wasn't helping. Clutching the strange envelope to her chest, she took two deep breaths and knocked.

A great crash erupted from inside. Pounding footsteps. She stumbled backward off the porch. Another crash, more footsteps, then the door flung open. A shirtless young man, eighteen at the most, peered out.

Pale, almost translucent skin stretched over his prominent rib cage. Brown hair shot out of his head at all sorts of lengths and angles, as though he'd taken scissors to it himself in the dark. His head twitched on his neck like a bird examining a stranger holding food. His clear, sunflower blue eyes blinked rapidly. When he looked down and saw that his toes had breached the line of sunlight from the open door, he shrieked and scrambled back into the pitch black of the cabin.

Okay. Strange, yes, but not dangerous. His Secondary signature burned hot and wavy, like the desert sun, and she was relieved to learn that *nelicoda* didn't affect that part of her. The young man's signature wasn't at all like Nora's and Xavier's, which carried with them an air of unrepentant revenge and hurt. Beneath Genesai's odd behavior there lay a line of . . . peace. Of innocence.

She turned to see if Reed was watching, but he was no longer visible. He wasn't worried about her escaping apparently; the narrow path was the only way up or down. The shack or the Range Rover, her only two options.

Gwen stepped tentatively forward. "Genesai?"

"Genesai!" With a giant smile displaying rows of browned teeth, he whirled back into the shack, arms and legs flailing. She took that as an invitation to go inside, shutting the door behind her.

Two early-twentieth-century gas lanterns sat in the far corners, emitting an unfamiliar odor and just barely lighting the tiny one room. She'd been right; the windows were slathered with a messy coat of thick black paint. Squinting, she could make out a table, two chairs tipped over on their sides, a narrow bed piled with frayed blankets, and an honest-to-goodness chamber pot.

Genesai jumped straight up onto the table and gargled in the back of his throat. Gwen's back hit the front door, but he didn't lunge for her. He leaped through the air, the force of his body moving the table, and landed on the bed. Like a child, he bounced on the weak mattress, his face contorted with what she assumed to be glee. He shouted, but the Translation didn't kick in so he was just making nonsensical sounds. He fell off the bed, picked himself up, and danced around the room, his knobby arms and legs wobbling like the limbs of a new colt.

Genesai started to babble, a short string of sounds that flew all around the pitch scale. They seeped into her ears and slammed into her brain. *This* was actual speech. She gripped the table edge, preparing for the roughest part of Translation, when all of a sudden it stopped. Not his talking, the Translation. Like a car that had driven about two feet out of park and promptly died. She realized why: he was only saying one phrase over and over and over.

"Down, down, down we come. Into fire, into water. Up, up, up we go. Together again, with blood."

The sounds and words were too limited and her mind couldn't complete the Translation. As Genesai bounced past, she grabbed his arms, the envelope dropping at her feet. She repeated the phrase in his language, her mouth and tongue feeling thick and heavy and tingly, like fingers regaining feeling after being numbed with ice.

Genesai's angular face alighted. He bounced out of her grasp and she trailed behind him, anxious for him to say more. Nora said she'd been trying to communicate with him for over a century, and Gwen was on the verge of a breakthrough. It was a powerful motivator, to gain something Nora wanted and only Gwen could unlock.

But Genesai just repeated the phrase. Gwen kept saying it back to him. He squealed with joy, hyping himself up so much he started to wheeze. She could see the energy starting to drain out of him.

"Wait, Genesai. Sit down and rest." She said it in English and Tedranish, knowing it was futile. But at least he let her guide him to the bed, where he sank with a great sigh. With each pump of his chest, she could count a new rib.

"I would very much like to talk with you," she said in English.

For the briefest of moments, she thought he might have understood. His face turned up to her and he smiled his version of a smile. She tried not to cringe in the cloud of his breath.

"Genesai," he whispered, and collapsed onto the bed.

His eyes rolled back in his head and his body went slack. Resonating snores filled the shack. Gwen shook him hard, called his name using the accent of his language, clapped in front of his face. No response.

Now what? Every second meant Nora crept closer to her goal of wiping out the Secondaries' secret existence. Every second in silence was a second lost to Gwen. She couldn't simply do *nothing*. When she did nothing, had nothing to say or offer, she was Nora's puppet. Those strings needed to be cut. Gwen just had to figure out how.

The envelope the Primary guard had handed her lay where she'd dropped it by the door. Gwen snatched it up and ripped it open. What the . . . office stationery and crayons?

A thin stream of mountain air leaked under the door. It tickled Gwen's legs then swirled up her body and throughout the cabin. There was movement in the corner of her eye, pale and fluttering. She turned toward the back corner, where the old lanterns still burned. Genesai's manic movements had distracted her before, but now she saw it. Or them, rather.

Every inch of wall and ceiling space in the shack was covered with Genesai's scribblings. Large sheets of old newspapers, ragged chunks of computer paper, painted-over coloring book pages, and torn corners of fast-food restaurant napkins. The air made the papers whisper, and Gwen moved closer to hear their secrets.

Translation had two branches: verbal and written. For the verbal, Gwen heard foreign words and absorbed them. Her brain was wired to sort everything out until the terms and grammar became as clear to her as her native tongue, and the muscles in her mouth and throat had been altered accordingly. The written part was a whole other ball of wax. It took longer, for one thing, and she had to hear the words spoken exactly as they appeared on paper in order to associate characters and combinations and punctuation with aural cues.

She only had to hear words once to remember them. She didn't even have to hear all the words in a language to know the complete tongue, but she needed a wide sample for her mind to make the necessary connections and draw the correct conclusions. The one time she'd rushed the process had led to an embarrassing mistake and a lengthy period of groveling. She'd learned to be patient. Except when it came to Genesai.

The pages taped to the cabin's walls held far, far more than what he'd spoken to her. She'd seen enough written languages to discern sentences and phrases, and the weird sentence he'd repeated to her had a specific cadence and used repetitive words. These wall scraps were the key to his consciousness, to communication. Nervous excitement bubbled inside her.

She moved from page to page—lifting one, sliding aside another—unsure exactly what she was looking for. Until she found it.

Ten pages of yellowed dot-matrix printer paper still tentatively attached. On it were rows upon rows of Genesai's bizarre scrawlings, drawings of something that looked half-woman, half-spaceship, and a large body of water.

The story of his arrival. Told not by Ofarians or Tedrans. Gasping, she whirled back to the bed, but Genesai was snoring like he was sawing the wood for his dream house, arms sticking out on either side of his bed. Had Nora seen these pages? When had he drawn it? Gwen carefully detached the long length of paper from the wall and folded it accordion-like. She opened the zipper of her cardigan sweater—where yesterday she'd stashed Xavier's photos of the Plant—and slid Genesai's drawings inside.

The origin of a plan—not Nora's, not Xavier's, but *her* plan—sprouted inside her.

This was why she'd been made, why she'd been chosen out of who knew how many Ofarians to be gifted that odd, elusive gene. When puberty had set in and the Translation took form alongside her water powers, the Board had dug up history on the Translators. It was a small bit of information, gleaned only from what the Translator who had first arrived on Earth had scribbled in brittle notebooks, but it was enough to know that Translators had once been the peacemakers. Made sense, really. The ones who could communicate between cultures were the ones to maintain the balance.

And now Nora wanted to use her ability as a weapon? Nothing about that seemed right.

But then, Gwen had been the one to start the international division of the Company. Turned out she had been anything but a peacemaker. She'd thought she was advancing the state of her people and solidifying their prosperity, but that was so far from the truth. *She* had been the one to increase the size of the Plant. *She* had been the one to drive them to breed more. Xavier had said they'd increased production five or six years ago. That correlated with the time she'd started up her division.

She could blame Jonah or the Board all she wanted, but she was the one who'd thrown the Company's genocide into overdrive. And she would have to be the one to fix it. But she had to get away from Nora. She had to get back to her father.

Everything pointed back to Chairman Ian Carroway, whether he was responsible or not.

Gwen threw open the front door. She'd entered in broad daylight and now stepped out into dusk. How long had she spent examining the walls, searching for her own weapon to use against Nora? The air had gone from daytime chilly to downright frigid. Thin strips of a purple and orange sunset pierced the thick forest. As she started back up the path to the Range Rover, Reed appeared at the top.

She avoided meeting his eyes, though she did give him a once-over. His nose was red and he'd pulled a skull cap over his shaved head. He watched her intently as she skirted around the SUV and climbed in without any order or provocation.

Sitting in the passenger seat, she had to order her knees to keep from bouncing. Underneath her clothes she carried the first major clues to saving both the Tedrans and the Ofarians. *Gwen* had them. Not Nora. The arrogant Tedran woman could dangle the Ofarians' demise over Gwen's head, but Nora would only ever know what Gwen told her.

Had the old woman ever thought of that?

Gwen's own agenda started to formulate. Whatever she was going to do, it would save the Tedrans *and* bring those responsible for the Plant to justice without compromising the Ofarians' existence.

Reed climbed behind the wheel. Even though Gwen stared out the windshield, her mind racing, she felt him staring at her profile.

Yeah, this trip to meet Genesai was probably the best thing Nora could have done to help Gwen's own scheme.

She just had to get past Reed.

NINETEEN

The Range Rover made a three-point turn and started back to the guard hut. Reed braked suddenly, throwing Gwen against her seat belt.

She calmly sat back, trying not to draw attention to the crinkle of pages between the poly-cotton blend of her sweater and her goose-bumped skin. "What?"

"I know I'm opening a can of worms with this," he said to the steering wheel, "but I have to know. Did they hurt you in there? I heard yelling, screaming."

She rolled her head on the seat cushion. The dashboard lights painted his face a soothing blue. His profile was as strong as his body. She tried to imagine him with hair and found it impossible. It would change too much about him, and not in a better way.

"Why, Reed. So you do care."

He squeezed his eyes shut and clenched the wheel. "Just answer the question."

He wouldn't ask if he didn't care, right? Then again, if he cared, he might actually look at her, or put some sort of concern in his voice.

She reached forward, poked up the heat a few degrees, and turned the vent so the hot blast hit her neck. "No, they didn't hurt me."

He nodded once and pulled out onto the mountain road. The swerves were harder to take in the dark. She closed her eyes and ran through everything that had happened in Genesai's shack. She was dying to take out his pages and study them.

The SUV pulled off the road and onto gravel, but it was

much too soon to be back at the lake house. Opening her eyes, she saw the Range Rover's headlights hitting a battered, wooden sign for MYRNA'S GENERAL STORE. Pine trees crowded the store on all sides, and gravel pads had been shoved between the tree trunks to serve as parking spaces. There were no other cars.

"What are we doing here?"

"I'm starving," he said. "And your stomach's been rumbling since we left that place."

She sat up, heart pounding. "You'd let me out?" One phone call to her father, or one word to the store clerk, and it would be over.

"No." He tapped the car keys. "Doors lock from the outside. Shatterproof glass."

Of course. Such foresight.

Reed veered into the darkest parking space to the left of the store. He hopped out and hit the locks, but Gwen tried them anyway. She was tempted to try to throw her elbow through the window, too, but she knew he spoke the truth about the glass. The Tedrans had considered everything far too well.

The store was a twenties-era house, compact and dotted with small windows. GOOD HUMOR and BUD LIGHT signs dangled from the porch eaves. Inside, through the glass door, a man pushed a broom across the floor. Reed bounded up the steps and disappeared inside.

Gwen channeled the Tasmanian Devil. She turned frantic. She ran her hands over every crevice in the passenger seat, turning the space inside out, searching for anything that might help her. The glove compartment was empty, so was the center console—clean and shiny like a brand-new car. She kept one eye on the store door as she bent forward and swept her hands under her seat. She crawled over the stick shift and shoved her hands between the leather cushions. Nothing. She could scream in frustration, but it wouldn't do any good.

A shadow flickered over the hood and she jumped, straightened. No Reed. An owl, backlit by the store lights, swooped over the moonroof and melded into the forest.

That was a precious three seconds lost. She stretched into the backseat, her fingers scraping at the floor mats. Then . . . there. Something small and hard and wooden stuck between the metal brackets of the driver's seat. She plucked out the familiar shape and tucked it underneath her thigh closest to the door.

A pencil. One of those tiny ones used on golf courses.

A bell chimed and Reed stepped out of the store carrying a small plastic bag and a liter of Coke. Inside, the storekeeper switched off the neon signs and flipped over the CLOSED placard.

"They didn't have much," Reed said, sliding behind the wheel. "Apple muffin okay?"

Her stomach growled in response. She thought she saw his mouth twitch, but she could have been wrong. "I guess I am hungry. Thanks."

Was her voice too loud? Did she respond too quickly or too enthusiastically? All of a sudden the heat in the car was too much and she punched it down a few notches.

Digging into the bag, she pulled out the muffin, but she also found what she needed even more. A white napkin. As Reed pulled back out onto the road, she fumbled with the noisy plastic wrap and stuffed the napkin under her thigh next to the pencil.

Reed drove with one hand and shoved pretzels into his mouth with the other. He kept his eye on the zigzagging road while she scarfed down the muffin. When she was finished, she focused on balancing the napkin on the seat edge, out of his sight. He'd given her an opening and she damn well was going to take it.

She held the pencil with shaking fingers. The napkin was flimsy and the pencil tip tore through several times as she tried to find the perfect pressure. Reed crunched pretzels and gulped Coke next to her. Darkness cloaked them both, but she managed to scrawl: *Kidnapped: Gwen Carroway, San Francisco. Call Ian Carroway.* And her father's private number. If someone called the cops instead, the Ofarian moles would be tasked with erasing any evidence. It was a chance she had to take.

She balled up the napkin in her fist and held it like a raw egg, precious and fragile. She held it all the way back down the mountain and into the busy, commercial area immediately surrounding the lake.

Not many people out at this hour, but as they sped past a

gas station lined with cars, she smacked the automatic window button. Her hand flew up to toss out the napkin. She opened her mouth to scream.

The part of her half-assed plan she hadn't considered? That not only did the doors not open, but neither did the windows.

Reed's reflexes were like a fly's: one of those nasty buggers who senses a swat and jumps away. He reached across the cab and snatched her hand before she realized the window never even cracked open.

The Range Rover swerved. Reed took back control, but he overcompensated and the SUV fishtailed. It skidded across the empty opposite lane, bounced over the shoulder and into a patch of grass. He slammed on the brakes. The SUV slid to a halt. A tree rose not two feet off the front bumper.

Had someone from the gas station seen? Were they now running over to see if anyone was hurt? Gwen could only hope so, and turned in her seat to see.

Reed took her cue, though. He threw the Range Rover in reverse and jounced back onto the road. They sped a mile or so, with him muttering, "What the hell, Gwen. What the *hell*," over and over.

He almost passed a darkened strip mall parking lot, then changed his mind at the last second and squealed into a space in front of a Laundromat. The lake loomed before them, the moon painting a stripe down its center. Any other night it might have been romantic.

Reed reached across and crushed her wrists in one hand.

"Ouch!"

"Oh, does that hurt?"

He pulled her torso awkwardly across the center console and stick shift, and pried open her fingers. The napkin inside revealed her guilt. Still holding her immobile, he flattened the napkin, read it, and then stuffed it into his pocket.

When he turned to look down at her, their faces were so close she could feel his short, angry breaths on her cheek.

"I saw you searching the car when I was in the store. You think I wasn't watching?"

"And you didn't come out? You didn't stop me?"

"I knew what was inside. I knew where that pencil was."

"Did you put it there?"

"Yes." He pulled her even closer. So close she practically sat on the center console. "I needed to know what you'd try to do."

She struggled. Pointlessly. "This was a *test*?"

"You tested me, didn't you? You thought I wouldn't give you the shot. You thought I'd sleep with you. You thought I'd go all stupid for you and just forget my orders. But I can't do that. I have a job to do and I'll do it, as long as you don't get hurt."

There was something else to his story, something big. She saw it lurking behind his eyes, in the way they shifted away.

"You don't understand, Reed." Desperation crept into her voice. "I *have* to get away from them." The plea died there. Everything she wanted to say to support her argument, she couldn't. Not to Reed.

She struggled again, another silly attempt, but this time he let go. She sat back on her heels on the passenger seat, hands on the console.

"Let's get a few things straight." He stared at her mouth. "First, I'm doing my job. I get paid extremely well to do it and I'm really good at it. You won't escape when I'm around."

God, the money thing again.

"And second"—his voice dropped so low it hit the pavement beneath the Range Rover—"I'm very, very attracted to you."

Every molecule in her body stopped moving.

"There's something between us, Gwen."

"But last night. This morning—"

"There's something there, but there can't be. Do you understand? It's why I left. It's why I pushed you away. Last night . . ." He scrubbed his knuckles along his jaw as his words died.

"I wasn't trying to use you. It wasn't an escape attempt." It had started off as an escape, but one of an entirely different kind.

He didn't say anything. Just searched her eyes. Something in them must have satisfied him, because his shoulders relaxed and he turned his big body toward her.

"There are two separate things going on here," he said. "There's us like we could've been in Manny's or even last night. And there's you and me how Nora wants us to be. I see you now—the way you're looking at me, the way you look in those jeans—and I know it's only going to get harder for me to keep them apart. But I can't let my guard down for you. I need you to understand that."

She didn't want to nod, but she did. Because if she wanted to keep her people secret, Reed could never be brought into her world. The time to submit to the Allure had expired. Now she was dancing on a high wire over a bonfire.

He drummed his fingers on the steering wheel. "But I also want you to know how torn I am. This has never, ever happened to me. Not in fifteen years. I've always been able to put up this wall between who I really am and who brings in the money. But with you . . ." He shook his head at his lap. "If we hadn't met before I brought you here, I'd have already been gone."

"Reed." She had no idea what else she wanted to say, only that his name sounded whole and reassuring on her lips.

He looked up, his blue eyes her own personal stars. "It's killing me not to know what they want with you. All right, there. I've said it. But I won't ask."

Her throat constricted. "I couldn't tell you, even if you did."

The heavy silence of the idling car pressed all around her. That iceman routine today hadn't been because he didn't want her. It was because he did. It confused her even more. And because she was a complete mess and a glutton for punishment, it pushed her closer to him. Shoved her, was more like it.

She leaned in. His lips parted; he sucked in a breath. She wanted to taste him again, this time slower, savoring. Just for a little bit, to soften the bite of what had happened between them last night. Something soft, to let him know that she was torn, too. To let him know that as much as she wanted to claim it was gone, the Allure hadn't died.

Closing her eyes, she went for it.

"No."

Her eyes flew open to find him tilted so far back his skull touched the window.

Her ass hit the passenger seat fast, like he'd physically shoved her away. "You think I'm trying to trick you? Use you?"

"I don't know," he snapped. "Are you?"

"No. I wasn't. I'm not."

She said it, but did she believe it? To work any sort of plan, she had to get around Reed.

"I'll keep you alive," he said, pushing the stick out of neutral and into reverse. "But that's it. Nothing more."

So he couldn't let his attraction interfere with what he'd been paid to do, and she couldn't let her attraction distract her from figuring out how to save and protect all Secondaries.

"You're right. You're absolutely right." She sank deep into the seat and stared, unseeing, out at the lake. "You need to keep your head and so do I."

"Okay, so it stops."

"Okay, then."

They hadn't mentioned trust. He didn't trust her not to try to use him. Her blood forbade her to trust anyone not like her.

Big difference.

TWENTY

They returned to an empty, dark lake house around eleven.
Reed used his scarily complex watch to open the front door. If
only she could get her hands on that thing . . . but it was practically molded to his skin and she'd have to get close to him to
do it. That definitely wasn't happening.

What the hell was going on at the Plant? Why were the
Tedrans still gone? She wondered—hoped?—if they'd been
caught. So, so much could change. She wouldn't mind Nora
being captured, but Xavier and Adine? The thought of the two
of them in Jonah's hands made her gut twist, and she wrestled
with the conflicting emotions.

Upstairs, Reed stood in the threshold to her bedroom cell
as she wandered inside, feeling strangely empty.

"Still hungry?" he asked, hand on the doorknob.

"Yes."

He nodded and left, the door locking behind him. She
unzipped her sweater and removed Genesai's papers. They'd
crinkled during her and Reed's little tussle in the car, and she
tried to smooth them on the edge of the dresser. The mysterious scribbles and shaky drawings stared back at her. Not knowing what was written made her want to scream. She'd never
been lost before, not when it came to languages, and she wondered how in the world anyone could stand it. She lifted up the
mattress and slipped the pages underneath.

Her clothes reeked of the mustiness of Genesai's cabin and
the unpleasant smell had transferred to her skin. She stripped
on the way to the shower. After she'd scrubbed herself clean,

she threw on one of the supplied T-shirts and the lone pair of sweatpants, and went back into the bathroom.

The door to Reed's bedroom was unlocked.

She listened for any footsteps on the creaking, narrow stairs and, when she didn't hear any, pushed open the door and stepped into Reed's half of their tiny little world. The bedroom mirrored hers: dramatically sloped ceiling, secondhand furniture, frayed rug. She went through every drawer, ran her hands over every crack. There was nothing in there to do with her or Nora, and very little, in fact, to do with him.

Packages of new white men's T-shirts and giant sweatshirts with the tags still attached lay crumpled near the foot of his bed. A pair of jeans had been thrown across the crooked chest of drawers. The bed was a messy pile of sheets and blankets that made her twitch. She tugged a corner back into place. Leaned down. Inhaled. How could she know his scent so distinctly already?

Don't go there, Gwen. She backed off and tried the hallway door. No luck.

In the bathroom she grabbed the green toothbrush she'd appropriated as hers and went at her teeth until her gums were sore. Bending over the sink, she swished water around and spit it out several times. She straightened, and almost jumped out of her skin. "Don't do that!"

Reed filled the doorway to his room. He held a tray piled with plates of food. "Find anything interesting in my room?"

"Since you asked, nope."

He studied her in that disconcerting way, his gaze sweeping across her face and down her body. Not sexual. Assessing.

A tiny lift of the tray. "Mashed potatoes, sliced turkey. Some carrots. Sound okay?" After she nodded, he nudged his chin toward her bedroom. "Go over there."

"Huh?"

"Just to the doorway. This bathroom, it's the demilitarized zone for us from now on." When she just stared, he added, "You stay there. I stay here. We're separate."

"So am I North or South?" She ambled to the threshold.

"North," he mumbled. "Definitely North." He took one plate off the tray and stepped into his room.

She came forward, feeling silly, and slid the tray off the

counter. She backed into her room and hooked a toe around the door to pull it shut.

"I need to watch you eat," he said from across the DMZ.

"Sorry?"

He gestured with a utensil. "The fork. The knife. I need to see them."

She held his eyes for a long moment, then sank to the floor, ass in her room, legs crossed on the bathroom tile. He did the same. They ate in silence, silverware clanking. They stole glances at each other between bites, the dim bulb over the sink the only light.

Halfway through his mashed potatoes, the screen on his watch lit up. He frowned at it, tapped a button, and resumed eating.

"Nora's back," he said, mouth full.

Gwen slid her plate up on the counter next to the sink and gestured to the Tedran device wrapped around his wrist. "That thing's pretty amazing." He merely grunted. "I liked your other watch." That got him to look up in surprise. "The Cartier. I noticed it in the bar. It made me wonder about you."

He lifted an eyebrow. "That was the first thing you wondered about? Considering how we met?"

Her mind circled back to the alley. "Not the first. Just one of many."

Another bite of potatoes. "I thought at that point we were past wondering."

Everything had stemmed from her wonder. She'd been ready to dive headfirst into the Allure. "I was trying to figure out why a guy like you had such an expensive watch."

He set his plate down, the fork clattering. "A guy like me?"

"Well. You know. A guy who looks like you."

Both sandy eyebrows shot up. "Do tell."

She gestured vaguely, thankful for the weak lighting so he couldn't see the heat creeping up her neck. "That body. The tattoo. The permanent scowl. The hair."

"And? Your point?"

"And . . . so you've pretty much cornered the market on badass."

"For the record . . ." He kicked aside his plate, leaned back onto his hands, and stretched out one leg far into the DMZ.

"I shave my head because I don't want to look like my eighth-grade science teacher with the horseshoe hair. Been doing it since I was twenty-five."

She wrinkled her nose. "Horseshoe hair? Okay, I get it now." Under her stare, he ran a hand over his bald top. His sudden, weird shyness made him seem like that twenty-five-year-old who'd first taken a razor to his head.

She turned sideways, pressing her back to one side of the doorway, her toes to the other, and wrapped her arms around her knees. "Know what else I wondered about that night?"

His eyes flashed. Even in the pale light she could tell. "We're not going there, Gwen."

"I know. I wasn't." Maybe not in her words, but definitely in her mind. "I wondered about the museums. You said you liked them, that you liked to learn." He nodded. "That surprised me. You surprised me. In a good way. I never knew I'd like being proven wrong so much."

"That damn painting on your phone." He blew out a breath and lazily shook his head. "Started a lot, didn't it?"

She could argue that whatever it was had started before that, but like he said, they weren't going to go there. He was right, though. Damn that Ed Ruscha and his crazy-good paintings.

She planted her chin on her knees. "Why do you like to learn?"

"Oh, boy," he said, chin to chest. Just when she didn't think he'd answer, he took a deep breath and added, "Because I didn't before. Education wasn't really my thing when I was younger. I wish it had been. Things might've been . . . different." He blinked away a far-off look. "Anyway, when I have downtime in a new city, I go to museums."

"Wait, I'm confused. You say you like to learn but education isn't your thing?"

"I said it *wasn't* my thing. Not when it mattered, at least." He drew a slow thumb up and down the leg of his jeans. "Sometimes I think about college. What I missed. Where my life would be if I'd done that instead of . . . other stuff."

Oh, this was fascinating. *He* was fascinating. "You could still go."

He made a sound of exasperation. "And do what?"

She shrugged. "What do you like to do?"

He pondered, opened his mouth to say something, then changed his mind, shaking his head.

"It's possible, Reed. It's always possible."

"Yeah? Well, the idea of going back to school scares the crap out of me. More than extracting. Can you believe that? I'm scared of starting over." He gave a wry grin. "And the homework. Can you imagine me doing homework?"

She smiled, and to her pleasure, he echoed it, the dimple making a cameo.

"Seriously," he said, "it's so different now. I don't know how well I'd do out there in the real world."

Such true words, she could have spoken them herself.

"So," she said, sensing he wanted to change the subject. "You just like going to art museums?" She couldn't dare to hope.

"Nah. All sorts. Started a few years ago when I got sick of hanging out in bars. I'm thirty-seven. That shit gets old real fast. I started with the Tate in London and, I don't know, I kind of got hooked." His lips tightened. "Obsessive personality that way, I guess. Anyway, there's a whole world out there I'd always ignored before in favor of . . . other things. I just started to pay attention."

Excitement burbled inside her. Reed was talking. About *himself*. She wrestled with why she enjoyed it so much. Was it more because he was giving her clues about his identity, so she could gamble with it later? Or was it more because his words had hit several marks all over her body? Her mind. Her heart. That place he'd almost buried himself in last night.

"Where else have you been?" she asked, to keep her brain from traveling down a path it shouldn't.

"Museums? Let's see. The Barbed Wire Museum in Kansas."

Gwen snorted embarrassingly.

"The Louvre, which was amazing. Spent two days in it. A couple of really interesting sex ones in Amsterdam."

Did he have to say sex? Because the way he was sitting back, his T-shirt stretched gorgeously across his chest, wasn't doing much to help derail her thoughts.

"How about you?" he asked after clearing his throat. "Do you get to go to museums a lot?"

"No, unfortunately. That's why I have all the books."

"Oh yeah. The books."

She couldn't decipher the meaning behind his frown. Then she remembered their conversation in Manny's and the fact that he'd been inside her apartment when she wasn't there. How could she have forgotten?

It'd been three days. What were her dad and Griffin doing now? Were they clearing out her apartment? Were they planning a funeral? An investigation? A war?

"So," she said, because the sudden silence placed terrible pressure on her ears and tear ducts. "You know where I live. You've seen my place. Tit for tat. Where do you live?"

"Live?"

She nudged her chin at the outer wall. "Live. Out there. When you're not working."

"Um . . ."

"Not Washington, I bet."

"You'd win that bet."

"Aha. We're getting somewhere. So where do you sleep at night when you're not"—she opened her arms—"here."

He tilted his head. Opened his mouth. Closed it. Then he rapped his knuckles twice on the doorjamb. "Check."

A poker player, eh? "Seems a bit unfair."

"Does anything about you and I seem fair?" His stare bored into her, frustratingly hot. She couldn't look away. And no, he wasn't being remotely fair, ordering them apart and then looking at her like that.

"Maybe I'll tell you." He sat up. "Someday. If you're a good girl."

Oh, God.

He looked down first. He ran a big hand up his forearm, using his fingernails to test the snaking lines of the vine tattoo that strayed out from under his shirtsleeve. Such a tease. She wanted to do that with her own nails, to know the texture of each and every leaf. Saliva filled her mouth. In her palms the phantom hardness of his body burned.

He looked up at her from under his lashes. "You want to ask me about the tat, don't you."

Her eyes widened. "Can I?"

His hand made a fist. He knocked.

TWENTY-ONE

Part of Reed enjoyed playing with her; it felt so real, so *normal*.
He'd had to stifle a smile on that last check.

Another part of him wanted to tell her more—tell her everything. But that could be more dangerous than the kissing or touching.

The first of his checks she'd tolerated with a gentle roll of the eyes. The second frustrated the hell out of her. She looked ready to crawl across the bathroom tile and smack the secrets of his tat right out of him. There were so many, it would make quite the mess, that was for sure.

He couldn't allow himself to think about her crawling toward him, that hair twisted over one shoulder, hiding one dark eye. Those sweats clinging to her ass. It would lead to him thinking about what else she'd do on her knees, and there wasn't enough money in the world to pay the fine that came with that infraction.

He shifted, trying to disguise his growing hard-on. Gwen had partly risen, now sitting primly on her heels, her hands in her lap. Her nipples were hard, though, and she wasn't wearing a bra.

It was easier, with this space between them. A silly idea, but it seemed to be working.

"Ask me something about myself," she dared, "so I can check you."

He understood her strategy. They fought on uneven ground, with him consistently above, forever having the advantage. It wouldn't get any better, as long as Nora kept her here. Gwen craved to have the upper hand in something. She did—with how she made Reed feel—but he couldn't even give her that tiny little amount or everything would crumble around both of them. That was why he'd pulled away from her earlier today. Why he should stand up right now and shut the doors between them.

He took his time rearranging himself: legs bent, wrists on knees, hands clasped together. "I don't really need to ask. I know a lot."

"How?" Fear swooped across her face. "From Nora?"

"No. Your apartment."

The apartment had seemed normal enough, if you were obsessively neat and didn't have much of a life outside work.

"I know you have a weird thing for shoes, but you seem to wear the same two or three pairs all the time."

"How do you—"

He tapped the bottom of his feet. "Worn soles."

"You looked at the soles of my shoes."

He took her in, the little ball of Gwen, arms wrapped around her waist. Guarded. Unsure. Scared to be here but comfortable enough to want to sit with him. Talking. "I looked at everything," he told her.

He had, too. And he'd almost walked out, because he saw her in every foot of that apartment. The tough, confident woman he'd encountered in the alley. The flirtatious, open woman he'd touched in the bar. The second he'd broken into her place, his target had become a person—a person who'd snagged something deep inside him on her way out of his life. A tough feat in such a short time, especially when his whole life was made up of quick, temporary episodes.

"Your collection of really bad teen movies is stellar, to say the least," he continued. "You have a killer kitchen but you must eat out a lot because there's not anything in your fridge or pantry."

Her lips parted, shocked. But not in a bad way. He clung to that, wanting more.

"You love your family. There are pictures of them everywhere. One sister?"

She nodded, holding her breath.

The photos with her mom stopped when Gwen couldn't have been more than fifteen or sixteen. Dead, he guessed, but he wouldn't bring it up, because he could see the sorrow in her eyes and knew she couldn't talk about it.

He wanted to kiss her for that.

Quick. Put something definite between them.

"Tell me about Griffin. The 'something like that' boyfriend."

"Ha!" She knocked, the sorrow kicking out of her expression. Bright challenge lit up her eyes.

He gladly took up the gauntlet.

"See, I don't think he's your boyfriend at all. I'm guessing, by the picture I saw of the two of you on your shelf, that you guys have been friends for a long time. I'm guessing that he wants something more from you, and maybe you feel a little trapped by that. I think you don't want to be with him. Which was why you were going to go home with me."

She knocked frantically, not realizing that, by doing so, she was answering in the affirmative.

He put a finger to his lips and tilted an ear toward the hall. Gwen watched him, wide-eyed, her hands braced on the door frame, ready to jump up at the slightest signal from him. If ever there was a perfect opportunity for them to cut off this conversation and separate, this was it.

He gave the all-clear sign. Her shoulders relaxed and she settled back into place. So did he.

"It's okay, you know," he said, lowering his voice.

She eyed him. "What is?"

"To feel trapped. To want something else."

"I thought we weren't going there."

He shook his head and waved a hand. "I'm not talking about me. I'm talking in generalities. I'm talking about when you get into something that makes you itch. Makes you feel tied down." Yeah, he knew that well. Too well. "So then you move on, thinking you've cured yourself, cut into the wound to relieve some of the pressure, until you start to get antsy again. And you find a situation exactly like the one you just got out of and it starts all over."

Wow, he hadn't meant to say all that. He scratched at the stubble on the back of his head.

Gwen fixated on a crack in the tile grout, lost in her own thoughts. Apparently he'd hit a nerve.

"We've been best friends since high school, Griffin and I. We've never slept together."

That shouldn't have mattered at all, but Reed had to hide his smile. "So why are you with him?"

She made a face. "Family?"

"Family."

"Yeah. Our families sort of . . . expect it."

Ah. One of those big money, powerful dynasties he'd only heard about or seen on TV. And she went along with that? The Gwen he knew?

"Wow. Okay." He chose his next words carefully. "So you don't want it. Maybe, when this is over, you can break it off with him."

Her head snapped up and she struck him with such a shocked and horrified expression that he actually recoiled. Anger tightened her mouth and set the slash of her eyebrows.

He could tell that she didn't think this would ever be over. She thought she would die here. Everything they couldn't say dropped between them like a rock.

"How did you get into kidnapping, Reed?"

He blinked, determined not to move any other part of his body except his eyelids. "I call it extraction. Or retrieving."

She held up a hand. "Call it whatever the hell you want. What makes you want to do this? What makes you want to destroy a person's life? Because you may not kill anyone, but you're destroying them, regardless."

"Um." He shifted his eyes to the shadowed ceiling and took a few deep breaths.

"Well?"

He could say this. He could. It had nothing to do with them. It wouldn't compromise himself or her.

"I fell into it," he told the ceiling. "When I was a teenager, I thought I was too cool for school, literally. Just barely graduated. Joined the Marines. After that, I had no prospects. A buddy of mine asked me to work security for some guy, some business bigwig. Boring as all hell. I did that for a couple of years in my early twenties, then my employer asked if I'd be willing to find and bring back someone who owed him money." He shrugged. "That's where it started."

Narrowed, accusatory eyes fell on him. "What happened between then and now? That's a pretty big time gap."

"I got really good at setting up extraction jobs—researching them, planning them, going in, and bringing someone out. I got good and I also got . . . addicted."

"Addicted?"

That's it. He'd disgusted her.

He'd never dealt with shame on the job before. Usually, well into the process like he was now, he'd have that interior wall firmly up. He'd be the Retriever until he walked away. But Gwen, true to form, had demolished that wall, and the guilt and shame he usually felt after he collapsed in his own bed now flowed around him.

"It's a rush, all that knowledge. All that power. All that fucking adrenaline. And it lasts for days, weeks. A massive surge, all the way up until final payment . . ." His voice died. Just dropped off.

"Sooner or later you'll crash."

He barked out a laugh. "I crash every time. Every single job. It ends and I sit in my place and wallow in what I've done. I can't stand it. Can't stand sitting around feeling sorry for myself. Can't stand the boredom. Can't stand all the damn thinking. Then another job comes and I stab myself with the needle, start the high all over again." It hurt so much, to tell her this, but he couldn't stop now. "So I know a thing or two about being trapped. About being caught in a machine you don't know how to turn off. Or aren't really sure you even want to stop."

At last he looked at her, and man, was she a sight. All fierce and beautiful, delicate and demanding. Everything he needed, all at once.

"Want to know something else?" he asked, because apparently he'd shocked her speechless.

"What?"

"I'm not sure I want to be cured. Or even if I can be. I keep thinking that I want out, that I want to stop the cycle, but I don't know if it's possible. It's how I'm wired."

And why, above everything else, he feared being caught by Tracker or the police. Because for someone else to end it all would destroy him. When he left, he'd do it on his terms. When he was capable.

"I don't understand what possible joy you get out of it. Isn't what you do supposed to fulfill you on some level?" She winced and pulled her arms tighter around her midsection, and he knew she'd just turned the spotlight on herself.

He considered that, head bent. "I've gone after a lot of people who owe money. I've extracted hostages so the police won't get involved, for whatever reason. All my clients are shady." He tilted his torso sideways, pressing his temple to the door frame. "All except this one job, nine or so years back."

"One?"

"There was this kid who left home. Eighteen years old and technically an adult, so legally his parents couldn't make him come back. And his parents weren't exactly law-abiding citizens so they didn't want to open themselves to police speculation. Anyway, the kid got sucked into a cult and claimed he wasn't being held against his will. His parents hired me to get him out of this crazy compound. Now that kid's a speaker and activist against cults."

He didn't know Gwen's reaction because he couldn't look at her. The whole speech felt strange . . . and strangely cathartic.

"I think about that a lot," he said into the silence. "Every job that comes in, I hope it might be something like that. But there's precious few opportunities for good among the people I know."

"Why can't you just leave?" she asked softly.

The look he threw at her was harder than he'd intended. "Because I've been off the government radar since leaving the service. Suddenly reappearing out of thin air? I just don't know what'll happen. How can I do it? Get back into . . . life? So I keep going and going with what I know. Like a fucking robot."

"So do something else." She didn't sound angry anymore, just frustrated. As frustrated as he was with himself.

He threw out his arms. "Like what? You think I wouldn't if I had the options? I limped through school. I've been a ghost for fifteen years. Convicted felons would have an easier time getting real work and would probably have more motivation." God, he sounded so weak. To think he was worthless and directionless and living a dead-end life was one thing, but to admit it out loud? To someone he actually liked?

"Know what? Never mind. Opening my mouth was a bad idea." He jumped to his feet and knocked on the door frame. "I'm done."

He whirled back to his room.

Her angry voice struck him in the back. "You know how to fix that guilt, don't you?"

He paused, looked over his shoulder. She'd risen to her feet, too.

"Get me out of here," she said.

He sighed, head hanging. He'd get Gwen through this and then he'd take off. Quit the game. Hide. But if he didn't see Gwen safely to the other side, he'd be Tracker's. Or the Feds'. He had to stick around and so did she.

"I can't."

He waited for her to slam the door in his face. Instead she lightly pressed the door shut. The click reverberated in his head. And in his heart.

TWENTY-TWO

"The phrase Genesai says over and over," Nora demanded. "What does it mean?"

Gwen stood with Nora at the end of the short pier extending out into the lake. A sharp bluff rose on the right, cutting off views of the neighbors. A boathouse squatted on the left, blocking the southern shoreline.

Distantly Gwen could hear the call of the water knocking at her subconscious, trying to get in, but the *nelicoda* Reed had made her swallow an hour ago had kicked in nice and strong. She could jump in and swim like a Primary, of course, but the guard with the rifle looked like he was a good shot. And she'd never really been a good swimmer with her arms and legs. Classic Ofarian arrogance.

Nora had brought Gwen here to taunt her, to show her what she could not touch. Because of that, Gwen took an even greater pleasure in lying. Against Nora, knowledge was a far more powerful weapon than water or a gun. She told Nora she had no idea what Genesai was saying.

"That's unacceptable," Nora spit. "Our window is closing. Rapidly."

Gwen threw out her arms. "I don't understand what more you want me to do. Genesai passed out. When he wakes up, I'll try again." *And I won't tell you a goddamn thing until I've figured out my own path.*

The dock vibrated as someone approached. Gwen held her breath, thinking—hoping?—it might be Reed. But it was Adine, her small footsteps making a big ruckus over the wooden slats. The tiny Tedran held two stainless steel coffee mugs. When she reached them, Nora took one mug without saying anything. Adine turned to Gwen and extended the other mug.

Gwen intended to refuse, but her body craved caffeine. She took the mug, curtly thanked Adine, and downed the thick black stuff in a couple of shots. As she lowered her arm, she saw Adine staring at her. Not just waiting for Gwen to finish drinking, but out-and-out staring. Opened jaw and stiff posture, to boot. Behind her rounded eyes there was something else. It wasn't anger, like with Xavier, or frustration and condescension, like with Nora. It wasn't fear. Wonder, maybe? Awe?

Gwen shifted uncomfortably. Was this what it would be like if Nora got her way and the world found out about Secondaries? Would people stop and stare at Gwen like she'd grown a third arm?

"You can go, Adine," Nora said.

Adine very nearly snapped to attention. Then she bent her head, took Gwen's mug without looking at her again, and hurried back to the house.

"Her father was a Primary," Nora said when Adine was out of earshot.

That explained Adine's lightened Secondary signature. Interbreeding wasn't something Ofarians ever did, so Gwen hadn't been able to readily explain it. Not for the first time, she wondered about Delia, whether her sister had had children with her Primary. Whether Gwen was an aunt.

Nora frowned into her mug. "He's the only man I ever loved. But he found out what I was, and then he couldn't exist anymore."

This woman just got more awful by the second.

"When was that?" Gwen asked.

"Beginning of last century. The Ofarians couldn't use Adine anyway. She has no glamour. But her mind . . . her mind is something extraordinary." She said *extraordinary* like the Brits did, dividing it into two words.

Nora sipped her coffee, her lips curling into a smile over the rim. "Reed knows about Adine. Not that she's Tedran, but what her mind can do—*has* done. He thinks he'll be able to hold it over us in case things don't go his way, but anything he knows will be worthless once we're gone." Another sip, another smile. "I think I got a good deal on him."

The pleasantly chilled autumn day turned arctic cold.

Gwen's eyes skated over the house's sloped grounds. Where was Reed? There, by the guard's hut, leaning on the wall near the door, speaking to the gruff-looking guy inside. Badass small talk. Gwen was learning Reed's body language, though, and no matter where he was positioned, he always kept an eye on her.

How could she convey to him to *get out now*? He was aiming a plastic toy gun at a charging tank. She was as good as dead anyway, and nothing he knew—or *thought* he knew—would save her. It would just keep him in the crosshairs, if not of Nora's weapon then of the Ofarians'. Because if Gwen got out of this alive and she had to tell her people everything that had happened here, Reed's life would be over anyway.

Griffin was very good at erasing Primary eyewitnesses.

Xavier stalked across the terrace then took the steps two at a time down to the water. Nora turned to watch him approach.

"Well?" she asked in Tedranish when he reached the two women.

"Still some unrest in the Plant," he replied in the same language. "They're asking for you. They need more proof."

Nora swore under her breath.

"It's so sudden," he added, remembering his own reaction to Nora two years ago and applying it to the dozens of wide-eyed Tedrans he and Nora had been secretly speaking to for days.

Nora pressed a hand to her forehead. "I can't afford to go back. I want to be available when Genesai wakes up. I need to go back with Gwen."

Xavier growled in frustration. She was losing sight of her priorities. "You can't afford not to go back. If they don't believe you—if they don't believe *in* you—all of this is pointless."

Nora pinched her lips, those midnight dark eyes dancing in thought.

"We have Muscle now, right?" He nodded disdainfully in Reed's direction. "Let him take Gwen back. Your people need you."

Nora locked eyes with Gwen, and after a few dreadfully long moments, the older woman nodded.

He exhaled and thrust a finger in Gwen's face. "Will the ship fly?"

She backed off a step and he enjoyed her retreat. "I don't know yet," she said. He liked hearing her speak Tedranish, like she had to come down to his level. "That's just what I was telling Nora."

"Get your ass moving. It could be any day now."

Gwen blanched. Good.

"Here's what's going to happen." Nora crossed her arms. "The Ofarians will follow the same protocol they did last time they moved the Plant. They'll do it at night, loading the slaves into a big truck. Adine's secured our own truck. She'll drive; I'll disguise it with glamour."

"And Xavier?" Gwen prompted.

He cleared his throat. "I'll be with the slaves."

He recalled the hushed, one-sided conversations he'd recently had with 111J and 003AC and every other grown Tedran as they'd lolled in their cells. Some of the men remembered him; all of the women did. They were in awe he'd escaped, but what they really wanted was to be touched and acknowledged by Nora, the mastermind behind their freedom. Their queen.

Then Gwen did something so unexpected he thought he might have been hallucinating.

She rounded on Nora. "I can't believe you keep making him go back there."

Even Nora seemed taken aback. She sputtered, "It's . . . it's what he knows. Where he's needed."

"And where he was *tortured*!"

Out of the corner of his eye, Xavier noticed Reed pull away from the guard hut. A small movement, one he masked by sweeping his eyes over the entire compound, but he'd reacted to Gwen's outburst, that was for sure.

Xavier hated that he'd shown Gwen so much of himself that day in the Plant. He wished he were anonymous. He wished he could look at this whole thing with distant eyes like Nora and Adine. But he couldn't, and he'd die before Gwen saw any more weakness in him.

He inserted himself between Gwen and Nora. "As the Tedrans are being moved outside, away from the neutralizers,

I'll give the signal and the quickest-reacting ones will cloak themselves and any others they can. They'll board the hidden truck, we'll bring them to the lake and Genesai's ship." He looked slyly at Gwen. "And the world will get a really interesting show."

She clamped her fingers on his arm, her pinch angry and electric. "What do you mean, the 'quickest-reacting ones'?"

He spun away from her, from what her awful proximity did to him. "Don't touch me." He rubbed his arm where she'd grabbed him. "Not everyone will have power. The children who haven't hit puberty, the pregnant women, the others who are coming off being drained—they need the strong ones, the ones who are waiting for the signal, to cloak them."

"The opening will be small," Nora mused, tapping her lips. "Outside there are no permanent neutralizers, but the Ofarian guards will have neutralizer guns."

"What if the Tedrans don't react in time?" Gwen's sharp eyes darted between Nora and Xavier. She'd figured it out: the big, giant hole in the plan. "What will happen?" she shouted.

Xavier looked to Nora, who met Gwen's demanding stare with cool regard. "Some of us will not be making the journey," Nora said.

Gwen grabbed two handfuls of her hair and whirled away, stamping to the end of the dock. Xavier flinched, fearing she'd make a dive for it. He couldn't go after her; neither could Nora.

But Gwen just stood at the edge, taking deep breaths. After gathering herself, she came back. "Your plan won't work."

"It's the only way," Nora said. "We may have to suffer losses. Leave behind a few to help the greater numbers."

"So the punishment you want my people to face—the fear, the scrutiny, the media circus—you are willing to inflict on your own people. The weaker ones, too." Neither Nora nor Xavier said anything, and Gwen barreled on. "It'll be a new kind of slavery. You know that, right? You'll rip your people out of one cage and shove them into another."

Nora lifted her chin. "Xavier has made all this known to them. They understand their sacrifice."

He dropped his head, watching the gray water shimmer through the cracks in the dock. When he'd told the slaves that part, almost all had cried. They understood because they'd been forced to. They had no other option. His heart was already broken, but this chiseled chunks off its hard lump. Gwen understood his pain, and he didn't know how to deal with that.

But if Nora believed this plan to be the best way, so did he.

"No." The anguished sound of Gwen's voice brought his head back up. "*No.* You're not using me the right way."

"What do you mean?" Xavier began, but Nora held up a hand to him.

"You took me because I'm the Translator, but I'm something more among my people. My dad is the Chairman. I'm the only family he has left. He will listen to me. My *people* listen to me. They respect me. Let me take what I know back to San Francisco. Let me confront the Board and figure out another way to—"

"Do you still honestly believe your father isn't fully aware of what goes on in the Plant?"

Gwen paused and Xavier held his breath. "I can't say what he knows, only that I know he's a good man and he loves me and will listen to me. The Board is divided, more on my dad's side than on Jonah's. All I have to do is get to the Chairman and we'll have the strongest ally imaginable on our side."

Our side. Xavier didn't know how he felt about those words on her lips.

Nora's head snapped back as though she'd been slapped. Even her eyes watered. "And you think that Chairman Ian Carroway would volunteer to help destroy the company he's built up? You're delusional. You've been infected by the Company mentality, the Ofarian arrogance."

"Every Ofarian I know outside the Board would be mortified to know what's happening to your people. That's the truth."

"Maybe. But they have no power against your Board, or against what the Board has built. Your culture, your whole existence, revolves around *Mendacia*. You think your people will want to destroy all that? What will they do then?"

Gwen's mouth opened for a swift retort, but Xavier got the feeling it was more a reflex, because she quickly closed it. By the slump in her shoulders, he knew what Nora had said had hit home.

"You think on that some more," Nora said, "then go back to Genesai and get us our ship."

TWENTY-THREE

The argument stopped as abruptly as it had started, making Reed uneasy. The echoes of that foreign language lasted long after Nora turned and walked away. Xavier loped after his diminutive leader.

Gwen stayed at the dock's edge. She looked ready to jump in and swim for it. Reed prepped himself to go in after her, boots and all.

Nora didn't spare Reed a glance as she swept past, but Xavier paused at the bottom of the stone steps going up to the house. Xavier looked pointedly between Reed and Gwen, frowning, then lumbered toward the terrace.

What was that all about?

"Hey, man." Frank, the ex-motorcycle gang member, ex-con hired guard with the missing fingers, slipped out of the hut Reed reclined against. "Gotta take a shit. You got eyes on this place for a few minutes?"

Reed had eyes for more than just this place. He nodded, nonchalant.

"Thanks," Frank said before dashing to the back of the boathouse, where, apparently, there was a toilet.

Reed surveyed the area. Frank, gone. Nora and Xavier, inside. Cameras sweeping all around.

The dock lurched under his feet. Gwen stood with her arms wrapped tightly around her stomach.

She whirled, bit out something in that weird language.

He held up his hands. "Just me."

Conflict rippled across her expression. She didn't want to

be happy to see him, yet she was. He couldn't put a word to the way that made him feel.

She swiveled back to the water. "They took me for the wrong reasons, Reed. And I'm not doing any good trapped here."

He recognized the dig at the tense way their conversation had ended last night. They really did stand on opposite sides of the DMZ. Suspicious, selfish, and passionate, the both of them.

He didn't say anything. Couldn't say anything.

They stood side by side for many long minutes, gazing across the lake. He could feel the vibration of her tension, the shiver of anger.

"It's my birthday today," he blurted out.

She looked up at him. "Nuh-uh."

He nodded. "It is. Thirty-eight. Happy birthday to me."

"Last night you said you were thirty-seven."

"I was. Last night." He nudged the zipper of his jacket to his chin, wishing he'd brought a hat out. Fall had kicked out Indian summer sometime during the night. He'd celebrated his birthday in all kinds of weather, all over the globe. "Know anything about Libra guys?"

She shook her head and returned her eyes to the water, but she was also biting her lip to keep from smiling. Good. The tension eased some. Her shoulders came down from around her ears.

"That's okay." He grinned. "Neither do I."

That time, she did smile. It died quickly, though, terrified eyes darting around.

"Camera is on top of the guard hut," he said. "Looking at our backs."

"Did you take some sort of class on this? 'Keeping Your Hostages Calm 101' or something like that?"

He took in the blue-gray of the mountains beyond and the relaxing sound of the waves, and imagined himself and Gwen in another time. Maybe lounging in deck chairs with a couple of beers, the same stunning scene stretching at their feet. He'd touch her hand, her hair, and she wouldn't have to hide her smile. Neither would he.

"No," he replied. "It's just for you."

A different kind of tension stiffened her body. "I want to go back inside."

She skirted around him and started back down the dock. As always, he was left to trot at her heels.

In daylight, everything about her was brighter. He liked the sway of her hair. A burgundy leaf swirled on the wind and got snagged in the layers that draped down her back. He wanted to reach over and comb it out.

As he trailed behind, the scent of her enveloped him. After she'd showered that morning—and out of her eyesight—he'd buried his face in her towel. They used the same soap, but something about that damp terry cloth smelled distinctly of her.

Space. They needed space. So he fell back a few steps, putting a good twenty feet between them.

In front of the guard hut she stopped, turned. Waited for him. Damn it, why'd she do that? Didn't she know what he was fighting here? If he could, he'd push her against the wall, slide his thigh between hers, and kiss her until every muscle in her body loosened. He'd pull that leaf from her hair and trail his mouth along her throat.

As though sensing what hot thoughts scored his mind, her lips parted. In the sunlight, the irises of her wicked bedroom eyes glowed the deepest amber. Being smarter than him, she was the first to snap out of their mutual haze.

She wheeled away and hurried into the house.

Midafternoon the faucet ran in the bathroom. Reed must have dozed off. His weird watch declared it 4 p.m. Gwen must have slept, too. He rolled off the bed and went to the bathroom door.

"Gwen?" He rapped softly with a knuckle. "You okay?"

No response. A hypersensitive mix of worry and Retriever instincts set in. Maybe she'd turned on the faucet to distract him while she tried to jimmy open the window or something. He flung open the door.

Gwen jumped back from the sink. "I told you to stop doing that!"

"Sorry. I knocked. Thought you'd heard."

Jesus, she was wearing his T-shirt again. Bare legs ending in toes with chipped red polish. She'd wrapped her long hair in a messy knot on top of her head, damp strands dangling around her face. Tousled and natural and touchable and hot beyond words.

"Ah-ah." She backed into her doorway, pointing to the tiled floor. "DMZ. Remember?"

He blinked, looked down, and realized he'd taken a half step into the bathroom.

How did they wind up back here so soon? Was this all they had? Cryptic, circular, sexually tense conversations over a bargain toilet and cheap towels?

Like last night, they watched each other across the small bathroom. No food between them this time. Instead there was something else, intangible but real, and it tingled every one of his nerves. Every inch of his skin.

He didn't want her to disappear. "I thought of something else to ask you."

She made a fist, ready to check with a knock. "Okay."

"Um. Can I ask what language you guys were speaking?" Good one, genius.

She eyed him. "You can. But I won't say."

"Fair enough. But you speak Japanese, too, right?"

She nodded without hesitation; she couldn't exactly deny that one.

"I'm guessing, for your job, you're an interpreter." He thought it was a safe topic; her real-life paycheck couldn't have anything to do with why Nora wanted her. Could it? Something odd and dangerous and fearful flashed in her eyes. "Do you speak a lot of languages?"

Her arms folded across her chest, drawing up the hem of the T-shirt. He lasered his eyes on hers to avoid the slopes of her inner thighs. She leaned casually against the door frame, one ankle crossed over the other. "Answer a question of mine first."

Oh boy. "I'll try. This could end in a draw, though."

He curled his fingers, ready to check.

"Why vines?"

He sucked in a breath. Held it. Unfurled his fingers. Where to begin?

"You know how some people have a bunch of different tats?" he began slowly, not really understanding where his mouth was going. "Lots of random stuff crowded all together?

Like whenever they think of something new they want, they just slap it up there?"

Her eyes positively shined. She nodded, the knot on top of her head bobbing.

"Well, I didn't want that. I knew a bunch of little stuff that I wanted on me, but I didn't want it to look like a big mess. I didn't want to just be painted. It had to come together, to have a bigger purpose. When I was in the Brazilian rain forest, I got this idea of connecting it all. It's easy to add to, too, when I want."

She pulled away from the door frame. "So . . . it's not just vines?"

He looked at her for a long time—just looked at her—before slowly shaking his head. "There's other stuff in there."

How long did she stare at him? Could have been forever and he'd be willing to commit to another day or two.

"Will you take your shirt off?" she whispered.

Bad idea. Such a bad idea.

He grabbed the T-shirt behind his neck and pulled it forward over his head. He considered the plain gray fabric and all that it hid from the world and from her, then tossed it to the side.

Gwen gasped, much like she had when she'd first seen his chest. One of her red-painted feet inched across the floor. Her legs shook, as did the air in her throat.

"Careful." He barely recognized his own voice. "Guns are trained on you. Dangerous crossing."

Her mouth teased a smile. Three steps away—safe, just out of his reach, thank God—she stopped. Still, her eyes swept over every inch of his tattoo. Shoulder, biceps, chest, obliques, ribs . . . Her virtual touch slowly killed him. He just stood there and took it, dying the very best kind of death.

Keeping her arms clasped tightly around her back, she leaned forward. "Oh, I see now. There are words in the vines. And pictures in the leaves."

He focused on the knot in her hair. On how he wanted to slide out that rubber band.

One hand snaked out from behind her back, fingers splayed wide. He inhaled, waiting—*Come on. Touch me. End this. Start this. Whatever*—but she snatched her arm back.

"It's beautiful, Reed. Like it's part of you. Like you were born with it."

He had to close his eyes for a second, to stamp down the memories of him, shirtless, hovering over her half-naked body. Here they were again, in the exact same state of undress.

"Pick one," she said, "and tell me about it."

He hadn't even told his tattoo artist, just handed over the idea or told him the word or whatnot, and let him go at it. But for Gwen . . . he was going to do it. He was actually going to do it.

Raising a hand, he touched his left pec. By memory he knew everything he'd put on his skin and exactly where. His fingers trailed across his marathon time from a decade ago; the name of his Marines unit; the image of Pikes Peak, near where he'd extracted that kid from the cult. His hand came to rest on three names.

"These," he declared.

"Edward and Elise and Page," she read, squinting.

It shouldn't be this difficult to talk. Not with Gwen. "Page is my sister. Edward and Elise are my parents."

The hand that had resisted touching him now rested on her lips. "I'm sorry. Are they dead?"

"No." He gave her a slow, reassuring smile. "They're in Virginia."

It felt good to tell her that. No, better than good. And he loved her reaction—the relief that came from knowing his family was still intact—followed by genuine, warm surprise.

"Virginia?" She scrunched up her nose. Don't know why he'd never noticed the faint freckles there before. "You're from Virginia?"

"Yeah. You find that hard to believe?"

"I guess. You don't have an accent."

He shrugged. "It sort of fell away after I left. Saw the world. I haven't lived there since I was eighteen and that was, what, twenty years ago now?"

"But your parents are still there? And your sister?"

"Yep. Go back and see them when I can. Which isn't a lot, unfortunately."

Bittersweetness tinged her smile and he remembered the photos on display in her apartment. The mom he guessed who was dead, the sister who apparently was no longer around, and her father.

"I send my parents money," he said. "They're getting up there in age and it's hard to maintain the farm. One day they'll sell, but I want to make sure they don't wear themselves out before their time. And Page has some learning disabilities, so she still lives with them even though she's only three years younger than me."

"Oh. I'm sorry to hear that."

He waved her off. No need to feel sorry for Page; that woman was endlessly happy. Now that he thought about it, Gwen would probably really like his sister.

"Naw, it's all good," he said. "I like to be a part of them, help them out, even if I can't be there."

"So you're a good son, huh?"

A veil of pure lust draped around her, pulling him into its confines. But then she checked herself, shook her head, and backed away.

Don't go, he silently begged.

"So how many?" he asked out loud.

She blinked, her hand absentmindedly smoothing her wispy hair. "What?"

He smiled. "How many languages do you speak?"

Her lips tightened. She wasn't going to tell him. Goddamn it, she'd played him.

"Twenty-two," she replied on an exhale. "Wait. Twenty-three." Then she turned and made a beeline for her room.

Reed's mind reeled. Twenty-three languages? No one spoke that many. *What the hell was going on in this house?*

"Gwen."

She halted, her back to him, the T-shirt draping delectably over the curve of her ass. As she slowly turned around, she toyed with the hem. More thigh, more skin. A pained look pulled her expression taut. He recognized it because he felt it, too.

His heavy head dropped, and he studied his own bare feet. A deep breath, in and out. Another. A slow lift of the chin. A heated meeting of their eyes.

He touched his chest again, where her presence had lodged itself. "Oh, who are we kidding?"

Who lunged first, he'd never know. The space between them shattered into a million pieces. They collided, a tangle of limbs and tongues. Her warm body at last against his. His hands slid all over her, ending at that soft, smooth place where her ass met her thighs. He lifted her with ease, adrenaline and desire making him feel like a giant. The slow wrap of her legs around his waist found some deep, hidden chord inside him and plucked it, the vibrations shuddering through him, centered in his dick. The taste of her mouth exploded in his brain. He groaned, deep and low.

She pulled away enough to whisper with a smile against his lips, "Shh," and then she took his mouth again.

He wouldn't fight it this time. There was no hope but for surrender.

The DMZ went up in flames.

TWENTY-FOUR

Her body soared within Reed's eager, urgent clutch. He held her like she might dissolve at any moment, and maybe she would. His mouth moved over hers, slow and wet. She clung to his hard body, the strength in his arms intensified by the way he supported her. Cradled her, almost, since she felt light as mist.

She slid her tongue against his, willfully defying their previous vow to stay away from each other, thumbing her nose at that idiot back in the Range Rover who actually thought she could keep such a promise. And damn, if it wasn't delicious defiance.

A stripe of dull pain slanted across her back and she pulled away in a daze, realizing he'd slammed her into the bathroom wall. One thick thigh pressed between hers, and his vines and cryptic words and history enveloped her. A dark, animal look clouded his eyes. Leaning in for more, his soft lips, surrounded by perpetual stubble, nipped at hers, teasing but not taking.

"I've been wanting to kiss you like this . . ." he began but didn't finish, the tip of his tongue instead tracing the corner of her mouth.

"You already have."

He shook his head. "Doesn't count. Your head wasn't in the right place. There was something huge between us. There isn't now." He sank his hands into the hair at the nape of her neck, tilting back her head, exposing her throat. She went after his mouth again but he held her skull firm against the wall. "Is there, Gwen?"

"No." And, stars' blessing, she spoke the truth.

The Allure caused temporary insanity. That was how the Ofarians had always billed it: mindless desire that dissipated after orgasm. Uncontrollable, fleeting, forgettable. Whatever this was between them, it had crushed the Allure under its boot heel and left it in the dust. And she hadn't even come. Yet.

"It's just us," she said.

He smiled, that dimple winking in and out. "Oh, thank God."

He sank against her, and even though she couldn't breathe, all she could think was that this would be the best way to go, with him stealing her breath and crushing her body. His erection felt harder than what was humanly possible, with her in only her underwear and him clad only in jeans. The rough ridge of the denim rode against her as he circled his hips, echoing the motion she longed to feel without anything between them.

His whole body started to shake, an earthquake consuming them both. Suddenly he went still, pulled away. Pressing his forehead to hers, his breath sawed raggedly.

"You're shaking." She pressed feebly at his shoulders. "You can put me down." Hoping that he wouldn't.

"It's not . . . you're not heavy." His eyes squeezed painfully shut. "God, I want to be in you. Say yes. If you say no, I won't touch you again, won't even look at you. Though it'll kill me."

It would kill her, too. Cinching her arms around his neck, she breathed hot into his ear, *"Yes,"* and prayed she wasn't making a colossal mistake.

A shudder traveled from his scalp to his feet. He ripped her away from the wall, spun, and charged into her bedroom. She held on as he collapsed backward onto the low bed, taking her with him. The severely slanted ceiling had other ideas and collided with her forehead in a loud *thud*.

"Ow!" She pressed a hand to her hairline.

Reed sat up, legs bent over the foot of the bed. She was straddling his lap, her knees still wrapped around his firm waist, and he was trying not to laugh. "That did not just happen."

"Unfortunately it did."

"I had this big, sexy, sweep-you-off-your-feet thing all planned in my head. How come it never works out exactly like your fantasy? Let me see."

"Well, you definitely got the sweeping part down."

He pried away her fingers, took her face in his hands, and stretched up to kiss the knob that hurt. "I think you'll live."

That statement hung between them, swaying in a nonexistent breeze. She'd live, yes. Today and maybe tomorrow. But after that?

As he tilted her head back down, their eyes met. His thumbs caressed her cheeks. "What are we doing?" he murmured.

The huge space behind her rib cage ached. "Don't say anything else." She slid her hands up his pecs, her fingers pale against the dark of his tattoo. He was so warm, and now that she finally got to touch the designs, she felt like she was touching a part of him no one else ever had.

He gave her a slight nod, understanding. Talking never seemed to work out for them. It always circled back to where they were. How they'd gotten there. Where they were going.

Trust.

She curled her fingers, digging her nails into him. It drew a tiny gasp from him, his eyes going cloudy. He was pure sex, raw desire, forcibly shoved into a man's gorgeously painted skin, forever trying to get out. The urge to tell him, over and over again, how roughly beautiful he was filled her brain and pressed against her tongue. How had she ever successfully ignored an attraction this intense?

Because . . . a tiny voice inside her offered.

Shut up. She quickly squashed that train of thought before it took off, instead concentrating on the gentle lift of his hand, the tug of his fingers as he pried loose the rubber band. The swish of her hair tickled her neck and back, sending vivid chills across her body. Then she realized it wasn't her hair doing that but his fingers, combing through the strands. He pulled sections of her hair forward over her shoulders and drew his fingers down to the ends, where they rested just above her nipples. There he froze. Lifted his blue, blue eyes to hers.

"You look good in my shirt."

"You look good in nothing."

His jaw circled, like an animal licking its chops. He toyed with the hem of her T-shirt. "Let me see you."

Raising her arms, he slowly lifted the shirt to reveal her, piece by piece. Arching, she offered herself to him. He used the fabric to tease her nipples, then replaced the thin cotton with his hot mouth.

"God, you're . . ." he croaked.

"What?" She didn't search for validation or a compliment. She craved knowing each of his thoughts, wanting to know where his head was at.

He drew a line with his palm from her neck, down between her breasts, to her stomach. "Beyond words."

The T-shirt might have disappeared into thin air for all she knew, because suddenly his big hands cupped her breasts from below, and he feasted on her sensitive nipples like a starved man. She reached behind her, clamped her fingers onto his thighs, and let him take what he wanted. Because she desired whatever he did, and everything he did or said sent shimmering waves over her skin to center at the place where her damp underwear rubbed against that incredible bulge.

She had to move. Had to feel more. Her hips circled, gyrated. She'd come that way if she kept it up, her tender clit hitting just the right spot. His fingers dug into her ass. The cool wetness on her chest brought her back to reality. She lifted her head to stare into his heated expression.

"Enough," he growled, "or I'll never last."

"I can't help it." Another slow circle, making them both shudder.

He inhaled all her breath when he took her mouth this time. He could have it all if he wanted; it was his for now. The kiss was hard and hot, and he held her so perfectly still. His hand slid around her ass and lifted her body slightly. He dipped around back and used the gentle pad of a finger to draw a long, slow line over her underwear from back to front and back again.

That was when she lost her mind, when all thought vanished and the only things she was aware of were the places their bodies touched. When she whimpered, he pulled away and whispered with a naughty grin, "Shh."

But then his fingers made mockery of the elastic in her underwear, sliding easily underneath. He lifted her more onto her knees and immediately slid two fingers between her slick skin and into the place that had gone liquid for him. He penetrated her, knuckle-deep, from behind. She moaned loud into his neck, letting his warm, taut skin bear the brunt of her verbal desire.

"God, you're so wet."

"For . . . you," she murmured in time with his down-tempo thrusts. "It's all for you."

He groaned. His whole body went limp. In a flurry of action, he flipped them over so she was sitting on the bed and he stood before her.

He pointed to her underwear. "Off."

She tossed him a smirk and pointed to his jeans. "Off yourself."

It turned into a frantic race to see who could get completely naked first. She, with only little white underwear, lost. Reed loomed above her, strong, painted, gloriously hard in all the right places. Eye level with his huge erection, all she could think was *That's for me*.

She went to her knees on the low bed. His abs contracted expectantly. Who was she to disappoint? Crawling forward, she filled her mouth with him. No preamble. Like his fingers inside her, she just went for him. His hips started to pump, and the thick slide of him against her tongue and lips made her mouth water. The taste of him, the suction, the withheld moans on both sides . . . it was too much.

His hands sank into her hair and pulled her off him with a pop and a gasp.

"I don't want to stop," she said, but he wasn't looking at her. His head was turned to the side, his eyes shut hard. His chest heaved with barely contained restraint.

"No." His eyes opened, searing her. "I said I wanted inside you." A wicked grin spread across his face. "But first . . ."

One second she was on her knees, the next he'd positioned her on her back. Reed pulled her bottom to the edge of the bed and sank between her thighs. He stretched his arms beneath her knees, pushing her legs back, and grabbed her wrists. The immobility scared her for about a half second, then his magic tongue made everything else go away.

Soft and teasing at first, taking a maddeningly long time, he licked her. Swirled her. Tasted her. He listened to her body, using deliberate strokes of his tongue and lips that built and built up to insistent. Masterful. His heavy breathing filled the small bedroom, and she got off on the fact that this turned him on as much as her.

When he released one of her arms and slid those fingers back inside her, she came instantly. Violently. She bit her lip before the cry escaped. His mouth kept moving, taking her up and up, and just when she thought they'd reached the top, her body tumbled into helpless movement. She gave it free rein, letting the little earthquakes and the starbursts of pleasure consume her.

After she'd calmed somewhat, he sat back on his heels, wiped his mouth with the back of his hand, and smiled. "Been wanting to see you quiver."

Moving as one, she scooted back on the bed as he crawled over her, his huge body hovering like it had the other night. He kissed her, her arms twining around his neck. One of his knees knocked her thigh out to the side and he settled into the cradle of her body, the tip of his cock pressing against where he'd made her melt.

He exhaled on a hiss, his head dropping to the crook of her neck.

"Please." She wrapped a leg around his hip.

"Oh, Gwen." His mouth curved against her skin. "You don't need to beg me."

He pushed himself inside. Gentle but firm. Millimeter by agonizing millimeter until he filled her and started to move. Curling his hips upward, he hit this amazing spot deep, deep inside her. Her body still pulsed from what he'd done earlier, and she grabbed fistfuls of the bed sheet to anchor herself. Even so, he felt like flying—the scary, sinking sensation on the descent coupled with the swoosh of adrenaline on takeoff.

"Better than I imagined," he stuttered. "Perfect."

The rhythm he found inside her was like music. A steady, deliberate beat. A little bit romantic, all the way hot. But soon it wasn't enough—for either of them. He rose up, tilting her ass higher with one hand, balancing himself on the other, and . . . stopped.

He looked down at her, and what she saw on his face was deeper than finally fulfilled desire. Stronger than perfunctory lust. She couldn't define it, but she understood.

She rocked her hips and he ran with the cue, slowly sliding out then plunging hard back in. Head back, back arched, she loved the deep stab, how he was pouring that hard-won emotion into the movement of his body and just letting it go.

Another completely unexpected orgasm barreled down on her. She had enough time to grab a pillow and bury her face in it, screaming her pleasure. This orgasm felt wonderfully different, its source emanating from that place deep inside he stroked so perfectly. And because it took a different path, started from a new origin than what he'd done with his tongue, it hit different points of pleasure. The shudders came slower, but their peaks and troughs were more pronounced and she rode them gladly.

There was another reason for the pillow. She didn't want him to see how much he affected her. In this raw, most naked of moments, she knew she couldn't hold it back.

"Jesus," he swore under his breath as her body subsided. "Another?" He plucked the pillow from her face, slanted his mouth across hers. "I could watch you come all day."

He started to move again. Easy at first, then building speed and pressure, until his hips pounded out his own desire, to his own rhythm. She made herself pliant, let him use her the way he'd dreamed, because she'd been dreaming about it, too.

Enraptured, she watched his powerful body buckle. Listened to the strangled sound of his own muffled orgasm. Felt him pulse inside her. He bared his teeth like an animal and never, not once, took his eyes off hers. He wanted her to see what he felt, and it was beautiful and overwhelming.

"You are . . ." he said with a great sigh. He fitted himself on top of her and his weight took them both deeper into the covers. But he never finished that thought. It was okay; she got it.

She slid her hands over the rasp of his skull stubble and turned his head to make him look directly at her. "You are, too," she said.

Starlight melted in his eyes; it was the only way to describe the warmth she saw in them. He kissed her with unapologetic reverence. When at last he pulled out of her, Gwen whimpered in the absence. He rolled over, and looked down.

"Oh, shit."

"I'm clean," she blurted out, feeling beyond awkward. "Been tested for everything." Ofarian policy, pending any engagement announcement. "You?"

"Me, too." He blinked, looking like a target in a gun range. "But what about the other part?"

"It's okay. I've got it covered." She really didn't want to explain the finer points of IUDs.

They remained frozen, inches apart on a tousled bed. He looked torn about what to do next, and glanced at her expectantly. Should he slide closer and hold her like a lover? Or back off, their needs satiated? Truth be told, she didn't have a clue. Too many *should* and *shouldn't*s rattled around in her brain, mixing haphazardly with the *want*s and *need to*s. One glance around the room told them exactly where they were and that what they'd just given in to compromised them both in too many ways to count.

But she did know one thing. He was right; they'd felt perfect together. And in more than just the physical way.

Fear must have shown on her face, because he suddenly reached for her. He pulled her on top of him, mingling their heat. His arms glided around her back, his muscles so thick and long they blanketed her from shoulder to hip. She drank in the smell of him—the soap they had to share, the starch of the sheets, the sex sweat—and tried to relax in his arms.

Warm fingers trailed up and down her spine.

"I've got you," he murmured. "I've got you."

Maybe he meant only in the context of his obligation to Nora, but she pretended he meant more.

They stayed like that for who knows how long, sweat gluing their bodies together. They searched each other's faces, Reed's big hand buried in her hair, fingers making lazy circles on her scalp. Their breathing synchronized.

This man was being paid to keep her from her real life, and the secrets she had to keep from him were too numerous to count, but they couldn't deny this connection any longer. It was deeper than physical attraction and wider than anything they could say to one another.

She finally broke the long, heavy silence. "This is so—"

"Intense," he finished for her.

"Intense," she whispered back.

The kiss that followed was deep and slow and lasted the rest of the night.

TWENTY-FIVE

Reed woke with no fewer than three parts of Gwen touching him. Dainty ankle around his. Silky arm across his waist. Her chilly little nose pressed to his shoulder, the one without the tat. It had been that way throughout the night, one or both of them periodically waking, realizing they'd separated, and then closing the gap.

His thumb drew a line down her cheek and her eyes flipped open. "Good morning" didn't seem appropriate. Maybe someday they could actually say that and mean it.

Whoa. Had his mind actually made that leap?

"You're awake," he said instead.

"Just been lying here. Liking it." But trouble lingered behind her eyes.

"Me, too." A blond hair got caught in her eyelashes and he pulled it free. "Thirsty?"

She nodded and he slipped into the bathroom to bring back two paper cups of mountain-cold tap water. They sat up in bed to drink, him finishing first. He watched her down hers. The second she lowered the cup, he was on her. Pushed her back into the pillow. Slid deftly between her legs and felt the hot place he'd been last night. He kissed her in the quiet light of a new day. Felt the soft, agonizing skate of her fingers on his back, making him compare it to the gentle tease of a whip before a lover snapped it.

Yeah, *whipped* was a good word for him.

She touched his mind. Commanded his blood. And every bit of it now headed straight for his cock, making it pulse. Beneath him, her hips rocked up, drawing him closer, telling him what she wanted. He rose to his knees and elbows, positioning himself, already feeling her heat. The tip of him caressed her inner thigh, and she held her breath in anticipation.

The watch, on his wrist positioned near Gwen's head, buzzed and flashed a message. They froze. Stared at each other.

This was not trying to zip up before your parents traipsed up the stairs. This was not pumping as hard as you could so you'd come before your roommates got home from the late movie.

This was life or death. His and Gwen's.

With a growl of frustration, he sat back on his heels and stared at Nora's message.

Take her back to the cabin ASAP. Back here by one. Photo proof at all locations.

Back to the lake house by one. With an hour's drive each way, they had to get a move on.

"What?" Gwen said, still stretched out gorgeously beneath him.

It was much easier to talk when he didn't have to look at her. "You have to go back. To that cabin."

"When?" Her hand gripped his thigh, saying, *We can make it fast. We can make it good.*

He wrenched away. He had no choice. The blood left his dick in a great, cold whoosh. "Now."

"Please don't turn away like that."

"I have to," he sighed, "because if I touch you, I'll never want to leave. And neither of us can afford that."

Then she was behind him, all naked softness, breasts against his back, hands curling around his shoulders.

He groaned and stepped away. "Don't."

"So nothing's changed between us. God, I'm so stupid for thinking—"

He whirled back around. "Are you kidding? *Everything's* changed. Between *us*. But for Nora, everything has to be the same. It has to look as it always had. And I've lost my handle on the separation for what I have to do for her and what I'm feeling for you. It's so fucked up. I've never, ever had an issue with being two different people because I've never had to be them at the same goddamn time. But now I do and I'm just barely hanging on. If she catches on, I'm a dead man. She'll get rid of me and then I couldn't look after you."

Gwen went a little wide-eyed, a little indignant. "Do you still think I'm trying to turn you?"

He gouged the heels of his palms into his eyes and didn't reply. Honestly, he had no idea what to think.

"Reed. Look at me. I'm not."

"I know." Did he? He peeled his hands away. "I'm just so . . . confused." He skittered away from her outstretched hand. "Gwen, I said don't touch me."

Now she was starting to get the hint, to share a little bit of his coldness. They had to use that to get out of the house without raising suspicion. If they walked out of this room right now, they'd be all over each other. He'd kiss her, touch her, every chance he got. He'd be Reed, not the Retriever, and everything would end.

The wall had to go up *now*, and they had to separate, physically and emotionally, for him to do it and protect them both.

He stormed back to his room and returned with a new yellow pill. He wasn't sure she'd be able to get it into her throat past the tight clench of her jaw, but she did it.

The door to the shack creaked open, throwing a shaft of harsh sunlight inside. Genesai hunched over the table, which had been pushed into a shadowed corner. Both hands shoveling food into his mouth, he was completely unaware Gwen had entered. She was surprised by the gusto of his eating. By his appearance, it looked as though he'd been scraping by on the bare minimum of nutrients for over a century.

She glanced back at Reed, who leaned against a pine tree at the top of the slope. He'd successfully reverted back to that detached kidnapper she knew so well, the one she hated. The Retriever's presence carved an awful hole in her chest, because every time she looked at him, she saw the man who'd grinned at her over a Guinness, who'd talked to her across the DMZ, and who'd moved so powerfully and so well inside her while touching her so gently.

She closed the shack door against Reed's image and blinked in the dimness. "Genesai?"

His head jerked up, his crazed eyes dancing over her. His

mouth fell open, half-eaten crackers tumbling out. She took a few tentative steps closer. If he remembered her, he didn't show it.

A clock ticked loudly in the back of her mind. Time with him was precious and short, and the window to figure out how to save the Tedrans and keep Ofarian society intact narrowed by the second. It was incredibly fortuitous that Nora had again been pulled away to the Plant and Gwen was here alone. She couldn't screw this up.

Gwen unzipped her jacket and pulled out the pages she'd taken from the cabin wall. Genesai saw them, and his head swiveled toward the exact place where they used to hang. She let the long piece unfold. He blinked at his drawings and scribblings. Blinked at her. She moved closer and he brushed timid fingers to the words and images she held, much like a child might when encouraged to touch something wondrous and new and a tad frightening.

She'd gone through Translation twenty-one times, the only exceptions being for English and Ofarian. Many Translations were similar. People took pride in their languages and they liked to know foreigners wanted to learn it. If she got words or structure or grammar wrong, they liked to correct her. So many were eager to teach. She placed her hope for Genesai on this principle. After one hundred and fifty years of solitude, she hoped he was itching for a little conversation with someone who might actually be able to communicate.

She smiled and spoke the phrase, in his language, he'd repeated over the years. *Down, down, down we come. Into fire, into water. Up, up, up we go. All together, with blood.*

Genesai's face lit like the sun breaking over the eastern horizon. It opened a door in him and he started to babble the phrase again, pointing to the ceiling and then the floor. He started to rise to do his twitchy jumping thing, but she couldn't let him get derailed and then wipe himself out again.

Since she already knew the writing on the long sheet of paper did not match what he said, she feigned ignorance, touched the first line of scribbles, and said, "Down?" in his language. He looked confused, so she repeated the phrase, touching a different symbol for each word. Questioning their meaning.

"Echa, echa, echa," he said, shaking his head with a goofy smile. One arm shot out in a jerky, snaky motion.

No, no, no.

They were getting somewhere. She took a deep breath and held it, trying to contain her excitement.

His long, pale fingers trailed over the symbols, moving vertically, not horizontally as she'd done. At the bottom he moved over to the next column and came back up. As he pointed, he read.

The words came so fast she gripped the edge of the table to steady herself, the Translation unfurling so quickly it tangled in her mind and made her dizzy. At the same time, it felt glorious.

Usually she Translated verbally first then moved to the written word. With Genesai, she absorbed both at once and she had to concentrate hard to keep them straight. The language was harsh, guttural. As Genesai's human tongue rolled around the sounds, the muscles in Gwen's mouth strained to create their echo. Her head pounded with the beat of syllables and accents, the rhythms of punctuation and verbs.

Every word was a weapon against Nora.

Someone suddenly flipped off Genesai's crazy switch, and his agitated fidgeting died.

"I first saw you when I was very young," Genesai began. "The dream was lifelike, intense, as if I had lived it before. But when I woke up, I knew it was a vision of the future. Our future together. It told me what I was meant to do: to create. You were the most spectacular thing I had ever seen and I knew you were my destiny."

The sound of his voice confused and intrigued her. The tone was high and childlike, but now that she understood his words, she detected the years, the wisdom, and the yearning inside him. The crazed young man was a shell for a lucid, heartbroken, lonely being. He was no more a boy than Gwen was a Tedran.

"Most of my people created their partners to stay on-world, but you and I were meant to travel into the dark above-world. We were meant to draw shimmering lines between the stars and planets. To discover, together. Ten cycles around the sun I spent designing and constructing you, correcting my mistakes, reinventing the science of my people. Then you finally worked. I will never forget the first time we connected and you drew power from me, coming fully to life. My partner, my life's companion. My love. No day or experience I have had since has matched it."

Rarely did Gwen question her Translations. Sometimes she was unsure, and that was where the teacher corrections came in handy. With Genesai, however, she was absolutely sure of what he'd said; she just couldn't wrap her brain around it.

He did not speak of a woman or a living, breathing partner. He was talking about—and to—his ship.

"We left my world," he went on, not pausing for her fascination, "and arced into the black. Time became inconsequential, a thing that flitted by outside your beautiful skin. I could not say how long we moved among the stars and hovered over planets both gorgeous and grotesque. I never wanted it to end. I did not miss my world or my people, for I did not belong to them anymore. I belonged to the universe. And you and I, we saw it all. You and I, we were never going to stop exploring. We were going to drift until our substance dissolved.

"But on the planet Tedra, riddled with war and slavery and death, we were stolen. Taken. Our curiosity became our bane. We drew too close and were pulled into its chaos. The warmongers, the Ofarians, commandeered us. They stole Tedrans from their home world and forced us to fly where they wanted. You became my moving prison. The planet to which the Ofarians made us go was one we had long avoided for fear of discovery. We crashed here and our captors ripped me from your embrace. Tore apart our blood connection. Divided me in half."

Gwen felt like she'd been flung into the stars herself. Only there was no joy in her suspension. She felt ill. Betrayed. Everything Nora had told her was true.

"I looked different from the Ofarians, and they wanted to avoid detection by the native race of humans. An Ofarian used his magic to transform me into water. They forced a simple boy to swallow me. They poured me into a new body and I do not know which hurt more: being separated from you or the constraints of my new body that fought so viciously against my true self."

The ugly truth clawed violently at Gwen's heart.

Is that how the Ofarian race on Earth began? Did they arrive, looking different from humans, and force themselves to be drunk by innocents?

What the hell was Gwen?

Though Genesai closed his eyes, his finger still trailed up and down his characters, and he recited from memory.

"It has been too long away from you. I do not know how long exactly. I do not know where you are. I do not know if you are well, or even if I survive without you. I still see you when I close my eyes. I am not the same. I fear I never will be again. I miss you."

This was no story. It was a love letter.

Gwen took a chance and reached out to cover Genesai's hands with her own. He jerked back. He started to squirm again. In her mind's eye, she saw a strange being beneath his skin, punching to get out.

"It's all right," she said in his language, because she finally could. She tested the sounds on her tongue, the movements of the muscle strange against her teeth and palate. "I'm here to help you."

The moment she said it, she knew it was absolutely true. He stared at her, eyes wide with unfettered hope and legs all jittery. Ignorantly, up until then, she'd only been concerned with maintaining the viability of the Ofarian race and giving the Tedrans their freedom. Genesai had only been a means to an end, a solution to her dual problems. Now she wanted to save him, too. She *needed* to give him back what her people had stolen.

"You will speak to me?" he rasped.

She smiled. "Yes, Genesai. I will speak to you. I am very, very happy to be able to speak to you."

A twitch of the head. "You said you are here to help me?"

As she nodded, she felt the lump in her throat. "I know where your ship is. I have come to help you get back to the stars."

She thought for sure he'd propel himself from the chair, bounce around the room like a racquetball, then pass out again. Yet he fell absolutely still. The only movement came in his bulbous eyes, which brimmed with tears. He lifted a finger, wiped away the salty drops, and looked at them in confusion.

"Where is she? Take me to her. Let us leave this horrible place."

This time when she stretched forward, he let her take his bony hands. She looked deep into his eyes and told him everything she knew about the war on Tedra and the settlement of the Ofarian and Tedran Secondaries on Earth. She told him about the slaves and how some rogue Tedrans wanted him and his ship to help them escape.

She *didn't* tell him that Nora wanted him to go back to Tedra. And she didn't tell him she herself was Ofarian. She feared he'd retreat if she revealed that, and she couldn't afford to negate all this progress.

"Can we go to her now?" Joy brightened his milk white skin like a lightbulb.

It killed Gwen to say no. "Not yet. We're working to free the slaves. Once that's done, we will come for you and take you to your ship."

His whole body started to shake. He rose, bouncing on the balls of his bare feet.

"I do not want to wait anymore."

Neither did she, but first, she needed a plan.

TWENTY-SIX

Reed had asked for this distance, this silence between Gwen and himself. In theory it would keep them both alive. In reality it sucked.

They'd returned from that bizarre cabin over an hour ago, but neither Nora nor Xavier was here. He'd made his report via watch, photographing, and time-stamping Gwen in the lake house foyer, then he'd locked them in the attic, in their separate rooms. Now he lay diagonally on his messy bed, feet somewhere near the pillows, arms cradling the corner of the mattress, cheek pressed to the cool sheets, when the bathroom door opened. No sense in locking the door when all he wanted was for her to come through. He lifted his head.

Gwen stood there looking at him, stiff arms braced on the door frame as though she held up the whole house. They were really good at acting cold toward one another. Perhaps too good.

His employers had been exceedingly distracted and terse lately. The part of Reed that wanted to be alone with Gwen was thankful for their absence. The part that belonged to the Retriever worried that their behavior meant the worst for their captive.

He had no idea if he should get up and go to her.

"Can I come in?"

Oh, thank God. He propped himself up on his elbows as she crossed to him. Had she ever looked better, with her hair hanging long over her shoulders, and the pine scent of the chilly mountain still clinging to her clothes?

The Retriever drifted away, if he'd ever managed to truly

come to the forefront at all that day. She must have been able
to sense the switch in him, see it on his face or something,
because she held out a hand.

"Come on."

"Where?" She couldn't go anywhere without him.

A nod toward the bathroom. "You're going to apologize
to me."

"What?" he began, a little angry, until he noticed the quirk
to her lips.

Then he slid his hand into hers and let her drag him into the
bathroom. They stood right in the middle of the demolished
DMZ. Late afternoon sunlight hit the surrounding bedrooms,
but she'd left the light off in the bathroom and it was so dim
he could just barely make out their shapes in the mirror.

"Gwen, I'm . . ."

. . . *sorry for what you've been pulled into and my role in it.*

. . . *obsessed with you.*

"No." She kissed him hard. "Not with words."

The surprise of her mouth and the heat it stoked in him
obliterated what he was going to say anyway. Slipping her arms
around his waist, she gave a little tug toward her room, but he
resisted.

"Don't I get a say in how I beg for forgiveness?"

"Maybe." She rubbed the flannel of his shirt between her
fingers.

With a deeply satisfied grin, he set her against the sink and
went to the shower. Spun the knob to *on*. When he turned back
around, she wasn't looking at him. She stared at the water
streaming out of the cheap showerhead with an emotion akin
to longing. A slight tremor danced along her fingers.

He had no idea what that was all about, but really didn't
care. Not at that moment. He stalked toward her, took her face
in his hands, and kissed her with everything he had. First her
lips yielded. Then, oh God, her tongue. It pushed out and tangled with his, and he was lost.

They went for each other's jeans' zippers at the same time,
fingers fumbling, lips still fused. His jeans fell down without
much effort. Hers were tighter and he loved tugging them down
her hips and thighs. He abandoned her mouth and dragged his
tongue over her newly revealed skin. He left her underwear

and T-shirt on, though, scooped her up into his arms, and deposited her in the steaming shower. Hurriedly he worked on the buttons of his flannel, whipped it to the side, then stopped in his tracks.

Gwen stood under the fall of water, drenched T-shirt plastered to her chest and waist, little white underwear gone entirely see-through. He shoved down his boxer briefs and stepped into the shower, immediately going to his knees, because that was where the sight of her sent him.

He loved the feel of the wet, tight fabric over her body, and he ran his hands everywhere until he'd had his fill. Then she needed to be naked. By the drop of her lower lip and the distant focus to her eyes, she needed skin on skin as badly as he. He peeled off her shirt and it landed with a plop somewhere behind him. He replaced the cotton with his tongue, taking a delicious nipple into his mouth.

She clung to his head. Water streamed between her fingers and down his face, mixing with the moisture of his mouth on her flesh.

Curving his hands around her divine ass, he pulled down her underwear and slid his hand into the slippery wetness so different from what the shower gave. She started to shake, to cry out, then bit her lip to keep the sound inside.

He'd watched her come twice already. He desperately wanted to hear her, too, but not in this house. Never here.

He leaned back, watching her with heavy eyes as he stroked her with one hand, pushed inside her with the other. Only their second time together and he could already read her body like a book. The water seemed to hug her as it streamed down her undulating body. She was riding his hands, getting ready to burst, and it was utterly beautiful . . . but he stopped just short of the goal. Her eyelids flickered open in frustration.

"Turn around," he murmured.

Dazed, she swiveled slowly. He rocked to his feet.

"Hands on the wall."

Not only did she do that, stretching high and wide, but she also arched her back. The most beautiful of shapes. The most perfect combination of lines and curves. He dragged a languid, worshipful hand down her back, from neck to ass.

He covered her from behind, his chest to her back, and let his mouth devour the sensitive place below her ear. His hand curled around her thigh and slipped into her from the front. Just for a second. Then he withdrew and replaced the pressure with his cock. Pushed against her, then into her. That quick, that amazing.

She moaned, long and low.

"Shhh," he said with a smile.

She buried her mouth in the crook of her elbow as he started to move inside her. Slowly at first, paying attention to every millimeter of friction she gave him. Deep, powerful strokes that shoved her forward so her tits touched the tile.

"Is this the kind of apology you wanted?" he said in her ear.

She looked over her shoulder and he took her mouth that way.

"Harder," she said against his lips.

His body complied before his brain processed the simple word. She must have been seriously primed, because she came so quickly he wasn't prepared when she shuddered and her legs started to go.

He wrapped an arm around her waist to keep her up. The fingers of his other hand dug into her hip as though he was afraid to lose her. Which he was.

His own orgasm rocketed through him, sending him forward, sagging against her back. The force of it stole bits of his soul and presented them to her as a gift. She accepted them with open arms and he knew his soul was better off in her care than his own.

He kept coming, little aftershocks licking his spine and making his extremities go numb. When they all dissipated, he pulled out, flipped her around, trapped her on the tile wall, and kissed her strongly—so strongly that when those little parts of his soul traveled back into his body, he could tell they were markedly better for having come in contact with her.

They kissed so long she started to shiver and her smooth skin transformed to a bristling mass of goose bumps. Unknowingly, he'd pushed her against the shower knob and had turned off the water.

He reached for a towel, wrapped it around her body, and pulled her to him again. She snaked her arms around his neck—his favorite way she touched him—and whispered, "Apology accepted."

"I'm willing to do more penance."

She ran her hands over his hairless scalp, brushing off droplets. Though they teased each other, neither one of them smiled, and it made his heart ache. She kissed him once. Swift and sweet.

"Dry me off and take me to bed," she said. "Your bed."

He slipped a hand between her legs. "I don't want you dry."

TWENTY-SEVEN

Gwen clung to this moment, because in the blink of an eye it could be gone. Reed didn't think he was good at handling the dual personalities he claimed to need. She thought the opposite; he was too good. But she knew it had to be that way.

The Tedrans could return any minute. Now, however, she'd stay locked in his arms, her body curled into his, his warm breath on the back of her neck. He pushed aside her hair and kissed her skin as though it were her mouth, his tongue finding every single point of pleasure.

The sun was setting. Through the window, mauve and gold streaks painted the sky. It was too easy to get lost in this, to think they had days and nights and days of being able to lie naked together. For now, she would. She'd concentrate on the solidity of his body contradicted by the softness of his touch. The low tones of his voice.

"This part of you"—his fingers traced her collarbone—"it's lovely. Don't know why I like it so much."

"That's sort of odd, considering what else you currently have access to."

He smiled and pressed his mouth to her skin again. "About this morning . . ."

"There's no need," she replied. "Everything you said was true. I hate this. You hate this."

"So you're saying the shower apology wasn't needed? Well, that was half an hour I'll never get back."

She laughed, but its strain was painfully obvious.

"What I hate the most," he said, "is being two people with you when I only want to show you one."

At first that made her angry. That's what he hated the *most*? Then she considered what he'd witnessed so far. Nora hadn't physically harmed her in any way. The Tedrans kept her locked in a fancy house on a beautiful lake. They made Reed take her to a weird cabin and she came out unscathed. To him, Gwen could be nothing more than an errand girl. He knew nothing about the real danger because he *couldn't* know anything. To him, she was safe because he was always there with her.

Things couldn't be farther from the truth, and it sent a sick feeling rolling through her belly.

"You've seen the real me, Gwen. I can't remember the last person who has, besides my family."

"Person? Or woman?"

He paused. "Either."

She didn't have to look at him to see his vulnerability, but she turned in his arms anyway. The sight of him—bald head resting on his big biceps—made her gasp. A melancholy smile touched his lips, an even sadder one in his blue eyes.

"You really are beautiful," he whispered, "do you know that?"

The words affected her more than they probably should have.

"That's a tough one to answer. Say no and I'm fishing for compliments. Say yes and I'm conceited."

"I'm telling you then. You really are."

Warmth spread through her body as unguarded flame. He inched closer, touched his mouth to hers.

"I like how you look after I kiss you." He raised a hand, fingers framing but not touching her face, as though he were examining a painting.

"Really?"

"I like where my chin scratches yours. Your lips swell, turn this bright red. Their edges blur. When we stop, you get this look in your eye, like . . . surrender."

He could make her shiver without touching her. "I wonder why."

Reed slid a hand onto the curve of her hip and just let it rest there. Possessive but gentle. It wasn't an overtly sexual gesture, not even meant to seduce, but she felt the passion start to coil inside her, widening and strengthening as it circled up. Then, underneath, rose a great wave of something else. Something far more potent than mere desire. It filled her body with fiery need and spread out through her veins until it reached her heart.

She sucked in a breath, shocked as all hell.

Dangerous. This man was the definition of temporary. He had a deadline stamped on him as plain as the black lines covering his torso.

So did she.

On her hip, his hand closed hard then opened, as if he, too, had just shared in her surprise. As though he were trying to tether her to him, then let her go. Claim and release. Claim and release.

They said nothing for a very, very long time. Outside, the sun disappeared. She was glad for the deepening darkness because his presence, physically surrounding her and emotionally invading her, dangled her over the edge of a bottomless ravine. If she fell, there was no climbing out. And she wasn't sure she'd want to. The ride down would be the scariest thing she'd ever experienced, but she'd never want it to end. And that frightened her most of all.

His hand suddenly stopped moving on her hip. His whole body tensed.

"What?" She tried to sit up, intent on lunging for her clothes then stumbling back into her bedroom before Nora or Xavier burst in.

But Reed pushed her onto her back, his great, decorated chest coming over her.

"Gwen." He kissed her delicately.

Something shifted in the space between them. Something monumental. She felt it as strongly as she felt his body on hers.

"When this is all over," he whispered, "I want to take you home with me."

His home. That city he refused to name.

When this is all over . . .

Her heart stumbled. When it finally recovered its rhythm, she slid her hands up his chest, tracing random vines with her fingertips. Dim light from the window settled like dust into the hard angles of his beautiful body.

"The something-like-that boyfriend. Will you go back to him?"

Unexpected tears pricked at her eyes but she repressed them. "That was over the moment Nora told me what this was all about."

Reed exhaled in obvious relief. There was a little tremble to his breath and it got to her. The tears gained some ground.

"I want to show you where I live," he said. "I think you'd like it. When you asked me where it was, I wanted to tell you. It's always been easy to lie about it, but not to you."

"Scared to trust me?"

He bent to touch his forehead to hers. "Scared of how I feel about you."

If the growing darkness had given him courage to ask such a thing, it gave her the courage to cry over him in his presence. She felt the tears leak out and sniffled.

"Hey," he said, wiping them away with his thumbs. "If things are rough for you when this is over, I can . . . I can make you disappear. I can make *us* disappear. I'm kind of good like that."

He laughed nervously, which brought on a new rush of silent tears.

"I know it's strange to hear. Hell, it's beyond strange to say. It doesn't have to be next week or even next month. It could be next year, though the wait might kill me. Just as long as you come. There's something about us, Gwen. I'm not ready to let it go."

She wrapped her arms around his neck and pulled him to her. Hard. She kept shifting her grip, because no way to hold him was strong or tight enough. He'd just told her exactly what she didn't know she wanted to hear, and she could extract no joy from it.

She felt him exhale. Felt him smile against her neck. *Oh, God.* He thought she'd just agreed.

"Reed." She pushed against him. "It can't happen."

It destroyed her to say it.

He stiffened, his chest halting mid-breath. He rolled off her. *Wait*, she was dying to say. *I didn't mean that.* He threw his legs over the side of the bed and sat there, elbows to knees. Pale light lay a white blanket across his broad shoulders, bunched near his ears.

"I shouldn't have said anything," he said to the floor.

She owed him an explanation. By opening his heart and translating what it said, he'd earned a reason. But she couldn't give him one.

He feared the Tedrans would kill her. He'd stayed on to make sure they didn't, but he didn't know that what they had planned for her was worse than death. He could never know. He had to go on believing in his system of checks and balances. He had to think that what he thought he knew about Adine would save his ass. If he knew his information was worthless, that Gwen really was in danger, he'd turn on the Tedrans so fast they'd bring up the U.S. government on speed dial and all would be lost.

Both he and Nora thought they held the better hand, and Gwen was relying on that stasis. Any disturbance in the current waters would upset the progress she'd made with Genesai. Any disturbance could destroy her chance to formulate her own plan. Any disturbance could set Nora off.

Besides, even if Gwen were to live through this and her culture retained its power, she couldn't ever be with a Primary.

None of it mattered anyway. If Reed learned who and what Gwen was, he'd take back all he just said and run the other way. She didn't think her heart would survive that.

Crawling across the bed, she slipped her arms around his waist and laid her head against his strong back. The need to constantly touch him was more potent than a heroin itch. Another name, Johnny Einhoven, threaded its way through the vines just beyond her nose. She wanted to know every fraction of every inch of his tattoo. What it all meant to him. How it had shaped him.

She never would, though, and she had to accept that sooner rather than later.

"I want to go with you. I want you to make us disappear," she said. He tilted back his head, exhaled, and slid his hands over hers. "That's no more crazy than you asking. It just can't happen."

"I understand. You don't have to say any more."

His watch jolted alive. When he raised his wrist, she saw the message, plain as day.

Bring her to the north garden. NOW.

* * *

The tiny garden north of the garage abutted a steep rise of rock that extended out into the water and became the promontory. A circular, brick path surrounded a dry fountain made of a pyramid of stones. It reminded Gwen of the enchanted fountain at Company HQ, but without the water running over it, it looked incomplete and lonely and made her long for her power.

Xavier stood on the far side of the fountain, next to a patch of blooming mums intermixed with withering plants at the end of their season. Small solar lamps threw weak circles of light around the little garden.

Reed took up position by the door into the house, leaning against the wall and staring out to the lake. Gwen walked to Xavier, who watched her approach with his arms behind his back. They hadn't been alone since the day he'd bared himself to her in the Plant.

He looked as cold and dry as the fountain.

"Are we waiting for Nora?" she asked Xavier in Tedranish.

"No."

"*You* called me out here?"

He just stared. She flashed a worried look at the door. At Reed. Too late she realized her mistake.

Xavier stepped between them, filling her vision. Accusatory eyes bored into her. "Why are you looking at him?"

"I wasn't . . . I just thought . . . where's Nora?" What the hell was going on? Was he accusing her of something? Or was he just trying to make her squirm?

"Still at the Plant. I came back with Adine. It's a mess there. The Tedrans . . . she's trying to reassure them, but it's hard to work around the guards' shifts and they have days, hours even, to understand when I had months . . ." He shook his shaggy head to clear his mumbling. "Tell me you spoke to Genesai."

She lied. She lied even as Genesai's language bubbled and grew inside her brain, and the bold strokes of his written words danced in her mind's eye. Xavier listened to it all with an unreadable face.

She had no plan of her own yet. She only knew that she couldn't tell Xavier the truth.

He crossed his arms and looked at her down his long nose. The garden lights made his pale, wavy hair into a halo. "You're lying."

"If I'm lying, I'm murdering a member of my own family and locking the rest of my people in a cage. You understand that, right?"

That's exactly what she'd be doing. Playing with everyone's lives like dice.

"What I understand is that you're very clever." Before she had time to process that, to think of a reaction or a retort, he blurted out, "You and the Primary spend a lot of time alone."

She tried not to trip over her stomach as it dropped to the gravel.

He leaned down, way too far into her space. "You're upstairs a lot."

To step back would scream guilt, to announce her weakness for Reed. "What are you saying?"

"What do you think I'm saying?"

She leaned so close to Xavier their noses almost touched. She jabbed an angry finger at Reed. "That man *kidnapped* me. He stole my life. He locks me in that room upstairs and keeps the entire world out of my reach. He's like a wall, Xavier. You think I want to have a conversation with him, let alone what you're insinuating?"

Xavier's wide eyes held hers in a long, uncomfortable stare.

"Are you trying to turn him?" he asked.

"*Turn* him? Didn't you hear what I said before? No matter what I do, my people are fucked. I can't win. There's nothing for me to turn him toward or against! How many times do I have to say it?"

And that was the absolute truth. She had nothing to give, nothing to work toward of her own.

He straightened to his full height and inhaled thinly through his nose. He didn't look convinced. Her only hope was to swerve his mind down a different road, get it away from Reed.

"Let me ask you something," she said. "Which is more important to you: freeing the slaves or getting off Earth?"

Disgust curled his lip. "They're one and the same."

"No. No, they're not. Not to Nora. Not in the idea of hers you endorsed." *There.* A flicker of doubt in his *Mendacia* silver eyes. She charged on. "You told me to make a choice. If I go along with the Genesai plan, the Tedrans will return to your home planet. If I plant a bomb in Company HQ during the weekly Board meeting and then go after the Plant workers, the Tedrans will be free, but they'll still live here on Earth. I'm asking you, Xavier, which would *you* prefer?"

He was a tortured, bitter man who viewed her as a representative of the people he hated most. He answered exactly as she expected.

"Above anything, I want justice. I want the Ofarians to acknowledge what they've done, that it's wrong. I want them to pay for their crimes."

"The Ofarians who are responsible for *Mendacia*, you mean."

His coolly handsome face twisted into something wild and vicious. "Aren't all of them?"

Her own ferocity rose to match his. "I had no idea what was happening until you took me into the Plant. You saw my reaction. Meryl Streep couldn't have faked that. I understand your plight, Xavier. I honestly do; it makes me ill to know what I've been a part of. What I don't understand is why I have to be the one to bring your revenge on my own people. I don't understand why *I* have to make this choice."

His wide shoulders lifted in the tiniest of shrugs. "Because you're the Translator."

A goddamn gene mutation in the Ofarian makeup that came randomly every couple of generations. It made her want to rip out her own tongue.

At last she looked away from Xavier, down to her feet. She didn't want to see his smugness any longer.

"I don't really have a choice, do I?" she finally said. "I mean, I have to help you no matter what happens. And if you're okay with the outcome, if you truly have no preference, it really is up to me, isn't it?"

When he didn't answer, she moved back a few steps. They'd

earned a bit of distance, and Xavier exhaled in obvious relief. His shoulders and hands relaxed. She thought back to the Plant, how the Circle had affected him, how he couldn't even stand to be attached to her by four feet of chain. Even now, he glared back at the house, chin jutted out.

"I know you would never say it, Xavier, but you depend on me. And you would never, ever admit it, but you place hope in me." That brought his head back around, but what she saw in his eyes wasn't anger. It was shock. And maybe a bit of truth. "I understand why you say the things you do to me. Why you treat me this way. I also know I'll never change your opinion of me until I fulfill what you brought me here for."

"If you betray us"—his harsh whisper magnified the wet chill in his stare—"if you keep my people in slavery, I swear on the stars that I will see every last one of your kind die. And you will be the last."

She planted her feet, laced her fingers, palms down, in the Ofarian prayer fashion meant to resemble water, and vowed in the Ofarian language: "I promise you I will free the slaves."

"What?" he snapped at the sound of her mother tongue.

Keeping her hands together, she repeated the oath in Tedranish.

He softened, even if only a fraction, then turned on his heel and stalked toward the house. As he passed Reed, Reed came forward without acknowledging the surly Tedran. Reed barely glanced at her as he took up position on the opposite side of the fountain.

A stone bench curved behind her knee and Gwen sank onto it, her back to the house and to Reed.

She replayed everything she'd said to Xavier. How she would do as the Tedrans said because she literally had no other options. Even if she continued to hide her communication with Genesai, it wouldn't do anything to free the slaves or lift her people from their dependence on *Mendacia*. What she'd told Nora and Xavier the other day was absolutely true: there were other ways she could remedy all that had been done wrong. But to free the Tedrans, punish the responsible Ofarians, and maintain the Secondaries' secret existence, she couldn't be in the lake house. She was trapped here. Except . . . what if she wasn't . . .

The seed of a plan nestled itself deep in her brain. She could see inside it, see how it would sprout, know what it would grow into. But the seed was broken and a few bits and pieces floated around in the ether, waiting for her to connect them. She needed glue, a bonding agent. Something—or some*one*—to bring it all together.

Behind her, Reed's subtle movements created photo-quality images in her mind. She closed her eyes and listened. As he shifted on his feet, his heavy boots moved dirt and tiny stones over brick. That deep *shush* was the sound of his denim-clad thighs rubbing together. He adjusted his neck in a small series of cracks. His arms were crossed and he drummed his fingers on his forearms.

That silence in between? That was him watching her. The very weight of it made her sag. Even in the chill of the evening, she could sense its heat.

Her head dropped, dread filling her fast.

No. There *had* to be another way. She sat there for what felt like forever, poring over ideas, turning them over and inside out. Agonizing. They all came back to one solution.

The timing for this could never be right, but it was especially awful now, given all that Reed had just said to her upstairs. Gwen drew a ragged breath, anxiety making her insides boil. He would think she was using him. He would assume she was manipulating his feelings to make him go against everything he said he wouldn't. The thought of it made her dig her elbows into her stomach, and she used the discomfort to keep everything down.

If the prospect of Reed's reaction didn't hurt enough, her birthright hung over them like a thunderhead. If she did this, she'd be disobeying one of the most important rules of her people. The same rule that had ordered Griffin to kill Yoshi and his henchman, and who knows how many others. No Primaries allowed inside. Ever.

There was no other way. She had to rely now on the truth— *veritas*, not *mendacia*.

"Reed." She kept her face averted from the cameras she knew were trained on her, but spoke loud enough so he could hear. "I need to tell you why I'm here."

TWENTY-EIGHT

Reed's panic came off him in a powerful blast. She didn't have to see him to know; she *felt* it.

"No. Do *not* tell me why you're here."

She fixated on a lightning-bolt-shaped crack in the rock face before her, despising herself for what she was about to say. "I'm going to talk, and since you have to be where I am, you're going to listen."

"I'll drag you up right now, lock you in your room."

"Xavier's grown suspicious. He questioned me about you, about us. That's what this meeting was all about. Don't take me anywhere outside of the camera's sight. You'll just make it worse."

He didn't say anything, and Gwen knew she had his reluctant attention.

"I'm asking you to listen. I didn't want to do this. Honestly, I didn't. I held out and held out . . . but there isn't another way. I'm asking for your help. Please, Reed. Please listen."

"Shit." Then, under his breath, "I knew I shouldn't have stayed."

She was not a religious person. She did not subscribe to any of Earth's faiths, and the devotions of her ancestors had been watered down to myths and fables. The rituals had scripts and specifics, but not much heart. The Ofarians' original, true religion had evolved into something completely secular, yet at that moment, she found herself praying. Praying that Reed didn't mean what he just said.

They were only two people. Thousands of Ofarians and hundreds of Tedrans needed her. It was a terrible choice, but the right one to make.

Sweeping his doubt under the rug stabbed her in the heart, but she had to do it to say what was needed. To go on, she couldn't be ruled by her feelings for him. Because what she was about to say would undoubtedly change his feelings for her.

Or destroy them.

"There are a lot of people in danger." She pressed her palms to the cold stone bench, locking her elbows. "People I love back in San Francisco, thousands of others I've never even met. They don't know it, but they need me. I'm all they have. Nora thinks she is the answer, but doing things her way would be . . . disastrous."

The autumn cold rode piggyback on the wind, shaking browned leaves off trees and shrubs and icing her bones. It didn't help that she felt that frosty separation slither between them again. She couldn't allow it to come back. She pushed at it with her words, hoping their severity and desperation would slow the division.

She drew a deep, shaking breath. "You asked me to go home with you. 'When this is all over,' you said. This will not end, Reed. That's why I said no. Not because I didn't want to."

"They told me you wouldn't be hurt." Threat darkened his tone, and she stole a bit of comfort from that.

She laughed to keep the tears at bay. "They lied to you. I'm as good as dead if Nora gets her way. Technically your agreement with her is valid. The danger to me comes after I'm done doing what she wants and you're long gone."

He made a low sound in his throat.

"The world will become dangerous for me and everyone I love unless I can work against Nora. Unless I can put my own plan into play. With your help. You said you stayed for me . . ."

"Don't." His anguish slashed at her with invisible knives. "Don't you dare use what I feel for you to make me do what you want."

"I swear I'm not!" She couldn't help it. She swiveled to get a glimpse of his face and immediately wished she hadn't. It was twisted with confusion and longing and anger. All directed at her. His eyes flashed in warning, telling her to turn back around.

She pretended to shift positions on the bench and stretched out her legs in front of her.

"I knew you would think that," she said, "and it's not true. Please. Just listen to what I have to say, then judge whether you still think I'm using you. But not before. It breaks my heart you think me so callous."

Even if his silence wasn't meant to be a prompt, she took it as such anyway. She inhaled through her nose. *Here we go.*

"What I'm about to tell you is the absolute truth. I am not crazy. I am not on medication." Reed had gone quiet and still as a rock. "That first day, when Nora and Xavier took me away without you, they drove me way out to the middle of nowhere Nevada. There . . . Nora's people are being held as slaves. She kidnapped me because she wants me to free them."

"Slaves." Disbelief dripped from his voice.

"They're being forced to create a product sold for more money than you could possibly imagine, to a worldwide clientele that is incredibly guarded and the elite among the elite. This product is sold by my company."

"The sales job you mentioned?"

"Yes."

"You're a *slave* owner."

As she shook her head, her hair fell across her face, and she welcomed the curtain. "I had no idea. I swear. I thought our product was created by carefully selected, highly skilled people in a legal manner. I really did." She thought of the last time she'd stood in front of the Board, desperate to sit among them. To help make their decisions, to know what they did. "Maybe I would've learned the truth in time. But instead I had to witness it through Nora and Xavier's eyes. He was one of them, you know. A slave. Nora broke him out. And she made him take me back there."

She heard the familiar scrape of Reed's palm against his grizzled cheek. She didn't realize how much she'd come to love the sound.

"That's why you were so upset when you got back."

Oh, thank the stars he was beginning to understand. "Yes. It was horrible. The worst thing I've ever seen. I couldn't—*still* can't—believe that people I know are responsible for it. That it's been going on right under my nose. That I've naively dedicated my life to keeping it going."

"Gwen, I shouldn't know this."

"You still worried about your paycheck?"

He paused. "I'm worried about a lot of things. Money isn't one of them."

She didn't know quite what to make of that.

"Nora wants me to free her people. But there's a price. Or else she wouldn't have had to kidnap me."

"You're important within the company," he pieced together.

She nodded. Important because she'd made it so. Pushed herself to the top. Expanded *Mendacia*'s markets fivefold. Created more jobs for the increased business and enabled the Company's prosperity to trickle down to the Ofarians who weren't directly involved. *Keep it together. Do not cry. Now more than ever, you need your head.*

"This product," he said, "what is it?"

"It's something that makes people look different than they actually do. Younger. Stronger. Smaller. Healthier. Uglier. Completely disguised. Whatever they want."

He didn't react for so long she feared he might have taken off or tuned her out. His boots moved over the path and around the fountain. When he lowered himself to the far end of her bench, facing diagonally away, it took all her power not to turn to him.

He rubbed his hands together. "So this product. It's makeup?"

I'm so sorry, Dad and Delia and Griffin. I'm sorry, Mom, for betraying all you taught me. This is the only way. "It's more like . . . magic."

His hands froze mid-swipe. The muscles in his thighs tensed up. He didn't even breathe. The entire garden paused.

"Magic?" he finally spit out. "What kind of asshole are you playing me for?"

The hostility and doubt didn't deflate her. Instead, it fed her strength and resolve.

"I'm not playing. Everything I'm saying is real. Everything is true." The words tasted like sandpaper. "All of Nora's people are slaves. They are . . . a different race. They're called Tedrans."

Reed forgot where they were and threw a disgusted look over his shoulder. He caught himself, snapped his eyes back to the dying garden. She wished she hadn't seen it. To know how he felt was one thing. To see it was another. She had no choice but to press on.

"Tedrans have the ability to make what's false seem like reality. To create illusions. It doesn't really change things, just alters someone's perception. And it's not permanent. When the glamour wears off, so does the illusion. The Tedrans can change anything, not just people and physical appearance, but that's how my company has been marketing it. We call it *Mendacia*."

"Latin for 'lies,'" Reed murmured. "Clever."

"It's incredibly expensive. We sell it to extremely wealthy people all over the world, and I'm not talking about C-list actresses. I'm talking about hedge fund billionaires and heirs to fortunes behind some of the largest and most powerful global companies. Royalty, even. You have to sign a pages-long agreement just to open a discussion with us. Iron-clad privacy clauses keep us exclusive and secretive, and no one wants to admit they use it in the first place. *Mendacia* turns them into whomever they need or want to be. It's made me, and us, very wealthy."

"Nice sales pitch. You notice you still talk about it in the present tense?"

"*Ah*. So I do." She dug her thumb into her forehead, where a dull throb had begun. "It has to stop, Reed. The production, the Company, everything. It has to end, and I'm the only one who can do it. But not from in here. Not how Nora wants it done."

He spit into the bushes, as if to expel the story from his body. But there was much more to go.

"A small group of my people have been holding Tedrans as slaves for generations. They have forced the Tedrans to drain their powers. Doing this drains their life. So to keep up supply, this group forces them to breed." That did it. She couldn't hold back the tears anymore. "My people make and steal *children*, Reed. I saw it with my own eyes."

He wasn't wholly made of stone. Out of the corner of her eye she saw him shaking his head in disgust.

"You keep saying 'my people.' Who the hell are you then?"

Oh, the fear in his voice. She couldn't talk about the Ofarians yet, so she wiped her nose on her sleeve and veered off course.

"I told you my job in the Company was sales. That's not entirely true. I'm really a Translator, with a capital T. I advance new markets, learn the language, then bring in my dad to make the sale while I serve as interpreter. I also translate the spells that come from the *Mendacia* Plant into the client's native language." She was doing it again, using the present tense. Her throat tightened up. "It's why Nora kidnapped me and not my dad."

"Twenty-three languages," he mumbled. "You did say that before. I didn't believe you."

She hadn't expected him to, but the thought of lying to him, after he'd told her about his tattoos, hadn't seemed fair. She'd wanted to share something real with him.

"So why exactly does Nora want you instead?"

She could say it in any one of twenty-three languages, but the hardest was English.

"There's a man being held in that cabin in the woods. He knows how to help the slaves escape and I'm the only one who can speak his language."

Reed opened his hands, frustrated. "The *only* one? Come on."

"Yes, the only one. I can speak any language in the universe. All I have to do is hear it, and then I know it as well as my mother tongue. It's a gift, a rare genetic trait that often skips generations. But I have it. I gave it to the Company and let them use me because I thought it was what was best for my people. I was wrong. And now Nora wants it."

He bent forward. "What exactly does she want you to do?"

The question came out haltingly. She realized it was probably the first time he'd ever out-and-out asked why his target had been extracted, to use his term. She wished it hadn't been her.

"Nora gave me two choices. I have to either destroy the Company and many people within it, or I have to help the Tedrans leave."

"Leave where? The place in Nevada that Xavier took you to? Seems like a no-brainer, Gwen. Escape over death."

"No." She stared at a crimson mum, completely numb. "Leave Earth."

He made a weird strangled sound, started to speak several times, then settled on this: "Here's what's going to happen.

You're going to jump up from that bench, act like you're angry and make a big scene, then run for the door to the garage. I'll be right behind you. Got it?"

No problem. She sprung from the bench and rounded on him. She faced the cameras now. If Adine or Xavier knew how to read lips, she had to be careful what she said. So she spoke the truth.

"I wish you'd never taken me," she snarled, then turned and bolted for the door.

She ran as though freedom were on the other side of that door. Reed's boots scrambled close behind. Though she knew it was all a ruse, those fleeting moments of letting loose, of pounding the earth and bursting into the garage, let her mind fly with possibilities and hope.

She charged into the garage and Reed followed, slamming the door behind him. They faced each other now. His chest pumped, his eyes hard. The dark place smelled of gasoline and garbage.

"Why here?" she asked.

"No cameras. But they'll come to check soon." He advanced on her like a man intent on attack, pushing her back against the white van. "You said you weren't crazy."

"I'm not!" Unconsciously, she stretched to take his face in her hands and he recoiled.

"Don't touch me."

"I'm sorry. I'm not trying to—"

"You're trying to tell me Nora wants you to take these . . . Tedrans . . . off *Earth*?"

She stood perfectly still. The picture of sanity. The definition of calm intelligence. "Yes. Using the same ship that brought the Tedrans and my people here a hundred and fifty years ago."

"You'd better explain that. Fast."

She barely recognized him, the harsh twist to his mouth. Not even in the alley had he looked this frightening, this animalistic. But his eyes were still the same, so she focused on those cool blues as she said, "My ancestors are from a planet called Ofaria."

He flung himself away. Whipped back around. "Holy shit. Holy fuck, Gwen. You're saying you're not *human*?"

She thought of what Genesai had revealed to her. How he'd been turned to water and forced down the throat of an unsuspecting human. She had no idea if the whole Ofarian race on Earth had started that way. It didn't matter. Her parents were human, and so were their parents.

"I am." She lifted her chin to Reed. "I'm as human as you are. I have gifts. That's it. That's all that's different between you and me."

He watched her, stoic mask in place, every muscle tight, including his fists.

Say something. Anything.

Suddenly he jerked. Grabbed her. Spun her around so her back was against his chest.

"Fight me," he growled.

No problem.

The door between the house and the garage flew open, banging back on its hinges. Xavier glowered in the opening, his face flushed. "What's going on?"

Reed tightened his grip as she wrestled to get out of it. "Tried to make a run for it. Went for one of the cars. I'll lock her upstairs."

As Xavier stepped back, Reed lugged her through the door. She dared to hope that her anger and Reed's harsh treatment would mollify Xavier. Reed was brilliant. But of course, deception was his thing.

Gwen kicked and struggled, not only because she was supposed to, but because her whole body wanted to scream in frustration. Reed dragged her upstairs, shoved her into her room, and locked the door behind them.

She opened her mouth to say something but he held up a hand. Alone at last, his entire body sagged. His big hands fell to his sides with a slap. The heaviness in his expression took her heart and snapped it in two. Silent as a ghost, he turned and walked through the bathroom to his own room. The lock clicked to red.

The Primary notion of souls had always seemed strange to her, but as she watched Reed walk away, she finally thought she understood. His denial and disappointment had just ripped the soul from her body.

Tentatively she crossed the bathroom. The tile was back to

being the demilitarized zone. *Careful. Guns are trained on you*, he'd said joking. But it was true now.

She pressed her hands to the door as if feeling the warmth of his skin through it. She spoke into the crack.

"You think I don't know how all of this sounds, but I do. I live in the same world as you. I know how things like this are perceived. Like fiction." She cleared her throat. "But I can give you proof. Nora keeps a bottle of *Mendacia* in the tall cabinet in the corner of the living room. I saw her put it there. I'm sure it's locked and I'm sure there are cameras on it, but I know that shouldn't stop a guy like you. If you bring it to me, I can prove everything I said."

She didn't expect an answer. Still, she waited. After many long minutes, she resigned and shuffled back to her room.

She must have fallen asleep, because when she woke up, the moon blazed bright right over the lake. A huge silhouette cut between the bed and the window, throwing her into shadow. A hard object plopped onto the pillow next to her head. She heard the distinctive *gloop* of viscous liquid inside.

Read cleared his throat. "Is this what you wanted?"

TWENTY-NINE

Gwen curled her legs beneath her and stretched for the wobbly table lamp next to the bed. When it clicked on, Reed was looking at the label-less *Mendacia* bottle in utter bewilderment. His gaze flicked up to meet hers, and he actually stumbled backward. He circled around to stand at the foot of the bed, as far away from her as he could get, and the movement was a club to the back of her head.

"I want proof," he said, "but I'm scared to death of it."

"Please don't be." She thought of the stigma surrounding magic in the modern world. "It's not evil or frightening. It's not demonic."

He was shaking his head before she even finished. "That's not what I'm scared of." Closing his eyes, he stood arrow straight and pumped his fists several times. "I look at you and I see this woman who has made me feel . . ." As his voice died, she tried to speak, but he cut her off. "I've told you more about myself than I've really ever told anyone—not even to the girl I once considered marrying. I'm not touching you, Gwen, but I can still feel your skin in my hands. I'm not kissing you, but I can still taste you. I've known you less than a week—because of my job, no less—and I can't imagine being without you, and then you drop this on me."

"Reed."

At last he opened his eyes. Found hers. The pain there . . . ah! It hurt her even more to know she was the cause.

"Everything you've said, I know it should change the way I feel about you," he said, "but it doesn't. It's like my feelings for you are inside this concrete block and your words are bouncing off it. There." He slashed the air with a hand. "There you have it. I've laid it out for you. Now you know how easy it could be to manipulate me, but I won't let that happen. I won't be made a fool of."

She pressed her hands to her chest, rose to her knees on the bed. "I'm not! I swear to you. I'm coming to you because I desperately need your help. Not because I want to use you."

The roll of his eyes made her stomach roll in echo. "Listen to what you just said. Do you understand how hard it is for me to know the difference?"

Yes, she did. But she couldn't retreat now.

"These stories, these crazy things you say"—he shook his head—"they aren't sinking in. They're hitting that concrete block and just laying there. I can't believe anything you've told me. Or maybe I just don't want to."

Her body felt like a balloon, buoyant in the emotion behind his words. She picked through all she needed to say, trying to find the best way in.

"You've asked me about my something-like-that boyfriend. Griffin. He's actually my assigned protector. We're old friends, but we're not in love."

"What's your point?" he said, exasperated. "Why the hell would you tell me this now? And do *not* say it's because you care about me, because it'll only confuse me."

She accepted the sting from his words, her buoyancy deflating. "Because I want you to know certain things about my people. It relates to what I need to do here."

He crossed his arms. "What exactly do you want me to know about him?"

"That we were supposed to get married. Marriages among my people are arranged. To create the strongest possible Ofarian bloodlines, to keep the race pure. The ruling Board chose Griffin and I for each other."

Reed shifted awkwardly on his feet.

"To be honest, I've never been truly comfortable with that aspect of our society, but I understood why it was done. I never wanted to go against them. Until you brought me here."

Silence.

"My sister was banished from Ofarian society. Not because she found out about *Mendacia*, but because she fell in love with a Primary and wanted to marry outside the race. His name was John; I've never even let myself say his name before because I've been trained to push it aside. I don't want to push any of it aside anymore because it's all part of the big lie. I haven't spoken to Delia in six years. I don't know where she is. I sided with my father when he sentenced her. I used to hate her for her decision. Now I envy her. I wish I'd had her strength."

"Am I a 'Primary'?" He spit out the word.

"Yes. You are."

He rubbed a hand over his head, refusing to meet her eyes.

"But my point is that now I'm not just questioning the marriage edict. I'm questioning *everything*. There are serious, serious problems with rules I've followed my whole life. We've based our existence on a product that can no longer exist. I know if I can just talk to my dad about what I've witnessed here, that he will question everything, too. He'll see things through my eyes. He can effect change. I believe he can bring the slaves justice, but not in the way Nora wants it. She's wrong. Justice shouldn't include death or torture for the majority of the Ofarians who never knew this was happening."

Reed looked at her from under his lashes. "What will happen if Nora gets her way?"

She told him about Nora's messy rescue plan that included leaving weak Tedrans behind. She told him how worldwide hysteria would follow. She told him about Genesai and the spaceship lying on the bottom of Lake Tahoe.

He thrust a finger at the darkened window. "*That* Lake Tahoe?"

With great pain, she nodded. "Do you see where I'm coming from? Even if I do exactly as Nora says and the Tedrans get away safely, I'll be locked away in a lab somewhere. I'm sure of it. And I won't be the only one. The whole world will have seen the ship rise from the lake. No Secondary will be a truly free person ever again. *That* is why I said I couldn't go home with you. Because I know, after the ship flies away, that even though I want to be with you, it can never happen."

The words just flew out. Instantly she regretted them.

Reed winced as he pressed his palms to his forehead. "Don't say that. Don't mix your feelings into this. Don't toy with mine."

"I'm sorry." She could say it ten more times and it wouldn't make any difference.

"I'm trying my best to believe you. To not, as you said, think you're on medication."

Her fingers wrapped around the bottle of *Mendacia*. "Can I prove it to you now?"

The slow, tense way he drew breath reminded Gwen of the way she'd felt before walking into her mom's funeral—dread very nearly overpowering courage. Reed nodded once, curtly.

Her turn to take a deep breath. "You remember when we were in the back of the van and the cops pulled us over and I screamed and kicked? Xavier didn't pay them off, as you thought. He used his glamour to hide our sounds and make the van appear still. He did the same to us when he took me through the Plant. He made us essentially invisible."

"You understand that is very, very hard to believe."

Gwen hadn't done *Mendacia* since she was ten. She and her friend David had found a bottle of it in her dad's office at home. They'd known about the product, of course. The reasons their families lived so well were not unknown. They dreamed of working for the Company one day, maybe even being chosen to be taught the supersecret process for making *Mendacia*.

Dad had been preparing to head to Houston to deliver an important order and the two ten-year-olds had snuck into his office. The bottle and spell words, customized to the client's specific desires, sat in his top desk drawer and David had dared her to try it. The client was a female oil CEO who was about to do a huge deal with a Saudi Arabian partner. Things would go easier all around if the Saudi dealt with a man, but rather than entrust the contact to one of her male vice presidents, the CEO wanted to do it herself. So she seamlessly disguised herself as a man.

The length of the glamour depended on either how much one used, or the speaking of cancellation words. Gwen only stole one drop that day, but David had had to hide her in the hall closet until it wore off and she looked like herself again, because they didn't know the words to cancel it out. It had been a close one, though. Dad had almost caught her and she was sufficiently freaked out to never go near it again. Until now.

She rose from the bed. Tipping the bottle, a single drop

beaded on her fingertip. She stared at it, haunted by the Tedran life it had cost to create. She told herself that by using it once now, it could stop all future use. It only made her feel partially better.

Tedranish filled her head. Before, when she had spent days translating the *Mendacia* instructions into their clients' native languages, she had known only what few Tedranish words had been supplied from the Plant. Now she knew the entire commanding language.

She licked the *Mendacia* off her finger. It tasted how it looked: like metal. Tedranish commands spilled from her mouth. She didn't feel any change to her body because it wasn't actually changing, but the sight of Reed's face confirmed the spell was working.

His eyes ballooned and he waved his arms in front of him. "Where'd you go?"

"I'm still here. It just looks like I'm not." The door beckoned to her. She held a slice of freedom in her hands. "I could walk right out of this room, out of this house, if I wanted. You'd never see me again."

"Gwen," he warned, sliding in front of the door.

"But I won't. I can't. If I escaped, Xavier would send his proof to the government. And"—she skirted around the bed, closer to Reed—"if I left, I'd never have your trust."

His eyebrows drew together. So much fear on his face.

Gwen reversed the invisibility glamour.

"Holy crap," he whispered.

"Do you believe me now?" she asked gently.

Still, he shook his head. An eternal doubter, scrutinizer. Just one thing that made him so good in his line of work.

"What type of woman do you like, Reed? Latinas?"

His head snapped up. "What?"

Another *Mendacia* drop touched her tongue. Another string of Tedranish commands.

She shook out her hair. Curly, jet-black strands fell around her shoulders. She held out her arm and watched her skin transform to dusky brown.

"Jesus Christ!" Reed backed away so fast he hit the wall.

"I didn't want to shock you like this." Then, she dared to say in Spanish, "Your pain and confusion are killing me, you have to know. When I look at you, I see the future I might have had. It's more than Allure for me now. It's strange, but I never would have had you, never would have been given this chance to know you, if none of this had ever happened. I feel incredibly guilty for being grateful for that. But there are greater things at work here. Things far more important than me and you, though I wish there weren't. And even though you look at me differently now, I won't ever want to go back to how things were before, when I was living in ignorance and you weren't in my life."

"*Gwen?*"

He was searching her face, alternately horrified and fascinated.

She switched to English. "How about a Scandinavian?"

She sucked another *Mendacia* drop from her palm. The Tedranish words told her hair to turn golden brown, her skin to creamy pale dotted with freckles. Reed's hand flew to his mouth.

In Norwegian she said, "Last night when you asked me to go away with you, my first response was to say yes. God, I want that. I didn't know I wanted that until you said it, because I never would have allowed myself to fantasize about something so impossible. But I want to see where you live. I want to go to museums with you. I want to be how we were in Manny's. I want to laugh with you. I want to . . . be with you."

"What are you saying?"

In English: "Everything you don't want to hear."

He hissed through his teeth, like she'd touched him with a hot poker. Like he wanted her to do it again.

Hesitantly, she moved closer. He didn't back away though he watched her with apprehension. Daring to reach out, she took his hand and gave it a gentle squeeze.

"It's all an illusion," she told him.

Reed shut his eyes, turned his face away. "I get it. I understand now."

"Do you? Do you believe what I've told you?"

"Yes." His hand twitched in hers. "How can I not? Now please, *please* change back to you."

She desperately wanted to press herself to him. Wanted him to hold her in the way she knew and loved. "Why?"

"Because I don't want anyone but you."

Immediately, she canceled the glamour. "Hey," she whispered, releasing his hand to brush her fingertips down his forearm. "Open your eyes. It's me."

When he did, and he saw her again as Gwen, his eyes churned with a mixture of desire and horror. He reached out and snatched her hands in his. They searched each other's faces as if meeting for the first time, and the round beauty of his, softening as the seconds ticked by, made her shiver.

She reached for the Ofarian language, the one her people used only in complete privacy or during the ritualistic Water Rites. She looked deep into his eyes and said, "I could love you very easily, and I know I won't get the chance."

He gasped and tugged his hands free, looking at her askance. For a heartbeat, she wondered if he might actually have understood.

"What language is that?" His voice was gorgeously hoarse.

"Ofarian."

He looked petrified, but in a completely new way. It had nothing to do with all she'd told him, and everything to do with *her.* "What did you say?"

She dared a step closer. They stood within each other's auras, inside that shimmer of energy that sparkled whenever they got close. She'd tried to deny that place existed since pretty much the moment they met, but she refused to do that anymore. If she could have, she'd stay there forever.

"I said that I'm still me."

And then *he* kissed *her.*

The kiss was hard and desperate, the entire force of his conflict behind it. She opened her mouth to him, and when their tongues met, he tasted of faith and torment, beauty and chaos. Emotion assaulted her, screaming in every language she knew. She wanted to ball his shirt in her fists and rip it from his pants. She wanted to slide down his zipper and touch what rose underneath. She wanted him to peel off her clothes and put his mouth to her ear, telling her what she meant to him, asking her to go away with him, if only to hear it again.

But she had to let him take the lead. Let him take what he thought he could handle.

The kiss deepened. Reed walked her backward until her

legs hit the bed. *Yes. Yes.* When he dragged his hands around her stomach and started to fumble with her jeans' zipper, she felt the shaking of his hands. Zipper loosened, he slid his hands down the back of her pants, under her panties, and gripped her ass in his palms. A long, low sound of need rolled up from deep inside her.

He froze. Pushed her away. Off-balance, she fell backward onto the bed. He towered over her, the back of one hand pressed to his still-moist lips. "I can't."

As he stumbled into the bathroom, he trampled all over her heart where it had fallen to the rug. He bent over the sink, splashed water on his face, and slapped off the faucet. Hands braced on either side of the basin, he stared down into it.

Using the fact he hadn't slammed the door in her face, she fastened her jeans and scrounged up the courage to stand. She only went as far as the doorway, though. The DMZ wasn't the DMZ anymore. It was a full-blown minefield.

"The information you have on Adine?" she said. "It's useless."

His head sagged between his shoulders. Then he snapped vertical, snatched a towel off the wall, dried his hands, and threw the towel to the floor. "Of course it is." He stood there with his hands on his hips. "How did you know about that?"

"Nora told me. She was gloating, saying you knew something big about Adine but that it didn't matter. She'd let you go on believing it gave you an advantage so you'd do what she asked."

"Fuck."

The exclamation slid down her spine, filling her with dread.

"I couldn't say anything when I found out because at that point I couldn't tell you anything about our world. And I didn't want you to leave." He threw her a warning glance, telling her not to venture into anything emotional. "I don't know what that information is exactly, but Nora's right. Even if you use what you think is your weapon, it won't make any difference. They'll be long gone before it gets where you want it to go. And I wouldn't be surprised if they destroyed you, too, on their way out."

He slowly shook his head.

"You're not questioning me," she added. "Which means you know I'm right."

"It means a lot of things. It means that what I know about Adine can't help you anymore." He lifted his eyes to hers.

Nothing could help her at this point, except him. She didn't say that, but she didn't have to. He looked away again, one whole side of his face scrunching up.

"Nora knows some things about me," he said at length. "One big thing, actually."

"Your name," she guessed, flipping through all the breadcrumbs he'd dropped since the moment they met. "Who you really are."

"Yep."

"Aren't you supposed to be good at hiding?"

He didn't answer that. He went to the toilet, flipped down the lid, and sat on it. "My last job, I reneged on the contract. I met with the guy, took his down payment, did all the target research possible, went in to get the kid, and . . ." He trailed off and his skin paled.

"What?"

"I got a strange feeling about it. A *bad* feeling. Like taking the kid would have been seriously wrong. Nora alluded it was something sexual, but I don't think so. I didn't get that vibe from Tracker. The job was more than I bargained for, and there was something else about it, something *off*. So I got out and I took his money with me."

"You could've given it back."

The guilty clasp of his fingers between his legs gave him away. No, he wouldn't have given the money back. He liked it too much. Gwen had, too, at one point, until she realized its cost. Now she thought of all those zeros in her bank account and wanted to vomit.

A tingling sensation—not so different from sensing Secondaries—flitted across her skin. "What felt off about the job?"

He just stared at her.

"It had something to do with magic. Didn't it."

"None that I ever actually saw, no." His cheeks puffed out. "Tracker wanted me to get this boy out from a hospital. I thought, okay fine, wouldn't be the first. But then once I dug further into the job, after accepting and taking his advance, I found out the hospital was a federal psych ward and this kid was under massive security."

She didn't want to ask. "Why?"

"He, uh, claimed to be a superhero. That he had . . . powers."

"Like mine?"

"No." He gave an uncomfortable laugh. "The intel said he claimed he could split himself in two. That he could become two completely different people at the same time."

That made her relax some. "Oh. You mean like multiple personality disorder."

He shrugged. "Dunno, never saw it. But if that was the case, why federal protection?"

She couldn't answer that, but the information settled awkwardly into her brain.

"Anyway"—he waved a hand—"I got out. Ran. Too much attention on one kid, and I started to wonder why Tracker wanted him. He's after me now, and Nora threatened to tell him my real name and how to find me if I didn't follow her orders."

Reed's behavior toward both Gwen and Nora now made a world of sense.

"I had to make this work two ways. I had to protect myself, yeah, but first and foremost, I wanted to protect you."

It took all her effort not to go to him. "You can still protect me," she murmured. "You can help me."

He sat up straight, planted his hands on his knees. "How do I know you aren't using my emotions to get me to do what you want?"

"How do I know you won't sell me out and take more money from Nora for telling her I lied to her face?"

It was a fair question, and his jaw tightened. "I wouldn't do that."

"Then we just have to trust each other. It's as simple as that."

"Or as hard."

He jumped from the toilet and spun around, scrubbing his head like mad. "This is crazy. This is insane. And I'm not even talking about all"—he waved a hand behind her—"*that* that you told me. Getting out of here will be tricky shit."

Tell her about it. According to Xavier, the Ofarians thought she was dead. If she somehow figured out how to contact her father, he'd immediately notify the Board. Jonah. The Vice Chairman didn't get to his position for being dense. He'd put two and two together. Gwen was taken to Nevada the same night she saw Tedrans in San Francisco. He'd know they were somehow connected. Jonah would do something with the Plant, which would tip off Nora.

All that dangerous proof of Secondary existence would fly right out of Nora's fingers.

"So you came to me." Reed stared hard. "What's your plan?"

Oxygen filled her lungs several times over. "Contact my father."

He actually laughed. "No way will that work."

"It's all I have."

He looked so huge in that tiny bathroom, standing there with his hands on his hips. "You actually believe that he doesn't know about the Plant?"

She searched deep inside herself for the answer to that question.

"You don't believe it," he said. "I can see it in your eyes."

She held up a hand and answered carefully, "Maybe he does, maybe he doesn't. Above all, I have to believe that he has doubts. Compassion. Or else I have nothing."

"You don't have anything anyway!" He checked his volume, tilting an ear toward the hall. Xavier would probably expect them to be fighting, given their violent show in the garage. Reed lowered his voice and continued, the back of one hand slapping the opposite palm. "You're talking about ending the slavery, but you also said this product rules your society. You're a fool if you think they're going to let that go so easily."

"The majority of my people will be disgusted—"

"But not the people in power. Not the ones who control the information. I know the types, Gwen. I know them very, very well, and I know them from the opposite side of the desk than you. If your culture is so ingrained, if this secret has been kept from thousands of people for generations, they won't let you waltz through the front doors, claiming to be back from the dead, and destroy their work and their revenue stream. They'll

spin your return like you've been brainwashed. They'll hide you away."

"They won't. They can't." But she could feel the cracks in her resolve widening.

"Yes, they will. Especially if you're talking about a shitload of money."

It wasn't just money. Reed had called it; it was about culture. *Mendacia* was all her people knew. Every Ofarian was connected to it somehow, however tangentially.

To end the product meant the end of Ofarian society as it had been for well over a century. The Board would never allow that. Could she?

Reed was right; she couldn't go straight for her dad. She turned and shuffled back into her bedroom, falling in a crooked heap on the bench opposite the bed.

"I have another idea," she said after sitting there for a few minutes. "You're not going to like it."

"I didn't think I would." His voice sounded so very far away.

"I have to be rescued."

"How?"

She licked her lips. There was too much doubt surrounding her father. There was only one other option. "Griffin."

Reed went into his room and shut the door.

THIRTY

The pounding on the hallway door reached into Gwen's hard
sleep and yanked her, kicking and screaming, into morning.
She came awake with a gasp, threw the covers off, and realized
that it was not her door being pounded on.

She heard Reed's footsteps cross his room, followed by his
muffled voice. Xavier's voice responded.

The two said about three words to each other in the hallway,
then the door to her bedroom flew open. Xavier stormed in,
his long legs eating up the small space. His eyes swept around
determinedly. What he was looking for, she couldn't guess,
until his gaze fell on the bed, with her still in it. Even though
she was fully clothed, she clutched the blankets higher on her
chest. Then she realized he wasn't looking at her, but at the
neat, blank space and fluffy pillow next to her.

Though it had pained her greatly to sleep alone last night,
now she could at least be grateful for Reed's silent treatment.
Xavier's suspicion received no confirmation. She didn't even
glance at Reed, though their ignoring of each other destroyed
her a little bit.

"Good morning." Xavier smiled, and his self-satisfaction
gave her chills. Then, in Tedranish, "I'm going with you to
Genesai's."

Someone swept her to the top of Mount Everest and dropped
her off the back end.

"I'm looking forward to meeting him," Xavier said, "and
also to see you work. Translation fascinates me. We'll be waiting for you in the hall."

She wanted to scream, to cry, to slam her fist into the wall, but she was crippled, unable to do anything but drag her ass out of bed and into the plainclothes prison uniform.

She could have told Xavier he was wasting his time, that Genesai would never say anything but nonsense. She could have tried to elaborate on the lies she'd spewed yesterday, but it wouldn't do any good. The moment that cabin door opened and Genesai saw her, the lie would crumble like a dry leaf.

And so would she. Here started the beginning of the end.

Everything she'd said to Reed last night was for nothing. All the truth, all his horror and hurt, all her begging . . . worthless.

Maybe he hadn't come back to her room last night because he was thinking things through. Or maybe the distance was his way of saying that he'd finish his job here, keep his identity safe from this Tracker person, and then disappear again.

As she knocked on the hallway door to be let out, she couldn't feel the wood beneath her knuckles. Every patch of her skin had gone numb, and when Reed opened the door without meeting her eyes, her heart took a high, hard dive into a bucket of ice.

He'd never given her any reason to hope, so why did she feel like it had been stolen from her anyway?

Xavier made her wait in the foyer while Reed pulled the Range Rover out of the garage. All she could think was, *what now, what now, what now?*

Reed rolled down the window as Xavier prodded her outside. "You want to drive?"

The pause in Xavier's step was only slightly detectable. "No." Scowling, he slid into shotgun.

Thinking back, Gwen realized she'd never seen Xavier behind a wheel. He'd lived in a cinder block building up until two years ago. Of course he couldn't drive.

"Gwen," Reed barked as he stepped from the driver's seat. "Back here." With one hand he held the door open to the seat behind him. The other hand tilted a water bottle to his lips. Just another day at the office.

Look at me, she silently demanded. *I'm sorry for telling you. I'm sorry for asking for your help.*

No response.

Then, as she climbed into the backseat, Reed touched her

hand. No, he passed her something. The feel of it was a fire-brand against her skin. She curled her fingers around it. Didn't question. She couldn't afford to.

Xavier stared out the windshield, oblivious. The door locks clicked, they pulled up and out to the main road, and she unfurled her hand in the crater between her thighs.

The golf pencil she'd used the other day and a tiny scrap of paper.

She loosely cradled the paper. Her hands were sweating and she didn't want to shred it. It was worth more than gold.

Her first thought should have been what to write on it, but it wasn't. All she could do was stare at the back of Reed's shiny head and trace the black vine lines curling around his nape with her eyes.

As usual, when he reverted into being the Retriever, he was impossible to read. But she knew one thing, and this she allowed herself to cling to for dear life. He was putting his trust in her, and it was the most precious thing in the world.

The Range Rover started its twisting climb into the mountains. As surreptitiously as possible, she kept watch on Xavier. When she deemed him sufficiently bored, she pressed the pencil to the paper. It poked through and she panicked. The tiny sound boomed like a cannon. Reed glanced at her in the rearview mirror, the connection no longer than half a second.

Elbow on the armrest, Xavier gazed out the window, unaware.

Gwen drew a deep breath to steady her hand. She wrote: *Griffin*. And his cell phone number.

The whole rest of the drive she held the little note against the outside of her thigh and stared down at it, into the faces of all of Earth's and Ofaria's and Tedra's gods. Praying. Hoping.

The road angled more steeply, its corners cutting more sharply, as they approached Genesai's corner of the forest. The trees crowded closer together and she fidgeted, thinking them all spies staring into the car. They knew what she was up to. That she'd coerced Reed into helping her. Apprehension fed into her fear, strengthening it.

She clutched her prize and waited. Waited. Steadied the entrance and exit of air through her lungs.

Reed started to shift uncomfortably in his seat. Xavier glanced over at him questioningly.

"Hey," Reed said to him. "Water's going right through me. Mind if we stop?"

It was all Gwen could do to keep from launching herself into the front seat and kissing Reed in gratitude.

Xavier eyed Reed sideways. "Aren't we almost there?"

Reed shook his head. "At least another half hour. There's an old general store just around the next bend. Secluded. I'll park where no one driving by can see us. The doors lock from the inside. You stay with Gwen. I'll just run in."

Gwen stared at Xavier. He glanced over his shoulder at her. Reed continued to dance in his seat.

Xavier waved an annoyed hand. "Fine, I guess."

The familiar gravel lot of Myrna's General Store appeared around the curve.

Reed's left hand dropped nonchalantly from the steering wheel and slid between his seat and door. He tapped there twice, silently. She shoved the paper into the slot, her heart throwing itself against her rib cage. Everything about the world felt heightened, exaggerated. And every single pair of eyes was focused on her.

The gravel under the Range Rover wheels crunched loud as gunshots. Reed killed the engine and pocketed the keys so he could lock Xavier and her inside. As he slid out of the seat, he smoothly shoved the paper scrap into his jeans' pocket.

"Won't be a moment." He nodded to Xavier, then limped up to the store to keep up the charade that he had to pee.

Through the store's dusty front window she watched the guy behind the counter direct Reed to someplace out of sight. Xavier would think it was the bathroom. Gwen prayed it was a phone.

Xavier hooked a long piece of his blond hair behind his ear and turned in the seat, the leather of his jacket creaking. "Is Muscle as dumb as he looks?"

Oh, the effort to keep a straight face. "Haven't we already covered this? I wouldn't know." Then, because she couldn't resist, "I'll bet he's not nearly as dumb as you think."

His eyes narrowed. "What did he say to make you try to take off last night? Don't say 'nothing.' I saw you two talking in the garden."

She held his stare. To look away would be telling. She'd learned that much from Reed. "I was upset about Nora's choices. I took it out on him. He pissed me off. So I ran."

"Uh-huh." His suspicion hung between them as translucent and hazardous as toxic smoke.

He watched her for a moment. When his face wasn't marred by a scowl, she imagined that the softness in his gunmetal eyes and his pale, European-style beauty might have assuaged some of the women he'd been forced to lie with. Maybe they'd reached for him. Maybe he'd been gentle with them.

"Will you miss Earth?" she asked, trying to get his mind away from Reed and her. "The parts of it you've seen, I mean. The beautiful parts. No one knows what Tedra looks like anyway. No one but Nora, and that was a hundred and fifty years ago when there was a war on."

He arched his neck to gaze up through the moonroof, at the harsh bursts of sunlight stabbing their way through the shifting tree branches. "I wish I could answer that. I don't know what's beautiful in this world and what's not," he said.

With a hard pang, she realized she didn't hate him.

She wanted to. Stars, she tried to. He was too astute and he was ruining everything. He was making things worse for himself and his people, and he wouldn't listen to any reasons why. Yet she couldn't bring herself to blame him, given all that he'd been through—was still going through. Her people hadn't just bred Tedrans in the Circle; they'd bred sorrow and bitterness, and Xavier was one of their finest accomplishments.

Gwen's presence fed his fire. When he walked into Genesai's with her and discovered she'd been lying, it would just be another load of wood and a generous squirt of lighter fluid on the flames.

The store door creaked open. Reed bounded down the steps. Such a short time inside. A good or bad sign?

Reed climbed behind the wheel, the car lurching under his weight. "Thanks, man," he said to Xavier, ignoring her.

Give me a sign. What just happened in there? What did you do?

He started the car and threw it into reverse. With a thick arm stretched behind the passenger seat headrest, he backed out of the lot and onto the road. And completely avoided her eyes.

She stared at the space between the seat and the door where she'd stuffed Griffin's number. No finger taps. No new note.

She stared into the rearview mirror, positioning herself so the rectangular glass perfectly framed Reed's blue eyes. They shifted left and right as he drove, but never up. Never up to meet hers.

Look at me! Tell me.

Why wasn't he giving her a sign? What was he waiting for? She'd told him everything there was to know about Genesai. He could deduce what was about to happen once Xavier and she went inside. Before she went in there, she needed to know where she stood.

Oh, God.

Reed's nonreaction *was* the sign. The worst one possible.

He hadn't reached Griffin. Or maybe he had, and Griffin hadn't believed him. Or Griffin had run to her father. Any way you read it, she'd lost.

She sank deep into her seat and closed her eyes. Only when she sensed the car stop did she open them, and even that much was a chore. They parked near the iron grill at the top of the cliff above the cabin. Reed jumped out and opened her door. It took a few seconds for her legs to find their gear. When she finally got out, Reed didn't look at her, but then she didn't expect him to. His silence said enough.

She would have to watch Xavier now. If Nora got wind of anything going down with the Plant, she'd contact Xavier first.

Xavier took her by the elbow and turned to Reed.

"I know the drill," Reed said, shoving his hands into his pockets and squinting into the trees.

Xavier's heavy gaze shifted between her and Reed, then his fingers tightened and he steered her down the steep path. Her feet dragged. She stumbled more than once.

Xavier pounded on Genesai's door without any sort of greeting. There was no time for Gwen to gather herself, no time to prepare.

The door flew open. A trapezoid of daylight tumbled into the shack and Genesai jumped away from it, a forearm shading his eyes. He was naked from the waist up again, his flour white skin covered in goose bumps. He didn't seem to notice he was shivering.

"Gwen!" he cried. "You came back! Will you take me to her now?"

It didn't matter which language was spoken, her name would always sound the same. She wore her defeat like handcuffs and leg irons: debilitating and obvious.

"I knew it!" Xavier roared. His fingers bit hard into her arm as he spun her around and shoved her inside.

Just before the door slammed shut, she glimpsed Reed up on the rise. He leaned against the Range Rover, pretending not to look at her. By the clench of his fists, though, he was. She'd never wished herself back in that San Francisco alley before, but just then she really needed the Reed that had appeared to her that dawn. She wanted him to charge down the hill and get her out of this.

He didn't.

THIRTY-ONE

Inside the cabin, Gwen coughed on clouds of dust. Xavier rounded on her.

"You lied to me, Gwen. You lied to Nora." Behind his fury lay the shadow of a deep, cutting hurt.

Denying it was pointless. The willpower to fight was starting to deflate, especially after Reed's nonverbal cues. If Griffin wasn't coming, if her father found out where she was, if Nora was readying her arsenal of photographic weapons . . . what was the point?

"You know what? You caught me."

"Why?" Xavier prowled closer. "Why lie when so many lives are dependent on you?"

"Gwen?" Genesai squeaked behind her. She could hear his breath quickening, sense his fear rising.

"I'm all right," she told Genesai as calmly as possible. Then, to Xavier, "I told you and Nora that there are other ways to end this. Other ways that don't end in death, or more slavery. I was buying myself time. Trying to figure out a way to help *everyone*."

"There *is* no time!"

"Gwennnnnn . . ." Genesai began to stamp his feet and pull at his hair. Mistrustful eyes bulged at Xavier.

She planted herself between the two men and took Genesai's shoulders. "Genesai. Genesai, look at me, not at him. Everything is all right. Please stay calm."

He vibrated in her grip. "He is hurting you."

"What the hell is wrong with him?" Xavier demanded.

"You are," she snapped over her shoulder. "You've upset

him. He gets worked up and passes out sometimes. If that happens, who knows when he'll wake up. Then we're all screwed."

She gently took Genesai's face in her hands. "He isn't hurting me. We're just arguing."

A deep, shuddering breath rattled his bones. "What does that mean?"

"It means nothing. We're just sorting some things out."

Genesai pointed a finger as white and knobby as bone. "Who is he? Why is he here?"

Xavier shuffled behind her. "What's he saying? Why is he pointing at me?"

"Enough." She shoved a hand in Xavier's face. "If you want what we came here for, keep your mouth shut and stand back unless I ask for you."

Xavier may have been desperate, angry, and uncouth, but he wasn't dumb. He nodded and backed up a step.

"This is Xavier. He's a . . . friend," she told Genesai, hoping he wouldn't pick up on the pause before that last word. "Remember what I told you about the Tedrans being held in captivity by the Ofarians?"

Genesai's face darkened. "Yes."

"Xavier was one of those slaves. He escaped. Now he's trying to help the others. He needs you."

Genesai gazed at Xavier with new, clear eyes, his wariness dissolving into compassion. "If he is Tedran, then he hurts like I do."

Well said. Almost too much so, because the pressure in her chest hindered her ability to talk. "Yes. Very much so."

Genesai's arms dropped to his sides, serenity erasing the shaking of his limbs, a dramatic and sudden shift from agitated to sympathetic.

"You told him who I am?" Xavier murmured.

She nodded.

"I am pleased to meet you, Genesai," he said, and Gwen translated, her heart warming unexpectedly at Xavier's gentle tone.

"I will be honored to help you," Genesai replied.

She fell into the easy rhythm of interpretation, one language flowing into her ears, another streaming from her lips.

Xavier cleared his throat, ventured closer. "Will the ship fly even if it's been underwater for a century and a half?"

Genesai chose his words carefully. "I have always believed she would fly for me in any condition, on any world, in any circumstance. But now I will need to make sure before I say such a thing. Water is unpredictable."

He wasn't accusing her of anything—he didn't even know what she was—but Gwen sensed the tension in his words and the hatred for the element associated with his altered form and his greatest enemy: her people.

Beside her, Xavier sank to his knees. The way he looked up at Genesai, glassy eyes alighting upon a savior, knocked the breath from her chest.

"We're so close," whispered the Tedran. He raised his palms as though asking for some sort of benediction. "And if it doesn't work . . . if the ship won't run . . . if he can't take us back to Tedra . . ."

Would Nora give her another chance? If Reed's contact attempt had failed and her people were not, indeed, coming for her, would they let Gwen go back to the Board on her own terms? Could this really end in everyone's favor?

Genesai's train of thought was far different from hers. Like a person's name, the name of a planet sounded the same in any language.

"Tedra?" Genesai narrowed his eyes. "Why does he mention Tedra?"

"Because . . . because . . ." A cold sweat broke out over her skin, stealing her words. Genesai's head tilted like a dog's. She stepped closer. "We are asking you to return the enslaved Tedrans to their homeworld."

Genesai stumbled backward, knocking aside a chair, until his back struck the wall. "No, no, no. We will not go back there."

"He says—"

"He doesn't want to go back to Tedra. Yeah, I think I got that." Xavier rocked to his feet and looked down at her, incredulous and disgusted. "You didn't tell him that before?"

"War on Tedra," Genesai mumbled. "Ofarian invaders. Ofarian thieves. Ofarian slavers."

Each mention of her people's name, spewed in that repulsed

tone, was a punch in her gut. She couldn't move, couldn't find any more words in Genesai's tongue.

Xavier came to her side, spoke low. "And you didn't tell him what you are, did you?"

Razors cut her throat as she swallowed. "No. He won't do it if he knows. Don't say anything or you'll be stuck here."

Xavier walked past her, his steps light and nonthreatening, straight for Genesai. Xavier placed a hand on his own chest. "Tell him," he said, "that there are no more Ofarians on Tedra. Tell him that if he helps us, all he has to do is set down, let us go, and then he and his ship can go anywhere they like. No one will harm him."

"Xavier, you don't know if that's true. No one has any clue what's happened on Tedra since we left."

"You left. We were taken."

She looked away, thinking how incredibly difficult it would be to convince her whole race to adjust their knowledge about history.

"I believe we were about to win our freedom," Xavier said quietly. "I believe that my people were winning the war, which is why the Ofarians fled. There are no more Ofarians there. We are free. Tell him. Please."

She told Genesai what Xavier wanted him to hear. Not because she was forced to, but because, for once, there was no malice in Xavier's tone. Just heartbreak. And hope.

Hundreds of lives rode on that hope.

Genesai believed her, a rotten-toothy grin providing proof. It ripped her in half.

Part of her didn't want him to believe. That same part told her to tell him what she was. No matter what had happened with Reed in the general store, this whole situation wasn't in her favor. It never really had been, but at least, for a few moments, she'd had a chance. What had she to lose if she tripped up Nora's plan right here and now? She was back to square one anyway. Maybe, if Genesai knew the truth, he'd stall, giving her more time to figure something else out on her own.

Then she caught sight of Genesai, his head slowly moving back and forth, up and down to take in the fluttering wallpaper of drawings he'd made of his ship. Such love in his eyes. Such longing. Seeing that, she knew what she had to do.

Maybe, just maybe, *someone* could have a happy ending in this mess.

Wearily, she turned to Xavier. "What now?"

He looked at his watch as if their success came down to minutes, not days. Perhaps it did.

The thing hadn't gone off while they'd been in the cabin. The Secondaries' secrets were still their own.

Xavier nodded at Genesai. "We take him to Nora. And then to his ship. We have to know if it'll fly."

She resisted correcting Xavier. It was not *the* ship, but *Genesai's* ship. It was not an *it*, but a *her*.

Xavier flung open the door. Sunlight and cold mountain air streamed inside. Genesai jumped back, staring with terror at the dust motes swirling inside the sunbeam.

"It's time to go." She touched Genesai's shoulder. "It's time to finally see her."

He took a tentative step forward then a giant leap back. Every time she tried to steer him toward the door, he eluded her. He started to sob, snot running into his mouth.

"What's the matter?" she asked soothingly. "Don't you want to see her?"

His sharp face jerked to the corners of the shack. "I've been here, in this room, for so long. The world outside scares me. It scared me when we first flew over it so long ago. It scared me when I was forced to land here. It's filled with people who look like you." He gazed down at his pasty body as if seeing it for the first time. "And like me. I feel stuffed into skin that is too small." One leg started to kick repeatedly out to the side.

"No one will know who you are," she assured him. "No one on Earth knows about the Tedrans and Ofarians."

But they will, regardless of what I do.

Xavier came forward. "You're safe with us."

The dual reassurances seemed to pacify Genesai for a moment, but when his toe pierced a sunbeam, he jolted as if burned.

"We prefer the dark," he hissed through gritted teeth. "We like the black and the stars."

He spoke as though he were already reunited with his ship, and it hardened Gwen's resolve to make that come true.

She went to the bed and retrieved his scratchy, holey blanket. She shook it out, adding more dust to the light, and draped it over his head. Instantly he relaxed. Putting her arm around his shoulders, she nudged him into the daylight.

"You're in the sun now," she told him. "How do you feel?"

She heard the smile in his voice. "The light coming through the blanket looks like stars."

Xavier stopped next to them, his face turned up the cliff side toward Reed. Examining. Thinking.

Even though Reed leaned against the car, the false disinterest plastered on his face and evident in his posture, Xavier frowned and asked her in Tedranish, "What does the Primary know?"

"Nothing."

"You lied to us about Genesai. Which makes me think you lied to me about him."

Oh no. "He has nothing to do with this."

She guided Genesai up the steep path before Xavier could ask any more. At the top, Reed took in the sight of a blanketed Genesai in stride and twirled the key ring on a finger. "We all set?"

"Gwen," Xavier ordered. "Get in the car."

She couldn't protest, couldn't resist, without revealing her hand. So she pressed Genesai into the backseat and stared out the windshield. Inside, Genesai could not sit still, every limb shooting out to test its limits. Outside, her lover and her jailer each had a hand on the Range Rover's hood. She could hear their conversation.

"What do you know?" Xavier asked.

Gwen dug her fingers into the seat edge. Leaned forward.

Reed looked Xavier right in the eye. "Nothing, man."

Xavier shook his head at the ground. When he raised it, he wore an ugly smile. "I'll ask you again. What do you know?"

"I'm *paid* to know nothing. You think I'd jeopardize that?"

Reed swiped off his skull cap and scrubbed at his head. She recognized that sign; she'd seen it several times since they'd met, but only now just pieced it together. He may be a poker player, but he wasn't a good one. What a tell. He was uncomfortable, not anywhere near at ease as what he was projecting.

Xavier turned his head and found her eyes through the windshield. "She's gorgeous."

Reed did *not* look at her. "Yeah. So?"

Xavier's pause was as long and cold as winter on the tundra. "So I guess we'll have to see whether you earned that pay."

As the Range Rover descended down the lake house driveway, Gwen spotted Nora and Adine waiting for them on the front stoop. She'd been distracted by soothing Genesai during the trip back and hadn't paid attention to Xavier. What had that stupid watch told him? What had he typed into it?

Nora was waiting for her. That couldn't be anything but bad.

The wind blew hard, snatching leaves from trees and throwing them around the circular drive. It smelled like snow might be near. The two women—mother and daughter—looked so very different. Adine's dull brown hair whipped about her head and she fruitlessly kept trying to shove it behind her ears. Nora had abandoned her regular loose garb for leggings and a plain, long-sleeved T-shirt. With her tighter clothing and close-cropped hair, the wind seemed not to touch her. *Nothing* seemed to touch her.

Xavier hopped out of the car. For about one point three seconds, it was just Genesai, Reed, and her in the Range Rover. She imagined Reed gunning the engine, swooping back up the drive, and busting out of the black gate. They'd race toward San Francisco at warp speed. She had Genesai, she had Reed; she'd find a way to make this end the way it should.

Then she caught Nora's stare through the tinted windows and that fantasy vanished.

In a daze and using him as a crutch, Gwen guided a blanketed Genesai over to Nora.

"Tell him I am glad he is here," Nora said, her hands clasped together like the fakest of kindly grandmothers.

"I recognize that voice," Genesai said with wonder. "She used to visit me. I never understood her and she never understood me."

Gwen translated between them without thinking, staring at an unseemly crack in the stoop brickwork.

"It's wonderful he remembers." Nora laughed. "Everything in this world is still so new to him. Think about it. He doesn't know how a telephone works. He doesn't know to look both ways before crossing a street."

Gwen glanced at Xavier, who was shifting on his feet, his jaw clenching tightly. Not too long ago, Nora could have said the same about him.

"And," Nora added, drawing Gwen's attention with her raspy bite, "he doesn't know how to lie. Isn't that amazing?"

That Gwen didn't translate.

Her soul was weary. She couldn't even muster a sneer. Nora had her by the balls and the little Tedran knew it.

Nora's false smile vanished. "Adine will take you and Genesai down to the ship."

Gwen blinked. "Now?"

"Yes. Now."

"This way." Adine gestured around the south edge of the house, still trying to get control of her hair.

Arm still around Genesai's shoulders, Gwen whispered where they were going. He shivered in excitement.

Out of the corner of her eye, she saw Reed move to follow them—follow *her*—as he'd been paid to do.

Nora called out, "Not you, Reed. We need to talk."

THIRTY-TWO

Without thought, Gwen swiveled toward Reed.

He shrugged at Nora. "Sure." One hand reached up and scrubbed at his head.

Gwen watched him turn into the house, Nora at his heels, and a terrible sinking feeling threatened to level her.

Xavier stepped in front of her, blocking her view of the door. He examined her face, and she feared what he saw there because at that point she was incapable of disguising her dread. He looked satisfied, sure of himself.

"Go." He prodded her toward Adine.

Did she have any other choice?

The ground passed under her feet in a blur. Genesai shifted under her arm, and she loosened her intense grip. Adine led them to the end of the dock and told them to wait while she went to the boathouse.

The gray choppiness of Lake Tahoe called to Gwen. In the rush that morning, neither Reed nor Xavier had remembered to give her *nelicoda*. For the first time in nearly a week, she could sense the greatness of the water's pull, listen to its language that rang like music. Like people, each body of water—no matter how great or how small—had its own voice. So, so easily she could dive into it, blend into the lake, touch what made her Ofarian. Disappear.

Except that Genesai and the Tedrans depended on her. And Nora had Reed up at the house.

Last night she'd wholeheartedly, unquestioningly given Reed her trust. It was now his to protect or disregard. She refused to believe that Nora would drag out his duplicity. Gwen had glimpsed Reed's gentle soul. He wouldn't sell her out to save himself from Tracker.

Would he?

The door of the boathouse rolled up and back into the roof on a near-silent mechanism. Out chugged a sleek, silver bullet-shaped watercraft. It smoothly parted the water on its way to the end of the dock. Adine popped out of the hatch, smiling shyly.

"This submarine," Gwen told Genesai, stumbling to find an appropriate word in his language, "is going to take us down to your ship. I need to remove the blanket."

"Yes." Genesai shook with excitement. "Yes, yes. Take it off."

When she did, he didn't look with fear up at the big, sunny sky, but with astonishment at the submarine bobbing before him.

Gwen and Genesai climbed in, then crouched knees to chest in the small space. Adine sat in a swiveling seat, her hands dancing over the controls. Pinprick interior lights blinked to life. Water sloshed against the small, circular portholes.

The craft pulled away from the dock and dove. Down and down. Slithering, shadowy weeds slid off the submarine's sides like snakes. Looking up, Gwen could see diffused light dancing on the top layer of the lake. The feeling of traveling in the submarine was similar to what *nelicoda* did to her body—so close to water and yet unable to touch it.

As they descended, they passed through a watery twilight and into a starless night. The portholes darkened to black. The craft hissed, its systems adjusting to Adine's commands.

Genesai couldn't stop touching the bulkhead. He never sat still. Eyes wide with fascination, he rattled off questions about the sub's construction and operation. Gwen translated for him, and then repeated Adine's enthusiastic responses. It was the most she'd ever heard Adine say, and Gwen was surprised to learn the petite half-Tedran owned a dry wit.

Gwen let her mouth participate in the exchange, but her thoughts were back at the house, with Reed.

Unexpectedly, Genesai slid his hand over hers. Such a human gesture.

Adine maneuvered the submarine in slow, smooth movements

through the murk and blindness. Never once did she consult a map or diagram, which made Gwen wonder just how many times she'd visited the ship while Genesai had been longing to see her for over a century.

"Almost there," Adine whispered.

Genesai pressed his nose to a porthole and Gwen joined him. The submarine's headlamps swept diffused light into the depths. Dark fish darted out of their way, scattering the lake particles that resembled swirling snow.

Genesai gasped and pointed. Gwen stared hard into the gloom, unable to discern anything. "I don't see her," she said.

"There. There."

Her eyes adjusted . . . and there she was. Genesai's ship rested on the lake bottom. Imposing. Stirring. Monumental.

"She looks like part of the lake," Gwen murmured. "Like she belongs here."

"Camouflage," Genesai replied, his voice choking. "When we are in the sky, she looks like she belongs *there*."

Though Ofarian by blood, Gwen was still a product of Earth and her imagination had been shaped by pop culture. She'd pictured the spacecraft that had carried her ancestors as hulking and gray, a cold machine made of hard angles and sharp edges. Genesai's ship was none of those things.

The submarine approached her from the bow. Even though she had been created on another world, through the eyes and mind and hands of a nonhuman, there was an undeniable femininity about the ship. A *humanity*.

The bow resembled a face. A wide, squat front porthole posed as a seductively curved mouth. The great dome of her forehead swooped back like a brilliant mane of hair swirling in the waves. The hull rippled like a dress fluttering in the breeze. Her beauty equaled that of an exquisitely carved statue. She was a woman through and through, destined to soar through the sky and make men weep.

"She is so beautiful," she told Genesai.

"Yes." Then he addressed Adine. "Move along starboard. There's an airlock halfway back."

Adine shook off her surprise; clearly she'd never noticed any airlock before. As she swooped the little craft down the right side of the ship, Gwen got a good look at its size. It could easily hold two Plants' worth of Tedrans. Camouflage or no, how its presence managed to stay secret all these years was beyond her.

"There!" Genesai's finger thrust toward a pale oval set into the hull. "There's the door!" If that tiny thing was the door, there was no way any of them was getting in. "Is there an extendable arm on this craft?"

Adine looked playfully offended. "Of course there is."

A motor whirred to life, and the submarine bobbed as the arm loosened itself from the side. It looked just like a human arm, with a hand and everything. Adine gave Genesai a special glove, which he slid onto his right hand. When he opened and closed his fingers, the arm in the water echoed his movements. Adine looked exceptionally proud, while Genesai murmured something about fascinating but clunky technology. Gwen spared Adine that translation.

Genesai stretched the arm toward the white oval. With one finger he drew characters in his language on its surface. Midnight blue lines appeared briefly in the finger's wake then dissipated, but not before Gwen could read them.

My love. I have come back.

The water shivered. Adine's hands scrambled over the sub's controls to keep it steady.

Outside, Genesai's ship sprang to life. Hundreds of tiny lights along the bulkhead sparked and rose to a dull glow. They lined her underbelly, accentuated the sensuous curves of her shape, and gave gorgeous accent to her feminine bow.

Gwen dreamed of how she'd look soaring between the stars.

Open the airlock, please, Genesai wrote on the white oval.

A mass of huge bubbles lurched out from the hull. The airlock door, easily twice as large as the sub, slid upward. Water surged into the ship, dragging them with it.

"This is incredible," Adine murmured as she steadied the sub in the ship's dark interior. "Better than when Pong came out."

A crown of lights beamed down from the ceiling, turning the water around them from pitch black to merely cloudy. The airlock door slid shut. Water began to drain from the chamber. As the water level lowered, the sub came to rest, tilted like an egg, on the ship floor.

Gwen itched to get out, to explore. She wasn't the only one. Adine lunged for the hatch lock but Genesai stopped her with a curt gesture. He stretched the robotic arm out and touched another white oval set into the chamber wall. "I need to tell her how to calibrate the air for our bodies," he said. "It's different for me now."

"Fascinating." Adine was practically licking the glass.

Genesai drew complex equations and calculations. When he was done, he nodded at Adine, who popped the hatch. A whoosh of manufactured air circulated inside. It smelled wet and stale, like a towel soaked in lake water and left out to dry.

Genesai scrambled out, Adine and Gwen on his heels. The floor wasn't hard like metal or wood, but slightly pliant. The walls were midnight blue, smooth and seamless, as though she'd been scooped out of some fantastical material and molded like clay. Water dripped down the walls in shimmering waves on its way to an unseen drain. The effect, paired with the dark walls and pale overhead lighting, was eerie and spectacular.

Genesai fell against the wall near the white oval. Cheek pressed to the blue surface, he extended both arms out, caressing her. The sigh that escaped his body was deep and long and a hundred and fifty years in the making.

Gwen thought she felt the ship sigh, too.

Deep red words appeared inside the white oval. *I have missed you. What took you so long?*

Genesai smiled through his tears.

You seem different, the ship said.

"I'm not," he whispered as his fingers drew the same words onto the oval. "I may look different, but inside I am not."

It would never matter to the ship what Genesai looked like, what form he took. She was not influenced by what had happened to him or how he lived, what he was or was not capable of. *Devotion* was an impenetrable word, trust an indestructible link.

All Gwen could think of was Reed's horror as she'd showed him *Mendacia*. How he'd shoved her away in disgust from that kiss.

The water separating them felt as formidable as concrete.

Genesai reluctantly pushed away from the wall and beckoned Adine and Gwen to follow him. The passageways rose twice as tall as an average human. Gingerly taking steps over the strange floor, Gwen understood how Earth's astronauts must have felt when they first walked on the moon. Or how her own ancestors must have reacted upon finding Tedra and then Earth. They walked through something magical, something *alive*.

Gentle light filtered from somewhere unseen. All along the walls, at regular intervals, were placed white communication ovals. As Genesai stopped to draw something on one of them, Gwen reached out, without thought, toward the wall. She snatched her hand back before she made contact.

Red characters danced on a nearby oval.

Let the yellow-haired one touch me. Let her know what you created.

Gwen gasped. The ship could see her?

Genesai turned, wearing a knowing smile. "Would you like to touch her?"

"Very much," she breathed.

Adine lunged for the wall the same moment as Gwen. Together they pressed both palms to the wall. Its substrate was the same as the floor, deep blue and with a slight give, but strong. Its warmth shocked, but also soothed. Gwen could swear the ship hummed, and not from hidden machinery.

Adine took a deep breath and Gwen braced herself for the Tedran's barrage of questions. Only one came: "What's she made of?"

"Nothing you've seen in this world." Genesai ran his knuckles around a white oval. "Nothing your ancestors saw in theirs."

Gwen pushed herself away. "Will she fly?"

Genesai indicated the meandering passage before them. "Let's find out."

They entered a perfectly round room with a high, domed ceiling. At the far end was the short, wide porthole Gwen recognized as the bow. They were in the cockpit, only there was no seat, no hand controls, not even a single computer or screen. Just one white communication oval.

Genesai motioned for the women to remain in the doorway and went to stand in the center of the room. There the floor wasn't midnight blue, but white. He stretched for the wall oval then dropped his arm, frowning.

"What is it?" Adine poked Gwen. "What's going on?"

"I used to be able to stand here and touch it," he said, looking down at his hands in dismay.

"His new body," Gwen whispered to Adine. "It doesn't match with how he designed the ship."

"Does that actually matter?"

Gwen raised a hand to hush her.

Genesai fumbled with the tie of his baggy pants, let them drop to his ankles, then kicked them away. He wore no underwear. His ghostly teenage body stood in stark contrast to the dark room. He started to examine himself, walking his fingers over his limbs and mumbling. When he was satisfied, he approached the white oval and skated his fingers over it.

Adine jabbed Gwen's ribs again. "What now? What's he telling it?"

"What he looks like. How tall he is, how long his limbs are." Gwen squinted to follow the mad dash of blue words. "Now he's talking about his blood."

"Why?"

Gwen didn't have to answer. Genesai showed them.

In the center of the room, his powder white feet blended in with the floor. He stood so still she wondered if he breathed. Adine nudged her, but she barely felt it. Genesai transfixed her.

The floor moved, cracked. Two thin white tubes detached themselves from the floor. Swaying in a nonexistent breeze, they rose, snakelike, to stretch for Genesai's body. They wrapped themselves around his arms, elongating. White ribbons against white flesh.

Little thorns popped out of the tubes, injecting into Genesai's skin. She and Adine jumped, hissing in sympathetic pain, but Genesai just smiled in rapture and basked in this bittersweet homecoming.

Swirls of blood flowed from Genesai into the tubes. The red was sucked into the ship's belly.

Down, down, down we come. Into fire, into water. Up, up, up we go. All together, with blood.

With blood.

"I'm checking her diagnostics." Genesai's conversational tone startled her. "I need to make sure she's healthy. And I need to adjust some systems so she can accept and use my new blood."

She translated before Adine could poke her again.

The entire room exploded into a myriad of lights, colors, and shapes. The warm, pliant wall burst into graphs and charts, numbers and lists, and hundreds of other images Gwen had no way to classify.

Genesai went to the wall, the tubes still attached, slowly leeching his blood. He touched a yellow squiggle here, traced the path of a pink dot there. He recited columns of foreign words—foreign even to Gwen. He played the wall like a concert pianist. When he was done with one chart, it disappeared and a new one swooped in to take its place.

At last he sighed, stepped away, and the room plunged back into darkness. Before Gwen's eyes readjusted, a million stars swept in to blanket the walls and ceiling.

There was Earth's moon and sun. And Mars and Jupiter. Genesai stood in the middle of a virtual solar system. He turned in a careful circle, palms raised up, to study the star map.

Adine and Gwen shared a wordless look. They may have been Secondaries, but there, inside Genesai's amazing ship, they were as dumbfounded and awestruck as any Primary.

The star map gradually faded. Genesai stretched as if to grab one of the illusionary spots of light.

You'll get back there, she wanted to tell him.

The thorns withdrew from his arms and the thin, snaky tubes unwound themselves from his body. Tiny puncture marks dotted his skin. He frowned at them, running his hands over the spots. The tubes flailed then snapped back into the ship's floor.

Genesai met Gwen's eyes and smiled wearily. "She is well. She can fly."

His legs wobbled. She lunged to catch him, but he collapsed before she could reach him. She stretched him out and pressed a hand to his neck. "She took a lot of your blood," Gwen said. "It's different, when you're human. You'll need to rest, to get some iron in you to help replenish it."

Adine fell to her knees beside them, breathless in awe. "Your blood? It's the fuel for the ship?"

At first Gwen was reluctant to translate, knowing Genesai's weakness. But he looked at her expectantly, and she knew he was anxious to speak with Adine, too.

"She uses my blood as the catalyst to create her own fuel," he answered.

Adine smiled. "Holy crap."

Genesai rolled his head to Gwen. "Can we bring her to the surface? Can we leave now?"

"No. We have to wait. Everything depends on the slaves." And Nora's awful plan.

The women helped Genesai rise, but he gently pushed them away and stumbled over to the smooth wall. He stroked the surface, reminding Gwen of a groom combing down a horse after a hard ride. His lips moved silently; she wasn't meant to hear what he said.

She nudged Adine. "Let's wait in the passage."

"Why? What's going on?" Adine kept trying to peer over her shoulder as Gwen steered her backward.

Gwen smiled, but her heart twisted with jealousy. "They've earned a moment alone."

Time slowed as they pushed back up through the water. Every second seemed longer than the last. Genesai leaned against her, quietly singing, but she didn't hear the words. She only thought of Reed.

The need to see him—to speak with him, to touch him—threw off her equilibrium. What exactly had happened inside the general store? What was Nora asking him? How was he answering?

After the submarine broke the surface, and Adine popped open the hatch, the three stepped out onto a nighttime dock. They'd been down below all afternoon and evening, and a new wave of panic rolled over Gwen. Anything could have happened.

"This way," came a gruff voice from the end of the dock.

She looked up with hope, heart in her throat, but it was useless hope because the voice wasn't Reed's. It belonged to a hired Primary guard—not Frank, the fingerless one—and he held his rifle at the ready. Why was he there instead of Reed?

Gwen rushed down the dock, her footsteps loud and hollow on the wood.

Two figures stood on the lowest stone step leading up to the brightly lit house. Gwen pulled up, terror hardening in her bloodstream.

"So." Nora's diamond black eyes glittered. "Thought you would try to find a way behind my back, did you?"

Every single word Gwen ever knew in any language vanished.

"There are too many people on my side—too many *loyal* people—my dear, to ever accomplish anything outside of my awareness."

What did that mean? That Reed had betrayed her? No. She couldn't believe that. *Wouldn't* believe that.

Xavier came down a step, to her level, wearing a strangely blank expression. So unlike him, not to wear his hate like a mask.

What did you do? she wanted to scream.

She didn't have to.

Xavier looked her right in the eye and lifted up the Tedran watch Reed had been wearing. "He's dead."

THIRTY-THREE

And there it was, plastered all over Gwen's face: confirmation.
Proof of what Xavier had suspected had been going on between
her and Muscle.

Gwen looked like she wanted to scream. She looked
ready to lunge for Nora and wrap her hands around the Tedran
leader's throat. Withheld tears twisted Gwen's mouth and
nose. But she was nothing if not strong, and she just stood
there, sturdy and tall as a robust tree refusing to fall amid
the storm.

Calm as ever, Nora addressed Adine. "Take our guest up to
the house. Get him settled in and see that he has something
to eat."

Adine stiffened, her dark eyes darting from her mother to
Gwen and back. Like Xavier, Adine was beholden to Nora.
Like him, Adine was beginning to believe that that wasn't
always a good thing.

Gwen went to Genesai and spoke to him in low tones. Xavier
had no idea what she was saying, but her actions and intent
were clear: she wanted to help Genesai. She wanted to see him
off Earth. And if she wanted that, that meant she was on the
Tedrans' side, too.

After Gwen finished talking, Adine slid an arm around
Genesai's shoulders and started him up the steps.

"I should have known," Nora sneered to Gwen after Adine
had led Genesai out of earshot, "that you'd use a whore's tricks
to try to turn Reed. You're arrogant. You're beautiful. You tried
to use it."

Gwen locked stares with Nora, sword striking sword. "Fuck. You. You don't know how wrong you are."

One thin, silver eyebrow arched high into Nora's forehead. "Oh, really?" She clasped her hands at her waist. "It doesn't matter anymore. Reed's *gone*. I have Genesai. And I have you. Wearing a tighter leash."

Xavier's watch chimed the same moment as Nora's. Adine up at the house: *Need some help with Genesai.*

Nora raised a hand to him. "I'll go. I've said what I needed to say to *her*."

Gwen watched Nora climb the steps. If Gwen's expression were a weapon, Nora would be dead in an instant. A mighty warrior, this Gwen. A mighty *surprising* warrior.

As Nora's little figure disappeared over the terrace, Gwen's shoulders sagged and her head dropped. A weird feeling settled in Xavier's chest. Sort of heavy and sour. He didn't like it.

He moved closer, spoke low. "You two thought you hid it so well." When Gwen tilted her face away, he knew he'd struck the right, tender spot. "And you did, from Nora, who's so singularly focused, and from Adine, whose innocence baffles me. But you couldn't hide it from me."

She slowly straightened, pushed back her long hair. After days and days of denial, she wasn't trying to hide it anymore. She knew she'd been discovered, and the bare emotion he witnessed on her face was too strong to be covered.

"You forget," he said. "Sex was my life from the day I was able to get it up."

"I didn't forget. I will never forget." She was trying to force strength into her voice, but it wasn't working very well.

"I also know every emotion that goes with sex. Tenderness. Revulsion. Fear. Mindless desire. Frustration. Obsession. Love, even. I've owned every one—or *think* I've owned them— so many times I've lost count." He scuffed a stone with his shoe. "Sometimes, when they were taking me in and out of the Circle, I'd peek into the other cells. When they saw that, they let me watch because they knew it would excite me. But when I watched, I also studied what I saw between men and women. I noticed who connected with who. I could see the signs, the emotions. See who was true and who was dead inside."

She didn't say a word, just lifted her chin. She wasn't going to give him anything and that was okay; Xavier knew it all anyway.

"I had an inkling about you two even though I never said anything to Nora. But it was just a feeling so I kept watching. And watching. When I found out you'd lied about being able to talk to Genesai, I knew I was right. I knew you were going behind our backs with Reed, too."

"Stop." Her face was so blank it almost scared him, this woman who had never feared hiding her emotions before. "Just stop."

He couldn't stop now. "I bet you thought he was this total statue, completely devoid of emotion. And he was, to an extent. He played the dumb muscle role really well, especially when he was alone. But when he came around with you, I sensed it. He changed. Little things like the way he stood, the shift of his eyes. Even when he was pretending to ignore you, he was listening to every word you said, even though he couldn't understand them all. I recognized his reactions. That building expectation of what could happen when you were alone. That sense of protection when you weren't."

He allowed himself to bend a little closer to her. "Even that scent, when you want someone so badly it comes off your skin. Sex is sex. It changes you, no matter the situation."

She didn't back away, and though their proximity was doing unwanted things to his body, despite his self-control, neither did he.

"I didn't tell him anything about . . . all this." She waved a hand at the house. "It was just sex."

That brought up a new bubble of anger. He laughed, but there was zero humor behind it. "That was the difference, wasn't it? He wanted you—truly wanted you—and you were just using him."

That brought out the reaction in her he was looking for. "No! That's not true."

He still needed more from her. She still needed to convince him.

"He may have been a dumbass Primary," he goaded, "but he was not a part of this. The only thing he was guilty of was fucking you."

"Stop." Tears made her dark eyes shimmer, but she pressed her thumbs to her eyelids so they wouldn't fall.

"You slept with him to win his sympathy. Then after you got Genesai, you were going to try to get him to help you escape."

"No! I never used him. I just wanted . . . him. He and I had nothing to do with Tedrans or Ofarians or anything else like that. Those emotions you mentioned? I've felt all of them for him. I still do. And now . . ." She started to cry.

That was what he needed to hear. It matched what Reed had told them once Nora had confronted him: that he'd met Gwen by chance before he'd been hired. That they'd become lovers while here, but that she'd kept quiet on the reasons behind her kidnapping.

Xavier tried to convince himself that was the only reason why he needed to hear her confession, but it wasn't really working.

Gwen sank to the step, her legs cast out messily in front of her. "If I tell the truth to my enemy," she murmured, "does it matter if I tell the truth at all?"

Xavier surprised himself by sitting next to her. "No. I think it makes it even more true."

A few of her tears dripped onto the stone between her legs. In the distance, the lake slapped against the side of the submarine still tethered to the dock. Water everywhere. The sign of his enemy. Yet here he was, talking to one of them.

She looked absolutely desolate. More hurt and lost than the day he'd taken her through the Plant. More terrified than the night of her kidnapping.

"Do you know why I'm doing this?" he asked, pushing his hair away from his face.

Red-rimmed eyes turned up to him and she snapped, "Because you don't want to be a slave anymore?"

"No." He pursed his lips. "None of this is for me. It's all for them. For the women who were forced to be with me. The mothers of my kids. The children themselves. I think about them constantly. In there, in the Plant, we didn't know the meaning of family. Now that I'm out, I know they should have that family. And I want to give it to them. Maybe I could do that, back on Tedra. I deserve that. So do they."

"There are other ways to get that, Xavier. Other, easier ways that don't risk shoving Ofarians—and Tedrans—under a giant microscope. We can figure out how to let all Secondaries live here in secrecy. Give me a chance—"

"I did—"

"No, you didn't!"

"—and look how you screwed it up. Now we have you and Genesai. Are you going to disappoint him?"

She jumped to her feet and growled in frustration. "Look at you. You're acting like you've just won some great battle."

"I haven't?"

"Don't all wars come with prices? Rarely is one side one hundred percent pure in their desires or their tactics. And it's never just the soldiers who get wounded."

He rose, ordering himself to remain calm. "You're talking about the Tedrans."

"Of course I am. You claim to want them all back on Tedra, holding hands and singing 'Kumbaya,' but you're not even sure you can get them all on the ship!"

His blood pressure started to rise. "We've covered this. We're taking steps to make sure every single one of them has the chance to escape."

She was shaking her head. "Chances aren't good enough. Not in my book. Given what you've just told me, I'm surprised they are in yours."

Every retort he thought of died on his tongue.

"Unless," she pressed on, "you've been forced to swallow whatever Nora says and believes like I've been forced to swallow *nelicoda*."

Anger broke through his blockade. "She got me out of there. I have no reason to believe she won't be able to do the same for all the others."

Her inspection of him was blatant and nerve-wracking. "I see you trying to believe it. I'm not sure you're entirely sold."

"I am." Was he?

"You can step away from me now."

He looked down, noticing for the first time that he'd backed her almost into the bushes. Blindly, he shuffled to the other side of the staircase. A cold wind came off the lake, but he discovered he liked it and turned his face into it.

Was Gwen right? He knew he was like a child, with twenty-plus years of experiences to make up for. Had Nora taken advantage of that? She claimed to have chosen him because he was the fiercest, the strongest of heart. Did she truly want to see him safe and free like she claimed, or had she plucked him out of the Plant to help her because he seemed the most damaged? The most malleable?

That made him shiver. Not the winds of coming winter.

Gwen brushed past him to head up to the house.

"He may not be dead," he said to her back.

She froze. Swiveled around. *"What?"*

Above, the terrace was dark and quiet, but he lowered his voice anyway. "Reed. There's a chance he survived."

She raced back down the stairs. He wondered if any of the women he'd procreated with would react the same if they'd thought him dead. Probably not.

"What are you talking about? Tell me what happened."

Oddly enough, it felt good to say. "In the car on the way back with Genesai, I contacted Nora and told her I suspected Reed wasn't one hundred percent on our side. She threatened to tell this guy—Tracker, I think she said his name was—Reed's real name if he didn't admit he was involved with you. So he did. But that's all he'd admit to."

By her distress, she must have known who this Tracker was and what he meant to Reed. Which told Xavier that her and Reed's relationship was definitely more than just sex.

"She ordered me to do it," Xavier went on. "Told me to shoot him. Take him back to the mountains. Bury his body."

Gwen's hands flew to her mouth as she sucked down breath after breath. "But you didn't do it?"

This thing called human interaction would never come easy to him. Pretending and posturing, honesty and trust . . . they were mysteries. He'd only followed Nora because her goal, to him, was the right of the world. He thought himself a hero. In Gwen's eyes, he was something else entirely, and he was forced to admit that it wounded him.

"Do you know why your people think you're dead?" He didn't give her a chance to answer. "Because Nora made me feed *Mendacia* to a homeless guy and then kill him. I couldn't just cloak him in my glamour because the second someone touched the body, it would dissolve. But if he drank *Mendacia*, the illusion would live until they cremated the body they thought was yours." He clenched his fists. "I stabbed him and it was the most horrible feeling in the world."

She stared back at him, wide-eyed. "I don't understand. What happened to Reed?"

He shook his head, hair falling over his shoulders. "I saw so much death in the Plant. All of it slow and agonizing. Though I hated killing that homeless man, when Nora told me to take care of Reed, I thought I could do it again, for her. But I couldn't. I ordered one of the Primary guards to do it—Frank, the guy with the messed-up ear and half a hand."

Gwen glanced down the hill toward the dimly lit hut housing a different Primary guard. "But Nora thinks he's dead?"

Xavier tried to nod with confidence, but he was starting to shake with the fear of discovery. "I told her that, yes. You don't think he'll come back for you, do you? Because if he does, we're both good as dead."

"No." Another surge of unshed tears. "He won't. He'll disappear."

She hugged herself tightly. The cold he didn't feel made her teeth chatter. "Thank you," she murmured, though he wasn't sure she was aware she'd said it.

It made him a bit indignant. He hadn't done it for her; he'd done it because his own fears wouldn't let him take another life.

She started up the stairs again.

"Wait." He couldn't believe what he was about to say. The words just sort of lodged in his throat. "If you help us get out of here, if you help my people and my . . . kids . . . I want to ask Nora if it would be all right if you came with us."

She turned as pale as a Plant Tedran. When she didn't say anything, he kept going.

"I know you didn't know about the slaves. I didn't want to believe you at first, but I believe it now. And I understand that you want to make things right. I see it in the way you handle Genesai, the way you're thinking about my people and your own. We forced you into this situation and you're helping us. I think you deserve a place on the ship. I don't think you deserve what will happen after we're gone."

Her face went from bloodless to tomato red in less than a second. Advancing fast on him, she jabbed a finger into his chest. "You want me to leave them? You want me to betray my people, then abandon them to public fear and government investigation while I sail off into the sunset?"

He threw up his hands in defense, utterly speechless, but she plowed on.

"I know you think you're offering me something good, some sort of twisted 'thank you' for a job well done, but I'm not a fucking coward. You think I'd give the government the match to ignite the bomb then fly away to avoid the blast? No, Xavier. I'm not going with you. I want every single Ofarian to know what I was forced to do here. I want them to know my shame over how we've used the Tedrans. I want them to know I tried to make it better for both races. I'm sure as hell not turning my back on them."

As she stomped up the steps, all Xavier could think was that he could not wait to get off Earth.

THIRTY-FOUR

Xavier locked her in the bedroom she was so very sick of. When she closed her eyes, the small, clean space retained Reed's image like pencil marks that clung to a piece of paper even after the drawing had been erased.

He'd told her once, during the night after their joint shower, as he'd folded her against his body, that he always traveled lightly for a job. So lightly that he rarely brought anything but the clothes on his back. It added to the anonymity, he claimed, and helped to maintain the separation between the Retriever and his true self. She wondered what had been left behind next door. Some socks, maybe. A pair of jeans.

The thought buckled her body and she collapsed onto the bed. In the rush and worry of that morning, she hadn't straightened the sheets. For once in her life she didn't care. She cursed the tears that came as she burrowed into the wrinkled sheets and encased herself in the dark of the piled blankets.

Her fingers brushed something hard and cold.

The object in one hand, she stretched for the lamp and clicked it on. She blinked at what rested in her palm.

Reed's watch. Not the strange Tedran device, but the Cartier Chronograph. *His* watch.

Night came and she clenched it all through the dark. Not even sleep allowed her to let go of him. The next morning, the watch band and time set knob had gouged into her skin. When the marks faded, she squeezed the watch again to make new dents.

Xavier dosed her with *nelicoda* and marched her downstairs. They didn't look at each other, didn't acknowledge in the slightest way their conversation from last night. He confused the hell out of her. One second he was Nora's pawn, the angry former Tedran slave. The next he was trying to help her, in his own twisted way. Still, his actions would result in her end and that of the Ofarians.

That's why she'd taken the *nelicoda* that morning without argument. Because when it dulled her and hollowed her out, at least she wouldn't be connected to the powers that made her Ofarian. At least she wouldn't feel completely like a traitor.

All day she translated for Adine and Genesai. By the appearance of their bleary eyes and the scads of nonsensical drawings, they'd stayed up the better part of the night trying to communicate. Gwen sat on the floor next to the coffee table in the living room, mindlessly interpreting Genesai's explanations about his ship, and describing Adine's blueprints for some truly remarkable inventions.

Across the room, near the fireplace, Xavier and Nora huddled, whispering. Though his attention was fixed on his leader, every now and then he'd glance her way.

Through it all, Gwen kept one hand in her sweater pocket, where she'd secreted Reed's watch.

She was laden with reminders that day; before following Xavier downstairs, she'd stuffed the photographs of the Plant he'd given her into her bra. They itched, but she wanted to be reminded of whom, in the end, she was helping.

Through the glass wall she watched the sun creep down, millimeter by millimeter. Every now and then, Genesai would stare out at the lake, too, and they'd share a knowing look. She'd nod in reassurance, and then go back to watching the sun, how it changed minute by minute on the water. When it fell behind the mountains, backlighting the peaks in stunning color and staining the sky in hot pink and orange, she sighed. Another day gone. Another day closer to the end.

The glass wall exploded.

A terrible, metallic sound roared through the house. Cold wind rushed inside. Pointed glass shards rained down, stabbing into the carpet.

Adine was screaming, scrambling over the back of the couch, pulling Genesai with her. Nora wailed behind Xavier's back as he pressed her into a corner, his eyes wide with fear and bewilderment.

Gwen calmly rose to her feet. Smiling. Jubilant. She sensed them before she saw them.

Ofarians.

There. Movement by the terrace stairs. An arm extended around the staircase opening, a gun clutched in a meaty hand. The man attached to it swept into view. Another appeared, then another. Five black-clad soldiers swarmed across the terrace, crouching low, gun arms extended. Two knocked out the remainder of the glass. The other three hurdled through the ragged hole. Glass crunched under their boots as they fanned out through the living room, shouting to see everyone's hands.

Tedranish whispered in the air as Xavier and Nora tried to form two different enchantments—one for invisibility, one for a confusing distraction—but nothing happened.

"They've neutralized us," Xavier shouted. He lunged for an Ofarian, throwing a punch that had little skill but a long reach and lots of passion. The Ofarian staggered, but another soldier came up, threw his arms around Xavier from behind, and subdued him.

Nora slyly lowered her arms, one hand going for her watch. A soldier swung around, aiming his gun at her chest. "Don't move."

Gwen knew that voice. David.

"Gwennie," David said over his shoulder. "You okay?"

Hands pressed to her lips, Gwen nodded exuberantly. They were here. Her people. Which meant that Reed had somehow succeeded. He'd reached Griffin.

It also meant that her father knew where she was and who had taken her. And if he knew, so did the Board. The Plant . . . the Tedrans . . .

One issue at a time. Get out of there. Find out what Griffin knew.

"Get their wrist devices," she told David, who promptly gave the order to strip the three Tedrans of their gadgets.

Faintly, in the distance, started a gentle and repetitive *whump whump whump*. The sound crescendoed, drawing closer. Helicopter.

A rubber-melting squeal whipped her attention to the large semicircular window above the front door. It framed the driveway as it slanted up to the road. Two black vans screeched down the drive, busting through the gate, and swerved to a stop. House alarms came to ear-splitting life.

The front door burst inward. More Ofarian soldiers poured inside like black water after a dam break. They flowed around the main floor and up the stairs. One even broke the lock to Adine's basement and descended into it.

The *whump whump whump* grew louder and louder.

Gwen whirled in every direction, searching for Reed in every soldier. If he'd gotten a hold of Griffin, maybe that meant he'd come back for her. If he wasn't here, she told herself, it didn't mean he was dead. No. He could just be gone. In hiding to protect himself from Tracker. Or from her.

It was counterproductive to jump to conclusions at this stage. She mentally slapped herself and turned toward the sound of Xavier's Tedranish cursing. David knocked Xavier to his knees, and the Tedran hit hard. Instantly Xavier's shoulders slumped, his chin dropping to his chest. David slapped a black adhesive patch over Xavier's mouth and clamped handcuffs outfitted with a glowing green neutralizer around his wrists.

Though appalled by David's treatment, Gwen said nothing for fear of tipping her hand. It might be better to let her people continue to believe that the established roles of staunch enemies were still alive. She couldn't explain it; it was just a feeling, and one she intended to follow until she found out what the hell was going on.

Adine and Nora looked so small and fragile in their restraints. Adine kept her eyes on the carpet. Nora looked her captors right in the face.

When Xavier lifted his eyes and found Gwen, the resignation in his posture cut deep. David roughly hauled Xavier to his feet. She went to Xavier, plastered a false sneer on her face, and spit out in Tedranish, so the Ofarians wouldn't understand, "You think this is the end, but it isn't. I'll stop *Mendacia*. I'll free your people. I promise you."

She pivoted away before she could see his reaction.

"Gwen!"

That dear, dear voice, back from her past. Griffin stalked across the foyer. Dark hair combed back, black uniform crisp, weapons holstered, he headed right for her. She vaulted up the two steps into the foyer. They met in a crushing embrace, the various doodads attached to his vest digging into her chest.

"You're alive," he whispered into her hair. Even under the screeching alarm, she heard him.

"You came." *Because of Reed*. She pulled back, hands on his shoulders. "Where's—"

"Don't." Jaw clamped shut, Griffin's lips barely moved. His eyes flickered from side to side, like he was ten and sneaking a beer. "Not here."

The *WHUMP WHUMP WHUMP* devoured the house now, fighting with the blare of the alarm. Outside the air churned, whipping the trees around the house in their own little tornado. Through the busted front door, she watched a great black helicopter land on the main road, its blades slicing the air and throwing the surrounding foliage into a fury.

Griffin circled one arm in the air, keeping the other firmly around her shoulders. "Move out!" Even standing right next to him, Gwen could barely hear the order over the cacophony.

Underneath the din of the copter and the house alarm cut the first high whine of distant Primary police sirens.

A sea of black ebbed back through the front door. Uniformed men and women streamed out from the corners of the house, heading for the vans. One carried a laptop computer up from the basement. David and others pushed the three Tedrans toward the waiting vehicles. One Ofarian dragged a writhing, howling Genesai.

"No! Wait!" Gwen peeled free from Griffin's embrace and went for Genesai.

She pried him from the Ofarian's clutches, but she recognized the first signs of him about to pass out.

"Genesai." She took his face in her hands. "It's going to be all right. These people are with me." *These people. Who are Ofarians*.

His eyes rolled back. "They took Nora. They took Adine!"

"Gwen," came Griffin's warning. The sirens were drawing closer.

"My ship . . . my ship . . ." Genesai wailed. His bound hands grabbed at the air toward the shattered window.

"Look at me, Genesai. I will bring you to her. You will fly with her again. I promise."

So many promises. She prayed she wouldn't have to pick and choose which ones to keep.

He passed out. An Ofarian lugged him over his shoulder.

They fled the house. Outside, the vans loaded up, circled the drive, and gunned it up the steep hill back to the road. They jumped the curb and swerved around the helicopter, heading north. The sirens and flashing lights approached from the south.

Griffin pulled her up the steep drive, sprinting right into the gale created by the copter. Her calves and thighs burned. Her lungs pressed flat against her ribs. She fell into the helicopter, Griffin following suit half a second later. He yanked the door shut and the craft lifted with a jolt.

Up, up they rose. The sun had set, and the blue and red lights of the Primary police sparkled brightly in the new darkness below. She wondered what they would find in the lake house when they investigated. She wondered what, if anything, they would make of it.

Had the Ofarian soldiers royally screwed up? By coming after her in the way they had, had they compromised themselves?

The copter careened southwest, back toward San Francisco. Back to the only place she'd ever called home. Back to the place she dreaded. *This must be what it feels like,* she thought, *to have your arm ripped off then reattached, only to have your body reject it.*

She sensed eyes on her and turned from the window to find Griffin watching her with a dark, guarded expression. What had Reed told him? Where *was* Reed?

Griffin gave her a small but firm shake of the head, echoing what he'd conveyed in the house. *Not here.*

A terrible *BOOM* shook the entire valley. Overtook the deafening buzz of the helicopter. Vibrated in her chest.

"Fuck, what was that?" Griffin screamed, motioning for the pilot to circle and check it out.

The pilot banked sharply to the right. When they came about, a great fireball tumbled upward, smoke and flame unfolding, swallowing every inch of the rocky promontory where the lake house had sat.

She couldn't breathe. Couldn't feel her skin. Couldn't hear. The helicopter froze in midair.

Another explosion consumed the boathouse. The submarine had been in there. A hideous wail filled the helicopter cabin and she realized, seconds later, that it was hers.

Nora's final statement. Her fail-safe, should anything go wrong. If returning to Tedra wasn't going to happen on her terms, it wasn't going to happen at all.

THIRTY-FIVE

The helicopter touched down on a circular cement pad some-where on the peninsula. It wasn't San Francisco International; it didn't even feel municipal. Another of the Company's hidden places secured with money bled from Tedran lives.

A huge silver BMW waited at the edge of the pad.

"My dad?" she gasped as the helicopter blades whined to a stop.

Griffin shook his head. "The Chairman is on his way back from Saint Petersburg. A few others have to fly in on red-eyes. The Board'll gather tomorrow."

That left her a little speechless. She'd only been "dead" a week and the Board was already back at work? She could understand the others, but her dad? He'd mourned Delia's exile for weeks. But then, Delia had never been nearly as involved in the Company as Gwen.

As they hurried to the waiting car, Griffin pressed the com-munication piece in his ear. "That kid's still out," he reported to her.

She worried about Genesai. "He may be for a while. Can they get him to me? I should be the first person he sees when he wakes up."

Griffin eyed her, then nodded before relaying the order. "Who is he?"

"Not a Tedran."

The fact that Griffin didn't ask another question said that he knew far more than he was letting on. Everything she needed to say bubbled up inside her, threatening to split her skin. As they tumbled into the waiting BMW, she opened her mouth to let out a barrage of her own questions, but he gave that little shake of his head again and pointed to the ceiling. Company car. Of course it was bugged.

Griffin directed the driver to the fluorescent-lit corner diner the two of them had always turned to in their early twenties when their late-night, alcohol-filled stomachs demanded it. They wedged themselves into a booth, their butts barely touching the vinyl before their voices overlapped.

"What the *hell* is going on, Gwen?"

"What do you know?"

"I can't believe you're alive."

"How did you find me?"

"What are we supposed to do now?"

"Did you talk to Reed? Where is he?"

"Reed." Griffin leaned back. "You want to start with *him*?"

She swallowed, trying to bring moisture to her dry mouth. "You knew where I was, which means you must have talked to him. Have you seen him? Is he alive?"

She'd only been gone a week, but Griffin's eyes seemed much darker than she remembered. He just sat there, staring at her.

"Oh, God." Her breath hitched. "Just tell me."

"He's alive."

She started to laugh. A hysterical, crazy sort of laughter.

"He's being held with the Tedrans at the Plant."

The laughter died. "What?"

Jaw set tight, Griffin ground out, "It was the only way. I had to tell the Board we caught the kidnapper. How would that look if I hadn't?"

"You captured him?"

"At least I know where he is now."

"Yeah, but you *captured* him?"

Griffin showed her his palms. "Whoa. I think you need to back up and start from the beginning. I'm flying blind here."

She twisted the zipper on her sweater. "Can you tell me what he said to you when he called? I'll fill in the rest."

He ran a hand through his glossy brown hair. The pieces around his ears and neck curled a bit. Stubble shadowed his cheeks and chin. So unusual for Griffin, who'd always made a point to be styled and shaved.

"I almost didn't pick up the phone." He stared at his hands, fingers spread on the table. "The number came through as 'private,' but I just had a feeling. I can't explain it. It was almost a premonition. Like how, even when my back is to the door, I know when you walk into a room."

Though he said it matter-of-factly, an uncomfortable flush crept up her neck.

"I thought you were dead—we all did—but I knew the phone call had something to do with you. Then I heard this guy's voice and my stomach dropped. He said there wasn't time to talk but that you were still alive, being held hostage by the Tedrans. I asked him if he was one of them and he said no. Then he told me I couldn't go after you until he told me the whole story. *Only* me.

"He said, 'I don't care about your fucking war. I'm concerned about Gwen and want her safe, and if you bust in now with guns drawn, she won't be.' I remember exactly what he said because of the way he said it, like he had everything to lose. I demanded to know who he was and he told me his name. Then he said he'd contact me again. That was the first time we talked, yesterday morning."

Her nose tingled. "The first time?"

"Yeah. I waited the whole day to hear from him again. Almost went out of my mind with fear for you. I told myself if I didn't hear back from him in twenty-four hours, I'd go to the Board. Then last night he called back. He sounded out of breath, shaken. Told me to get up to Tahoe to meet him. Alone."

She stretched across the table and covered Griffin's hands with her own.

"I could've set a detail on him, could've brought the entire security force with me." He still didn't meet her eyes.

"But you didn't."

He shook his head. "It was the fact that he'd called me and not your father. It was the desperation in his voice. And"—he finally lifted his eyes to hers, and they were haunted—"that I already knew who he was."

Huh?

"I remembered his name. When you told the Board about the night you first saw the Tedrans, you said the Primary who met with them was named Reed. When he said that was his name, I knew he wasn't lying because I remembered he'd been talking to you before the Tedrans ever came in. I remembered he was the guy who'd attacked Yoshi."

She didn't like the wary look on Griffin's face. Her hands turned clammy but she didn't want to let his go.

"So I drove up to Tahoe and met him. Gwen, he told me everything."

A huge sigh of relief left her body. She knew Reed would have been quick and direct; it wasn't in his nature to bullshit or skate around the issues. That meant Griffin knew all about the Tedrans and the Plant and *Mendacia*.

But when Griffin's expression turned rock hard, dread dropped like a stone into her gut. "Wait." Her voice went hollow. "Everything?"

Griffin withdrew his hands.

A waitress plopped sloshing cups of coffee between them. Gwen regarded them with surprise even though she and Griffin had ordered them the second they'd walked in the diner.

"Gwen, you *slept* with him? The Primary who kidnapped you? The man working for the Tedrans?" The disgust in his voice hardened as ice on her skin. "Please tell me you did it so he'd help you escape. Please tell me you used him."

Stars, she wanted to. "I can't."

He punched hard into the booth cushion, air whooshing out of it. "Do you understand how this sounds? How this makes me feel?"

"Of course I do." Only the truth would help them now. Sort of like breaking a bone again to set it right. "It's more than the Allure. Maybe it started out as Allure, but sometime in the past week it shifted."

His hands started to shake, and he tried to hide them under the table. "I don't know if I want to hear this."

"I think you have to." He cringed. "It'll help you make some sense of this mess. I knew someday I'd have to tell you. It won't be easy to hear. Hell, I can't even believe it happened."

So she told Griffin about Reed. The whole story. She started with the scene in the alley and described their conversation in Manny's. Everything she hadn't told the Board. Everything she'd kept to herself.

She went through all their interactions at the lake house,

everything but the erotic details. Griffin had to know that her and Reed's relationship wasn't just circumstantial, that you couldn't have thrown a different kidnapper at her and gotten the same outcome. That it had started out as the Allure and ended up someplace else entirely.

Through it all, Griffin stared at his smeared reflection in the metal napkin dispenser.

When she finished, ending with Xavier's admission that he hadn't killed Reed, she opened her arms. "There. Now you know everything I do."

He pulled out a napkin and started to pick it to pieces. "Not true. I know something you don't."

Her heartbeat stuttered. Something about the Plant or her father or the Board. Something that would render the slaves' rescue impossible. Something that would prevent her from going after Reed . . .

"What is it?"

Griffin laughed without any bit of humor. "You know, at first I thought I was imagining it, that I was reading too much into it. I thought you were dead. I was still grieving and my thoughts weren't exactly straight. Then all of a sudden here was the very guy who'd taken you, talking to me about someone who I considered to be a ghost. He couldn't possibly be for real, I thought. He couldn't possibly know you as well as it seemed."

The napkin disintegrated in his fingers. He cupped his jaw in the crook of his hand. He still wouldn't look at her.

"I tried to talk myself out of believing it, but it was pretty damn persistent. I saw it in his eyes. It came through in the tension in his voice, how he told me your story." Griffin ducked his chin. "Reed doesn't give a flying fuck about Ofarians or Tedrans. It's all for you."

She could only sit there as Griffin's word tsunami bore down on her. At last he met her eyes.

"He's in love with you, Gwen."

This, from the man the Board wanted her to marry.

"I . . . I don't think so. We've known each other a week."

"Took me less time than that to fall in love with you. The first hint from the Board about our match, and bam, it just hit me. So I know what it looks like, to love you. I saw it in him."

She pressed her forehead to the Formica table, which smelled of eggs and coffee.

"Do you love him?"

Her fingers found Reed's watch, still hiding in her sweater pocket. She pictured him lying back on that low bed in the attic cell, one big arm draped behind his head, tattooed mysteries wrapping themselves around his hard chest. She heard his voice in her head, telling her about his drive to learn and his life's regrets, about what was written on his body. She saw that slash of a dimple, meant only for her.

"I don't know," she said to the table. "Maybe."

But as she raised her head and met Griffin's expectant gaze, they both knew she was lying.

The coffee between them was getting cold but she clenched the mug, dying for it to give her warmth and strength. As she shook her head, greasy strands of hair brushed her face.

"I'm sorry," she said. "I'm so sorry to do this to you."

Griffin looked like a deflated balloon. Boneless, resigned, and brokenhearted. He slid out of the booth.

She panicked. "Where are you going?"

A thumb jutted toward the back. "The bathroom. Give me a minute."

She watched the bathroom door with a twisted stomach. When he shuffled back, his hairline was damp. For a moment he stood motionless at the end of the table, and she worried he was deciding whether or not to sit back down. She needed him. What they had to do was much, much bigger than their personal relationship, even if she had made some wrong choices.

"I won't pretend to understand what's happened between you two," he said, finally flopping back onto the cushioned bench.

A sick feeling rolled through her. "Is that why you took Reed?"

His pause lasted forever. "No." Then his head twisted and he sneered at his reflection in the window. "Maybe partly. I don't know. When I walked away after first meeting him, I was so confused. I was angry at the Board, at our ancestors. Angry at you and Reed . . ."

"So you took him because of that?"

He pinched the bridge of his nose. "That first meeting, he

and I hashed out a plan to go in and get you without involving the Board. He's good. Really good. Ex-military, obviously. I was supposed to go back to San Francisco, make up some excuse for my absence, then rendezvous with him again. But once I was away, I knew having him around us wouldn't work at all. He's the Primary who kidnapped you, for chrissakes. No one would ever believe he'd switch sides. No Ofarian would allow him in. So I had to make like he gave me the tip but that I didn't trust him. So right before we were supposed to go in for you, I had him ambushed." He gave a short laugh. "Can't say it didn't give me little bit of satisfaction."

Reed had to be seething. Enraged at Griffin's duplicity and furious at Gwen for ever dragging him into this. She couldn't be more grateful for Reed's trust and his risk, and look how she'd repaid him. One good thing about it, though? At least now he was out of bounds for Tracker.

"Did he say how he got away?"

Griffin grinned awkwardly. "Said it wasn't too difficult. Bribed the guy who was supposed to have pulled the trigger."

Of course. Those guards were all Primary misfits. Frank the Fingerless was probably hiding from something, like Reed.

"When we get the slaves out," she said quietly, "I'm taking Reed with me."

He just stared. "Are you forgetting something?"

"What?"

"Reed *knows*. About us, Gwen. He's a Primary."

She straightened. "You wouldn't. Not after how he helped me."

"I wouldn't?" But even he didn't look so sure.

She wanted to lie down right there on the cracked vinyl, close her eyes, and wake up a week ago. If she'd known then that all this would happen, would she have let Reed pull her into his arms on the sidewalk?

Yes. Yes, she would have.

"Tell me you didn't know anything about the slaves," she said.

"God, Gwen, no. Not a thing. I mean, I knew where the Plant was for security purposes, but as far as production went, I knew as much as you."

"Do you think my dad does? Know everything, I mean."

He shifted on his seat, his gaze dropping.

"You do, don't you. *Shit,* Griffin. He can't."

" 'Can't,' Gwen? Come on. Of course he can. And he does. You just don't want to believe it. Don't be stupid."

She chewed on her lower lip, her mind ping-ponging, her senses in hyperdrive. The smell of burgers on the griddle assaulted her nostrils. The stickiness of the tabletop permeated her skin. The lights glared harshly and the inane chatter of the late-night crowd poked a headache into her skull.

"I'm going to end this," she said, "and I need your help."

For the first time in her whole life, she saw fear darken Griffin's eyes. "That's treason."

She unzipped her sweater a few inches, reached inside her bra, and whipped out the photos she'd stashed there. She tossed them in front of Griffin. "And that's slavery."

He looked at them. Recoiled. "Jesus."

"Take them."

To him they were poisonous, and his hands hovered inches above the images. "What do you want me to do with them?"

She told him her plan.

The horrible consequences of that plan flashed in Vegas lights across his face. If they failed, they'd face a punishment worthy of treason. A *nelicoda* overdose at the very least. Banishment from Ofarian society. Possibly death. Griffin's whole life had been service. He'd trained incredibly hard to rise as high as he had. And she was, for all intents and purposes, an Ofarian princess.

She hoped against hope that he'd see things her way.

"I'm sorry, Gwen." He pushed the photos back to her. "I can't."

THIRTY-SIX

"There's been a mistake."

One Ofarian soldier in black fatigues stood in the shadowed corridor next to the double doors, ignoring him. Reed tapped his wrist restraints against the bars, aggravating the throbbing at the back of his skull. That'd been a good hit. Solid, on the mark. The men at Griffin's rendezvous had taken full advantage of the element of surprise. He'd suspected Griffin might double-cross him, but at least not until after they'd rescued Gwen. This had to be some kind of colossal mistake. Griffin hadn't been at the rendezvous. Somewhere wires had gotten crossed.

Reed had to get out of here. Had to get to Gwen.

He tapped the bars again. The lone soldier dismissed Reed with a quick side glance, then shuffled a half step away.

"Hey, I'm talking to you. Get Griffin."

"Griffin who?" the soldier smirked.

Reed growled in frustration. "Jesus. I don't know his damn last name."

The soldier grinned. His top two teeth slanted slightly inward. "Orders came straight from the captain. No mistake at all."

Mother*fucker*. The bastard took him on purpose. He'd believed everything Reed had to say about Gwen then locked him up for it. Cocky, jealous asshole. What was Reed thinking, telling Griffin everything? What was Reed thinking, believing Gwen when she said Griffin was the key to getting her out and the start to sorting out this whole mess?

"Face it, Primary," came Xavier's monotone from behind him. "She used you."

Reed turned his back to the bars, pulsating scalp grinding into the iron, to face Xavier, who was sprawled against the far wall. The sickly green overhead light bathed his pale hair and skin, making him look demon-like.

When Reed had first come to, he'd had no idea where he was. One look at Xavier's tormented expression and Reed figured out he was in the Plant.

"She screwed you," Xavier said. "Literally and figuratively."

She didn't. She didn't. She didn't.

"You think she's really going to come back for you? For us?" Xavier's eyes went frighteningly blank. A shudder coursed through him. "She's a liar. This whole time, she lied to both of us."

Reed shifted his gaze to Adine and Nora, who huddled in opposite corners. Nora was shooting eye daggers at Xavier. Adine looked, well, hurt. And lost. Like she'd been betrayed by her best friend.

"Don't feel stupid." Xavier's clipped tone stabbed at Reed, hard and sure. "She screwed us, too."

"What did she promise you?" Reed asked.

Xavier's eyes swept across the green-gray walls, but he didn't answer.

"To end this," Nora sneered. Her little backbone was made of steel. She sat perfectly upright, cross-legged, hands on her knees. "She lied. She's made of lies, from blood to bone."

Reed pulled away from the bars. "How is this any worse than what you did to her?"

"Nora, she tried," Adine said shortly. "She really did. You didn't see her down there with Genesai and the ship. She honestly wanted to help him, to help us."

Reed had never seen Adine snap at Nora like that. As the two women glared at each other, he said to Adine, "I noticed you don't call Nora Mom."

Adine shifted, eyes on the floor. "No. Not for a long time."

Nora sniffed and fixated her stare on Xavier, as though this was all his fault. Maybe it was. If he'd actually pulled the trigger instead of handing the gun to Frank, none of this would've happened. Reed wanted to tell Xavier that he'd done the right thing, but had he? If Xavier had followed Nora's orders, the slaves might be out by now . . . but Gwen and her people would still be in danger.

Was trading the safety of one race for another the only way?

Gwen hadn't believed that. Reed wouldn't either.

He crouched in front of Xavier. "We can still try to get out of this."

"We have nothing." The desolation in his face echoed that statement.

"Not true. You have me."

Xavier's head came away from the cinder block wall.

Reed rattled his cuffs, lowered his voice. "This little green light doesn't do shit for me. It's an opportunity. When they move us . . ."

Xavier laughed though it was devoid of anything but hopelessness. "You really are nothing but muscle. You're not getting out of here, away from *them*. You know what they do to Primaries who find out about them?"

Reed glanced at Nora, who turned her superior gaze toward the bars.

"You don't, do you?" Xavier sat up, his bitter face inches from Reed's. "They kill them. Anyone who's ever gotten a whiff of the Ofarian world dies. Aside from protecting Gwen, that's Griffin's *job*."

Reed's mind circled back to the scene in the alley. If he hadn't shown up, the Japanese guy would've died. That's why she hadn't wanted to call the cops; she was biding her time to wait for Griffin to arrive.

But Gwen wouldn't've told Reed all that she had, knowing that would be his fate. No way. She hadn't *wanted* to tell him; she'd held out until she had no other options. He'd witnessed her desperation. By nature, she wasn't deceitful. She'd convinced him she wasn't using him. He had looked into those beautiful, beautiful eyes and believed her.

He swept to his feet and surged toward the bars.

"Hey," Reed called out again to the soldier in the corridor. "Does Gwen know I'm here?" The soldier raised an eyebrow. "Gwen Carroway. Contact her directly. Ask her if I'm supposed to be here."

With a roll of his eyes, the soldier peeled away from the doors and went to a corner to mumble into his shoulder radio. Reed couldn't hear a word of the exchange. Xavier smirked on the floor. The whole thing took forever. If Reed had had hair, he would have been gray by now.

The soldier sauntered back, stood right in front of the bars. "Well?" Reed demanded.

"Ms. Carroway says you're exactly where you belong."

Reed felt as if a giant, invisible football player had tackled him from behind. His body hit the concrete floor with a terrible force his numbed nerves didn't feel. As his eyelids dropped, his last thought was of his mom and dad and Page, and how devastated they would be when he didn't come home for Thanksgiving.

Gwen swept through Company HQ. Coworkers, kinsmen, and friends swarmed her, enveloping her in a cocoon of warmth. Despite her sick heart and the spiked ball of dread slowly dragging its way through her veins, she was genuinely glad to see them. She spoke to each of them, sharing tears and hugs. But when she pulled back, looked into their happy faces, and then glimpsed their computer screens or the stacks of paper on their desks, all she could think was: *You don't know what you've been perpetuating.*

"Gwennie!"

Dad.

The Chairman stepped from the boardroom at the far end of the corridor. The crowd around her parted. In that moment he wasn't anything but her father, and the need to go to him was instinctual. She hurried toward him, the weight of their past hardships and present problems trailing just a nose behind. He was sobbing as he pulled her into his big dad bear hug. Too tight for comfort, but too wonderful to matter.

"I thought I'd lost you, too," he murmured, only for her ears. "Oh, Gwennie, I didn't know how I'd go on. Your mom, Delia, you . . ."

"I'm here, Dad. I'm okay."

When he stepped back, his hands firmly on her shoulders as though she might disappear again, she saw the extent of his grief. Uncharacteristic stubble dusted his chin and cheeks. His

Italian suit was rumpled and he smelled faintly like the cabin of an airplane. But the most disconcerting detail of all was the fact that he wasn't using *Mendacia*.

There he stood, Chairman Ian Carroway, laid bare with his own face and wearing his grief, for all the Company to see. He took her face in one hand and nodded toward the boardroom. "You don't have to do this now. You can rest—"

"No." She *definitely* had to do this now. Reed was trapped in the Plant with the Tedrans, and Griffin feared committing treason. She was the last fighter standing, and she was going in with weapons hot.

The whole Board waited inside. She noticed, as she crossed the threshold into the boardroom, that the waterglass had already been activated. How long had they been all together, waiting for her?

As the door closed behind her, she made the rounds, clasping hands and accepting gentle embraces from men and women she'd long considered superior. Despite their caring words and benevolent smiles, a chill hung in the air, enhanced by the consistent murmur of the waterglass.

At last she shook Jonah's hand. She flashed back to seeing him in the Plant, when authority and tension had buzzed around him, and he'd glossed over the Tedrans as though they were unfeeling machines. His grip on her hand was disturbingly normal, though he held her eyes for a beat longer than he ever had.

"Welcome home," Jonah said. "We're glad you're back."

And she thought: *But you were the reason I was taken*.

Her father patted the chair next to him and she sat, gazing over the group of men and women she'd once longed to be a part of. Was that only a week ago? A week and a lifetime ago. A week and *thousands* of lifetimes ago, because that's what had been wedged between her and her former aspirations: the truth behind thousands of Tedran and Ofarian lives.

She sifted through everything she'd learned and everything she thought she knew. If she was the last warrior capable of doing what's right, she wouldn't back down, even while being hopelessly outnumbered. She thought of Xavier and how he'd offered her a place on Genesai's ship. He hadn't done it to hurt her; he'd done it because deep down he believed in her. What she did now, she did to erase the reasons why he'd flinched from her that day in the Plant.

She took her dad's hand and squeezed it once. He looked at her questioningly, the curve of his wrinkled mouth troubled.

She faced the Board and announced, "I know about *Mendacia*."

Inside her fingers, her dad's hand went slack. "What do you mean?" he asked, and his voice sounded lower than she'd ever heard.

"I mean I know everything. Where it's made. *How* it's made."

As she spoke, the story of the Plant came out true and hit its mark. She looked every one of the Board members in the eye and related the horrors she saw. The most satisfactory part was the sheen in her father's eyes. She hated to take solace in his devastation, but his reaction was exactly what she'd needed to see. He wasn't heartless.

He pressed his lips together to keep his chin from quivering, but it wasn't working. "What did they want with you? Out of all of us, why take you?"

Here she paused, considering where she wanted her words to steer her elders. Nora had once told her that *Mendacia* was nothing but liquid lies. She'd been right, but right now that term also applied to Gwen, because she was made of water and the time for telling the truth to the Board had ended.

"Nora thought I would be able to speak with the pilot of the ship of the First Immigration. She believed he could take the Tedrans home, but Genesai is useless without his ship. It no longer exists."

The limo pulled up in front of the stunning white, three-story Victorian manor in Pacific Heights. She'd practically grown up there and had never thought of it as ridiculous or opulent, but now, staring up the grandly curved front steps, all she could see were the faces of glamour-drained Tedrans in the stained-glass windows and sex-dead men and women in the carved porch posts.

"What are we doing here?" she asked her dad. They hadn't said anything on the short ride from HQ. Just sat next to each other, her head on his shoulder like she was twelve again. "I thought I was staying with Griffin."

He gave her knee a pat. "Why don't you stay here tonight? It would make me feel better."

It rankled her, but she pushed the feeling away. She'd sleep in the second-floor bedroom that had once been hers and think about what to do next. Think about how to get Griffin on her side. How to get around the Board. How to save the Tedrans.

In a daze she trudged up the steep front steps and into the warm, rich interior of the Chairman's manor. Two members of the security team followed her and her dad up the creaking staircase to the second floor. She didn't recognize either of the soldiers.

She paused at the door that had once been decorated with puffy stickers and teen pinups. "Where's Griffin?"

"Away on my business."

That was fast. She frowned as an itch started on the back of her neck. Dad swept an arm into the bedroom that had been redecorated in rich jewel tones. She went inside, lost in thought.

Griffin would hate to be away now. Even in the light of their strained conversation at the diner, he wouldn't want to be away from her. She was still his responsibility. She hoped the Board wasn't punishing him for "failing" to protect her.

"Won't he expect me back at his place? He'll worry if I'm not there."

"He knows where you are and that you're safe." Dad shut the door and leaned against it. They were alone in her old bedroom. "I can't even imagine what you've been through."

She stood in the center of the room, tightening her arms around her waist. "You need to see it, Dad. You need to go." Nothing like the truth. It was her strongest weapon now. "And we need to stop it. You and I."

That weight settled on his shoulders again. He stuffed his hands into his pockets, looking his age. He shook his head with great sorrow. "I'm so, so sorry you had to find out like that."

"Find out . . . Oh, God." Her legs fell out from beneath her, and she sank into a brocade-upholstered, wing-backed chair. "You knew. You knew everything and did nothing."

He lifted his eyes to hers, and there was unfathomable sadness behind them. "Of course I knew. I'm the Chairman."

Nora and Xavier had been right. Reed had tried to tell

her—Griffin, too—and she hadn't listened. She deserved a silver medal for foolishness and a gold in naïveté.

Instinctively, her hand went for her pocket. She wrapped her fingers around Reed's watch and squeezed. Hard.

An open wound yawned in her spirit where Reed had been ripped away from her. Griffin's absence burned like acid poured into the crevice. And her own father's treachery lit the whole thing on fire.

"Dad, how could you . . ."

He came toward her and rubbed her numb arms in an achingly fatherly gesture. When she looked into his weathered face, she could barely see straight she was shaking so hard from anger and hurt.

"You have such a good heart, Gwennie. Your people are everything to you, as they are to me." His voice was too soft, too compassionate. It was making her think he was someone he actually wasn't. "We had to ease you into it."

"*Ease* me?"

"Yes. The internships, the opportunities for advancement. We wanted you to be as involved with the Company as possible. Become invested in it, heart and soul."

She ripped herself from his touch and he let her go with the opening of his hands. The misery in his eyes, paired with the awfulness of his words, confounded her.

"Wait." Her voice was nearly as dead as she felt. "The international division was my idea. I came to you and Jonah and wanted to give my gift to the Company. To the Ofarian people."

He put a hand to his chest, and he actually had the audacity to have tears in his eyes. "And we were so happy you did that."

"Oh, my *God*, you planned that, too? Stay where you are!" she shrieked when he came for her again with the hugging arms and tormented expression.

He settled back into place, drawing himself up like the Chairman he was. "We didn't plan it. We wanted it. But we wanted you to want it more."

And she had. Her ambition had overridden everything.

"Haven't you seen how much you've helped your people?" he said. "You gave more wealth to more Ofarians. By expanding internationally you did so much. Our future is more financially secure, thanks to you."

The sympathy in his eyes was terrifyingly real, because it meant he was too far gone into the world he'd created—the one she'd expanded with her own ignorance.

"I made them make more babies." The statement sliced at her throat because it was the first time she'd said it out loud.

"Sweetie. Gwennie. You have to stop thinking of them as babies."

"Excuse me?"

"I know it's hard. Believe me, I do." Was this for real? Was she really hearing this out of her own father's mouth? "You don't think every one of us struggled when we found out the secret behind *Mendacia*?"

She put the wing-back chair between her and Dad. "And you did *nothing*?"

He considered the floor, chewed the inside of his cheek, which meant he was choosing his words carefully. "We have rules for a reason," he said slowly. "Do you think I liked exiling Delia? It *destroyed* me to do that to my own daughter. But she chose not to be a part of us and we did what we had to to protect ourselves." He'd advanced several steps without her knowing. She circled around the chair. "Do you think I *like* knowing there are living things being kept in a dark building for our benefit?"

She tasted salt and realized she was crying. "They're not things. They're Tedrans."

His palms came together, as though praying in the Christian religion. "No. They are things. And their purpose is to help Ofarians. Don't you understand? Everything we've ever done since coming here is to keep ourselves hidden and safe from the Primaries. If the Tedrans were suddenly just allowed to . . . run about, they'd compromise everything."

She literally had no words. It didn't matter; he had enough for both of them.

"We've been safe for a hundred and fifty years. Who am I to say that it's time to stop *Mendacia*?"

"You, Dad, are the Chairman."

"And it's my job, my life's calling, to serve my people."

It might have been easier to react to if he yelled or

maniacally rubbed his hands together or cackled evilly at the sky. But Ian Carroway carried a bone-deep conviction that he was a philanthropist through and through. He believed every word he said. And that screwed with her head even more.

"You know," he said, "I had a similar conversation with the Chairman before me."

That shoved her into motion. She exploded. "Don't say that like you want me to take your place. I'll never lead. Not this. Not what we've created."

That injured him. She recognized the agony. She'd witnessed something similar the day he learned Delia's affair with John was more than the Allure.

She skirted around the chair, advancing on him. "I won't 'come around.' I won't 'ease into it.'"

His chest shuddered beneath his Italian suit. He stared at the tasseled rug, hands still in his pockets. She tried to convince herself that this was not her father, that this was a man who'd been brainwashed into being upset over her treasonous words.

"When were you going to tell me?" she demanded.

"You would have learned when the Board voted you in. You were close, too."

She wanted to believe that, even if she hadn't been kidnapped and her previous life's dream came to fruition, she wouldn't ever have fallen victim to the Board's propaganda.

"Who else knows?" he asked, his voice markedly sharper. "Who did you tell? Griffin? That Primary?"

The two men she cared most for in the world were as good as dead if she admitted that. Her lips remained closed, her face impassive.

Her father backed toward the door and put his hand on the doorknob. "These are your people, Gwen. Choose your side very, very carefully."

She glared. "You can't keep me here. I'm your *daughter*. I'm all you have."

A lightning bolt of pain crossed his face. "You're an Ofarian first."

He left. The lock clicked from the outside.

THIRTY-SEVEN

Closing in on eleven o'clock, and sleep was a thousand hours away. Gwen lay curled on her side atop the burgundy coverlet on the huge canopied bed. Reed's watch indented a fringed pillow next to her face. She'd been staring at it so long she saw his face in the crystal.

He wasn't smiling.

Last night she'd been sleeping in Griffin's guest bedroom—because the thought of going back to her place was way too scary and odd—when he got a secure call from inside the Plant. A guard had asked if Gwen wanted her kidnapper kept prisoner. Her immediate reaction had been to demand Reed's release, but with Griffin looking on and remembering what he'd said about keeping up appearances in front of the Board, she'd checked herself. She told the Plant guard that Reed was where he belonged. She needed the Board to think she was still on their side. Fat lot of good it had done her.

She'd tried the bedroom door many times since her father had left. Banged the crap out of her hand. Shouted her throat raw. No response. She gave up pounding but didn't give up thinking.

Tap tap tap. It came from the window. At the lake house she might have attributed the sound to tree branches or squirrels. It took her a moment to remember that she was trapped in her old bedroom on a treeless lot in downtown San Francisco.

Tap tap tap.

With a gasp she snatched the watch from the pillow and swiveled to the narrow corner window near the bathroom door.

A dark figure loomed on the other side of the glass. Feet propped on the steep incline of the roof, rope extending from his waist up to who-knows-where, she knew his shape, the cut of his hair.

She scrambled to the window and tried to open it. Sealed shut; the perfect cell.

Outside, Griffin waved her away from the glass. Still dangling from the rope, his hand skated around his black vest, taking out tools that glinted in the city lights. He fiddled with the window frame and snipped some nearby wires. When the bottom half of the window finally slid upward, fresh air and the faint hum of the city leaked inside.

"Griffin, what . . . how . . ."

"No time. Cameras on this side of the house are out for a few minutes. Any more and they'll notice." He extended a hand.

She took it but stood firm. "Genesai?"

"David's got him."

David. Stars. She'd dragged Reed into this, then Griffin. And now David.

She put her foot on the window ledge and Griffin pulled her up and out so she balanced over the back patio.

"I only have eight others," he said.

It was eight more people than she'd had on her side two minutes ago.

"If I'm caught . . . if *we're* caught . . ."

Griffin drew a sad, strained smile. "Then at least I'll know I was one of the good guys."

Wrapping an arm around her waist, he curled her body into his, locked her in with his legs, and rappelled down the side of the house. Wind rushed through her hair, her stomach dropped, and she clung to his neck.

On the patio, he released the rope from his belt and pulled the entire length of it back in a flurry of his arms. Looping the thick coil diagonally across his body, he sprinted across the patch of back garden with her in tow. He hoisted her over the garden wall and scrambled over after her. They darted through strangers' backyards and burst out onto the street the next block over. A dark green sedan—plain, not one of the Company's—waited and she threw herself inside.

The red-haired woman behind the wheel slammed her foot

on the gas, and they peeled out of Pacific Heights. God, he'd brought Zoe in, too. What could Griffin have said to his soldiers to turn them against their people so fast? And what had changed his mind to help Gwen? He'd left the diner with such steadfast denial, and aside from the phone call coming from the Plant, they hadn't spoken at all since then.

Genesai and David huddled in the backseat. David nodded at her, his mouth drawn tight. Genesai grinned and embraced her awkwardly. She clung to him.

As the sedan swerved onto the Bay Bridge, Gwen tapped Griffin on the shoulder. "Do they all know?"

"Yeah," Zoe replied, raising her troubled eyes to meet Gwen's in the rearview mirror. "We know."

"How did you know where I was?"

Griffin turned in the front seat. "I didn't. When you weren't at my place, I knew something was wrong. I knew the Board had you."

"No." She pressed her forehead to the seat back, ground it in nice and hard. "My dad had me."

Griffin said nothing. He didn't have to. He knew he'd been right and he took no joy in it. The time for tears had passed. Even if she dug for days, she knew she wouldn't find any more. And that was fine by her, because she had to be focused to get to the slaves and Reed. She was sick of being jerked around and this time she'd be on the offensive.

The watch in her pocket had grown hot from her clutching it so consistently.

"What's the plan?" she asked.

Griffin gestured through the windshield. "Copter's up there. We're working your plan, Gwennie."

The one she'd outlined for him in the diner. The one he'd shot down.

She gasped. "We can make it work?"

He patted her hand next to the headrest. "We're going to have to."

Three additional Ofarian soldiers waited in the helicopter. Gwen knew them by face but not by name. They nodded deeply to her, almost reverently. Their courage and sacrifice overwhelmed her. The helicopter started up, a great whine and a blast of wind stealing her words.

As everyone donned bulbous sets of headphones, Griffin's voice crackled in her ear. "Three others are already in Nevada, working the plan from their end. We'll rendezvous upon touchdown. Listen up. Here's what's going to happen . . ."

He'd changed the plan somewhat from how she'd imagined it in her head, but then he was the soldier and she was the executive. People were given jobs for a reason, and Griffin was excellent at his. Every layer to his revised plan excited her. Every layer increased her fear. Inside her pocket she tightly clenched Reed's watch, then realized she didn't have to hide it anymore.

She pulled it out and slipped it on. A welcome weight, a big and beautiful reminder. Griffin saw it and looked away, but she couldn't concern herself with how he felt about Reed. Not when she was hours or minutes away from getting Reed back.

After a ride that felt both agonizingly slow and incredibly swift, they touched down and immediately splintered into groups. David sped away in a nondescript four-door with the waiting three soldiers. Zoe prodded two of the men who'd ridden in the copter into a brisk jog, and they melted into the night.

The helicopter lifted off and disappeared into specks of light blinking in the blackness. They'd been dropped in the center of the Nevada nothingness. She could barely see her hands in front of her face, but she recognized the feel of the expanse around her, could taste the briskness of the air.

A black pickup truck waited for them. An Ofarian soldier—Sam, she learned—slid behind the wheel. She guided Genesai into the cab and Griffin hopped in the bed. The vehicle jounced along the rough terrain with only its parking lights on. Gwen tried desperately to make out any distinguishing landmarks—how close were they to the Plant?—but to no avail. Genesai pressed his cheek to the cold window and drew lines between the stars with his fingers, his limbs continually twitching.

The truck stopped in a cloud of dirt on a ridge overlooking a two-lane road. Griffin opened the cab door from the outside and took Gwen's arm when she exited. He pulled her to the lip of the drop-off. From inside his soldier's vest he produced a cell phone.

"Turn it on."

She did. And stared down at the color screen in all its high-def glory.

"They're all on there. And everything else you wanted, it's all loaded up."

"Griffin . . ." Her whole life had been made up of words—she'd been born to talk—and he'd rendered her completely speechless.

He waved off her unspoken gratitude. "You don't have to go down there."

She rubbed gentle fingers over the Cartier. "Yes, I do."

Clenching his jaw between thumb and forefinger, he stared down the steep slope. "For me, Gwen. For our friendship. Stay at the truck with Genesai. There are so few of us; I can't say for sure you'll be safe."

For our friendship.

"If there's so few of you, you'll need me. And I could never, ever live with myself if I sent you and the others down without fighting myself." When he refused to look at her, she added, "You, of all people, should understand that. Could you give the order to fight and then step back to watch?"

"Gwen . . ."

Griffin's radio sputtered to life and Zoe's voice crackled, "They're coming. From the south. Ten minutes out."

He loosed a small set of night-vision binoculars from his plethora of vest doohickeys and peered south into the darkness.

"Teams A and B," he barked, "move into position."

She and Griffin were Team C. Sam was staying behind with Genesai. If anything were to go wrong down there, Sam had orders where to take Genesai to keep him safe.

"Team C," Griffin murmured to her, radio off. "You ready?"

She took a deep breath and nodded. He leaned over and kissed her on the cheek, his lips lingering. As if realizing what he was doing, he broke the contact fast, like ripping off a bandage.

The way he cleared his throat was simultaneously awkward and endearing and bittersweet. "See you down there. Stay covered."

He stepped back, whispered Ofarian words, and collapsed into water. She watched his liquid form splash and burble over-land, swift as whitewater, down toward the road at the bottom of the quiet valley.

A piercing scream cleaved the night.

She whirled. Genesai, ten paces behind her, had gone skeleton white, his eyes wide as moons. One shaking hand pointed to where Griffin had turned liquid, and he screamed again. To make a sound so anguished, so potent, he must have reached far, far back into his past. Into his former self. It didn't sound entirely human.

She started for him, arms outstretched to soothe. Stupid move.

He stumbled backward as if she were on fire. "Ofarians! You've aligned me with Ofarians!"

How could she have let it come to this?

"Genesai." She dropped her arms and advanced carefully. "Please let me explain."

Dust plumed under his bare feet as he scrambled for the truck. The doors were locked and he fell to the ground, huddling near the wheel well like a wounded and trapped animal. His terror froze her.

Sam hopped out of the pickup cab, but Gwen waved him back inside. The last thing Genesai needed was another Ofarian in sight.

"You're one of them, too, aren't you?" Genesai hugged the rubber now, his eyes squeezed shut as if bracing for an execution. "I listened to your words. I trusted you. And you are my enemy."

"No, Genesai, no. I am not your enemy."

"If I hadn't listened to you, I would already be with her. We would be in the sky. I should be with Nora."

Another step closer. Genesai flinched.

"Everything I told you back in your cabin is true. The Ofarians who forced you to come to Earth and the Ofarians who are still keeping Tedrans as slaves, they are my enemies, too. The few of us who brought you here tonight, we are fighting them."

Genesai was shaking his head, not hearing anything she said. "You're not going to let me leave this awful planet, are you?" Tears drew wet lines down his dusty cheeks and glistened in the moonlight.

"Yes! Yes, I am. I want to send you and your ship back to the stars, just like we talked about."

"I don't believe you."

As she stepped closer, he winced as though she held a bull-whip, ready to strike.

"Nora is the one who kept you captive all these years. She wants to free her people, and so do I. But her motives are not all good. That is why Griffin and I are here right now. There are only eight other Ofarians with us. We are not with the Tedrans or the Ofarian majority. But we know what's right, and we want to help you get back to your ship."

At last he opened his eyes and peered up at her through their wetness. "We were so close. I touched her. I was *inside* her."

She sighed and crouched down before him. "The Ofarians and Tedrans are still at war. I am caught in the middle. *We* are caught in the middle."

He must have picked up on the despair in her voice, because suddenly he stilled and looked at her with what she could only hope was empathy. Then he peered down the hill.

"What's happening down there? Why are Ofarians attacking Ofarians?"

"Because I want the Tedrans freed, and the other Ofarians—the ones who kept the slaves—don't like that." *My father doesn't like that.* "Griffin and I, we're trying to do what we believe is right for the Tedrans, not what Nora wants and not what the Ofarian leaders want. I want to end the war, Genesai. Nora does not. I didn't tell you this before because I really, truly wanted you to take the freed Tedrans back to their homeworld. I didn't tell you what I am because I desperately needed your help."

A line of headlights appeared on the road in the distance. She needed to get down there. Fast.

Genesai at last released his grip on the tire and stood. "And now? Now that you've declared yourself for no side, what happens to me? What happens to us?"

The approaching headlights reminded her of being deep, deep in Lake Tahoe, where the light pierced the dark in wavering spots. For a brief moment she was transported back there, surrounded by the thick movement of the water and the dullness of sound. The narrow valley fell away from the present and she pictured Genesai's beautiful ship looming before her.

"What happens?" she said. "What happens is that I'm going to get you back where you belong."

THIRTY-EIGHT

Gwen threw her watery body down the hill. Scrubby, itchy grass flew beneath her. She flowed around large rocks and bridged broken parts of the land. She stretched herself thin, parts of her trailing behind, but she had to hurry. The world passed quickly, too quickly to watch the progress of the caravan barreling toward them on the road.

Griffin wouldn't wait for her, and he didn't. She was still a good distance away from where she needed to be, when a spout of water shot up from the ground, as powerful and determined as the man who controlled it. The shimmering liquid expanded to Griffin's familiar, lean silhouette, then hardened into his true shape.

His re-formation gave the signal to everyone else.

Gwen stopped where she was, still twenty yards up the slope from the road. Touching the water, speaking its language, she commanded it to return to her true body. Up the road a bit, out of sight, Zoe and her team would be assuming form, weapons trained. Across the road, lining the shoulder, David and his team spouted into being.

Griffin told them the Ofarians driving the caravan used heat-seeking and night-scope vision whenever they traveled in the dark. That had been the reason for staying in water form. But it had taken a bit of a toll; Griffin gritted his teeth and caught himself from swaying on his feet. Changing the molecules of clothing was one thing. Altering weaponry and ammo and other articles sapped strength. The more you changed, the more it took. And every soldier was loaded down.

Gwen didn't have a gun, but she wasn't there to shoot.

David reached over his shoulder and slid out a long-range rifle. Impeccable timing. A huge black SUV crested a rise, charging toward them. Just behind it came a gray van, then a giant semi-truck rumbling like an earthquake. Another black SUV brought up the rear. Their headlights were no longer fuzzy points in the distance. They were clear and close, and Gwen's stomach leaped into her throat.

David lifted the rifle scope to his eye, aimed, and fired.

The single bullet snapped like a whip, the great *crack* echoing off the hills. The gray, windowless van swerved violently. It crossed the yellow line. Veered back. The rubber of its left front wheel flapped.

The semi's brakes squealed and hissed, the trailer bobbing as the whole thing tried to avoid hitting the erratic van. The van skidded to a messy stop halfway onto the shoulder, right in front of Zoe's team.

The semi jackknifed, straightened, and then halted across the deserted road with a considerable jerk. The lead SUV slowed, screeched around a U-turn, and doubled back. The tail SUV sped up, passed the semi, and stopped alongside the tilted and disabled van. Smart of Griffin. Taking out one of the guard SUVs would only send the caravan fleeing. But handicap the van carrying the entire supply of *Mendacia* and everyone would have to stop.

Ofarian guards poured from every vehicle, moonlight glinting off their drawn weapons. They sprinted for the downed van—protect the product at all cost—equipment jingling on their person, boots slapping the asphalt. They shouted for status reports, bellowed orders to search the nearby area.

They never got the chance. Griffin fired first.

The *nelicoda*-laced bullet exploded from the barrel and found its target in the leg of a *Mendacia* guard. The guy crumpled, howling in pain. The *nelicoda* bullets had been Griffin's suggestion; she hadn't even known they existed. The order to disable, not kill, had been at Gwen's insistence. But as the world exploded in gunfire, she began to second-guess herself.

She dove behind a rock just barely big enough to cover her curled-up body. A bullet struck its top, tearing off a chunk. Another bullet buried itself in the ground by her ankle. The ungodly noise of violence and shouting sent her hands flying to her ears.

She managed to peer around the rock. The semi stood huge and unprotected. Inside was her purpose in the form of three hundred innocent, defenseless people. If they had Reed, if they'd obeyed her orders to keep him with the Tedrans, that was where he would be.

Griffin had retreated up the hill, higher up into the dark, away from the headlights. Fifteen feet from Gwen, he flattened himself to the ground, propped himself on his elbows, and fired away. His arms jerked with every shot. He was fast but careful, taking aim, using the benefit of higher ground and the advantage of the shadows.

Another of their own wasn't so lucky.

"I'm hit!" Even from that distance, Gwen heard the pain and fear in Zoe's cry. The *Mendacia* guards weren't aiming to injure.

It should have made Gwen cower. It should have made her regret joining the front line. It should have made her want to turn to water again, flow back up the hill and hide with Genesai.

"Griffin. Throw me a gun."

She couldn't sit there in a shaking, useless heap. The fight wasn't going in their favor. She didn't have to be a soldier to know that.

"What?" He didn't look at her, and got off another shot. Someone down at the caravan wailed. "You don't know how to use it!"

A bullet tore between them, exploding a stone into shards.

"No," she agreed. "But I know someone who does."

The gun slackened in his hand. He quickly corrected it, popped off another shot. "No, Gwen."

"You don't always know what's best for me, what I'm capable of."

Three hard, fast shots. His mouth was grim, his eyes hard.

"All the gunfire is focused here and to the west. If I stay low, circle around to the east, I can make it to the semi."

"Turn to water," he growled.

"Running's faster at this distance. And I won't be tired from changing the weapon."

"No. Stay here. Stay covered."

"We're getting nowhere fast. Just give me the fucking gun."

He breathed hard, shooting on every exhale.

"Now, Griffin!"

Though his hand slowly slid to his sidearm, he was shaking his head. "The safety's on."

He flung the gun at the exact moment another bullet streaked between them. It caught Griffin's left forearm in a burst of flesh and blood. He didn't even cry out, just cradled his arm to his chest.

"Griffin!"

"Don't worry about me." His clenched teeth gleamed white. "Just go."

The whole thing suddenly became horrifying real. If she sat there and thought about it too much, she'd never get up. So she closed her eyes for a second, took a deep breath, and pushed herself out from behind the rock.

She sprinted east, away from the fire.

At the same time, she got her first complete look at the scene. Every headlight in the caravan had been switched to bright. Ofarian *Mendacia* guards writhed on the ground, clutching legs or arms or both. A few took cover between the SUVs and the *Mendacia* van, and they showered the hills with rounds. So many more of the caravan's guards than of Griffin's crew . . .

The semi was a beacon in the darkness. She dug deep and hurtled over rocks and dirt. The truck stood fifty yards away. Then forty. Twenty.

A lone guard stood at the rear of the trailer, his attention on the firefight. She didn't know why she hadn't seen him before, or had assumed they'd leave the semi unprotected. Precious cargo, of course. Couldn't have the product without the labor.

She didn't recognize the guard. It didn't make raising her weapon to him any easier. She fumbled with the safety, figured out how to flick it off, then started toward the guard. Closer, closer. Her feet sent rocks skittering and the guard jumped.

His gun found her before his eyes.

Her first shot was lucky, one for the storybooks. Her finger pressed the trigger more out of reflex than with any sort of aim.

No one had ever told her about a gun's kickback. A giant dug his fingers into her shoulder and yanked her back about a foot.

The guard went down with a yelp, hands pressed to his thigh and blood flowing between his fingers. She hurried over to him, worried she'd struck the artery, but he was bleeding from just above the knee.

His eyes widened then narrowed. "You."

She saw the calculation cross his face, the realization that she was corporate, not a soldier with combat skills. He stretched for his gun. She fired again, the bullet smashing a hole in the asphalt inches from his crotch.

"Jesus!" he screamed.

She kicked his gun into the gravel on the side of the road. "How do I open the doors?" He smirked up at her, and she knew he assumed she had no real fight in her. That her talents lay in typing and schmoozing. She leveled the gun right at his chest and hoped against hope that he'd never be able to see that she couldn't ever shoot anyone like that. "You're surrounded. The quicker we get what we came for, the quicker you can get help for that leg. The doors."

He grimaced. His face was going pale. One hand left his bleeding thigh to unclick a set of keys from his belt.

"You're letting them out?" he snarled. "Is that what this is about? You don't want the *Mendacia*?"

The fact that he thought the Tedrans and the product two separate things set her blood afire.

She slammed the key into the padlock, wrenched the lock apart, and yanked on the door handle. The trailer door rattled and clanged as it rolled up.

She saw Reed's boots first. Such a silly thing, but she'd know them anywhere, those beat-up workman's boots with the fat laces and thick soles. The door kept rising, revealing him inch by inch. Powerful legs clad in dirty jeans. Expansive chest and strong shoulders covered by a black, long-sleeved shirt and an unzipped fleece jacket—what he'd been wearing the last time she'd seen him. Fists bound by neutralizer handcuffs. Sharp blue eyes staring down at her in quiet disbelief.

He was literally an angel appearing out of the dark. And like something heavenly or otherworldly, she didn't quite believe he was standing there before her. Her chest went tight with the sight of him. Her head spun.

Reed jumped off the truck, a lion leaping from its trap, sprung by the mouse. Though his hands were bound, he landed easily. Straightening, they stared at each other. Less than two days apart and it felt like two years. It had been eons since they'd touched, since she'd heard his voice.

A surge of emotion cascaded over her. As powerful as the moment when they'd lunged for each other in the lake house's bathroom. As unrelenting as ocean waves.

She didn't see the same on his face. Just a hard, impenetrable expression and heart-rending wariness. God, what he must think of her.

"Reed, about the Plant . . ."

Gunfire popped all around. Reed impatiently rattled his handcuffs as he peered over her shoulder. "No time for that. Unlock me."

She trapped the gun between her knees and, with shaking hands, paged through the keys to find the one for his cuffs.

"We came for the Tedrans." She glanced up at him. He was beautiful and scary, all coiled with purpose and calculation, like that moment in the alley when she'd first seen him. "And I came for you."

The cuffs fell to the pavement with a clatter. His eyes flickered to his watch on her wrist and he went still.

They faced each other, physically unfettered but a sea of unspoken words swimming between them.

The gunfire rose and rose. Reed shook his head, focus replacing emotion. "Secure the caravan?" he said. "That's the idea?"

"Yeah. Disable the guards and it's ours." She jerked her chin to the hilly roadside. "Griffin's up there, wounded. We only have nine total." She remembered Zoe with a pang. "Maybe eight."

Reed scratched the heavy stubble on his cheek. "They've got eighteen."

Of course he'd have paid attention to that. "They're down a few, but we're not aiming to kill."

He seemed a little disappointed at that. "Got it. Weapons?"

She loosed the one between her knees and held it out. "This

one has *nelicoda* bullets." Then pointed to the one in the gravel. "That one doesn't."

He looked at her funny for a moment. He still didn't know *nelicoda*'s purpose. Another obstacle between them. A big one.

He checked the bullet chambers of each gun and swore. Sidling to the edge of the semi-trailer, he ventured one lightning-quick peek around the corner.

"Don't move from this spot until I call for you."

And then he was gone. Again.

The gunfire escalated. She heard Reed shouting for Griffin, and Griffin answering. Against the truck, she squeezed shut her eyes, imagining them both safe.

With a sickening lurch of her heart, she thought of what Griffin had insinuated back in the diner. What she'd feared even as she'd spilled everything to Reed. Her Primary didn't just know about Secondaries now. He was a part of them. Among them.

Her next battle would be to save his life.

"Gwen."

She whirled. Xavier had come down from the trailer. She never thought she'd be so happy to see his artful good looks and mistrustful eyes. Despite what was going on at her back, she smiled, because his eyes were no longer mistrustful.

He couldn't speak for several long moments. "You came for us."

"I promised you I would."

All the Tedrans inside pressed to the front of the trailer, quiet in their fear of what lay outside. The little green lights of their neutralizers glowed like sickly fireflies.

Xavier lifted his hands. "These handcuffs are new since I escaped. We didn't know . . . if we'd have tried to go through with Nora's plan, it wouldn't have worked."

Without thinking, Gwen touched his arm. When he didn't recoil, she gave him a reassuring squeeze.

A lithe figure in loose, pale clothing stepped to the edge of the trailer bed. Chin lifted, Nora looked down her nose at Gwen, as if they were back in the lake house and she still had the right.

Gwen looked her former captor right in the eye and pointed to the hilltop. "Genesai is up there. Waiting to take you home. All of you."

"The fighting? What's going on?" Xavier asked.

She thought back to their conversation on the terrace steps, where she'd confronted him about buying into Nora's my-way-or-the-highway bullshit.

She looked up at him sadly. "I'm as much a pariah to my people as you are. But I'm going to change that."

"You *think* you'll change," Nora spit. "But you won't."

The gunfire abruptly stopped.

"Gwen!" Reed's voice cut through the night.

She scrambled for the key to Xavier's cuffs and pointed to the wounded Ofarian guard on the ground. "Bring him," she told Xavier, then dashed out onto the battlefield, not thinking to check if it was safe, trusting Reed implicitly.

The Ofarian guards had been herded up against one of the SUVs. The barrier of the skewed *Mendacia* truck kept them packed tightly together. Most clutched their wounded parts, moaning. Some sat with hands behind their heads, glaring. Xavier added the one Gwen had shot to the pile, then backed away fast, watching the scene with wide eyes.

A pile of confiscated weapons and radios lay in the roadside ditch. Other Ofarians—Gwen's Ofarians—surrounded the captives. Seven of their original nine. She didn't see Zoe. But David was there, and Griffin, pressing his wounded arm to his side. He needed to get to a doctor, but the Ofarian ones were all back in San Francisco. The Plant had had doctors, but they weren't among the captured guards or sitting with the Tedrans in the semi.

Gwen smelled a hunt to come.

Reed stood before them all, legs spread, hand clutching the one gun she guessed hadn't run out of bullets. He glanced her way, the mask she recognized as belonging to the Retriever firmly in place.

A surge of elation flowed through her, making her light as air. All the desperation and isolation and fury she'd felt in Nora's captivity—and the uselessness she'd despaired over while trapped in her father's manor—all seemed so very far away. Victory was within her reach. They just needed to get to the lake.

She nodded at Reed, so very, very grateful for everything he'd done. All that he'd sacrificed. But he just tightened his lips and returned his attention to his targets.

And she realized, with a suddenness that sent her reeling, that she *had* used him. Why else would she have asked for his help in the first place, if she hadn't wanted his strength, his abilities?

"What now?" Griffin asked behind her.

Inventory, she thought. She headed for the *Mendacia* van. She never actually got there.

One of the caravan guards grabbed her as she passed. He was fast, too fast even for Griffin and Reed. The guard rolled to his feet, smashing her body against his chest, a knife point pricking the skin just below her ear.

Reed's gun swept around, but it was too late.

"Stay where you are," snapped the guard. "We don't want you. Just her."

There was something familiar about his voice. She didn't have time to think on it, however, because he whistled and the rear doors of the *Mendacia* van opened.

Her father stepped out.

THIRTY-NINE

"Gwen." *Keep her calm*, Reed thought. She needed her head to get out of this, and she had one of the best minds he knew. *"Gwen."*

Her eyes finally found his, but she still clawed at the arm of the guy holding a knife to her throat, panic twitching through her body.

"That's it," Reed told her, nice and easy. "Keep looking at me. Keep it together."

She didn't let go of the asshole's arm, but the longer she looked at Reed, the easier and steadier her breathing became.

Jesus, what she'd done tonight . . . She'd escaped from Nora, gone back to San Francisco, been reunited with her people, and then risked her life to go against them and do what she believed was right. He'd never doubted her conviction, just his role in her plan, especially since she'd kept him locked in the Plant.

And what had been the first thing she'd done when Griffin and his team teetered on the brink of defeat? She'd come to Reed looking for help. Is that all he was good for to her?

Yet she was wearing his watch.

"Dad," Gwen begged the man who'd emerged from the van. "Dad, you don't have to do this."

An eerie quiet fell over the scene. Every Ofarian—those captured, those holding guns—watched Gwen's father in expectation. Reed got the feeling that in any other situation, they might have bowed. Even Griffin looked doubtful. Fearful.

Strange, but the Chairman looked incredibly young, late forties at best. He took a few steps toward his daughter, hands in his pockets, the corners of his eyes drawn down in distress.

"I did listen to you, Gwennie. And now I'm doing what's best for our people. That will always be my priority. As it should be yours." The look he gave the soldier holding Gwen was filled with regret and heartache. "You were right, Jonah."

The soldier said something in that strange, rolling language Gwen had used back in the lake house bedroom, the one that reminded Reed of water tripping over stones. The soldier's body and face shivered, shifting between illusion and reality, the way Gwen's had done that night when she'd revealed everything. The soldier disappeared; in his place stood a middle-aged man in sleek trousers and a pricey sweater.

The sight of this guy—Jonah, apparently—lit a fire under Gwen's ass. The fear in her expression switched to loathing, and she started to struggle again. Jonah said something in Ofarian in her ear. The knife pricked her skin, drawing blood, and she went still. The fight burned strongly in her eyes, though. Good girl.

"Right about what?" she spit at her father.

"I told him you'd pull in Griffin," Jonah sneered. "That Griffin's pathetic love for you would obliterate any intelligence or Ofarian loyalty."

Reed snuck a glance at Griffin, whose face had gone red with rage.

The Chairman held up a hand. "I had to know if we could trust the protector of the Translator—and head of my security force—to not let his emotions get in the way." He slowly came forward, and he did not look happy about this scene at all. Not angry, just sad and disappointed. "I would not call it pathetic, but love is the reason why we rely on our marriage system. Love is too unpredictable. Marriage is deliberately based on advantage, not emotions."

"You can't just ignore emotions," Gwen said.

The Chairman gestured to the hill. "And look how you've compromised Griffin and David, and all the others."

"I'd do this again," Griffin said, shifting his gun from Jonah to the Chairman, "knowing what I know now. Gwen is better than all of us combined."

Reed searched Gwen's face for a reaction, but she was focused solely on her dad.

Jonah started to wrangle her backward toward the van. He'd

been hit in the leg during the firefight and limped. "I was wrong about one thing," Jonah said to her. "I thought you'd go for the kill." He used his chin to indicate the injured Ofarian soldiers still writhing on the ground. "You know, eye for an eye."

"I'm not like you," she snarled.

Jonah was trying to get Gwen into one of the SUVs, Reed realized. Yeah, that wasn't going to happen.

Reed inched to the right, improving his target angle on Jonah. "Stop. Right now."

Jonah raised his eyebrows, his tanned skin wrinkling over his forehead. "Shoot me and the knife goes in."

"Jonah, no!" The Chairman thrust out a hand.

"You won't hurt me," Gwen blurted. "I'm the only Translator you've got."

"She's right, you know," Reed told Jonah. "I'm just one of the people here with a gun and they're all on you. You're outnumbered. Let her go or this ends badly for you."

The Chairman reached for something in his pocket. Reed swiveled, barrel aimed at Gwen's dad.

"I'm on Jonah," Griffin said behind him.

Good, because Reed wanted the man who'd manipulate and sell out his own daughter.

The Chairman whipped out a phone. "I didn't want to do this, Gwennie. I really, really didn't." He pressed a button. "Reinforcements."

The Ofarian called David pivoted and ran a short distance up the hill, binoculars to his eyes. No headlights yet, but they'd come.

"So this was all a test?" Gwen's voice had evened out into the deep, hard tone of someone seriously pissed off. She'd gotten her spark back, that defiance he'd witnessed the night he'd tied her up in the back of Nora's van. *Hold on to that*, Reed silently ordered her. *Use it.*

"Yes," Jonah said, sweeping a satisfied look over Griffin and his team. "To weed out the traitors."

The Chairman moved closer to his daughter. Reed could see the emotional battle in her expression: disgust fought with love.

"The protest ends tonight, Gwen," the Chairman said. "You will come back to the city with me. Be a part of the people you love. *Lead* them. If you do that, we'll pardon the treason. Please. Please don't make me lose a second daughter."

The Chairman looked on the verge of tears, but Gwen was spitting mad. She struggled again. A stripe of blood wept from the cut by her ear and stained the neck of her sweater. Jonah clung to her, clearly vacillating between wanting to hurt her and appeasing his Chairman.

Through it all, Reed watched Gwen make her move. Her struggle masked the movement of her hand as it worked its way into her pocket. Man, she was brilliant. Courageous. What did she have in there? Gun? Knife?

"*Mendacia* is wrong." She pulled hard against Jonah's clutch. Whatever she had in that pocket was now in her hand; Reed could see the bulge of her fist through the cream-colored knit. "Everything about it is wrong. Don't you have any sense of guilt? That truck is filled with people, not product."

The Chairman's face frosted over. "They're paying for their ancestors' atrocities."

"You believe in lies!" she shouted.

If there had been an Ofarian on that road who hadn't already been staring at the Chairman and his daughter, they did so now.

Gwen looked into the upturned faces of the soldiers. Her voice carried easily, surely. "We've all believed the lies. Our ancestors saw in the Tedrans the same thing you see now: profit. Even on Tedra we used them. No, we were not their slaves. No, we did not revolt and instigate the war. It's always been the other way around. Our people rewrote history to satisfy themselves."

No one moved. Not the Chairman, not Jonah. *Now*, Reed wanted to shout to Gwen. *Get away while he's distracted*. Reed would shoot Jonah if he knew that was what she wanted, but this was her op and she clearly had a plan.

She gazed into the eyes of the guards. The injured men and women exchanged questioning glances and looked up at the Chairman. They wondered if his own daughter spoke the truth. She'd planted the seed of doubt and Reed thought it was a clever strategy.

"Shut up," Jonah said, regaining his focus and pulling her back toward the van.

But her dad edged closer, eyes narrowed. "Why should we

believe you? Why should we believe what you say over what's
been passed down through generations? What gives you the
right to question what can't be proved?"

"There's a woman in that truck who remembers. She was
on Tedra when it all happened. She was part of the immigration here. She knows."

Jonah snorted. The Chairman went eerily still. Several
Ofarian soldiers craned their necks toward the semi.

"That woman kidnapped me," Gwen said. She was so
strong. So lovely. "She wanted me to destroy you and the Board
to bring about change. But I believe in our ability to change
ourselves. No more death. No more lies."

"Our people have built their lives around *Mendacia*," the
Chairman said. "You can't just rip it away from them."

"Wrong. Our people have built their lives around what
makes us different from Primaries. We want to be special. We
want to be proud of our culture and uphold its secrecy. We can
do that without *Mendacia*."

"No, Gwen. It's the cornerstone of our existence."

"You and the Board have used our fear of the Primary world
to lasso us into your control. You've allowed so few Ofarians
to work in the Primary world, and those that do still answer to
the Company. You've arranged it so the Ofarian teachers and
bankers and construction workers are all dependent on the success of *Mendacia*. Only when the Company did well, did they
do well, too. And you think that because of this, we will throw
our conscience into the gutter to maintain the status quo. But
do you know what *I* think? I think that the Board has kept the
secret behind *Mendacia* for so long because you knew that if
the Ofarians ever found out, they'd turn on you. End it all."

"No. They'd turn the other cheek and hold out their hands
for their paycheck."

She gasped. "You really believe that, don't you?"

The Chairman lifted his chin and Reed saw where Gwen
had learned that little gesture.

"Well," she said. "Let's test that theory."

Jonah chuckled and glanced down the road. "That's the best
part of your little speech. They'll never find out."

Gwen smiled. Reed held his breath.

"That's what you think." She lifted her foot and kicked back, *hard*, into Jonah's injured leg. Jonah howled, the knife tumbling from his hand and clattering to the asphalt. He reached for the wound, his body buckling.

"Bitch!" Jonah spit.

Gwen wheeled away, putting space between her and the two Board members.

Reed charged into the opening, propelled by intense pride. He leaped onto Jonah, knocking him backward, one boot pressing Jonah's arm into the ground. The other foot kicked the knife under the van with such force it skittered out on the other side. He aimed his gun right at Jonah's heart.

"Don't move, Chairman," Griffin said.

Reed looked over his shoulder to see Griffin holding Gwen's father at point-blank range. But the Chairman's defeated, murderous eyes clung to Reed.

"I don't believe we've been introduced," Reed said to the Chairman. "I'm Gwen's."

The Chairman started to shake with fury. "You're Gwen's what?"

Reed grinned. "I'm just hers."

And there it is, said Reed's ice blue eyes. *It's yours to do with as you please, even if it destroys me.*

He actually believed, Gwen realized, that she'd destroy him on her way to getting what she wanted. That was her own fault, for approaching him in the lake house the way she had.

Wrenching her focus from Reed, she closed in on the Chairman. She had to view him as that right now, because to think of him as her father, as the man who'd taught her how to hit baseballs in the park and played Barbies with her without protest, she wouldn't get anywhere.

Sometime between their confrontation in the manor and now, he'd dosed himself with *Mendacia*. The forty-something man she barely knew watched her with fearful anticipation. She pulled from her pocket the most powerful weapon on that battlefield: the cell phone Griffin had given her on top of the hill.

Raising the phone to the Chairman's eye level, she pushed *on*. The photo that came up, bright and disgusting, made him gasp.

She looked over her shoulder at Griffin, who nodded solemnly.

The morning before the Board meeting, she'd secretly left the photos—the ones he'd denied in the diner—on his bed, in a place he couldn't ignore, hoping for his compassion to kick in. And it had. He'd come through for her spectacularly.

"Photos inside the Plant," she said. Thumbing through the barrage of awful images, she lowered the phone and slowly walked back and forth in front of the Ofarian soldiers. "Imprisoned Tedrans. Drained of their powers. Dying before their time. Forced to procreate to increase inventory."

Xavier leaned heavily against the giant wheel of the semi. His ashen face was half buried in the crook of his elbow. When her gaze met his tortured eyes, he closed his so tightly his eyelashes disappeared.

Many Ofarians leaned closer to the ghastly images. Most grimaced. All murmured in shock.

"How did you . . ." the Chairman began, crimson staining through his glamour. He couldn't even finish. Him, the man who could bullshit his way out of a Colombian prison.

Gwen moved to stand between him and Jonah. She couldn't tell if the Chairman's *Mendacia* spell was actually fading, or if his true, aging self was pushing through in his time of exposure. Either way, she glimpsed his real face, wrinkled and spotted. Desperate. Hurt. Livid. His sagging, reddened eyes glared like a dragon's, but she wasn't remotely afraid of his fire. Two weeks ago, maybe. But not now. Not ever again.

"I'm sending these to every Ofarian," she told him.

"No," he breathed. "For us. For your people. Don't."

"They deserve to know."

Jonah's hand, the one not trapped by Reed's boot, clawed for Gwen's shin. Reed flexed his thighs, crouched down, and pressed the barrel of his gun to the Vice Chairman's forehead.

"Do what you have to do, Gwen," Reed said.

Her finger hovered over the phone's *send* button. She wanted the Chairman to watch her every movement.

He stretched out a hand, his voice trembling. "Think about what you're doing, Gwennie. What it will mean to all of us. To everyone who depends on *Mendacia*."

"I have." She met his pleading eyes dead on. "And the difference between you and me is that I have deep enough faith in my people that we will be able to grow and prosper without it. I believe we will be able to find our individual ways in the Primary world and not be so dependent on one such thing as this. I believe in the future, not the past."

She couldn't have made this move any earlier, though her trigger finger had itched. If she'd blasted the Ofarians with the images the second Griffin had handed her the phone, the guards in the caravan would have received them, turned the vehicles around, and disappeared with the Tedrans and the product. Waiting had killed her, but it had paid off.

She pressed *send*.

The Chairman crumpled forward, hands braced on his knees.

She liked to think that she could feel the weight of that message launch from the phone. She liked to think she saw its power rise from the constraints of circuits and plastic, fly over her head, and search out each and every one of her people. The ultimate truth bearer.

Various ringtones chimed throughout the Ofarian crowd huddled at her feet. Some soldiers reached into their vests to get another look at the proof she offered. Some just let their phones sit, the evidence too awful to see more than once.

And she wasn't done yet.

Her thumbs danced across the phone's keypad. "Now I'm telling all our clients the Company has folded and *Mendacia* production has been shut down."

The Chairman exploded back to life. "No!" He lunged.

Reed wheeled off Jonah, charging to intercept the Chairman's attack. Jonah took full advantage, scrambling to his feet and diving for Gwen's arm holding the phone.

The same enemy with the same purpose. Two assaults. Two angles.

Two gunshots.

She screamed, the surrounding hills throwing back the sound in screeching echo.

Jonah fell smack to the pavement, face first. A flower of blood bloomed aggressively on his back.

A half-second later her father collapsed to his knees, gasping. He clutched at his shoulder where blood seeped across his pin-striped Italian suit. Then his ass hit the ground. She'd never seen him look so small or so lost.

"Dad," she began, but all her words ran out, because that was who he was again—her father—and the enormity of the space between them became achingly apparent. He closed his eyes, hissing through his pain.

Jonah Yarbrough's body twitched, then went utterly still. Beneath him, blood turned the asphalt to glittering ebony.

She looked at Reed, who held up his hands and shook his head. Together, they swiveled to Griffin.

Griffin's gun was still outstretched, death reflected in his dark features, his eyes black orbs. Gwen stumbled over to him. "Hey," she said, pressing down his gun arm then prying the weapon from his fingers.

"Stars," he murmured. "I shot them." He blinked and shook his head as though waking from a dream. "Gwen, I'm so sorry. I should've known the Chairman was setting a trap when he sent me away on that shit job. I should've guessed."

"Don't. We both should've known."

"Headlights!" David called from his position on the slope.

The Chairman's reinforcements. More Ofarians, whose phones had also gone off moments ago.

"Guys." Reed trotted up. "What next?"

She scanned the length of the caravan. "We're taking everything with us. The vehicles, the *Mendacia*, everything." She'd figure out what the hell to do with it later, it just couldn't be left there. "Except the guards. They stay."

Griffin snapped his fingers at one of his men and ordered him to load all the *Mendacia* boxes into one of the drivable SUVs.

"I've got the semi," Reed said.

She did a double take. "You can drive a semi?"

His small smile hinted at the dimple. "Where to?"

She looked to the southwest. "The lake."

Griffin radioed Sam in the pickup truck atop the hill. "Lake Tahoe. Bring Genesai."

Reed jogged for the semi and Gwen watched him go, amazed he was still here. Amazed he'd remained on their side, even after Griffin had locked him up and she'd kept him there.

Griffin went to the Chairman and bound his hands. The *nelicoda*-laced bullet and the wound it had inflicted might keep him from trying to run, but Gwen didn't blame Griffin for being extra careful. Still, the sight of her father, injured and defeated and shackled, destroyed the image of the hero she'd created over her lifetime.

A very small part of her wanted to apologize to him. She got over that really fast. "We have a lot more to say to one another," she told him. But the prospect of that made her heartsick. He lifted his chin in his signature gesture, and for the first time in her life, she didn't bristle under his intense look of disappointment.

"I still love you, Dad, despite all this. And I did the right thing."

"I love you, too, kiddo," he whispered. Or maybe she just heard it in her head, because she wanted to.

She went to stand next to Griffin, who was checking on the disabled Ofarians. She lifted her voice to address everyone. "Backup is on its way. They'll help you because they're Ofarians, and if they don't, they'll answer to me. I want the Chairman taken into custody and all remaining members of the Board arrested. As protector to the Translator and security liaison to the Board, I give Griffin seniority over all Ofarian soldiers."

Griffin picked up her cue and pointed at the slope behind him. "Two of your own have fallen. Don't forget them. And do not let the Chairman's backup go after Gwen. Let her do what she has to do."

Gwen turned to watch the last of the *Mendacia* being transferred from the van to an SUV, when one of the Ofarian caravan guards grabbed her hand.

"It's true, isn't it." He breathed hard; he'd taken a hit high in the thigh. "You didn't make this up. These photos are real."

It was like going back in time, stepping outside her body and looking into her own face the day Xavier had dragged her through the Plant.

"I wish it weren't true," she said. "But it is."

The soldier sank into himself, eyes dropping to his blood spattered on the road shoulder.

She lifted her face to the semi, Reed poised behind the huge steering wheel.

Griffin touched her arm. "You want to ride with him?"

"Not with Reed. With the Tedrans. They need to know what's happened. What's going to happen."

He nodded tightly. "Then go. Hurry."

The headlights of the Ofarian backup drew closer and closer. Even with Griffin's orders to stand down, who knew what they'd do when they saw the injured Chairman. Gwen needed to get the hell out of there.

She ran for the back of the semi and pulled up when she saw Xavier propped heavily against the trailer, the events of that night clearly riding high and hard on his back.

"I saw everything." His voice was full of wonder, full of regret. "You . . . you . . ."

"No time for that," she said, stealing Reed's words. "Boost me up. I'm sending you home."

FORTY

The semi-trailer was cold despite the press of hundreds of bodies around her. To stave off claustrophobia, Gwen talked the
length of the bumpy ride. No one else said a word. She spoke in
Tedranish, outlining her whole story, leaving nothing out. Above
everything, the Tedrans deserved honesty. It was too dark
inside the trailer to gauge their reactions. Nora stood somewhere in the mass, but wherever she was, she remained quiet.

Xavier wedged himself through the crowd, unlocking
neutralizer handcuffs one by one, and the floor became luminescent with tiny green lights. The Tedrans stood there,
confused. They didn't know what to do with their freedom.
They had no idea that, as soon as they were well away from
the neutralizer magic, the glamour was now theirs to command
as they willed.

When the truck finally stopped, the Tedrans pushed Gwen
to the door. The back rolled up and this time it was Reed on
the ground and her inside. He looked up at her, extended a
hand, and helped her down.

The moment her feet hit the ground, he tugged his hand
from hers. The expression on his face was maddeningly blank.
She owed him a zillion explanations, none of which she could
give now.

Xavier hopped down next, and together the three of them
helped the Tedrans out of the truck.

The semi had braked diagonally across an empty harbor
parking lot on the shore of Lake Tahoe. A sign at the lot
entrance read: NO PARKING BETWEEN 2 AND 6 A.M. It was

closing in on three, and the parking spaces were all taken up by milling, nervous Tedrans.

It had been beyond difficult to try to explain the concept of a spaceship, let alone a lake, to people who'd never even seen the stars. Now the Tedrans huddled together in a wide-open space, pointing at mundane things like road signs and bushes. Some cried, bemoaning the loss of walls. It was close to freezing outside, and none had been in a temperature other than seventy-two degrees.

One third of them were children. None, save for Nora, was elderly. Many of the teenage girls were pregnant.

Xavier swept around the outside of the group, murmuring reassuring words, trying to keep the group calm. Telling them to trust Gwen.

She heard him ask several women if they knew which kids they'd made together. The women only shook their heads, looking as lost as he. But by gazing over the towheads and the taller ones, Gwen could take a pretty good guess. She sincerely hoped they'd figure it out.

Gwen finally caught sight of Nora in the throng. She was holding children's hands, smiling, smoothing hair. Whatever misguided plans Nora might have had, she was still a leader. She still wanted her people to be happy and free. So had Ian Carroway.

Adine milled around, too, speaking Tedranish to confused adults, but looking overwhelmed and unsure herself.

Reed stood alone, off to the side, but she instead went for Griffin and David, who were hopping out of the SUV that held all the *Mendacia*.

"We need a boat," she told them. "I don't care if we have to make a million trips in a dinghy. Just get something."

"I'll handle that," Griffin said. To David he ordered, "Take the SUV that doesn't have the *Mendacia* and get the rest of our guys back to San Francisco. You're on point for going after the Board. I also want anyone and everyone associated with the Plant—doctors, guards, fucking janitors—and I want it done yesterday."

David nodded and went off without question. The pickup truck carrying Genesai swerved into the lot. Sam killed the engine, hopped into the SUV with David and the others, and it sped south.

"They're leaving?" Xavier said quietly, just behind her.

She glanced at Griffin, who was already halfway across the lot, heading for the very few remaining boats tethered to the harbor cans. She just realized what he'd done.

"Yes," she said to Xavier. "It's better this way. The last thing your people need is a bunch of Ofarians circling them, telling them what to do."

Xavier sighed, and the sound was saturated with gratitude and relief.

She looked at the expanse of weathered wood stretching out into the black, choppy water. "I need everyone on the dock. Reed?" She turned to find he'd edged closer, arms across his chest.

"Yes?" That voice, with no challenge, sank deep into her bones.

"Can you help get everyone to the docks?"

She'd explained to the Tedrans that Reed was a harmless Primary, so they listened as he started to guide them across the road. Xavier moved to follow but Gwen took his arm and held him back. "I need your help, too. But with something else."

She told him what she needed. He nodded and disappeared into the crowd.

Genesai still sat in the pickup, hands splayed on the glass, staring out at the water. She rushed to the vehicle and opened the door. Off balance, he tumbled out and hit the ground in a pile of awkward limbs. She lifted him to his feet, looped her arm through his elbow, and said, "Come with me. I'm about to bring up your ship."

She and the pilot pressed through the crowd of Tedrans until they came to the very end of the dock. Genesai shook with anticipation.

Xavier was already there, standing at the head of a line of seven Tedrans. Of all the Tedrans present, those seven looked the oldest and healthiest. Xavier nodded to her. All was ready on his end.

Reed stood to her right. Slowly she turned to him. His chin

dipped low. Those intense eyes didn't blink as they searched her face.

"I didn't want to bring you into this," she said. "I really didn't."

He clenched his jaw hard.

"You said I used you. Maybe I did. And I'm sorry. So very, very sorry."

"Gwen, I know—"

"No, you don't know. Not all of it. There shouldn't be any more secrets between us. You said . . . you said you were mine. So you should know exactly who's laying claim to you."

With that, she inched backward, heels poised over the edge of the dock, and whispered Ofarian words.

The magic swept up from her toes, transforming her body part by part to shimmering water. The last thing she saw before she let go of her bodily mold and splashed into the cold lake was Reed's wide eyes and the exaggerated O of his mouth.

Gwen didn't need Adine's submarine or her fancy instruments or her enviable memory to find Genesai's ship again.

Deep under the lake's surface, she expanded her water body into a thin net of droplets. She opened herself to the lake's voice, and it was as welcoming as the embrace of a dearest friend—the one who'd never judge or abandon. She'd been so worried, when the Tedrans had kept making her take *nelicoda*, that the drug would permanently damage her magic and she'd never again get to feel her liquid self slide through water. Truly, there was nothing like it.

She tested her surroundings, asking the water to tell her where the ship lay. The response came in vibrations that drifted across her liquid body, describing disturbances and outlining the placement of rocks and wildlife and sunken boats.

In the lake's deepest canyon, she found her prize.

Gathering her body in close, she streamed like an arrow toward the ship. There it rested, gorgeous and patient, just as Gwen remembered. She flowed right for the white communication oval near the airlock. Manipulating the water pressure, she drew words in Genesai's language to introduce herself and outline her intent.

Red words of reply streaked across the oval. *Welcome,*

Gwen, friend of Genesai. I remember you. The blood of my love has fed me well. To the surface I will rise.

The ship lurched and shook, dislodging itself from over a century of lake-bottom sludge. She rose and rose, and Gwen followed, drafting in her powerful wake, loving being surrounded by something other than air. For a few seconds, Gwen thought of nothing but being Ofarian, her mind gloriously empty and soaring.

They burst to the surface in a mountain of white, burbling water. No one on land would be able to miss that. Gwen prayed Xavier and his people were doing what she'd asked.

She slithered back through the water, aiming for the antsy crowd on the dock, and wound herself up and around one of the posts. Several Tedrans anxiously crept back, pointing to where she stretched her liquid form in a long puddle atop one of the wide slats. She let go of the water form, her body shooting straight up, to rematerialize in front of the gasping crowd.

Reed wasn't among them.

"Look," Xavier said, and she was thankful for the yank back to the task at hand.

She turned and gazed out at the water. The calm, unaffected water.

"Wow," she murmured. There was no trace of the alien behemoth that had emerged from the lake depths.

Xavier kept his attention on the water. "The mask will dissolve for anyone who touches her. It's like when we went through the Plant, why I couldn't let anyone touch us."

And like the homeless man who'd been forced to drink *Mendacia* to keep the illusion alive regardless of touch.

"The ship is floating at my eleven o'clock," Xavier said. "Tell Griffin to head that way. He'll feel it when the bow of his boat strikes the ship. If any part of the illusion fails, we'll fix it."

He nodded toward an idling, barnacled tourist boat roped to the dock, Griffin at the controls. How he'd swung that, she never knew. She started for the boat.

"Gwen."

She turned back to Xavier. He glanced down the row of Tedrans standing next to him. "There are eight of us working the illusion, but it's huge. And it shifts constantly. I don't know how long we can hold it."

"We'll hurry. I promise."

She found Genesai pacing on the edge of the dock, like a dog who hates water dying to jump in after a favorite toy.

"She's there!" he cried. "I see her! How do I get to her?"

Apparently Xavier's magic meant nothing to the ship's creator. Gwen guided Genesai to a rickety ladder and showed him how to climb down into the waiting boat. He could barely hold himself steady on the rungs, he was shaking so intensely from the excitement. Standing in the boat, Griffin tried to keep Genesai steady. When Genesai had gone halfway down the ladder and only his head poked above the dock, Gwen wrapped her hands around the ladder posts and crouched.

"I just realized," she said, eye level with him, "that I'll never see you again."

He stopped, confusion lifting his upper lip high into his cheek. "Is that a good thing or a bad thing?"

"Good point," she muttered to herself in Ofarian. Then, to him in his language, "It's both, I suppose. It's happy for you, but sad for me, in a way. What I'm trying to say is that I think I'll miss you."

For a moment she didn't know if he understood, or if she'd incorrectly translated her emotions. Then he gazed back at her with such clarity that she knew he comprehended a hell of a lot more than she gave him credit for.

"Gwen," he said. "You are not your people."

The words squeezed her heart so tightly she could barely breathe. He gave her his version of a dirty, lopsided, youthful smile, and half jumped, half fell to the boat.

She straightened and turned. Nora stood right behind her, chin lifted, spidery hands clasped at her waist. The milling Tedrans gaped at her as though she were queen. Every quarter second Nora's expression shifted. Fury to pride, frustration to hatred, fear to relief. But never, ever gratitude.

Gwen didn't expect it, and didn't need it.

"My father and the Board will be brought to justice. I promise you." That was one promise Gwen knew she could keep.

Nora's cold, doubtful eyes flickered out to the nothingness in the middle of the lake. "How do I know the ship's really out there? How do I know Genesai will take us home? How can you assure me your kinsman won't drown us out there?"

Gwen sighed and gestured to the Tedrans and the vehicles parked across the road. "You can't trust me, not even now?"

The black diamond stare hit her hard. "I will never be able to trust an Ofarian. Surely you can understand that much."

Gwen supposed she could, though it made her sad to hear.

Nora had no idea what awaited her back on Tedra. Could be anything. More war. Exquisite peace. Who could possibly say? But Gwen didn't say that, allowing Nora to keep a firm grasp on her concept of Utopia. Truthfully, the Tedrans had never felt hope before, and to squash that now would be the most evil thing Gwen could do. She could no more promise the Tedrans a tidy existence here on Earth than she could on their home world.

Nora looked over her shoulder. The Tedrans shifted, awaiting her attention and direction. "Adine," she called, extending her hand. "Let's go home."

Adine pulled away from the crowd edge. As usual, she'd blended in with everyone else. The half-Tedran stared at Nora's hand as though it were Pandora's box.

"I'm not going," Adine declared.

"What?" Nora exclaimed.

Whoa, Gwen mouthed.

Adine kept tucking her hair behind her ears, forever losing the battle with the wind, but doing a great job of establishing her defensive position otherwise.

Nora stood toe to toe with her daughter. "This is what we've been working for."

For once, Adine did not look away. "No. It's what *you've* been working for. It took me a while to realize that." Her brown eyes swept across the star-filled sky. "I always thought it would be incredibly exciting to go up there, to see Tedra. But as I got older, I became aware that those thoughts weren't mine. I believed them because you'd drilled them into my head since I was old enough to listen."

Nora puckered her lips, ready to spit. "This place is wicked."

Adine held up a hand. "And it's the only home I've ever known. I'm not a Tedran, Nora. I'm not a Primary either, but I know I belong here, not up there. *This* is home, and I'm not leaving it."

Adine smiled—actually smiled—turned on her heel, and

walked away. It was the first time Gwen had ever seen Adine turn her back on her mother. Apparently, by the stunned and hurt look on Nora's face, it was a first for her, too.

Adine pushed through a resisting crowd, the Tedrans scowling at her in confusion. Why would a Tedran not trust Nora, and her own daughter to boot? They turned their hopeful, devoted faces to Nora, who lifted her chin even higher and gave them a sad smile that seemed to reassure them.

Good leaders, Gwen thought, loved their people. She could blame Nora for nearsightedness and a twisted sense of vengeance, but Gwen would always believe that Nora held the survival of her people above all. She could never begrudge Nora that, because it was exactly how Gwen felt about her own people, despite their flaws.

"I wish the best for you and yours," Gwen told Nora. "I hope you can at least trust in that."

Nora inhaled deeply and swept a dreamy look over her huddled masses, on their way to a new life. "You know, I think I do." Then she went to the ladder and lowered herself into the boat, refusing Griffin's assistance.

FORTY-ONE

Gwen supervised as Griffin packed the boat with Tedrans, who clung to one another and pressed away from the railings, away from the water. The boat backed up with an engine whine, then it *put-put-putted* into the open expanse, toward Xavier's eleven o'clock.

Everyone on the dock held their breath. Gwen didn't realize how close she'd moved to Xavier until her arm brushed against his. He startled but didn't move away. He and the other Tedrans stared intently out at their illusion, some with arms wrapped around their middles. One ground his fingers into his temple.

All Gwen could see was the pain of Tedrans in the draining room. These eight here on the dock hated using their power, but they did it for their people. It was one of the bravest, most selfless acts Gwen had ever witnessed.

Far out in the water, the boat stopped. Jerked. A whisper of magic drifted across the waves, a warm breeze in the midst of the cold September night. The black atmosphere above the boat wavered, rippling. Gwen squinted, trying to discern the ship's lovely shape. One of the Tedrans groaned. The illusion snapped back into place.

The moonlight was just barely bright enough to illuminate the Tedrans on the boat. They were tiny, shadowed shapes shuffling about the deck. And then they weren't there at all. The illusion engulfed them. As they climbed into the ship's airlock, they disappeared into nothingness, sucked into the Tedrans' apparition.

Gwen watched, heart in her throat. When the boat was empty, Griffin gunned it back toward the dock and they started the whole process again. And again.

As the crowd thinned, she recognized the feel of eyes upon her. She'd know it anywhere. Her whole body had been tuned to it, an instrument awaiting its player.

Turning, she saw Reed leaning against a post, a yellow, bug-filled light hanging above his round head. His posture did an okay job of pretending to be casual, but she knew what those tight arm muscles meant, the intense train of thought drawing together his eyebrows. She'd seen it all the night she'd told him what she was.

She couldn't swallow, couldn't breathe, couldn't move. The rough edges to him were more beautiful than ever, and it hurt to look at him. He knew everything about her now, had seen it with his own eyes.

I'm just hers.

She felt like she knew him well enough to say that his tension wasn't focused on her ancestry or anything that had happened here tonight. It was drilling inward. Hard, eating at him. She remembered what Griffin had told her, about Reed doing everything he had for her, not for her people. Even if it took her the rest of her life, she'd make him believe that she wanted *him*, not only what he could do for her.

After all, she was his, too.

He pulled away from the post. His lips parted, his eyes softened, as if preparing for a kiss. A giant invisible spaceship bobbed out in the middle of Lake Tahoe, swallowing an alien race in preparation to leave Earth, and Reed looked only at her.

She started toward him. The rigidity of his body shattered. The dimple flashed. He broke into a jog.

"Gwen!" Xavier's strangled voice came from behind her. He sounded on the verge of breaking, and when she whirled back around, that was indeed what he was.

The final boat filled with Tedrans sped off toward Genesai's ship. The illusion was cracking, tiny flickers of reality starting to show through. Xavier had fallen to his knees, face red from severe exertion, his hair soaked to the roots. He was Atlas, assuming his terrific burden alone.

Alone. Why was he alone?

She sped over to him.

"It's getting . . . really hard . . . to hold this." The tendons in Xavier's neck popped out. He was crying, and seeing his tears might have affected her most of all.

He was close to empty, and the ship had yet to break away from Earth.

She had not come this far to fail in the final step. Xavier needed help. He needed more power.

She wheeled around and sprinted back down the dock. Legs pumping, she could honestly say she'd never run this fast or for a greater purpose.

"Where . . ." Reed called as she blew right past him.

When she got to the parking lot, she could barely see for the stars pricking at her periphery, and she could barely breathe for the constriction of her lungs. It didn't matter. She ignored it.

The keys to the black SUV were in the ignition. She revved the engine, threw the shift into gear, did a jerky three-point turn, and squealed in reverse down the entire length of the dock at thirty miles an hour. The deckboards rattled angrily beneath the tires. The brakes screeched, stopping the SUV feet off the edge of the dock.

Jumping out, she saw Xavier now sat on his heels, his tall body listing to one side. Griffin was heading back with the empty boat.

Reed jogged to meet her at the back hatch. "What do you need me to do?"

She threw open the door, snatched out a box of *Mendacia*, and ripped open its top. "Dump it. All of it. Into the lake."

Without a moment's hesitation, Reed's big hands snatched two bottles at a time, his thumbs popping open the tops.

"Xavier." She knelt next to the Tedran. "I'm getting in the water. I know Tedranish. I can take over the illusion if I use all the *Mendacia* as it mixes with the water."

"No . . . Gwen . . ." He couldn't even shake his head.

"No arguments. When Griffin comes back, I want you on that boat. I'll take over from here."

The plan made sense in her head. She'd get in the water, utilize the *Mendacia* floating there, and then take over command of the illusion. Xavier would get on Genesai's ship and she'd mask the craft's rise into the sky. Easy as pie.

She rocked to her feet and went to help Reed.

So much power in a bottle the size of a nail polish. Hundreds of them were glugging into the lake. In the moonlight, the thick, metallic *Mendacia* clung close to the top of the water, riding the waves in a crude, silver oil. How appropriate: the Tedrans' magic refusing to mix with the Ofarians'.

Xavier collapsed to all fours.

"Hold on," she begged him. "We're almost done."

Xavier didn't hold on. He started crawling toward the edge of the dock. Griffin was still fifty yards away. Without warning, Xavier threw himself over the side, landing with a flat, hollow splash in the middle of the thick *Mendacia* puddle.

"Wait!" She lunged for him. "What are you doing?"

Xavier came to the surface, gasping and flailing. He struggled through the liquid, looking like a child who'd only been to a handful of swimming lessons. He opened his mouth and swallowed a great gulp of silver.

His long arms stretched for the ladder and he pulled himself against it. Fingers curled around the top rungs, his legs wrapped around the bottom, he clung to it for his life. The thick *Mendacia* dripped slowly off the ends of his hair and rolled off his clothes like they were made of plastic.

Gwen kept calling to him, telling him to come back up. He wasn't listening to her. He mumbled in Tedranish, but the sound of the waves and the approaching boat and her own panic drowned out his words.

Out in the lake, the illusion solidified again.

Gwen flattened on her stomach at the dock edge. "Xavier. What are you doing? Let me do it. Get your ass on that boat."

He lifted his face up to her. Strength had come back to him courtesy of that singular drink, taking the strain from his face and bringing clarity to his eyes.

"The illusion needs more than words," he said. "It's too big and you can't swallow all this. It wouldn't work for you anyway, not for an illusion created far away. You can only work on your own body. When the ship flies, it'll need me."

Shivering violently in the cold water, he turned his attention to the illusion. He reached up, grabbed the collar of his plaid flannel shirt in both hands, and ripped it off his body. Half-naked, he submerged himself up to his collarbone. Giant goose-flesh popped out on his wide shoulders.

"You'll freeze," she begged, but deep down she knew protesting was hopeless and counterproductive. He'd made up his mind.

The floating *Mendacia* gathered to him, encircled him. He was commanding it, the lives of his brothers and sisters and mates and children. The struggle of his people. With a gasp, she watched the *Mendacia* soak into his skin. Drop after drop, it crawled up his neck and extended down his arms—coating his skin, burrowing in. He rose from the water to his waist, legs braced on the ladder, and his whole torso glowed molten silver. His gray eyes shined like crystal, lit from within. Water dripped from his blond, wavy hair and rolled off his platinum body.

He looked beautifully alien. He *was Mendacia*.

And through it all, he smiled. His luminous silver eyes drifted far away, staring someplace beyond the illusion. Beyond Earth.

She finally understood what he meant to do. "Oh, God, Xavier."

"This is how I can help them," he said. "I can help them get away safely and they can have true lives, the lives I gave them."

Stars' blessings upon them—the women he'd been forced to impregnate and the children he'd never know, who should wear their resemblance to him with pride.

Griffin pulled up in the boat, maneuvering it sidelong against the dock. "Xavier," he called. "Come on."

Xavier sighed. "Tell the ship to go, Gwen. I've got it." When she hesitated, he barked, "Do it."

There had to be another way. Xavier hated Earth, hated Ofarians. He deserved his place on that ship.

"*Now,* Gwen."

She pushed to her feet, her body heavy. Yet she managed to stand on her tiptoes, wave her arms toward the unseen ghost of Genesai's ship, and shout, "Go! Go now!"

Below her on the ladder, Xavier pushed his metallic body completely from the water. No more *Mendacia* floated in the lake. Now it sheathed him in magically metallic armor.

Griffin appeared at her side. "What's happening? Why is he still here?"

Fingers to her mouth and throat, she murmured, "He has his reasons."

Xavier gasped. Tears leaked from his silver eyes, but this time they came from unmistakable joy.

"The ship . . . it's moving . . . it's lifting. Ah!"

Minutes swept by. The tint of his skin started to fade as he channeled all the stored power of his people. Though she wished there had been another way, Xavier was the rightful wielder of this magic. For anyone to touch it other than a Tedran, it would have been nothing short of sacrilege.

Gwen turned her eyes to the open water. She yearned to see Genesai's love in motion, hear her sounds. The only thing Gwen heard, however, was the boat knocking against the dock and the early autumn wind tangling in tree branches. The only movement came from the far side of the lake, where a single car's headlights made a slow turn on the road.

Yet she felt something. An *absence*.

When she'd feared Reed was dead, his absence had filled her with awful hate and deep despair. There, standing on the quiet dock watching absolutely nothing, this new absence brought her a sincere happiness she'd never be able to quantify.

She stood there forever, watching. She could have stood through ten more forevers.

Xavier's hand flailed on the ladder. The top of his head appeared. Shaking arms tried to pull his body onto the dock. Gwen dove and grabbed one side of him, Griffin the other. Xavier's skin had returned to its regular pale color, and it was ice cold to touch. Reed whipped off his fleece and draped it over Xavier's convulsing body.

All the *Mendacia* in the world as assistance, and it still wiped him out. She wondered how many years he'd shaved off his life.

"It's done." Xavier's teeth chattered so hard she could barely understand him. He struggled to keep his eyelids open. "The ship's gone. Away. You saved my people."

She took his hand in one of hers, and touched his face with the other. His eyes rolled up to hers, briefly flashing pure white. "And then you saved mine," she told him. "Thank you."

Unconsciousness was winning the battle. He tried to speak but no sound came out.

No, he mouthed. *Thank you.*

FORTY-TWO

For the second time that night, Reed stepped away from the scene. Primaries definitely weren't meant to be here, to witness this.

But he was strangely glad he had.

Xavier shuddered and passed out. Griffin hauled the taller man over his shoulder in a skillful fireman's lift and started for the SUV littered with empty *Mendacia* boxes and vials.

Gwen still stared out at the water, arms around her waist. When she finally turned, she looked strangely shocked to see Reed still standing on the dock. The hesitation in her body, the fear in her eyes, made his stomach churn. Did she honestly think he'd leave because of what she was, or because of what he'd seen? Maybe he'd thought of leaving that night in the lake house when she'd started it all, but not now. Never again.

"Say something." The wind nearly stole her voice.

Ear to shoulder, hands on hips, he said, "Come here."

She lurched forward as though he'd pulled on her leash. But she stopped two feet away, looked up at him with those giant, reflective brown eyes. With her gold hair swirling around her face and courage shining through her skin like what had just happened with Xavier, she had never, ever looked more stunning.

He reached out, slid a hand around her neck, and pulled her mouth to his. Her kiss . . . if there was ever a drug as powerful as it, he'd never want out of addiction. Wrapping an arm around her hips, he heaved her against him, forcing her arms around his head and neck.

They kissed hard. Greedy. The first meal after famine.

Different, now that they were away from Nora and that house. Better.

She tasted of cool, crisp, sweet water. Water . . . hell, she *was* water. He'd seen it with his own eyes.

When he finally forced himself away, her eyes had gone all dreamy, like he'd once told her. If he wasn't holding her up, she'd melt again into a puddle. And wasn't that the best compliment you could give a man? To see how you affected a woman like her?

"Oh, I'm sorry." He grinned, loving the way her gaze traveled to his cheek with the dimple. "You wanted me to say something, didn't you?"

She laughed. He framed her face in his hands, his fingers sinking into the softest part of her hair. "Holy shit, that was *you*? You . . . *melted*."

She blew out a shaky breath. "Yeah. I did."

"How come you didn't tell me about that before?"

"Figured I'd reached my quota of weird shit to throw at you."

"Is it like the Translator thing? Or can all of you do it?"

She searched his eyes. "It's us. It's what makes us special. Ofarians."

Suddenly everything calmed between them. The swirl of storms made up of questions and secrets, hidden layers and deception, just blew apart. The atoms of doubt scattered in the wind, flying up to the atmosphere like the spaceship he never saw but completely and totally believed in.

It was just them now. Gwen and Reed. Not the Retriever and the Translator. Not captor and captive. Not user and used.

The realization drew his mouth to hers, and he slanted across her lips with unquenchable fervor. They kissed as if they were alone. They kissed like they didn't care they weren't. She fed him her drug through her lips. Three or four days ago it might have gone solely to his dick. Now it swelled his heart.

In the next two seconds, he remembered every word they'd ever said to each other. Every heated glance of longing across the DMZ. Every stroke of his hand across her bare back. Every thrust inside her. Every withheld sound as she came . . . It all slammed together, transforming his body into a tempest of *need* and *want*.

He pulled back for breath, his lungs sawing. If he didn't stop now, there'd be no stopping until he was inside her.

Their foreheads came together. No, every part of their bodies came together, ankles to chests.

"You did it," he whispered.

"Not without you." She inhaled and slid her hands up his arms. Even without his fleece he didn't feel a single degree of cold.

She blinked long, shook her head, and turned serious. "What Griffin did . . . he said he took you to avoid suspicion. He was thinking about what would be best for me."

Reed kept his smirk to himself. "And maybe he didn't like what I told him about us."

One corner of her full mouth ticked up. She turned her head, smooth skin sliding under his hands, and kissed the center of his palm. "He didn't like it. Can you blame him?"

Not at all. Look who was at stake.

He scrolled back to the scene in the Plant, when he'd tried to get the Ofarian guard to let him out by dropping Gwen's name. His face must have changed—man, he really was slipping around her—because she asked, "What?"

"Did you know where I was? After they jumped me?"

Her throat moved. "Yes. What happened in there?"

"I tried to drop your name, tell them they'd made a mistake. They said they called you and that you told them I was where I needed to be. Was that true?"

"Yes." Her warm hands went flat on his chest. "And I'm sorry. It was for the same reasons Griffin had you captured in the first place, to protect your involvement from the Board. It killed me to lie."

"Doesn't matter anymore anyway."

She smiled. "Oh, thank God."

Over her shoulder, Reed noticed Griffin approaching.

Reed smoothed Gwen's hair away from her face. Kissed her once again. *Yeah, Griffin, she's mine.* Childish? Absolutely. He really didn't care.

Griffin stopped halfway between them and the SUV. Even decked out in his soldier gear, he was one of those pretty men. He looked from Gwen to Reed, his injured stare hardening.

Gwen jumped in front of Reed. "No, Griffin."

No what? Oh. That. What Xavier had told him about Ofarians taking out Primaries who found out about them. Griffin looked like a model, but it also looked like he could hold his own. It would be a good fight, but Griffin would still lose.

Griffin held up his hands. "I hated killing for the Board. I won't do it on my own. Not ever again, even if you order it, Gwen."

Gwen exhaled forcefully. "Thank you. Thank you."

"It's a new world." Griffin's voice sounded drowsy and loose. "New players. New rules."

"Everything will be different now." Her voice, in contrast, sounded hopeful.

"Everything," he echoed.

"Better," she asserted.

Griffin cleared his throat and came forward, extending a hand toward Reed. "Sorry for what happened. The ambush . . ."

Reed gently moved Gwen aside and stretched for Griffin's hand. Shook it. Griffin squeezed a bit too hard, but Reed got it. It was all good.

"Thank you," Griffin said, looking Reed squarely in the eye. Then he glanced at Gwen. "I don't know if I'll ever be able to thank you enough. For our people. For her."

Why was Griffin thanking him? Reed had made a phone call to get Gwen out of a dangerous situation. He'd aimed a gun at the asshole who'd put a knife to her throat. It was a no-brainer.

Griffin withdrew his hand first.

Reed nodded. "You would have done the same."

"Yes, I would have."

Gwen went to Griffin then, pulled him into a big hug that tugged a bit at Reed's jealousy. He heard her murmur something to Griffin about the Board. He nodded into her shoulder and patted her back.

"Yes, sir," he said. "Right away, sir."

She stepped back. "Oh, so you're going to listen to me now?"

"Hey," Griffin said, "if I hadn't've saved your ass at the fountain, none of this would've happened in the first place."

Reed had no idea what that meant, but he watched Gwen's eyes cloud over and a deep crease etch itself between her eyebrows.

"You know?" she said. "You're absolutely right."

"I'll call for someone to come get that pickup." Griffin turned to Reed. "Can you drive the semi to the city?" Reed nodded. "We have a secure location. Follow me."

Gwen's fingers pressed against her lips in surprise. Not only did Reed know about Ofarians now, but apparently they were letting him into their secret lair. He wondered if there was a magic handshake or something.

Gwen slid her hand into Reed's, their fingers intertwining. "I'm going with him in the semi," she told Griffin. And this time, she wouldn't ride in back.

Griffin nodded, climbed behind the SUV's wheel, and started the engine. He sat with his hands at ten and two, staring at the dashboard.

She was looking at Griffin when she said to Reed, "He thinks you're in love with me."

Reed paled; he actually physically felt the blood drain from his face and land heavily in his boots. Vertigo swooped in, almost knocked him on his ass.

Her face reddened as she slowly turned to Reed. "Oh, God, that was out loud, wasn't it?" She waved a dramatic hand and barreled through her next words. "Don't respond to that. Really."

Reed glared at Griffin's profile. The Ofarian man now sat with his elbow against the window, head in his hand. *Not* looking at the woman he was supposed to marry and the guy who was supposedly in love with her.

Jesus. Was he? Was that even possible in a week? And during all the whacked-out crap that happened to them during that time?

"Come on." She tugged him toward the semi, unsuccessfully trying to keep her blushing cheeks averted. "Show me how you drive that big rig."

FORTY-THREE

"The Board." Griffin snapped his cell phone shut. "We got 'em all. Just found Elaine Montag in Cabo."

Gwen sat across from Griffin, Reed to her left, at the breakfast bar in Griffin's Telegraph Hill apartment. She'd forgotten how nice his place was—how nice *all* their places were. Since returning from the land of the dead, she couldn't even cross the threshold to her own apartment. The whole thing smelled of death and deceit. She and Reed had taken a room at the Four Seasons. Seemed appropriate to come full circle.

The manhunt for the Board and anyone who'd ever worked at the Plant had taken three days. Anyone who knew about the slaves and said nothing was in the crosshairs. Many Ofarians volunteered to help, and Gwen wasn't remotely surprised at the majority of her people's resolve to right what had been done wrong. She'd clung to that belief in captivity and it had been proven true.

Against all odds, they'd succeeded in keeping the strange happenings in bumfuck Nevada and in the middle of Lake Tahoe under wraps. Xavier had used the last of the Tedrans' magic well. And now *he* was the last.

None of the *Mendacia* clients could raise a stink about the dissolution of the Company. The contracts still bound them to keep quiet, and no one wanted to admit to using the product either.

It truly was over, and one end opened up into another beginning.

"Where are you keeping them?" she asked Griffin.

"At the old Plant. Seemed appropriate." His hand slid over hers. "Do you want to see him?"

"No." That came out much stronger than she'd intended. "Not yet."

There were about a Dickens novel's worth of issues for her to page through before she could face her father in person.

"Whatever you want, Gwen," Griffin said. "He'll be there whenever you're ready."

She traced a jagged black line in the marble countertop with a finger. "Any lead on Delia?"

His pause twisted in her stomach. "Still looking. The Board seems to have lost her trail a few years ago. But it doesn't mean she's not out there. There's no proof of death."

She nodded, but more because it was expected, not because she believed they'd find her sister.

Griffin spun his phone on the counter, using the hand that wasn't in a sling. "There's generations of info to sift through. Thousands of things the Board was hiding from us."

"Get Casey, Dad's secretary, to head up the task force to go through all the files. She practically owns that office anyway." As Griffin nodded, she remembered something else. "And have her keep an eye out for anything labeled 'Others.'"

He raised an eyebrow. "'Others? That's all we have to go on?"

She told him what she'd glimpsed in the boardroom the morning after Yoshi's attack—the weird map, the strange labels and color codes, paired with the Board's argument.

"Yeah, okay." He laughed humorlessly. "I'll add that to the list."

"You took Adine's computer, right?" Reed chimed in.

Griffin nodded. "About a thousand levels of security in that thing, but we're working on it."

"Let me know if I can help," Reed said. "I have contacts."

The men shared a look that translated as an awkward sort of truce. It was a start.

Griffin said, "All right. Thanks."

Griffin's phone went off again. She'd gotten used to the persistent sound over the past few days. Right now he was acting as her go-between, but that couldn't go on forever. Her people wanted to hear from her, and she needed to lead. At least until they could establish a new ruling party.

As Griffin spun away from the kitchen and disappeared into

the bedroom, phone plastered to his ear, she meandered over to the bar. She dug out a bottle of the good stuff, poured herself a glass of Napa Cabernet, and ventured out onto the terrace. Coit Tower rose above the roofs only a few blocks away, warm exterior lights lifting the round, ivory structure high into the sky. Surrounded by the white noise of traffic, she leaned on the terrace wall and breathed in the salty air. She'd grown up here, but everything felt different. She no longer belonged.

Glass clinked on stone as Reed set down the wine bottle. He poured his own glass and stared into the ruby red. "Tell me what you want to do."

She inhaled through her nose, lifted her face to the breeze. "I don't want to stay here. In San Francisco."

He nodded, staring up at the tower. "You don't think you should?"

"I need to stick around for a bit to see some things through, but I can't live here." She shook her head. "My old life . . . it isn't mine anymore. Maybe someday I'll find my way back."

"But your people."

She closed her eyes, smelling the water to the east. "I was thinking that what could possibly be a better way to convince them to get out into the Primary world than to see me doing it myself? I can still be involved with the Ofarians from anywhere in the world. The magic of the Internet, and all that."

"Griffin needs you." It killed Reed to say that, she knew, and she loved him for it.

Stars, she did. She loved him.

They'd both managed to ignore her little outburst on the dock a few nights back. When her mouth had opened before her mind could catch up, Reed had looked like she'd run over him in that giant semi he'd looked so sexy driving. It was okay; she didn't blame him. She was in no hurry. For once in her life, no hurry whatsoever.

Silence draped itself over their shoulders, but it wasn't awkward. Nothing about the two of them felt forced or uncomfortable.

"Griffin does need me," she acquiesced. "And we work well together."

Reed swirled and sipped his wine. "Remember what I told

you back at the lake house? That I wanted to show you where I lived?"

"Of course I remember."

He scrubbed a hand over his head, and the fact he was nervous made her belly flutter in the best possible way. "If I asked you to come home with me now, would you?"

"What about Tracker?"

They'd talked about him a bit as they got tangled in the ridiculously soft hotel sheets. Reed was worried but not scared. Nora had never contacted Tracker.

"I can always move us to Alaska. Change my name again."

"Again?"

"Well, I could still be Reed Scott to you."

"Damn." She snapped her fingers. "Was hoping to get two for the price of one."

He smiled brightly. She would never, ever get tired of the dimple. "So what do you say?"

Scrunching up her face, she pretended to consider. "Depends on where this mysterious home is."

Another sip. "It's east."

She pressed her hip into the wall. "East of what?"

"East of here."

They laughed together. He really wasn't going to tell her, the impossible, mysterious man.

"I've been thinking about something," he said in earnest.

"Yeah? What about?"

"How we met. Where we are now." He leaned closer. Though they'd spent the better part of three days naked or kissing, his proximity still made her dizzy. "Can you think of a crazier situation in which two people have tried to start a relationship? Think about the shit we've been through. Our atmosphere could hardly be called normal."

"What are you saying exactly?"

He leaned both elbows on the wall, kicked his long legs out. "I know we can survive anything, but I think we should test it out."

"Test *what* out?"

"Normalcy. Us, inside normalcy."

She laughed. "So you want to take me back to Virginia? Meet the parents?"

"No, not that. Not yet, at least. I want to take you back to my home, not theirs."

"So how do you want to work this test of yours?"

The dimple flashed. "My mom once told me there are two ways to test a relationship, to see the other person's true colors. One was to wallpaper a room together."

She snorted. "And the other?"

"Road trip."

They left two days later.

Reed rented a generic blue two-door for the drive he cryptically described as "long." She'd sent him into her old apartment to get clothes and things while she'd stayed out in the hall and shouted directions. He didn't mind at all. Even took along a few of her gigantic art books out of his own interest.

Griffin was under orders to put the place on the market. When she came back for meetings and rituals and such, she'd stay at a hotel.

The rental car idled in the street, Reed leaning casually against the driver's side door. Gwen and Griffin stood facing each other in his open front door, warm September San Francisco sunshine on their faces.

He reached up, grabbed the door frame with one hand. "You know, I think I'm a little scared."

"I don't think I've heard you say that since the day we graduated high school."

He chuckled. "You know what I mean."

"I do," she said seriously.

"I wish you were staying. At least for a little longer."

She glanced at Reed, who was trying not to watch them but wasn't doing a very good job. He'd firmly left the Retriever—and apparently all his cover abilities—behind. "I can't."

Griffin mistook her meaning and glared at Reed. "If he's making you . . ."

She placed a calming hand in the center of Griffin's chest. "He's not. Not at all. We don't feel the way we do about each other because we were thrown into the lion pit and clawed our way out. But we'd like the chance to prove it to ourselves. I think we deserve that. That's why we're leaving."

"That's it. Throw the Ofarian world into upheaval and take off. Nice one, Carroway."

She laughed lightly. "That's right, I'm a coward." Then, soberly, "So. Conference call tomorrow with the new finance group? I'll make sure I'm somewhere with good cell reception."

He nodded. "Your suggestion makes sense: dividing the Company assets among all innocent Ofarians. The audit committee will approve it, I'm sure."

"I hope so."

He laughed. "After your incredible address yesterday, they'll do whatever you want."

That's not what she'd hoped for at all. She hadn't deposed one ruler to take over herself. The Ofarians needed to start from a clean slate.

That was why, in yesterday's video address securely sent to all Ofarians, she appointed Griffin as her interim spokesperson until they could establish a new government outside the Company. She agreed to sit on the restructuring task force—and embraced being able to help the people she loved—but they needed someone other than another Carroway at the head of the table.

It had taken her an entire day to write that speech. Much of it she'd already told her father and everyone else after the caravan attack. Griffin had said the response was overwhelmingly positive.

There, in the open doorway, Gwen looked at her dearest friend. "However we restructure, however we go forward, it will be on a better road than the one we traveled before. Besides"—she cupped his smooth cheek in her hand—"they'll have a strong leader."

He shifted uncomfortably. "I would never say this to anyone else but you, but why would they want a failure to lead them?"

She drew back. "Failure?"

"I had a responsibility to keep you safe, Gwen. My *only* responsibility. And then I let a Primary go with knowledge of us." He coughed. "I couldn't even keep the girl."

"You know what I think? I think sometimes the most reluctant of leaders turns out to be the most fair and able."

"You don't know if they'll vote me in."

She smiled. "Yes, I do."

"Thank you. For your faith."

They embraced for a long time, rocking, then she backed out into the sun.

"I want you to come back in January," he said, "and lead the Ice Rites."

She let out a little gasp. "You don't know if the people will choose me for such an honor."

His turn to smile. "Yes, I do."

She started to back down the walkway toward the street. "You know where to find me."

He raised a dark eyebrow. "I do? *You* don't even know where he's taking you."

She waggled the shiny new cell phone Reed had bought her when he'd gone out for the car. Only three people had its number. "I meant that I'm never far."

He put a hand to his heart. "No. You aren't."

She had to turn then, to walk away.

"So." She plopped into the passenger seat of the sedan as Reed stuffed himself behind the wheel. "Where we headed?"

Reed's grin was borderline evil.

FORTY-FOUR

Six weeks of sitting on the edge of her seat. Of asking, every time they crossed a state line or entered a city's limits, whether or not this was the place, if *this* was where he called home. Every time he'd throw her an impish smile, which meant no.

Then, depending on where they were, they'd check into a hotel, shower, fuck until they were hungry, grab something to eat, hit some crazy-hilarious regional museum, or hang out in a local bar to chat with the townies.

She saw parts of the United States she'd never even heard of before. One afternoon, just outside Jackson, Wyoming, she found herself looking up at an airplane with distaste. Why would anyone choose to travel with a view of only the seat in front of you? Why couldn't everyone have Reed as a traveling companion?

He cracked inappropriate jokes when she demanded he pull over and let her pee. Somewhere in Idaho he coaxed her out of her fear of horses, and she was hooked. She made him ride every day for the three they were in town. Across the barren stretches of South Dakota, he turned off the radio to listen as she told him all about her life. He didn't pressure her when she really, truly didn't want to eat venison at a roadside diner on the Wisconsin-Minnesota border. She even learned the Lakota language.

She spent long stretches of empty highway e-mailing back every Ofarian who contacted her directly, most of whom she'd never met but was honored to know.

It was the best six weeks of her life.

One evening, as they pulled into a boutique hotel in Minneapolis, her phone rang. The screen showed a San Francisco area code. The third person who knew her number.

"Gwen?"

She wondered if he'd call. "Xavier. Hi."

"I . . ." Even over the fuzzy cell phone line, she detected the shaking in his voice. "Gwen, I don't know what to say."

"Then don't say anything." She looked at her lap as Reed glanced over questioningly. "Just take it. It's yours, the way I see it."

"*All* your money?"

"I don't want it. I don't need it. Most of all, I don't deserve it."

"But it's so much!"

"And now it's yours." A few seconds passed in silence. "Do you know what you're going to do?"

Xavier exhaled. She pictured him running his hands through his tangled hair. "Adine's helping me get settled. There's so much to know . . . so much to think about . . ."

"I'm glad Adine's with you."

"She said she'll stick around for a bit. She's got plans of her own, though. I don't know what they are."

In the background she heard waves crashing against land.

"Thank you, Gwen. A thousand times, thank you."

"If you ever need anything . . ."

The line went dead.

She shut the phone and cradled it in her lap.

"Xavier?" Reed asked softly.

"I gave him my money."

He whistled in a high arc then nodded. "It was the right thing to do." He reached over and took her hand. "You won't need it anyway."

That brought a smile. "Plan to take care of me, do you?"

"Hell no. I'm retired. Figured you'd be the one taking care of me. Get your ass back to work, missy. Someone always needs translators."

She loved the way he could make her laugh when she least expected it. Whenever he did, she flashed back to the moment they met, and how the man in that dark alley was so very, very opposite from the man sitting next to her now.

He still didn't make any move to get out of the car. "I was thinking," he said to the steering wheel, "of going to school."

Pride swept through her in a warm glow. "To do what?"

He shrugged. "Don't know. Something else."

She crawled into his lap and pressed her lips to his, slowly tracing his mouth with her tongue, her body coming alive. "That," she whispered, "is a wonderful idea."

She figured out where Reed lived before they ever entered the state. Their travel route had taken them up through northern California and Oregon, across Idaho and Wyoming and South Dakota. He'd been as excited as she to see those areas, but when they crossed into Minnesota, she noticed a change in him. A calm like he'd been there before, perhaps often. After a few days in upper and central Wisconsin, that calm transformed into excitement.

They drove leisurely south through Wisconsin, enjoying the autumn color. Reed practically danced in the driver's seat. They crossed the Illinois border and Reed groaned, "Oh, my God, *yes*." He veered off the highway and pulled into a flashy diner-style eatery in the heart of bustling suburbia. "Come on. I've been dying for an Italian beef with hot peppers. You'll love it. I promise."

"Yeah, that's what you said about ostrich burgers."

But he was right this time, and she understood the reason behind his food-lust orgasm. The taste of the dripping sandwich made of thin-cut beef danced on her tongue. The mound of hot peppers made her lips sting and tingle. It felt like when he kissed her.

He grinned at her over his second sandwich. "Now this . . . *this* is Chicago."

And that was where they ended up.

Reed owned the penthouse apartment in a twenty-story building overlooking Lincoln Park. The park showed off for Gwen, wearing its autumn best. Thanks to the shedding trees, she could see down into the nearby zoo. A still, straight lagoon cut through the park, perpendicular to the expansive, cobalt blue Lake Michigan.

All that water, so close.

No matter the weather, there were always a few souls

running or biking along the beachfront path. To the south rose downtown, a sparkling and stunning skyline. She spent a lot of time out on his terrace, memorizing the city that had captivated him. The city he called home.

It was there he found her at sunset on Halloween.

"What are you doing out here? It's freezing."

She turned, smiling. "I can't get over the view. It doesn't have the same feeling from inside."

"Don't expect me to open these doors come February."

She waved away the ominous words. He'd warned her about the winters here, that her Californian blood wouldn't be able to handle it, but with him beside her, she could handle anything.

She clapped her hands like a little girl and bounced on the balls of her feet. "So do I get my surprise now? You've been gone all day."

He rewarded her with a flash of dimple, and the sight of it pulled her inside like a tractor beam. He reached for her, crushed her against him. Their tongues stroked and she felt the familiar, delicious pulsing between her legs. On a groan, he pushed her away.

"Please don't stop now," she begged.

He raised a falsely innocent eyebrow while adjusting his jeans around his growing erection. "I thought you wanted your surprise."

"I do, but I've decided it can wait."

He peeled off his shirt, his fierce blue eyes holding hers the whole time. He tossed the shirt onto the stack of college brochures fanned out on the coffee table.

"Mmm," she purred, her gaze raking over his abs. "I like the delay already."

Then she saw the white gauze taped over his left shoulder and biceps, and her breath caught in her throat. "What's that?"

Reed inhaled, deep and long. "Come closer. Let me show you."

Almost eight weeks they'd been together. Eight weeks to memorize every inch of his massive tattoo. All the leaves, the hidden images, the tiny words. He'd told her most of their meanings. For some he remained tight-lipped, and she was all right with that.

But that spot trailing down his shoulder to his elbow, now covered with gauze, had always been blank.

She eyed him. "It's not my name, is it? That's so cheesy."

"No, I'm not that stupid."

She punched him in the opposite shoulder. Like a rock, he barely moved, but instead grabbed her around the waist and kissed her again. Heat blazed in his eyes as he leaned back and slowly began to peel off the gauze. She stared at the new black lines, speechless.

A new vine roped down his shoulder and twined around his biceps. At first she thought it a simple branch, lined with the same leaves that decorated his torso, but there was never anything simple about Reed. She leaned closer. The vine was not a solid stalk, but many, many words packed tightly together.

He pointed. "Start here."

She squinted. "Two million dollars? Is that what it says?"

Reed never took his eyes from her face.

"That what I'm worth?"

"You're worth more." The huskiness in his voice reached deep inside, wrapped her heart, and pulled tight. "Keep going."

She did, reading aloud. "Two million dollars. San Francisco. Lake Tahoe. Oregon. Idaho. Wyoming. South Dakota. Minnesota. Wisconsin. Chicago . . ." Her voice trailed off to a whisper.

Their story, on his flesh. Forever.

"You like it?" He sounded a little scared.

She kissed his arm, right below the name of the city in which they stood. "I love it."

He took her face in his hand, thumb brushing her lips, fingers digging deep into her hair in a gesture she'd come to know as both possessive and adoring. "There's room for more."

She touched his warm chest. His nipples hardened and she trailed her nails down his stomach to the snap of his jeans.

"You know," she said, "someone once told me that you love me."

He didn't go pale this time. Didn't retreat. He bent closer. "Whoever that was is a damn smart bastard."

"So it's true?" Absolutely nothing else existed in the world outside of that apartment.

"I'm so in love with you," he said, "I just may stamp your name across my scalp."

She reached up and ran a hand over his smooth head. At the

same time, she snagged moisture droplets from the air and slammed them together to create thin rivulets. She used them to swirl glistening, tantalizing lines over his scalp and neck, down his pecs, and around his ribs. They were like extensions of her own nerves, these liquid teases. She could feel more of his skin at once and it was exquisite.

A rumble rose up from deep within his chest. "Oh, God. You know I love that."

She dried him off, curled her fingers inside his jeans, and pulled open the fly. His breath hitched.

"And I love you," she said against his mouth.

They were completely and utterly alone. No one to fear hearing them from the next room or the floor below. No more worrying about maids wanting to clean their room. No more burying their orgasms against their arms or in pillows.

"Reed." She smiled wickedly. "Make me scream."

Turn the page for a preview of
Hanna Martine's next Elementals book

A TASTE OF ICE

Coming soon from Berkley Sensation!

The first morning of the Turnkorner Film Festival and already you could throw a rock and hit a celebrity. For two weeks each winter, that's exactly what Xavier wanted to do.

He hadn't moved to White Clover Creek, Colorado five years ago for the swarms of film lovers and demanding Hollywood types, but for the other fifty weeks of the year when the insular world of the nineteenth-century mountain town helped him forget what needed to be forgotten.

Today, strangers hogged the ice- and salt-covered sidewalks, jostling him from all sides. He ducked his head, hunched his shoulders, soldiered on. He hated the crowds but he loved the cold: that stinging cloud of air sucked deep into his lungs, the hurt of freezing toes. Anything to remind him he lived free.

Just one more block up Waterleaf Avenue. Just fifty more yards and then he could hide himself in Shed's restaurant kitchen. He'd tie back his hair, grip his knives with an intense sigh of relief, and then spend the next fourteen hours thinking only about the three-by-three-foot station in front of him.

Except that about a thousand people mingled between where he stood in front of the Tea Shoppe and where he longed to be . . . and more than half of them were women.

A hole in the crowd opened up and he pushed into it. On the steps of the Tea Shoppe to his left, two girls in puffy jackets sipped from steaming paper cups. He could smell the pungent Earl Grey, and just underneath it, the scents of their skin and their flowery shampoo.

His body reacted to them as it had been trained. Every

muscle, no matter how small, tightened with expectation. Every blood cell raced faster. He *wanted*.

One of the girls slapped the other on the arm and pointed to Xavier. "Hey, check him out."

He'd never get used to this, to the bold women of the outside world who lusted on their own terms and displayed that lust for all to see. Before, *inside*, he'd been the one with the desires. His captors, the Ofarians, had done a damn fine job of creating that monster, and he was still trying to exorcise it.

Three seconds. That's the maximum amount of time he let himself look at any woman.

You could learn a lot about someone in three seconds. For instance, the two on the steps were here for the scene. And to be seen. They stared at Xavier because he just happened to have walked by. In another minute or so, their attention would drift elsewhere. Though his eyes saw their beauty was plastic—made, not born—his body didn't know the difference. It didn't care.

Three seconds came to an end. He looked away.

Man, he was messed up. He was still learning about this world and about himself, but that much was pretty clear. Normal Primary guys didn't sprint the other way when a woman showed interest. Normal Primary guys didn't spend half their days obsessing over cooking and the other half pounding the ever-loving shit out of a boxing bag just to avoid getting naked with someone.

But then, he wasn't a Primary. He wasn't human.

And even though he wanted nothing more than to be "normal," he certainly wasn't that either.

"Excuse me. Pardon me. Excuse me."

Xavier recognized the reedy voice and sought it out—a note of familiarity in the chaos. He searched the crowd for the source, thankful, for once, that he was just about the tallest person on the street. A crooked little man, silver hair partially covered by a tweed cap, slid along the brick front of the Tea Shoppe, trying to reach the stairs. Mr. Elias Traeger, as much a fixture in White Clover Creek as the bronze statue of the work-hardened miners in the middle of the garden square. The old man had worked at the Tea Shoppe for twenty years and would probably totter from local job to local job until his life gave out. Crazy, but that's what Xavier dreamed of.

The crowd shifted. A tourist with a cell phone plastered to

his ear shoved hard into Traeger's shoulder and the elderly man tipped to one side. His eyes went wide, his thin arms scrambling for purchase on the smooth brick.

Five years ago, Xavier would've let Traeger go down and then walked on without a second thought. But Xavier wasn't that man anymore. At least there was that.

Xavier lunged forward and caught Traeger under his arms before his brittle kneecaps could hit the ice. Traeger found his feet, and Xavier helped him right himself. Traeger blinked up into the sunshine.

"Ah. Mr. Jones," Traeger chuckled, his slight British accent coming through. "My thanks. Reaction times aren't quite what they used to be."

Xavier nodded, pleased Traeger remembered his name. "You should've taken the day off," he said. "The first day is always the craziest."

Traeger waved him off with a brilliant smile full of false teeth. "Never sit idle, I always say."

Well, if that wasn't the truth.

"Excuse him," Xavier said sharply to the girls still loitering on the steps. He'd perfected the art of talking to people without looking at them. The girls moved aside with a huff, but at least they moved, and the second they disappeared into the crowd Xavier felt his body calm. Traeger entered the shop and removed his cap.

Xavier slipped back into the crowd and started to press toward Shed again, but the going was painfully slow. What the hell was the hold up? He craned his neck above the sea of bobbing heads made taller by colorful hats. Ah, there. Two massive pockets of people, gaping at two different things, had converged and no one could get through.

Shed's entrance was tucked into the back of a cobblestone alley that ran alongside the historic Gold Rush theater, used as the festival's main venue. Some young, grizzled guy stood under the triangular theater marquee, getting interviewed and photographed by no fewer than five camera teams. The gaggle of fans surrounding him elbowed for space with the people who'd formed a giant circle around a street performer who was, literally, performing in the street.

Waterleaf had been barricaded on both ends, and no cars

were allowed around the main square for the whole festival. Now a middle-aged man wearing a beige North Face jacket and a cheap, felt jester's hat danced along the street's yellow road divider. Normally Xavier didn't pay a second of attention to anything related to the festival, but what Jester was doing made him stop and watch.

Jester juggled a mass of colored balls—hands blurring, balls flying. Some disappeared then reappeared. The audience gasped. Xavier did, too.

Was this guy like him—a Tedran, a Secondary—capable of true magic, true illusion?

No. That would be impossible. Xavier was the last.

He looked closer, following the intricacies of Jester's hands. When Xavier caught the deft slip of Jester's fingers into the folds of his coat, Xavier exhaled. He watched a charlatan, nothing more. He started to turn away, to head back into the thick of the crowd, then stopped. He wanted to be normal, right?

Primaries, he told himself, *like to be entertained.*

Xavier rooted his feet. Closed his eyes. Shoved away the feel of strangers around him and pretended he was weightless and invisible. He drew in a deep breath through his nose and pushed it out. Opened his eyes.

Jester was storing the balls in a suitcase to the sound of applause. He pulled out a deck of cards from his coat pocket and shuffled them in an impressively high arc. He started to go around the circle, asking random people to pick a card, look at it, then put it back in the deck. His marks all happened to be women.

Jester offered the deck to Xavier with a flourish, then pretended he'd made a mistake. "Whoa. Not you, big guy." He tried to play it off for laughs, but Xavier noted Jester's reaction. He'd seen it plenty of times before.

Some people edged away from Xavier because of his size. Since escaping the Plant and finding therapy in throwing his fists into a bag, he'd probably put on a good thirty pounds of muscle. Add that to his six-foot-plus frame, and he understood why he got wary looks.

Other people saw his eyes and just stared.

Pam, his boss, said it was because his eyes were the color of guns—shiny, gray, and full of don't-fuck-with-me. The loathed color reminded Xavier of death. That's why he never looked in the mirror.

Jester offered the card deck to the person standing immediately to Xavier's left. "Well hello, beautiful. Care to pick a card?"

Three seconds.

The woman on his left watched Jester with genuine excitement. Pure joy lit her eyes, which were the color of the caramel Xavier had made at two o'clock in the morning last week. Laughter cast her in a spotlight. She clapped like a kid about to get a cookie—so unlike the attention hounds he'd encountered on the steps.

Somewhere in another world Jester was doing magic tricks, but Xavier only saw her. He forgot how long a second lasted.

Her deep brown hair, streaked with gold and wavy like a stormy ocean, streamed out from beneath a knitted red hat topped with a pompon. She was tanned, like so many Hollywood people traipsing through White Clover Creek, and also freckled. A price tag stuck to the sleeve of her green, fur-trimmed coat.

Vaguely, he felt his skin start to tighten, a heat rising from deep inside. His heart rate started to kick up, but it felt goddamn amazing. Too fucking long to deny himself this day after day.

She must have felt the weight of his stare because suddenly she got this funny look on her face. Glanced over her shoulder at him. Did a double take. Their eyes met and hers widened. Not with wonder or apprehension, like he'd seen on the faces of so many other strangers, but with surprise. Like she'd been expecting to see him and, suddenly, there he was.

She turned toward him and his body went haywire. "Hi," she said.

He didn't say anything out loud. Inside, he screamed, *Walk away, Xavier. Walk away* now.

No. Stay. You're getting hard, slithered a voice from the past, one he hadn't heard in a very, very long time. *I brought her for you,* said the Burned Man, the sadistic Ofarian guard once in charge of Xavier's cellblock. *She's yours. Take her.*

Five years free from the hallucinations. Five years gone.

Xavier's mind flipped back in time. He was in his cell in the Plant's breeding block again. The Burned Man had always brought him the Tedran females. This time, in the waking nightmare, he brought Xavier the freckled woman. She crossed the cold, white floor willingly, but without enthusiasm or even emotion. Xavier took the red hat off her head and tossed it to the side; then he went for the zipper of her coat. Pulled it down. Like all the Tedran women he'd been made to lie with, this woman just stood there, her face agonizingly blank. She was naked underneath the coat and he peeled the thick garment off her body. Anticipation made his skin come alive. The rest of her was as tan as her face, but he'd been trained to only care about the heaven between her legs.

The Xavier that still stood on Waterleaf knew the images in his mind were a twisted combination of past and present. Those three seconds stole a beautiful, laughing face and thrust her into his hell.

In his head, he pulled the woman to the lone mattress in his brightly lit cell. His clothes dissolved. He pushed inside her without any sort of preparation. He shouted at the feel of her and took what he'd been made for. Hated himself because of it. Years without release built and built and built inside him, propelling his thrusts. Beneath him she was limp, but she didn't protest. Her eyes stared far away.

Xavier—the man he had become since escaping this torture, the man that knew this was wrong—ordered the hallucinations away. But in the horror-filled world of his past, his body still worked inside hers. Long-denied fulfillment—because it would never, ever be called pleasure—and self-loathing colliding at a violent crossroads.

He threw his head back, pleading for mercy. *She doesn't want this. I don't want to want this.*

The square window he knew should belong to the White Clover Creek Tea Shoppe morphed into the wire-crossed observation holes in the breeding block cells. The Burned Man appeared on the other side of the glass. The scarred cheek and chin, the distorted ear, the webbed hands . . .

Don't stop, said the Burned Man, the puckered skin on his neck working. *If you do, I'll just bring you another.*

In the waking nightmares, as in life, Xavier always came. This is what he'd been bred for, to create new generations of Tedrans. New slaves for the Ofarians.

It's okay, what you're doing, the Burned Man soothed, his tone syrupy false. Xavier had always suspected he'd enjoyed watching. *Her life will be better if she gets pregnant anyway.*

A red-mittened hand touched Xavier's arm, snapping him back to Colorado.

He gasped as though he'd been held underwater for minutes, and gulped down the sweet, cold air. The buzz of the festival filled his ears in a painful rush. Dance music now thumped from speakers set up around the square and it drove into his brain. The sun bounced off the snow, blinding him. Xavier knuckled his eyes, hard enough to hurt. When he opened them, she was still there in front of him, gorgeously and hideously innocent.

"Are you okay?"

Her voice was smoky, sexy, and it tugged him between reality and evil memories. She wasn't naked beneath him, taking it because she had to. But the possibility of it terrified him.

He ripped away from her touch. "Fine. I'm fine."

Apparently an even bigger celebrity had sauntered under the theater marquee because the crowd had gone from unbearable to insane. He couldn't move unless he put his shoulder into someone's back and barreled through. The old Xavier would have done that. Maybe now would be a perfect time for that asshole to return.

"I'm sorry, but"—her freckled nose crinkled and a curious smile lit her candy-colored eyes—"I know this'll sound weird, but do I know you? You seem . . . familiar."

Since he'd given up women, whenever temptation or panic gnawed at him, he'd picture himself in the kitchen. A pristine cutting board. The handle of a scary-sharp chef's knife cradled loosely in his palm. Rows upon rows of meats and vegetables lined up, waiting. He'd poise the knife over a green pepper, make the first cut, then let his hand fly through the strokes, blocking out everything else.

He did this now, and calm rippled through him.

"No, you don't," he said, finally able to look at her without picturing her suffering underneath him. But that didn't mean he was about to stay and chat.

He wheeled away, found the tiniest crack between bodies, and shoved himself into it. He hated to use his size, but he was desperate. The tourists parted for him because they had no choice, and he apologized as he angled for freedom.

"Are you sure?" the freckled woman called after him, but he barely heard her over the thud thud thud of blood in his ears.

The alley mouth was thirty yards and thirty thousand miles away. At last he broke the edge of the crowd, the yellow-and-white striped awning over Shed's entrance in his sight. He hurried toward it.

"Hey, wait." That smoky voice. Following him. "Can you hold up a sec?"

Giant pots, holding mature yews and decorated with bows in Shed's signature yellow and white, dotted the wide alley, and he wove among them. Stupid to think he could actually lose her, given that the alley came to a dead end, but he was grasping for any way out. When he ducked under the awning and still heard her footsteps crossing the cobblestones, he knew there was only one option left.

The day he'd arrived in White Clover Creek, he'd given up not just sex but magic, cold turkey. But there, standing in the shadowed cold, shaking with fear, he reached deep inside and pulled out the rusty words of the Tedran language.

No reason to speak it anymore, since there was only one person left on Earth who could understand him, and he hadn't spoken to Gwen since she'd freed his people and started a new life. A better life. No reason to use the words of his birth if he'd abandoned using illusions. Yet the language sprang up inside him like the quick gush of blood after a pinprick. Filled him.

He chose his illusion, imagining the face and body he wanted, and whispered the Tedran words to bring it about. Glamour enveloped him in a light, airy caress. Head to foot, the new image fell around him in a shimmering cloak made of the thinnest material. Touch it and it would dissolve.

He couldn't deny that for some part of him, using his birthright after all this time comforted him.

He grabbed hold of the thick, iron bar on the restaurant's original granary shed wood door, and slid it wide on oiled rails. Rushing through the little foyer that blocked the winter wind, he pushed open the restaurant's main door and waddled inside, shouldering a huge purse that wasn't really there.

Pam, Shed's owner and executive chef, sat hunched over

table eighteen studying receipts and supply orders in neat little piles. By the way her fingers toyed with her short, platinum hair, he knew that something wasn't adding up in the ledgers.

The only reason Xavier could work for Pam, a woman, was because she sent out zero sexual vibes toward him. Probably had to do with the fact he had a penis.

Xavier shuffled through the dining room, making a point to be noticed. Pam glanced up. "Hey, Rosa," she said, distracted.

"Hola," he replied in the lilting voice of Shed's cleaning lady. Magic tingled on his skin.

Veiled in the disguise of a tiny Hispanic woman, he slipped into the back room where Pam stored her linens and cutlery. He shut the door behind him and sagged against the shelves.

Shed's front door opened.

Pam's shoes clicked across the dining room floor. "We're not open for lunch for another two hours."

"Oh. I'm sorry." *Her.*

Xavier groaned, her voice slicing through him like a newly sharpened blade. Desire flowed into the open wound, and despite his mind's direct orders to stay away, his arm reached out and cracked the door open.

She stood by the hostess podium, her eyes darting around the dim dining room. The cold touched her cheeks with a gentle pink. "I was looking for someone. Really tall, wavy blond hair to his shoulders? Navy blue down coat?"

Pam nodded and half smiled in the way that looked like she was laughing at some private joke. "You mean Xavier? Hasn't come in yet."

The woman tilted her head, the red pompon flopping to one side. What was it about that silly hat that forced Xavier to conjure images of tomatoes being diced to hell?

"I thought I just saw him come in here."

"Nope." Pam fiddled with the menus on the hostess stand, perfectly aligning their edges. She wasn't very good at casual conversations. Not such a great trait to have in the hospitality business, but it made her incredible back in the kitchen. Good thing she recognized that and gave front of the house to someone else to run.

"But he works here?"

"Yeah. He's my saucier." When the freckled woman looked confused, Pam added, "One of my line cooks."

The woman shifted her weight and a snow chunk slid off her fuzzy boot. "Any chance you have a reservation open for tonight?"

Pam flipped open the mahogany leather reservation book and lazily dragged her finger down the page. "So. How do you know Xavier?"

The woman blushed almost as red as her hat. Xavier was horrible at guessing ages, considering his own was about as twisted as a screw, but she was younger than him. Mid-twenties, most likely. She kicked at the dislodged snow. "I . . . I don't."

Oh shit.

Pam looked like the fox who'd swallowed a chicken. Wrong person to learn a woman was looking for him. She'd been trying to get him to date since he'd aced his job interview. Even got her girlfriend to badger him. Between the two of them the barrage was endless. *Let's get the quiet cook laid.* They thought it funny, a game.

To Xavier, it was anything but.

Pam arched an eyebrow at the freckled woman, her wicked smile tipping toward flirtatious. "Oh, really?" She tapped the reservation book. "Look at this. Lucky for you. We have an opening at eight. For how many?"

Shed had been booked up for weeks, if not months.

"Um. Two. Put it under my name. Heddig."

"Got a first name? Just in case I need it?"

Pam would need it all right—to needle Xavier all shift. He considered calling in sick but knew he couldn't. Not during the festival, when every table would be full from lunch through close. Not when being alone and unoccupied in his house would throw open the doors and invite the Burned Man to take up permanent residence.

"My name's Cat," said the woman.

"Great, Cat." Pam clicked the pen closed and grinned. "See you tonight."

From New York Times *Bestselling Author*

NALINI SINGH

Kiss of Snow

A Psy-Changeling Novel

Since the moment of her defection from the PsyNet and into the SnowDancer wolf pack, Sienna Lauren has had one weakness. *Hawke*. Alpha and dangerous, he compels her to madness.

Hawke is used to walking alone, having lost the woman who would've been his mate long ago. But Sienna fascinates the primal heart of him, even as he tells himself she is far too young to handle the wild fury of the wolf.

Then Sienna changes the rules, and suddenly, there is no more distance, only the most intimate of battles between two people who were never meant to meet. Yet as they strip away each other's secrets in a storm of raw emotion, they must also ready themselves for a far more vicious fight . . .

A deadly enemy is out to destroy SnowDancer, striking at everything the pack holds dear, but it is Sienna's darkest secret that may yet savage the pack that is her home . . . and the alpha who is its heartbeat.

penguin.com